FLOODTIDE

FLOODTIDE

Roger Mark

JAVELIN BOOKS

POOLE · NEW YORK · SYDNEY

First published in the UK 1987 by Javelin Books,
Link House, West Street, Poole, Dorset, BH15 1LL

This novelisation © Anthony Fowles 1987.
Based on the scripts of *Floodtide* © Granada Television 1987.

Distributed in the United States by
Sterling Publishing Co., Inc.,
2 Park Avenue, New York, NY 10016

Distributed in Australia by
Capricorn Link (Australia) Pty Ltd,
PO Box 665, Lane Cove, NSW 2066

British Library Cataloguing in Publication Data

Mark, Roger
  Floodtide.
  I. Title
  823'.914[F]   PR606.A64

  I. Title II. Series

ISBN 0 7137 1967-2

Typeset by Nene Phototypesetters Ltd, Northampton
Printed in Great Britain by
Cox & Wyman Ltd, Reading, Berks.

FLOODTIDE

The anticipation was nearly the best thing about it. Nearly. It was like when you were young and had the certain knowledge that soon you would be having sex. Well, those heady climaxes of the flesh were far behind him now but this . . . this was unfailing. Better.

Prolong the foreplay! He made his impeccably manicured fingers work slowly at unfolding the wrap. Doubling in number, gleaming white crystals spilled across the small mirror and obliterated the reflection of his own confident face. So pure! He reached for the silver spoon in the saucer of the untouched coffee cup. He'd not been born with it in his mouth but, by God, he'd earned it!

Still he hesitated. No supply problems, so tease yourself! Wring the last savour from the self-enforced wait! The spoon in his hand stayed motionless above the tooled green leather of the desk. From beneath the crystals the blurred suggestion of a still youngish smile grinned back at him. This was all a further plus. The refined bookcases, the Liberty fabrics of this serenely expensive upstairs study on the Chelsea-Westminster borders added to the hype. It was like having your host's wife while he was just outside tinkering with the Volvo.

And all so easy! A few moments before, the coffee cup secure in his hand, he had risen from the dining table downstairs.

'And *à propos* of this damned by-election,' he had lied, 'there are a couple of calls I must make before the evening's over. Jean, I wonder . . .'

'Of course. Use Ted's study,' she'd replied at once. What dinner-party hostess would baulk a Government Minister, he so practised a liar and her husband his hard-working agent? As he'd edged the balloon-backed chair aside he'd seen a 'he's overdoing it' frown stiffening Tessa's quicksilver face. Yes, well. There were no other secrets between them and one day, no doubt . . . Bennet had caught his eye.

'Give the PM my regards,' he said with heavy wit, 'and say that as form-sheets opinion polls aren't worth the studying.'

He'd smiled and the momentary pang had passed away. A buffoon, really, Bennet, for a top person's quack, but able to keep his mouth shut where it mattered.

Now then . . . with gentle firmness he began to crush the crystals on the mirror. There! He wiped his finger across the back of the spoon and then, lips bared, rubbed its tip across his gums. He reached the pen-knife out of his dinner-jacket pocket – for an instant feeling distaste. Also silver, it clashed with his gold cuff links. But who was there to see?! Patiently he chopped the crushed crystals into still finer particles. Then – careful now, no blowing it away! – he used the blade edge to divide the fine powdery flatness into two straight lines. Once again the finger, the sour friction against the gums, the hint of what was to come.

And now go for it! From his dress-wallet he extracted a twenty-pound note. Crisp, virgin – and a good joke. A fitting coke tube for a top person. He rolled it tightly and bending to the mirror snorted a line of powder into his left nostril.

And now the second. There! He straightened waiting for the rush, the surge of euphoria, the chemical orgasm, to embrace him totally. Yes, here came that indescribable – Jesus! My God! An invisible scalpel was scything across his chest sending a gushing heat out from his belly that flooded his whole body. There was a hook through his heart, which was leaping like a salmon. Iron bands were tightening about his lungs. Sweet Jesus! He tried to call out but the cry stuck in his locked throat. The complacent room reeled and, flailing in his agony, as he crashed forward and across the desk, all he could hear was the pounding surf-beat of his deafening pulse.

Downstairs, Jean Adams was becoming cross. It was too bad – and not the first time – for Exton to pull ministerial rank like this and deflate a very hard-worked-at dinner-party. Probably only calling Isabel.

'The by-election is clearly going to be a damned hard-run thing,' Bennet was sententiously declaring. But without the centre-piece, the arbiter guest, the remark fell into emptiness. Ted was doing the liqueur bit. Jean would play a card to certain strength.

'Tessa,' she said, 'Armagnac's Exton's tipple, isn't it? Be an angel and run one up to him. And tell him we don't sanction over-time working in this house. Not even for him!'

Tessa flashed her a grateful smile and then looked across at her mother. But Beryl Waite, *toujours noblesse oblige*, was pretending to take Bennet seriously.

'All by-elections come at a bad time,' she was responding.

Ted had done the honours with the flat, black bottle. Tessa took the glass from him and left the room.

'It'll be a damned close-run thing but we'll –'

Beryl Waite couldn't complete the sentence. Against such a scream nobody could.

'*Daddy!*'

In the study Tessa Waite stood looking down on her father's flushed, sweat-drenched face. Croakings seemed to be coming from

6

the spittle-flecked mouth but she couldn't be sure. A scream was burning into her brain like a hot wire. From somewhere far away it came to her that the scream was her own and that the juddering trip-hammer trying to disjoint her was powered by her father's pulse.

ONE

The stylish veteran of the Light Fifteen, the Maigret Citroën was in exactly the same place, so he hadn't come back. She could sense it. The cottage was still empty. Tessa Waite's heart clenched. It was unfair! After the last two days God owed it to her for Ramsey to be in. Again the temptation to collapse and cry, be mindlessly helpless, welled up. But with nobody there it would be more than an indulgence, it would be silly. Instead, for the second time that day she reached into the hanging basket of dying petunias and felt for the spare key and let herself in. She'd tried everywhere. They'd said he wasn't away. All she could do was wait.

Three hours before, she'd hardly taken in the interior. Ramsey wasn't in so she'd turned right around to go looking for him: the hospital, the '*Bar de la Marée*', Ramsey's old mooring on the Barfleur quayside. His boat wasn't there. The hospital receptionist had seemed to say he was off duty that day. The best guess was he was off fishing with Marcel and Gabin. He could be hours yet! Now, steady . . . she made herself look round the room.

It was less feminine and less British than two years ago. It was becoming like the car outside. The cane flyrods hanging alongside the gruff chimney breast, the stocked wine-rack where the grate should have been, the pipe-rack on the mantelpiece were cliché-masculine and international. The over-wrought sombre-wooded desk, and the green-shaded brass lamp upon it were clearly French. So were the stiff and high backed chairs about the oak dining table in the corner. It was all leather and brown and dark in here. No colour. No flowers in vase or bowl. No splash of Matisse-evoking fabric. Anne's shrine was clearly in Ramsey's brain. One glance and any detective from fiction would have instantly put this room down as the den of a confirmed old bachelor and never begun to apply the adjective *Anglo-Scots*. Yet the age-confirming records – shellac 78s in stiff vertical row along this shelf – were all American and British labels. Brunswick, Polydor, Columbia. The one horizontal record – still on a player that seemed barely electric – was by Artie Shaw, *Crescendo in Blue*. Two years ago Tessa had come to quivering climax as that soaring clarinet – but forget that! The fictional detective was still pressing his case. 'This is the collection of a hobbyist of a certain age. As to nationality – is it not a well-known fact that the French are the greatest, how you say, jazz buffs in the world? *Voilà, M'selle.*' Yes, *voilà* and wrong!

8

Detectives. The small fantasy vanished away as the grey-black misery of the past two days swirled about her once again. At Southampton, on the endless yet somehow too-soon-over night crossing she had all the time had that feeling of being watched.

It was what she had grown used to, of course and almost expected. With her father's accession to Cabinet status had come the wide-shouldered men in inferior suits and matching haircuts. In the car behind, in the wings of the Assembly Rooms stage, further down the plane in Economy. Only for him, of course. But on those occasions when she'd been with him they'd been blatant in their unobtrusive presence. Perhaps if her father had been promoted earlier she'd have been a kid enjoying the reflected importance of having bodyguards. But they had come on the scene just as she was discovering boys, flirting with dope and booze. It had been inhibiting. It had made for the posting of letters in random boxes; of making the rendezvous away from the house. Never using the 'official' phone at home, she had made fewer and fewer calls on the 'private' line. Why? It was all unnecessary. She wasn't one of the Christ Church crowd. Only . . . if it was private then it ought to be private and not shared by . . . whomever. No other council should be privy to it . . .

As she had driven on to the ferry at Southampton, the feeling of there being eyes on the back of her neck had briefly bored a sense of present surroundings through her frozen, displacing grief. Locking eyes with that man in the ship's observation lounge had also brought her back off automatic pilot. But thickset, inferior rain-coated, he had looked so like a detective in a television series, she had shrugged away her paranoia. This wasn't Strudwick, the one who'd questioned her, making her thoughts run on so. He had got under her nails so painfully she'd wanted to rake them across his face just to get one expression to come to its surface. Not thick in any sense, that one, knowing he could leave his smooth, unsettling image hanging glassily in her mind. Not even the darkness of grief could completely black it out. Although that was the reason she felt so brittle, of course. Grief made you self-conscious. You felt that everyone was looking at you because they must all know your father, your husband, your sister, your lover had died. It showed in your face. Oh, God!

Burning back in her brain had come that dreadful, irradicable etching of her father's last seconds. Those final galvanised jerkings as – how ghastly the slang was when you'd seen it happen! – he literally croaked to death. His upside down eyes had enclosed a silent scream in which terror and, somehow, guilt were inextricably – no, don't! Stop it now! Don't think about it!

To drive away the image of those eyes that any second now would roll upwards and freeze she must use her own. She walked to the wide

9

sea-facing window and forced herself to stare through it.

It was like being back on the ferry. There was, in fact, a falling away of scrubby garden, a road of sorts, a further incline of rock face down to the stony beach. But you could choose to overlook all this and, the captain on the bridge, let yourself be drawn into the panoramic sweep of sea and clouded sky. It was a day neither warm nor cold, rough nor calm. Towards the horizon the sea seemed choppy but closer in the protection of the long, concrete, somehow wartime, mole stretching out from the shore on the far side of the water-front brought smoothness to its surface. It was along the length of the mole that many of the fishing boats tied up: along there she had gone earlier to seek out Ramsey's boat. Two years ago she had fallen in love with the picturesque, working scruffiness of Barfleur, the slapdash combination of bright paint and rust on the dogged little fishing boats. But that, no doubt, was because she fancied herself in love with Ramsey. Two years is a long time between intimacies. Now the view was no longer picture-postcard quaint but alien and grey. It was grey because the day was too, and because the awareness of death, of everyone's mortality, hung like a brooding spectre just beyond the edge of vision. She found herself blinking. Not from tears this time, but because of the glare from the slanting pewter sea. And tiredness. She yawned. Unaccustomed oxygen, like sadness, can make you feel tired. As can, of course, a fitful, over-night cat-nap just a few seats along from the Ministry of Whatever's man in mid-channel. Another yawn cut short what would have been her first smile in long hours. Silly. He was a traveller in – what was it they always said? – ah yes, ladies' underwear. And she . . . she was going to lie down.

Before she had thought further she had entered the cottage's one bedroom and found herself halted by the cross-fire of memories its walls boxed in – the furious summer heat distanced by the thick stone walls, Ramsey tautly brown all over, herself frightened at first, awkward, coming to pant, to gasp and finally shriek unabandonedly as his patience gave place to like passion. But so briefly. Seventeen days. Then back to England and in all the time between, another summer and now this, only one short, impersonal letter. Everything had changed, for her. But not the room. It was exactly as, in detail, she had remembered it: the low, pine dressing table; the bookshelf crowded with the yellow paperbacks; the simple double bed. The photograph of Anne at the bed's side had not been moved by so much as a single millimetre.

She crossed and looked at what she had already got by heart. A calm face beneath short, expensively simple, hair. Hollowed cheeks that seemed to extend the amused generosity of the mouth. Gentle, probing, untroubled eyes. A beautiful face. Anne. Nine years dead. And nine hundred might go by before Ramsey would confer on any other woman – let alone her – a fraction of the love he had given to the wife whom, a powerless doctor, he had watched cancer waste away. Dammit!

Tessa flounced down on the bed and, doing so, displaced a pillow. At last a touch of colour was revealed. Pale blue. Ah, yes – Ramsey's pyjamas. And beneath the other pillow? She shouldn't but she would. It was a double bed after all. Slewing around she lifted the second pillow and, discovering nothing beneath, felt mean and cheap. To dispel the feeling by an action she swung her feet up on to the bed and stretched herself full length. The tactic worked. The beams that she had once idly looked at through an unfocused haze of pleasure looked back at her and she knew then that she had fled to France because she still loved Ramsey.

There was no reason for her flight, and every reason. It was unnatural and yet quite natural. The natural thing would have seemed to be to stay dutifully and sustained in the bosom of her family. But when your father was struck down wasn't it natural to seek out, regardless, the figure your instinct said could best replace him? When your mother's *comme il faut* correctness coldly disdained any healing outpouring of tears wasn't it only reasonable to run to someone with whom, unashamed, you could cry your heart out? Probably not, Ramsey would have argued. That was why she had not phoned him until across the Channel and well down the road from Cherbourg. A call from England establishing he was away from Barfleur or, worse, telling her to stay put, would have locked her back into the plucky, dutiful daughter role. It would have robbed her of the luxury of the headlong journey where the miles said you needn't think. Yes, it was a self-dramatising role to – Wait a minute. The telephone! There was a concession to contemporary living in the place.

She swung off the bed. Next to the phone on the desk in the main room was an answering machine. Perhaps it would hold a clue to where Ramsey was hiding out. A small red light shone. The question was how to work it. Well, when in doubt, press the forward pointing arrow. Click! The machine whirred into life.

First came Ramsey's voice, the French flawless, no doubt, and seeming to be the bog-standard message in any language. Certainly the equivalent of 'dealing with your message as soon as I get back'. A promise in that, at least. More tape hiss meanwhile and now a bored woman's voice utterly redolent of French hotel receptionists at their 'take it or leave it' worst. But something about '*traumatologie*' and '*de l'après-midi.*' The hospital then. More hiss. And now herself,

11

from that strange smelling phone box.

'Ramsey, this is Tessa . . . Oh God, I hate these machines . . .
Look, I'm over here. In France. Gateville I think this place is. I'm on
my way to see you. Something's happened. Something awful . . .
You may know already . . . I need to see you . . . Ramsey, I'm
scared . . . I'll – well I'll see you soon I hope, and tell you.'

God! How incoherent! Young! And, yes, she was lonely and if
Ramsey didn't come soon – A third message diverted her from a
fresh burst of self-pity.

She didn't take in a single one of its words after '*chéri*'. But the
voice was female and huskily cooing and provocatively mocking and
put her in mind of impossibly chic French women strolling with
magnificent posture in the Paris spring. Before the voice could finish
she had pressed the re-wind button.

As if as a result the phone rang. Her heart leapt into her chest and
she all but jumped out of her skin. The hand she reached out seemed
a long way from her eyes.

'Hello? Er, Allo?'

'Tessa? Ramsey.'

As he started to give her instructions she became aware that, for
whatever reasons, she was crying again. And somehow, thereby, that
even if there were no assurance of rekindled love in her life, the first
return of comfort and of hope was in that nearby voice.

TWO

Ramsey was playing *boules*. She had screeched down the hill – on the wrong side of the road for ten metres after a quick left-hander – and slid amid a shower of gravel into a parking slot on the south side of the square. One or two heads had turned, but not his. As she jumped out of the Fiat she saw that it was his turn. His back was to her. Across the square he was caught in the motionless split-second before the release. His arm swung back. The heavy silver ball arc'd through the air in a high defensive strike. There was a metallic smack, a cry, but meanwhile Gabin was hurtling blackly toward her, all but knocking her off her feet. His huge paws were on her shoulders, his tongue licking at her face with feverish friendship.

'Hey, Gabin – stop it!' she was laughing. Yes, actually laughing. 'Good boy now, good dog! *Couchez*!'

Somehow she got the huge Labrador down on to tail-wagging all fours and then, as she was bending forward to pat his head, oil-stained corduroys walked in to her line of vision. She looked up and there, as if he always had been there, was Ramsey.

'Don't believe a word,' he said. 'He flatters to deceive.'

She straightened up. 'At least he remembers me,' she said. 'Goes to the trouble of pretending he's glad to see me.'

Ramsey smiled an amused apology. '*Je m'excuse*,' he said. He took her in his tall thin height and kissed her. But it was *à la française*. She felt the stiffness in his manner as his lips did no more than brush passingly against her own. He held her at arms' length and looked at her.

'I like the hair,' he said. 'Short suits you.'

She smiled as she thought, it's like Anne's in the photo.

'Drink?' he said.

She nodded. Just what she needed! They crossed the square arm in arm. Then he freed his hand to signal to Marcel, and motioned towards Tessa. From amid the *boules* spectators Marcel grinned toothily at her and waved. As mutely, she waved back. Ramsey pointed to the game, and to Gabin padding at their feet. Marcel nodded. He moved forward to take Ramsey's place. He snapped his fingers and the dog obediently bounded towards him.

'You still look after him, then,' she said as they walked on.

'Marcel? He looks after me. I couldn't afford Walter Brennan. We've been out fishing since quite early.'

'Yes. I sort of guessed that. I –' She was too near all of it to go on.

13

'You've been here some time,' he said. 'They said at the bar here an English girl had come in looking for me.'

'Yes.'

'You should have dropped me a line. Or phoned. Then –'

'I did. Sort of. Ramsey, I –' Again she was lost for words. He looked at her appraisingly.

'First the drink, then we talk,' he said.

They went into the bar. A few hours earlier when she had been in here asking with faltering stupidity about *le médecin, er, le docteur* she had been a woman under threat. A foreign bit of stuff. There had been cocky glances from the film extra regulars summing up her sexual form. That was all gone now. Ramsey was known, was liked. Ramsey was safe. It was warm in here and as they sat in a booth across from the zinc-topped bar she realised she had been cold.

'*Deux fines,*' Ramsey called out.

She touched his arm. He turned to her. 'No,' he said, 'drinks first. Doctor's orders.'

In the end she timed it badly. The patron had just turned away from serving the two small glasses when she heard herself blurting it out.

'Daddy died two days ago.'

Ramsey's hand was half-way to his mouth on the point of proposing a toast. 'Oh,' he said. He replaced the brandy untouched on its saucer. His cheek muscles tautened and then his face went empty. He looked past her into space. Afraid of her clumsiness having aggravated the pain she looked numbly at him.

His face was tanned and not quite handsome, not quite lean. It was the sardonic, cynical twist to the full mouth that qualified the handsomeness. This is someone, his features said, who's been around and knows the score and doesn't care too much for the game in the first place. Except that was all wrong; not even the half of it. The eyes told you that. Amazingly blue-green under the dark, straight hair they suggested something very different. They belonged to a man who had been in the game for quite a while now and had been obliged to absorb a lot of punishment. But who hadn't gone sour. The eyes were not cynical at all. They were resigned, but not just to an uncaring Fate. They were resigned to the hard-learned awareness that the one counter to the bitterest personal loss was a warm commitment to the dozens around you also needing help. To playing the indifferent game with as much style as you could bring to it. Well, she thought, as his look focused back from the past on to her, I'm just being wise after the event.

'How?' he said.

In broad terms, trying hard to soft-pedal the brutal suddenness of it all, she told him. 'I even thought you might have heard,' she said.

14

It took him a moment to take that in.

'No,' he said. 'I'm very French these days. No World Service. Not even for the cricket. We caught the early tide this morning. I haven't seen today's *Figaro*. I'm glad, though.'

She looked at him sharply.

'Glad I heard from you.'

Ah, that was something. Abruptly he drank his brandy off in one sustained gulp. She sipped hers. It stung fierily down into emptiness. He signalled to the patron.

'So that's what politics does for you,' he said savagely.

'For some, it seems, yes. When did you last –' she hesitated but there seemed no point in avoiding the jokey echo '– see my father?' she finished.

'Last Christmas. In Paris.'

'He seemed so alive these days.'

'Alive going on frenetic. I tried to hint that Cabinet games are always won by stayers.'

'Yes. In every sense.'

'Mind you. He's been desperately unlucky.'

'I don't see how he could have been unluckier.'

'No, I'm sorry Tessa – what I mean is, he had a heart murmur. Mild *mitral regurgitation* as the books call it.'

'Rheumatic fever when he was a boy. Perhaps he was lucky to last this long.'

'No. Not at all. It seems a paradox but people with that condition almost never develop acute heart failure.'

'Well. He did.'

'That's what I mean. Damned unlucky. Poor old Exton.' Now it was his turn to look sharply at her. 'Poor old Beryl,' he ventured. She considered.

'I know what you mean,' she said. 'But I'm sure she's . . . well, terribly upset. More than twenty-five years of marriage. If not togetherness. It's just that, you know, she would never allow herself to appear devastated. Right now she'll be planning his Memorial Service down to the last pew.'

There was not much approval in the quick grimace Ramsey flicked at her. 'When did you last eat?' he asked abruptly.

'I . . .' She couldn't think when and she was, she realised, starving.

'You should eat now. They'll do something for us here.' And indeed the patron was back at the table with Ramsey's second *fine*.

Forty minutes later she was scraping juice from the plate with her last morsel of delicious, *real*, bread. She realised that for the last few minutes she had been virtually unconscious of anything else but the steak and *frites* right under her nose.

15

'I was starving,' she said, looking up.

'So I rather gathered.' Ramsey's light irony got to her. It brought her present circumstances right back home.

'I suppose . . .' she faltered.

'You suppose it seems callous to go on living when the dead are dead,' he supplied. 'To go on eating. Go on enjoying eating.' It was exactly her train of thought. It must have showed in her face. But she resented his providing the sentence for her.

'You're the one person, Ramsey,' she snapped bitterly, 'who treats me as though I were twelve and had a brace on my teeth.'

He inclined his head slightly in partial acknowledgement of the charge and thus apology.

'Do you have the remotest idea how old I am?' she continued. Now it was his turn to hesitate and hers to read his mind.

'Twenty-four.'

She nodded brusquely. She had another weapon now. 'Do you work out everything from the year she died?'

'Yes,' he said flatly. 'Who found the body?'

The needling change of subject hit her hard. 'I did,' she said.

The compassion came back into his eyes. The anger was gone.

'You never said,' he said gently.

No. She had purposely played that down.

'He was sprawled across this vast desk,' she said by way of amends, 'upstairs in Ted Adams' – his agent's – house. He was gasping for breath. His face was flushed. He was sweating –'

'Flushed?' Ramsey interrupted. Something in his own face seemed darker. 'Are you sure?'

Her father's twisted features confronted her again. 'Quite sure.'

Ramsey's stare returned her to the present. He seemed about to speak and then he didn't. 'Coffee at my place?' he said finally.

She nodded. The food, the wine, and the warmth had brought the sleepiness back. He got up to pay. She made no fuss about splitting the bill. Later they'd work something out.

The square was now deserted. They scrunched across its thinly gravelled centre. Night had almost come in full.

'A lift home,' Ramsey said. 'I'm privileged.'

'Would you rather –'

'No – you drive if you don't mind. It's a long time since I did the RHD bit.'

And quite a while since she had driven on the right. Still, it was no distance.

She was ultra-careful, all the same, as she backed out. Perhaps it was the excess of caution that caused her to glimpse the bobbing head in the Renault over her left shoulder. As she straightened on to the

16

road proper its engine fired and the lights came on. But as it too pulled out, a glance at its plates in her mirror told her it must be a local job.

Water hissed insistently through the cottage's pipes and he could hear it drumming in the shower. He finished straightening the sleeping bag on the camp bed and regained his glass from the desk. He moved to the record player. The needle dropped. For an instant vintage crackling replaced the water's hiss and then, sure in its lower register, full-blown with the first note, the jaunty control of Shaw's clarinet caught him by accustomed surprise yet again. *Begin the Beguine* had begun. He moved to the window. When his body blocked the glare of the desk lamp he could see out into the night. Two patly on cue lights bobbed towards the end of the mole. The bigger boats were setting out for the night's fishing. He saw them and forgot them. He sipped the brandy and looked right through his own reflection.

'A night of tropical splendour . . .' Hardly. This night in Barfleur would not mark the tropic of anything. In present circumstances trying to re-create the bedroom splendours of two summers ago was a no-go area. It would be too much like incest. It wasn't by accident Tessa had come running to someone old enough to be her father. To replace her father. Even if in a sense she had then taken advantage of him, he wasn't about to take advantage of her now. There were still rules of sorts . . . All the same it had been physically stunning. There had been too much long enforced celibacy, too much tamping down of all emotion for him not to explode. And she, lithe and ripe all at once, had magically found herself in bed with a man she hero-worshipped, a demi-god made flesh. Hell! Private. photographs skittered across his memory. He drained his glass the better to obliterate them. The record was right.

It had stopped. He realised that he had betrayed it by largely not listening. The water had stopped running too. The latch on the door from the kitchen clicked and Tessa came into the room.

'Night cap?' he asked.

She shook her head. He'd made up the spare bed while she was showering. He saw that she had clocked it and the implication at once. Her face had almost not changed.

'The water – it's so soft here,' she said. 'I'd forgotten.'

'They have very refined chemicals these days.'

She was wearing his towelling bathrobe and he was glad. A welter-weight in light-heavy's gear, she looked so like the gamine heroine in a so-so romantic comedy, his sense of individuality backed away at once. He didn't like life type-casting him. Fastidiousness now let him block off completely the sexual memories, the erotic anticipations he'd just been experiencing. All the same, she was something. Not pretty, no, but sometimes beautiful. Slight without being thin, she was, what? – a thinking man's Liza Minelli. Dark eyes to drown in, classic cheekbones, a wide mouth full of fun and expertise. Now with her still damp hair shiny and tight as a close-fitting helmet about her skull she might have passed for Cleopatra.

She had wandered to the record player. 'Artie Shaw – still!' she mock remonstrated.

'Old bands, old books, old habits,' he shrugged.

'And old friends?'

Ah. She wasn't going to let the sleeping past lie without some hint it might be revived. Time for priorities. 'One less than I realised,' he said.

She blinked just once.

'No new ones, I really meant.'

'You meet people,' he evaded. Once again he shrugged.

Her big eyes were suddenly matt and he could not tell that behind them she was listening again to a French woman's cooing huskiness. But his instinct told him to stay hard. 'Will it be a big funeral?' he said.

'No. Small. Family job.'

She had been dead-pan but he must have raised an eye-brow. 'St Martin's-in-the-Fields or the Palladium later on,' she explained. 'Top brass. Mellifluous reading. *News at Ten* and a back row full of body-guards.'

'I ran through the answering machine messages while you were in the shower,' he said.

'Oh, yes. . . ? 'Fraid mine was a bit all over the place.'

'You said somewhere in it you were "scared" . . .'

'Yes.'

'Why?'

'There was this police officer.'

'Police?'

'Oh, God, Ramsey, I don't know. Something. Plain clothes. Good at whispering to people in the corner. Horrible to me. My father hadn't been dead an hour and he was asking me all these questions as if I were a liar. As if he didn't believe me. He was . . . metallic.'

'Your father was a very important man. This cop or whatever would have wanted to get his homework dead right.'

'All the same.'

'All the same . . . When you found him, what did you do?'

'Scream.'

'Then what?'

'Screamed "doctor".'

'How long before one showed up?'

'Less than ten seconds.'

'Oh?'

'There was one downstairs at the dinner party.'

'Anyone I'd know?'

'Probably. Wyn Bennet. Daddy's tame one.'

'Oh yes. Rather hooray Harley Street, unless he's changed.'

'He hasn't.'

'Tessa – if he was immediately there, what did he do?'

'How do you mean?'

'Did he lie him down? Try to raise his legs? Cardiac massage? Give him mouth to mouth?'

'No.'

'Did he give him an injection?'

'No.'

'No?'

'Ramsey, he was dead in no time . . . I screamed for help. I was feeling his pulse. I –'

'*You*?'

'Yes.'

'Why?'

'I don't know. Shock reaction. People do it in films. I was bringing him a drink. I remember throwing the glass away. Then I was holding his arm and feeling his pulse.'

'Could you find it?'

'I could hardly help not. It was thumping like a steam shovel.'

'Thumping?'

'Crashing away. That was one of the things that Strudwick, this cut-glass bastard of a copper, kept coming back to.'

'Yes.'

'What do you mean, "yes"?'

'I just mean go on. Did he say he didn't believe you?'

'About the pulse? Not in so many words. He kept on about what had I seen in there.'

'What had you seen?'

'You're a doctor! I'd just seen my dad dying across a desk! Do I need to draw you the fucking picture!'

The proper tears came at last. For a long time, standing in the window, he held her tight until eventually, life again imitating Hollywood, he worked a handkerchief out of his pocket and into her hand. Awkwardly she blew her nose. As she moved away he could see that her eager face, bright from the shower, was now sticky from

19

the drying tears.

'Sorry,' she snuffled. 'All right now. Good thing, really. Needed to come out.'

Remembering his own grief he nodded.

'Won't do it at the funeral now,' she said smiling faintly.

'Where's that to be?'

'Brinkton.'

'Ah, yes, of course.'

'Cremation, Beryl decided. Cleaner-cut, you see.'

In spite of himself he grunted. But she seemed to take it as a comment on her dig. Almost certain as to what her own request would be he waited as passively as possible.

'Ramsey,' she said, 'come back to England with me. For the funeral. I know I won't cry then.'

He'd been dead right. He stayed silent a moment letting the other thoughts run in his head.

'Ramsey, he was your friend. You'd have gone to the funeral if you were back home, wouldn't you?'

'This is my home,' he said in genuine annoyance. 'People forget that all the time when they write,' he said more gently as her face began to work again.

'Please.'

'I'm not on duty tomorrow morning. I can spend it arranging a "locum",' he heard himself say. 'We'll go tomorrow evening.'

Her face lit up and he sensed her restraining herself from coming back into his arms.

'On one condition,' he hastened on.

'Of course.'

'You go through and into bed and take what I give you to get you through the night without another murmur.'

'Without another murmur. Cross my heart!'

And it won't be me, he was adding silently to himself. He pointed toward the bedroom door. A bedraggled girl again, her victory won, she crossed towards it.

In the kitchen, heating the milk on the Butane-served range, he wondered at his truer motives. It was a long time since he'd been back. Perhaps it was time – time since he would never forget her – to exorcise Anne's ghost from the old haunts. The Vauxhall stand. The Chelsea Flower Show. The Purcell Room and the Thames. . . . Cremation, of course, made his other thoughts academic. This was not the time to tell Tessa – perhaps no time would be. He caught the milk just before it boiled and poured it into a stone-ware beaker. Steam rose up smelling of the chocolate. He stirred the spoon around. Whatever Exton Waite had died of, it hadn't been a coronary.

THREE

Clinton shivered, and as if confirming the chilliness of the still early morning, the heat from his face misted up the binocular's lenses. He sighed, waited for the condensation to clear, and tried again. Much better. He pulled the cottage into sharp focus. There. And movement already! He swung the glasses slightly down and to the left to bring it into the centre of the field. Ah, just the big black dog making for the patch of sunlight. The folks were at home, then. Well, after a night *à deux* they'd hardly be in a hurry to rush out, would they?

It was supposed to have been a doddle. A civilian. Some punter of a girl not in the trade at all. But first there had been that moment on the ferry when he'd been sure she'd rumbled him and then, although trailing her along the roads had been strictly routine, it had all got too much like hard work again once she'd fetched up here. It was too small. Another English, he stood out like a sore thumb. They should've sent Lemerle. But God in his Curzon Street office had probably sent Lemerle to blend in with the Macclesfield landscape while he'd been obliged to trek thirty-odd kilometres down the road in search of a low profile auberge. All for no good reason! His call in last night had produced orders that might have saved him all that aggro.

Hang on – he was wrong about the long lie-in. The bloke was coming out of the front door. By himself, it seemed. Yes, he was calling back into the shoe-box in the 'shan't be long' way you do when someone's staying behind. The dog was bounding around now and, yes, scrambling into the car like there was a bitch inside. Something going into the boot. But in a cardboard box. Impossible to say what.

Clinton traversed the glasses to his right as the Light Fifteen moved off on its low-slung way. Tasty that. He swung them back on to the cottage. Cold though he was, crammed into the rented dodgem car of a Renault, he began to feel a little bit more like it. Bit of luck, in view of his over-night briefing, if the two of them should stay split up a while. She wouldn't like it but he'd make it stick. A little of what she didn't fancy would do her good, in fact. He allowed himself a quick grin.

Towards the end of morning Ramsey halted the Citroën outside the tall, wide, green-painted wooden gates set into the high mellow wall. With the key he took from his pocket he let himself in through the wicket. He opened the gates wide enough to admit the car. He drove in to the *manoir*.

The tyres crunched on well-kept gravel. Free-form fruit trees waved greetings from their irregular stations in about a half-acre or so of paddock-like grass. He halted the car again and got out. The sun was high and strong now. The garden seemed to wall it in and most of the wind out. It was a warm day.

'*Restez là.*'

Gabin's hopefully quivering muzzle relaxed into obedience and he slumped back down on the rear seat. Ramsey turned to the *manoir*. It was of the same serene, sand-yellow stone as the wall. Its very flush façade was relieved by the mid-green outer shutters flanking the windows of the first two floors and by the dormer windowed mansard roof above. Bright flowers spilled out from boxes beneath the lower windows and seemed to be trying to reach their look-alikes in the beds fronting the house at the edge of the grass. Classy but casual, Ramsey thought yet again. Full of upmarket historical charm. That impression of gentle, understanding ghosts – and in this day and age bloody expensive.

A flash of movement caught his eye. Not the sly shade of a rural *curé*, but Chen Ning. Ramsey smiled again, and bent his steps away from their path to the front door, toward the conservatory on the south side of the house. He approached it on tip-toe. He opened its outer door silently and stepped into the enhanced heat generated by the sun-struck panes of glass. At the change of light value Chen Ning looked up from his work but, prepared, Ramsey instantly put a finger to his lips.

Chen Ning's work was the naked, prone body of a fair-haired woman. He was in the process of massaging it. Ramsey did not find the spectacle either unduly shocking or titillating. He was familiar with both the process and the spectacle. The massage and the medium. The body belonged to the woman who was the owner of the house and who, for some eighteen months, had been his mistress.

Without missing a motion Chen Ning looked enquiringly at Ramsey, who signalled again. Chen Ning honoured his ancestors' reputation for inscrutability. He paused to pour more rubbing oil between the two dimples either side of the small of the back and stepped slightly to one side. When the laying on of hands recommenced they were Ramsey's.

The massively gentle Chinese pointed to the right clavicle and went silently away. Ramsey's fingers began probing the big muscle just under the collar-bone. Sustaining the joke he worked steadily and said nothing. It was the joke, of course, and not the voyeurism-plus that activated him. This was, after all, familiar territory. Only, you could almost say, he was feeling it through new fingers.

She really was delicious. The body, the texture of its skin, had been flawlessly maintained. The allocation of flesh upon bone had been set just provocatively short of plumpness. There was tone to vary the yielding in this body's curves. His hands roved across to the other collar-bone. As they did so she spoke.

'Ramsey. *Tu as les mains de boucher.*' Utterly matter of fact.

Merde, he thought. 'I thought I'd fooled you,' he said.

'Do you think I'm deaf as well as thick-skinned?' Dany said. The syntax was as impeccable as the knowing accent was charming. Her English was like the house. 'That wreck has a death rattle.'

'Nonsense. Good as the day it was made.'

'None of us is!' Simply, quite unabashed, she turned herself over to look him in the face. So that he looked at nothing else he resolutely held her gaze. She nodded towards the oil. 'Don't stop,' she said. He was the one put out. He backed away a step, rubbed his hands on the towel.

'If I don't stop,' he said as purposefully as he could manage, 'I won't be in a condition to say what I came to say.'

A shadow crossed her impish, superficially selfish, fundamentally giving face. But intent on teasing a while longer she postponed concern or curiosity. She levered herself up on her elbows and glanced appraisingly down. This time his eyes followed hers. Full, pert breasts and a flatness stretching on down below them.

'But you're a doctor, Doctor,' she said. 'You see things like this every day.'

He saw that on this day and in this thick, almost palpable hot-house atmosphere, her taut nipples had already stretched to point seven on the Reichian scale.

'Dany, please! Put them away!'

Pouting she gathered a bath towel to her. 'You flatter me, Doctor,' she said. 'I had no idea –'

'You have every idea,' he snapped. 'I tell you often enough.'

'Not recently.' Another pout, but it made him laugh.

'Tuesday isn't recent?'

'Not as recent as last night.'

'There was an emergency,' he lied.

'Perhaps even at the hospital. And today? *Ah, Ramsey, il y a du bon vin à la cave et d'ailleurs ça court à Deauville cet après-midi . . .*'

'*Dany, arrête!*'

'*Pourquoi?*'

'*Je t'ai déjà dit pourquoi.* I've got something to say.'

'*Pour commencer, des fraises au champagne.*'

'I have to go away.'

24

'*Ce soir, donc.*'

'I have to go to England.'

The towel tight about her by now she sat bolt upright. 'Why?!'

'Because.'

'You've been there. Who in their right mind goes twice?'

'You're a wicked old thing.'

She went serious at last. 'You just used my unfavourite word,' she said.

Old. He realised for the first time that she sensed the tide of her beauty was on the turn and that she mistrusted both of them sufficiently to believe it might make a difference. 'A friend of mine died. I must go to the funeral.'

'Naturally.' She chose to pretend that she did not believe him.

'I won't be gone more than two or three days.'

'Call me, please. So I know you're safe.'

'And thinking of you. Of course. On condition.'

'Oh! On condition is –'

'Could you look after Gabin for me?'

'I've done it before. I suppose I can do it again . . . My God – I suppose I must believe you. England. A funeral. No one could invent such a crippled excuse.'

'Lame.'

She shrugged and swung her feet round off the high massage table. She was unconcerned as the towel dropped away again. She held her arms wide and stretched her petiteness up on tip-toe towards his greater height. Her smile seemed naturally perfumed. She might have been modelling for Lalique. 'You'd better kiss me goodbye,' she said. 'By the time you get back you'll either have forgotten how or turned gay.'

'In three days! Albion isn't that perfidious!'

'But I've known some terrible English lovers. Kiss me.'

He did. Her body relaxed for an instant in his arms and then began to strain against him. Her hands went to the back of his head and pulled as her tongue pushed deep into his mouth. The ageless thickening at the base of his spine began to kindle. His tongue rasped against hers in a form of fiery communion. He pulled himself sharply away. How British! England, home and duty before bed!

'I'll keep it down to two days,' he said thickly.

Dany laughed richly, throatily. She realised he had spoken not simply to excuse his roughness but because his body made him want to say it. To mean it. He wanted to be back and in bed with her again as soon as possible and she knew it. She was confident of him again. With every reason. There seemed no part of his make-up that would quarrel with her assurance.

The cemetery was above the town. In the French fashion it was walled, but, lying as it did on an up-slant of land running into the lower slopes of the next march of cliffs, you could see orderly rows of graves at its top end as you climbed towards it. Tessa had walked the kilometre or so. Ramsey had said he would not be back until mid-afternoon. The kennels were some distance away.

'A lot of loose ends,' he had said. 'Snap decisions take time.'

She pushed open the wrought-iron gate. The graves that had dropped behind the wall as she'd drawn near reformed their ranks. Many of the plots were strangely large for so small an overall area. Family monuments, of course, vaguely Second Empire in the main and pompously ugly with it. The French regarded death as a serious affair.

She advanced down the central path to the first intersection and turned right. There was no one about but she needed no guiding. She made straight for the one grave with meaning to her. It was simpler than almost any other there. A headstone and a mound. At the foot a square stone holding a dull metal vase. The vase in turn held flowers. She knelt to inspect them. No more than three days old. For a moment she felt penitent she had brought none of her own and then glad she hadn't. The one-offness of her token gesture would have contaminated the continuity of the truly bereaved's. And Anne, as she could remember her from her early teens, had never set much store on costume jewellery. She lifted her eyes. A simple stone. Granite, she supposed. A simple inscription too. The simplest. 'A.R. 1947–1979.' What else could you have put that started to do justice?

Her shadow was sharp across the mound but it was chilly here. The cemetery was like a blanket laid out on the side of the hill and the wind coming steadily off the sea to dry it played nip and tuck with her bare neck and forearms. She turned her head into it. The sea seemed very close here. A mile away, at least, in reality, it lay stretched beyond the horizon created by the wall and the ongoing shoulder of hill. It was a benign presence today. Merry under the high sun, shimmery, it made everything seem clean. There was a sense of silver and bright bone that made death seem less corrupting. A good place to lie.

She looked back down on the grave. 'I know it's no contest,' she said, 'but as he knows that too perhaps. . . .' She cut the sentence short.

She had heard a footfall on the grass and a sharper scrunch of a shoe against pebble. Not Ramsey over-hearing! No, silly. He wouldn't hear a murmur in this breeze. Or know she was here. It would only be another mourner or perhaps the sexton. But then a long shadow fell over the grave and stayed still as if intent on

26

chaperoning her own. She twisted round, gaining an impression of an ugly, heavy shoe, and rose to her full height. The beat her heart missed churned through her stomach. She was confronted by the man from the ferry.

'I'm sorry I startled you, Miss Waite,' he said.

It didn't seem worth replying to. Despite the sunshine he wore what she always thought of as a Lewisham High Street raincoat. His eyes were puffy and a sort of less than transparent glaze seemed to cover features whose bland symmetry suggested a patiently malevolent wax-work.

'One of Strudwick's, are you?' she said.

With a composure that said he might be good at his job he neither confirmed nor denied. 'Isn't it time you went home?' he said. A sub-cockney, comprehensive school voice. Left after 'O' Levels, probably.

'What's that to you?'

'Officially – nothing.'

'What's that supposed to mean?'

'Unofficially, Miss Waite, I think you ought to be in London with your mother.'

'My mother?'

'Lending support. If you aren't at the funeral, people will speculate. I think they should be denied that opportunity, don't you?'

Behind her rising anger, she saw she had been wrong. He'd stayed on for his 'A's. 'What people?' she asked.

'A daughter of a father such as yours does have certain responsibilities,' he persisted.

'How do you know I didn't hate him?' For the first time he allowed himself the flicker of a reaction. Amusement. This time he did not side-step her question.

'I'm led to believe you idolised him. Almost as much, I'm told, as he idolised you.'

She told herself she would not lose control in front of an errand boy. 'You seem well informed, Mr . . . ?' she said.

'The name's not important.'

'Not like its owner? Self-important.'

The wax-work had reassumed control. Not a hint of anything. She felt like sticking pins in it.

'You can tell your bosses that if I ever feel in need of a "minder" I'm perfectly capable of choosing one for myself!'

'So it would seem, Miss Waite . . .'

'And you can mind your own business!'

'Ah . . .' To indicate how totally she had justified his present occupation he went so far as to spread his arms a little. Yet another flunky, she realised, was just obeying orders which presumed to make her his business.

'You can also tell them that I *am* going home. I will be at the funeral. I'm leaving on an evening ferry from Cherbourg. Where we will doubtless meet again.'

'Oh that is good news.' Never more dead-pan.

'Why wouldn't I be at the funeral?' she added with deliberate ice. 'I always loved charades.'

'And is Dr Ramsey going?'

'Why don't you ask him?'

'You could just save me the trouble.'

'I'm a tax-payer. I like to get some return on my money.'

'Well . . . it's not important.'

'Like your name,' she said dismissively and turned her back on him and his moon-faced nastiness. She heard in reverse order the scrunch of stones, the footfall on grass. To take a short cut he was walking over people's graves, stepping on their faces. Well, she thought, anger curtailing her breath, at least he's consistent. He treats everyone, alive or dead, the same.

It became compulsive. On the N13 up to Cherbourg they both must have looked in the rear-view mirror a dozen times. There was no sign of any cynically obvious tailing. For a while a grey Mercedes station wagon with English plates travelled just behind them, but when she deliberately slowed it carried its freight of suitcases, beach balls and quarrelling children straight on by. The other traffic all seemed random and changing. When Ramsey craned across to look once more she decided to puncture their tension.

'I told him we were crossing tonight,' she said. 'He's obviously believed me. They've probably checked our booking. He won't be behind us now.'

'Pity,' Ramsey said. The curtness struck her.

'Pity? Why a pity?'

'We're in plenty of time. We could stop and I could bend his face.' Perhaps she shouldn't have told him that it had happened above Anne's grave.

'I thought all doctors were healers,' she said.

'We're pledged to do away with malignant little growths,' Ramsey said darkly. 'It's part of the oath.'

FOUR

On the A3 coming up from Alton the next day he was followed. It was relatively easy to spot the vehicle this time. It was a white Rover which had go-faster stripes down its sides in red and yellow, and the driver had further customised it with a chunky blue excrescence in the centre of its roof. It came up very fast from nowhere, its light not flashing, and tucked in behind Tessa's Panda. Then, doggedly, it proceeded to sit there. Ramsey had sighed and ·slowed to a don't-lay-down-the-law-to-me four miles over the limit and kept the needle there. Not all bad. The Rover would be experiencing a nervous break-down over whether to be in second or third.

It was the second incident since they'd crossed. At Southampton nothing at all untoward had happened in Passports and Customs. But they could be so easily observed from afar there he'd hardly expected it to. Who knew whether the uniformed man with a transceiver was sheep-dogging cars or reporting in about their progress? But when about half-past ten they'd walked in to Tessa's tiny cottage on the edge of Alton – the inland, English equivalent of his own he realised – she had turned to him wide-eyed.

'Someone's been here,' she had said.

He had looked around. Cane furniture, bright curtains, an oil lamp, a splendid set of library steps – all he could detect was the heavy silence several days absence fills a house with.

'How can you tell?'

'I don't know. But I know. Something's different. Moved. Can you smell anything?'

'Polish, I think. A waxy smell.'

She grimaced and pointed. The surface of a period sidetable gleamed obviously back.

'Anything missing?' he said.

Slowly, standing in the small, low room's centre she swung round on her heels. She had all but completed a circle when she stopped. 'The telephone,' she said. 'The receiver's the wrong way round.'

Moving across to the shelf the phone was on, she picked up the receiver, turned it around, replaced it. 'I'm right-handed,' she added. 'I always hold the phone in my left hand so I can make notes.'

He stepped across and took the phone from her. With a doctor's precision he unscrewed the mouth piece.

'What is it?'

'Nothing that I can see,' he was obliged to say. 'Hang on, though.'

29

He put the mouthpiece back together and, remembering the 01, dialled Guy's Hospital. He held the receiver tight to his ear as each spin of the dial sent instructions chattering down the line towards the relays. The moment there was a ring the other end he hung up.

'What was all that about?' Tessa asked.

'If it's being tapped there's supposed to be an echo.'

'Was there?'

'I don't know. I don't know what the echo would sound like.' He saw that she didn't know whether to laugh or groan at this complete collapse of his Bogart image. It was self-esteem as much as anything that prompted his next remark. 'If it's important, though – private – I'd ring from somewhere else.'

A while later, having dropped her and taken the car on, he'd felt the whole trip was a mistake. The driving on the left, the floor mounted gear lever, was no sweat. It was like riding a bicycle. Once he'd stopped turning the wiper on each time he meant to signal, he'd remembered and gone over to automatic pilot . . . No, that was nothing. It was . . . everything else.

There was Tessa. Yes, she genuinely did need him for moral support right now. But hanging between them all the time was her indication, certain, however unspoken, that she thought she needed him in every other way as well. More generally . . . The walls of the Gents on the ferry had been covered with obscenities about a football manager's private life. When he'd bought pipe tobacco in the duty free shop he'd been jostled by two leather-jacketed, henna-haired teenagers of both sexes, who'd never questioned their right to reach across him. The country pub he'd stopped at for his first pint was no such thing. It was a road-house of a restaurant, incongruously 'themed' to resemble a boat house. Oars hung on the walls, skiffs and racing shells were suspended from the ceiling. The vestigial bar that remained – 'Would you like a drink before you eat, sir?' 'No, I'd like a drink' – had been space-invaded. Played on by loud young men with loud suits, predictable moustaches and credit cards, electronic bandits clattered and rang. The fizzy, soap-sudded suspension of chemicals of a 'pint of ordinary' had left him homesick for Pelikan. He had left the dimpled mug on the counter still two thirds filled with its over-engineered contents. . . . Yes, a mistake all round. Part of him would be sorry to say a last farewell to an old friend but this was the England he had not been at all sorry to leave . . . And now this tiresomeness.

After some six miles of self-conscious tandeming, the police car, its protruberance now flashing, had drawn alongside him on the gong. Sighing, he pulled over half onto the grassy verge. The Rover slewed across his bows in the text-book 'they shall not pass' Hendon fashion.

Two of them. Curiously it was the driver who got out and, taking his sizing-up time about it, came sauntering back. They'd picked a good spot. Country. Hedges and fields and not too much else on the road at this in-between hour. Ramsey wound down the Fiat's window.

'Afternoon, sir.'

Don't bother to reply. Just make the bastard stay outside bending down. Thirty plus. A touch older, then, and uniformed but otherwise a moustachioed clone of the cock-sure sales reps back in that ghastly Yeoman pub. Lucky he'd drunk so little.

'May I see your licence, please?'

Ramsey handed it across.

'Ah . . . Are you French then, sir?'

'I have the feeling you already know that I'm not.'

Not put off the policeman – 49 was the number to note on his shirt epaulette but it was hard to tell his rank – compared the mug shot on the licence with the original. 'Not a UK resident then, doctor?' he said.

'No. Not at present.'

'I wonder if you could tell me the registration number of this vehicle, sir . . .'

Not a question, an order. And damn his smug, petty, brief authority, he couldn't! It began with an A but as to what came after . . . Well, he would tough it out.

'I've absolutely no idea of what it might be.'

'May I see the insurance documents . . . sir?'

'I've no idea where they are either.' Again he used his Hospital Management Committee voice.

'Is there a current Test Certificate in issue?'

'Is that the MOT?'

'It is.'

'I imagine there's one somewhere.'

'You realise that according to the Road Traffic Act of 1972, Section 43, there must be one?'

'I thought it was Section 44?' That got to him. Two faint patches showed red among the incipiently broken veins on 49's cheeks. But it was suddenly all too tiresome.

'It's not my car, is it?' Ramsey said. 'I've borrowed it from a friend.'

'And who would that be?'

'A Miss Tessa Waite.'

'W-A-I-T-E?'

'Yes.'

'And her address?'

'Pett's Farm Cottage, Alton. But she works at the Mid-Hants Agricultural College. I've just dropped her there.'

'I see, . . . Can you prove that you're in possession of this vehicle with this Miss Waite's consent, sir?'

'One phone call will do that.'

The policeman thought about it. He straightened up and then bent forward again. He returned the licence to Ramsey. 'Do you intend staying in England long, doctor?' he asked.

Good Lord! Was it all just for that? 'Is that relevant?' Ramsey said. It caused a furrowing of the brows.

'Relevant, sir? How do you mean –'

'Relevant to whatever you're doing.'

'I don't follow you, sir.'

'You just did. For six or seven bloody miles. Aren't you supposed to tell me why you stopped me – provide a reason?'

'You were driving over the limit, sir.'

'And the stuff going by us? That Saab?'

'We can only attend to one matter at a time, sir.'

'My heart bleeds.'

'And it is in your own best interests to stay within the speed limit, sir.'

'You can tell them I'll be here no more than three days.'

Number 49 looked at him. Was it with satisfaction now? 'Drive carefully, sir,' he said.

Someone ought to write *The Tale of Two Houses*, Ramsey thought as he swung the Fiat into the driveway and behind the top of the range Volvo wagon. The price tags would be comparable but, otherwise, what a contrast! Dany's *manoir* had retired behind its wall but it was not stand-offish. Whatever faint traces of *ancien régime* aristocracy had once run in their veins the ghosts there were an amiable bunch. They would be in dishabille as they amusedly watched the present incumbents repeat all their own mistakes. Like the house they had, you would finally have to say, a human dimension. At the Blackheath abode of the late Exton Waite and his wife Beryl, however, the ghosts would be in bourgeois black tie. The house went back to the mid-eighteenth century and had once, no doubt, throughout its four double-fronted storeys been as graciously unbraced as the French. But some Edwardian precursor of David O. Selznick had caused a sort of white, columned Roman colonnade to be shot-gun married to the façade. Not in the least retiring, the house squatted squarely down on the west side of the heath proclaiming the four-square merits of hard work and application and, if you had it, money. The early ghosts would have long since taken the Dover Road. Those who

32

remained would be the ones happy to eavesdrop on the conversations of the solicitors and merchant bankers and Parliamentary hopefuls about the Arab take-over.

Ramsey took the off-white steps two at a time but as he approached the Number Ten-ish door its Brasenose knocker abruptly receded from him. Beryl Waite stood in the open doorway.

'Ramsey!' she said.

Everything threw him. Political animal as she'd long since become, and practised at masking her feelings, a sort of consecutive triptych of emotions had this time paraded across her face. Indignation had given way to undisguised surprise which had then been supplanted by a largely feigned pleasure.

'Hello, Beryl,' was all he could say.

'I'm totally surprised! I caught a glimpse of Tessa's car and . . . naturally . . . I thought it was her.'

'She's at the college. I dropped her off there earlier today.'

'Oh.'

'We got back this morning . . . You do know she came over and stayed with me in France . . .'

'No. I didn't . . . But I do understand now. Come in, please.'

And he understood now why indignation had occupied pole position as she opened the door. It was a mean trick to use mutual grief as a way of heading it off at the pass but the card was to hand. 'About Exton,' he said, as he stepped into the spacious, chandeliered hall, 'words aren't adequate, but –'

'Thank you,' she said, sincerely enough. 'I know you were good friends.'

'Since college. If there's anything I can do . . . anything . . .'

'I promise you'll be the first to know . . . For the moment, you've timed it well. We're just having tea. Pop in there and introduce yourself and I'll get another cup.'

Not a fat woman, but stocky, square, she turned towards the back of the house. He went through the door she had indicated and a trim man of medium height and age politely rose to meet him. As well as the black tie he wore a single-breasted suit in a faint Prince of Wales check, the overall greyness of which contrived to complement the greyness of his neatly parted full head of hair. He was extending his hand. 'We haven't met,' he said. 'My name's Adams. Ted Adams. I'm – I was Exton's agent.'

The accident of a full teapot apart, the visit's timing had not been convenient. Small talk had ensued. His gesture in crossing over for the funeral was given formal acknowledgement by an official, as it were, invitation. But as, with no further reference to Tessa, widow and agent proceeded to map out the funeral's logistics he felt uncomfortably *de trop*. Not that it was ever a comfortable room. In exquisite good taste, with its *eau de nil* walls, peacock satin drapes and white plastering, it was very Beryl, very Sanderson; but comfortable – never. That was it. It was uncomfortable because it was a room of only one person's own. Hers. He watched her as she fine-tuned the arrangements for the funeral bake meats. Never in her life attractive, she had had to convert her forward thrust of jaw and wide, almost Slavic face, into promises of dedication and dependability. Her early fifties were beginning to emphasise the masculine in her a little too much for comfort. He remembered hearing it said way back that without Beryl's pushing Exton Waite would have readily set his sights no higher than being a cheerily drunk lobby correspondent. Whereas, if he had lived, Beryl might have woken up one day knowing she had matched Nancy all the way to the top.

'So, Tessa came to see you,' the object of his thoughts now slightly startled him by turning and saying.

'Two days ago.'

'And why, do you suppose?'

He leaned forward and replaced his cup and saucer on the trolley before he replied. Whether by interrogation or intuition she would know about two years ago, of course. 'I'm not sure,' he said. 'Somewhere to run to. Rejection of the present by changing the geography since you can't put the clock back. You know, like refusing to drive a car you've put a dent in. And, of course, while you're running you can let your mind go blank.'

Without making a sound Beryl Waite contrived to suggest she had sniffed. 'Twenty-four years old. You expect more. I know I do.'

Ted Adams saw the sardonic-looking doctor use a non-commital smile, a quick inclining of the head to ride the conversational jab. A good bloke, he suspected. Beryl and Tessa, he thought for the thousandth time: no love lost there. The girl had got all of her looks and dash and openness from her father, of course. What Beryl had provided them both with was money.

'Beryl,' he said looking at his watch as he rose, 'if it's all right I'll have to collect Ingrid now.'

'Yes, I'll be fine,' Beryl said almost ignoring him. 'I should have thought, Ramsey, you could at least have phoned me.'

But the doctor could counter-punch as well. 'Beryl, it never for a moment struck me that she hadn't told you where she was.'

Hovering half-way between chaise-longue and door Ted Adams saw Beryl digest that reply and decide to swallow it. The sense of her rudeness towards him compelled him to make some further bid for attention.

'Did I tell you they've got a fourth Daimler?' he said.

'Yes, Ted, you did,' she said quickly. 'I'll phone you tomorrow and we'll work out the station detail then. Thank you so much for sacrificing this afternoon.'

'No. Not at all . . . My job at the end of the day. Not that . . . yes, well, I'll see myself out. Goodbye Doctor Ramsey, nice to have met you.'

'And to have met you.'

Wondering why Exton Waite's widow had been at such pains to show him who ruled the roost, Ted Adams saw himself out of the house.

'He's really quite excellent,' Beryl Waite was meanwhile saying while conveying otherwise. 'Exton swore by him. More tea?'

Ramsey shook his head. The Volvo outside rev'd and reflections slanted glancingly about the room.

'It was at his house, of course . . . it's so confining, you know, holding the funeral at Brinkton. Such a tiny place. No facilities.'

'He did love it down there.'

'Yes. The retreat to the green thought in a green shade. You know, today we were scheduled to drive up to Yorkshire for the by-election.'

'Oh. I didn't know there was one.'

'Oh, yes. And another one now, of course. Very touch and go, this one. Central Office was drafting in all the big guns.'

'He used to hate elections.'

'Who doesn't? Three weeks of "on the knocker". Of fatigue, boredom and anxiety.'

'He surely wasn't that worried about this one, was he?'

'Not in a personal way, no.'

'Had he had any warnings?'

She looked hard at him. 'With his heart, you mean?'

'Yes.'

'Well, yes and no. No attacks of any kind. But there was the whole rheumatic fever thing when he was a boy.' She stared at the stiff arrangement of dried ferns in the fireplace. 'I've already blamed myself ten dozen times over but with hindsight who doesn't? Now it seems obvious. He should have taken things easier.'

'Was he still golfing?'

'Oh, yes.'

'Was that wise – with angina?'

'Isn't mild exercise supposed to be good in such cases? Circulation and all that. Wyn used to play with him.'

'Your doctor?'

'Yes. Wyn Bennet.'

35

'What about medicines?'

'What sort?'

She levered herself up from the grandmother chair and moved to the secretaire. On its top was a small japanned box. She opened it and returning to Ramsey proferred him a bottle and a packet not unlike an old-style pack of cigarettes. 'I had them to hand for the other doctor,' she said. 'The one who signed the certificate.'

'Who was that?'

'Sir James Wakeley.'

Hmmn, he thought. Going out in style. He read the labels. *Trinitrate 0.5 mg . . . Transdermal patches of Glycerol Trinitrate.* 'Wyn Bennet prescribe these?' he asked.

'Yes.'

'When did he take them?'

'Whenever he felt he needed one, I suppose.'

The airiness of her reply surprised him. Wise after the event was one thing. Pig ignorance before and during it was something else. The one may be excusable if the other doesn't precede it. But how ignorant?

'How did he take them?'

'Swallowed them, of course.'

'Beryl, he didn't. Not these.'

'I'm not with you.'

'These are sub-lingual tablets. They're dissolved slowly under the tongue . . . At times of acute attack.'

And suddenly she had flared up. 'Ramsey! You think I haven't enough on my mind! A twopenny halfpenny cottage to invite people back to! An idiot vicar! The patches were to stick on his chest and not the car bumper. That I *do* remember!'

'Correct,' he said as drily as possible. Never give Beryl the first inch.

'And I'd be "correct", no doubt, in supposing you've come here to cross-examine me.'

'Why should I?' He had, of course. And she, in turn, knew it.

'I'm sorry, Ramsey. It's this sense of holding a funeral in a goldfish bowl. This afternoon's the first time the media haven't been camped on the heath outside. Ted's worked this trade-off with them. So long as we let them turn the memorial service into a circus they'll soft pedal the funeral.' She wrenched her gaze back from the windows. A touch of softness came into her eyes and, then, her voice. 'So they went under his tongue, not down his gullet,' she said. 'I didn't know. He'd want to keep things like that from me to stop me worrying. And to be brutal – so what? It's irrelevant now, isn't it? I was wrong but also, m'lud, I'm at the end of my string.'

He tried to look sympathetic. Privately he was thinking that she was holding herself together with precisely the tough-minded composure that had made her a Westminster conversation piece. There was a lot more string on the reel than she let on, he thought, and much of it used to mark the ways of political labyrinths. He wondered how Izzie was taking it.

FIVE

'I was blow-drying my hair – sitting over there,' Isabel Fleming said.
'I had Breakfast TV on but –'

'Breakfast TV?'

'Yes. We have it over here now. Pretty ghastly, but it pulls me up out of sleep when I'm doing the crack of dawn markets.'

'Sorry, interrupted you.'

'I was watching it but not listening. Because of the drier. I had the sound down. I was only half-watching. Some chat show pap. Suddenly it was the announcer and then his picture flashed up. It took me a moment to realise it was really Exton. You know how I mean.'

'Yes.'

'I grabbed the drier, grabbed the gun but I hit the wrong bloody button. I turned the set off. In the couple of seconds it took me to get it on again with the sound up it was the weather forecast . . . I didn't know what to think. Promotion? Resignation? IRA bomb? Answering a Private Member's Question . . . what? I didn't know what to think.'

'What did you do?'

'The programme repeats endlessly like some mindless conveyor belt. Every half hour or so. I said "stuff Bermondsey" this week and settled down to wait. Even forgot finishing my hair. After five minutes I wasn't really worrying. Just early in the morning over-reaction I told myself. Then the picture came back on and they were saying he'd died the night before from a heart attack. The night before that we were together . . . I couldn't believe it. Wouldn't. And then I could. Ramsey, I never felt so lonely in my life. Beryl . . . Tessa . . . they'd have each other. People. People would ring. Say how sorry they were. I had nobody. I knew it wouldn't alter anything, bring him back. But it would make it more endurable. I had nobody. It's the ultimate bugger of being a mistress, of course. All that "back street" anonymity really brought down on you squared.'

'You should have called me.'

'I nearly did. But I thought you'd been through the same scene once with Anne and . . . well, you deserved being missed out this time around.'

'That was kind, Izzie. But it would have been all right. You end up being stronger, you know. You will, too.'

She looked at him gratefully. A soft, round face framed by brown hair. The huge brown eyes were soft, too. Soft and somehow luminous. They gave an almost liquid quality to the features. But underneath there was the strength of enormous self-reliance. Her consideration towards him from the depths of her own grief was typical.

'I watched his maiden speech,' she said and for an instant was watching it again. 'Coming out into the sunshine and traffic afterwards I felt drunk. I wanted to shout . . . "Hey, that was my fella down there. Pretty good, wasn't he?" '

Back in the present, she smiled ruefully at Ramsey. 'But who to say it to? The 53 bus? He was still in the House and I was out on the street alone. There was no one. And now there's nothing. There was only him, Ramsey – and now he's gone.'

Abruptly she smashed a fist into a palm. 'Dead,' she said. 'Let's call a spade a spade.' She grinned, as the small eruption of violence provided release. 'Never did like the euphemisms,' she confirmed. 'More plonk?'

'Why not?'

'I'll get another bottle.' She went into the kitchen. He looked about him. Slightly sixty-ish in its reliance on naked wood, sealed floorboards, bright cushions and fibre mats, it gave no clue to the dark mahoganyesque feel of the shop below.

When, the bell tinkling, he'd pushed the door open an hour or so earlier there had been a customer, a tall, elderly woman, inside already. Izzie had looked up mechanically and then, her face coming alive, rapturously. But she had stuck to her last. As the woman handled the silver picture frame Izzie remained silently at her side. Willing to be patient too, he had pretended to be another customer and looked about. There was a big glass-fronted bookcase and a restored chaise longue, but in the main Izzie dealt in smaller pieces: Cranberry, Capo di Monte, antique jewellery. Less capital investment. She did well as a staging post to the big places on clocks. She'd long ago learnt what was what, as witness now.

The woman's dithering was obviously an act. She wanted the piece. In a Harvey Nicholsish voice she suggested a swingeing discount. Izzie countered with firm demureness and a nominal reduction. She was dying to see him, talk to him, he knew, but she wasn't going to be a doormat for anyone. Her all over. Vegetarian, Greenpeace and free-range eggs, Indian peasant fabrics, she seemed at first glance a small 'l' liberal pushover. But she wasn't. She was as determined in her gentle way as was Beryl in hard-nosed mode . . .

After decades, at Izzie's price, the woman bought the frame. The second the outward bound bell had rung, Izzie was in his arms.

'Ramsey! At last a person!' she had said. It was barely mid-morning but she'd put the 'Closed' sign eyes front.

'Come upstairs,' she'd said. 'The bar's open.' So was the second bottle of Frascati. She returned with it now.

'So you're staying with Tessa,' she said, suspiciously neutral.

'No. I thought that was a sleeping dog best left to lie.'

'I'd hardly call Tessa a dog'. She had that low, clear voice.

'Now, now. Don't be roguish.'

'Where then?'

'I booked in at some one-up from sleazy hotel on the Kensington borders. It's called the Kensington Carlton but it's really the Earls Court armpit.'

'I know,' she said, sitting down, 'they look sideways at you if you don't come back with a bird.'

'Got it in one. There's a butter ball of a night clerk – rancid butter, *bien entendu* – who within four minutes of my checking in had checked out whether I wanted a tart, boy or some dope.'

'I didn't realise it was so up front these days.'

'Well I've lost touch. A sense of scale. I told him I'd watch TV.'

'You could stay here, you know.'

'Thanks but – no pun intended – I'll hang loose. It's only a couple of nights.'

She put down her glass. 'Make me a promise,' she ordered.

'Of course.'

'Come back and tell me about the funeral.'

'Done.'

'In a while I'll go down there . . . they all got him wrong, you know.'

'Who?'

'The papers. The obits. "The PM's yes man." "Another Gaitskell or McLeod." None of them got the nice, caring, worried, *funny* man I knew.'

'You were the one who made him all those things.'

'Do you think so?'

'Yes.'

'Oh, I do hope you're right.'

'You know I am. Now don't think about crying . . . In a way, you can't have been totally surprised.'

'Ramsey! I was shattered!'

'But you knew he had angina.'

'Rubbish!'

'But he did.'

'Never. He'd have told me.' Where before her eyes had started to grow even more moist, she was now, a woman in her forties, blushing.

'Dr Ramsey – I shared a sex life with him. It was active, varied, er, imaginative. He didn't have angina.'

'What did he have?'

'Nothing. Oh, a bit of a back. A disc thing. A tendency to colds but I kept pushing the Vitamin C into him.'

'Booze?'

'No. Not *that* much. Social but not chronic.'

'Did he sleep well?'

'Didn't need to. Always citing Churchill's four hours a night ration. He used to get up in the small hours, potter around, draft memos. He'd make tea. Great tea drinker.'

'Food?'

'Not a lot, no. Not a big appetite.'

'Way back when he used to smoke pot.'

'Still did a bit. There was a nub of it in his electric razor.'

'Still got it?'

'I flushed it away.'

He paused a moment as he prepared to step on hallowed ground.

'Is there much of his stuff here?'

'A fair amount. Do you want to look?'

His delicacy had been unnecessary.

'Would you mind?'

She shook her head and stood up. She led him out on to the minuscule landing and pushed open the door to her spare room. 'Go in. I'll do us a salad.'

He went in. It was cluttered in a rather high-style way. Floor-standing stacks of shiny new books – ah, Exton had reviewed for the Sundays – Hansard, gallery catalogues. On the bleached pine desk note-pads. No jottings. And nothing in the waste bin. Of a sudden he felt foolish and ashamed. It was a sharp clear image of what he no doubt was, a prying interloper playing at detectives but with no idea of what he was looking for that fuelled his self-contempt. 'Dr Ramsey's Case-book.' What the hell gave him the right to be in here doing this? A vague professional disquiet didn't justify poking his – Case-book! Exton would have navigated his days courtesy of a whole slew of diaries. He opened the desk drawer nearest to hand and signposted for him by its discreetly gilt 'E.W.' a diary slid into view. He picked it up, flicked towards the pages Exton had turned, oblivious to the fact they marked the quickening count-down to his death. The last entry was cryptically geographic: SW3. He put the diary back in the drawer. Now, any more? What were those? Oh, of course, video cassettes. About eight of them on a shelf. Labelled. *'Panorama'. 'This Week'* . The one on the far right was simply dated: 19.3.87. Seized with an idea, he picked it up. He moved to the door to

41

find that something made him pause. He turned. For a while yet this was still a dead man's room. The objects within it waited with forlorn stubbornness as they tried to deny the growing weight of silence, implication. Bereft of their master, they had known him for a stranger. He closed the door on them.

Life bustled in the bright, white kitchen. Izzie was slicing a lettuce. 'You and Exton – were you in the habit of rendezvousing in Chelsea?' he asked. The knife froze for a moment in mid-stroke.

'No,' she said. 'Very much not. Too much on the beaten track. Why?'

'Oh, just a note he made . . .' He brought the cassette up into her line of vision. 'Is this him?' he asked softly.

'Yes,' she said not even glancing at the label. 'One of his television interviews. He used to ask me to do them.' She pulled a wry face. 'He could count on my being in to press the button.'

'Would you press it now for me?'

She looked sideways at him – grimly sideways.

'Can't you?'

'I wouldn't know which one.'

'All right.' She wiped her hands. 'I'll start it going. But you watch it by yourself.' She led him back into the living room.

'I'm sorry,' he said, as she bent over the video recorder, 'but the French aren't that big on these things. They still think it's possibly nice to sit opposite each other in the evening talking.'

'And I'm sorry too,' she said. 'But I know I'm just not ready yet to sit watching him face to face again, if you see what I mean.' Things clicked and whirred.

'We're a new generation really,' she went on, as she straightened. 'Evening after evening we get entertained – visibly – by dead people.' She pointed to a remote control. 'Zap,' she said. There was another click. She turned away and positively hurried from the room. Before any images had come she had shut the kitchen door.

It was a brief interview. A local, regional programme, he gathered. He watched clinically only half-hearing the words as a nervously ambitious reporter asked his tetchy devil's advocate questions. 'But, Minister, given the public's disquiet and the findings of this latest report, surely you'd agree . . .'

Exton didn't agree and he had scant trouble in explaining why not. . . . Midway through the salad Ramsey put down his fork and looked at Izzie very carefully.

'Did he always talk that fast?'

'Hmnph! You ever sit in the Visitor's Gallery?'

'No.'

'Or hear *Yesterday in Parliament*. "Order! Order!" If you don't talk fast you don't get heard.'

'Democratic government by the vocal bully-boys. Of whichever sex. You said he had a lot of colds.'

'Yes.'

'The tip of his nose. Was it often sore?'

'Isn't yours a sore point when you keep blowing it?'

'You told me about the cannabis – what else was there?'

She looked hard at him and had meant to. He held her stare and said nothing. 'Does it matter?' she at last conceded. 'Can it bring him back to life?'

'It could save a lot of other lives, Isabel.'

She was a very determined soul but even more a decent one. She sank down onto a kitchen stool. 'He was snorting cocaine,' she said.

He'd been almost certain. The over-achiever's drug.

'He got into it in Washington,' she went on, as if reading his mind. 'What would you like – brandy, port or coke? You name the dinner party, it's there. You think it killed him?'

'Yes. Tessa took his pulse. She said it was thumping, booming. He was sweating like a . . . He was sweating. If it had been a myocardial as the certificate states he'd've been blue. The pulse would have been thin, thready. Bennet would have tried to revive him . . . an aminophyline injection probably. He must have known.'

'There would have been a tube and things,' Izzie said in a distant voice.

'No one's mentioned them . . . he was sprawled across the desk.'

'I didn't think it would kill him. I thought he –' Her voice cracked completely. The soft face crumpled. She began to cry. He held her. After a while she pulled away, sniffing and wiping her face with the back of her hands. She reached for a tea-towel. 'Truth for truth's sake,' she said bitterly.

'I'm sorry. But you must –'

'No, don't apologise. I won't curse you, Ramsey. I don't blame you. It's your nature to be truthful.'

'Not always.'

'In big things, you are . . . You're right. His nasal septum was gone . . . He OD'd. And when they spelt that out in full it came as a "coronary".'

'But of course. Do you think any government could live with the truth? Especially these apostles of "law and order". They'd rationalise it to themselves and one another by saying they were protecting his memory.'

'But at bottom it's a conspiracy of silence.'

'And at the top. There has to have been a cover-up. Bennet, his GP certainly. Wakeley, the big gun they wheeled up because a *Sir* looks good on a certificate – almost certainly. Adams his agent, very likely.'

'And Beryl?'

They looked at each other with the same increasingly wild surmise. 'Beryl wouldn't countenance anything that would prejudice his health and so his career and so her ambition,' Izzie said.

She spoke flatly and out of a sense of reality, he acknowledged, not from rancour. 'All her investment,' she added. Well, some rancour, after all.

'But by the same token she'd then do everything to protect that reputation once he was dead.' he said.

'If she was in on it . . . do you think she was?'

'She might have seen something Tessa missed and put two and two together. She would have kept tighter control when she walked up and saw it all. Or Bennet or someone may have blurted it out in the middle of all the panic. Adams. There was a hell of a lot of constraint between her and him when I came in on them yesterday.'

'They might have had to tell her to clinch her agreeing to go the cremation route. It's not her, a cremation. Too unladylike.'

He looked closely at her. The Laura Ashley print belied her shrewdness.

'That makes a lot of sense,' he said. They fell silent. The kitchen clock measured the length of their thinking with a succession of 'tocks.'

'Why this time?' Izzie asked. 'Why did it kill him this time and not any other?'

'There has to be the one time. For all of us . . . I'm not sure otherwise. Could be it was so pure, so unadulterated it blew his head off.'

She winced but he hurried on.

'He'd have access to the best presumably. Or then again the complete reverse. Cut with something lethal – rat poison, battery acid, some amphetamines . . .'

'In which case . . .' she began. She paused. Again they were looking unblinkingly straight at each other as separately, but in perfect synchronisation, they made the same deductions. 'In which case we have to ask the question, since Exton's death wasn't natural was it accidental or was it . . . engineered.'

She had got through to the end of the sentence. The thought of murder only just having come to him he had not had the time to divert the earlier course of the conversation. The softness of her features was being drawn tighter by some inner constriction. It occurred to him it made her look exactly like he felt. His mouth, his throat were dry. And when she spoke again her voice was all but inaudible. 'The funeral . . . should we get it stopped . . . try to?'

44

'Izzie – Tessa was followed to France. We've both been tailed since she reached me. Her cottage has been searched – very discreetly, but searched. Almost certainly bugged . . .'

Her eyes were almost lemur-like.

'A proper post-mortem – they won't allow it. As we've said. The good name bit. Not his, when it comes right down to it, but the party's . . . And what about his? The desecration – would *you* want it?'

Mutely she shook her head.

'Thirty-six hours from now his body goes into a furnace,' he said. 'And that's the end of it.' She blanched. With reason.

SIX

It was the smell that irked him most, that got up his nose. The rest –
the faded bamboo-motif'd wallpaper, the chipped dresser in ill-
seasoned block-board, the token sliver of soap in the vertical coffin of
a bathroom – he could shut his eyes to. Locked into his own thoughts,
nagging away at the giant cross-word puzzle he seemed increasingly
intent on setting himself (all those blank squares; so few clues) he
could even ignore the chink of glasses, the slap and tickle giggles, the
bed creaks, that had come through the cardboard walls at irregular
intervals and, it seemed, from varying protagonists. But the smell!
There was an ancient foundation of cheap, pine-scented disinfectant,
then a layer of musty, frowsty dust, the over-spill of damp from the
bathroom, and finally a top-dressing from the cheapest of cover-
your-multitude-of-sins aerosols. Air-freshener! The aroma had the
sharp copper-wire tang of animal urine. You could all but taste it on
your lips and tongue.

Feeling his stomach threaten to heave, he diverted his attention
with a glance at his watch. Nearly nine. All over London public life
was just about beginning again. Time to start playing the longest of
shots. He quitted the evil little room and walked down the cheerless
corridor. First floor. No point in taking the lift. As the stairs began
the corridor's threadbare carpet gave way to another selected on the
basis of its knock-down price. Only the equality of the wear and tear
prevented the sunflowers utterly clashing with the waffle-patterned
rectangles.

As Ramsey rounded the last corner of the stair well, the back of a
bald head bobbed like an albino beach ball across the lobby. Good
Lord! The porter was cleaning the windows.

The last tread creaked and the head swivelled instantly round.
When he saw Ramsey the porter's face tightened. 'Good morning,'
Ramsey said.

Still tight-lipped, the porter nodded warily.

'Do you have a copy of the Yellow Pages behind the desk?'

'What are you after?' The question was delivered sideways on.

'A look in the Yellow Pages.' It took one to know one. Hostilities
were confirmed. Limping slightly the porter crossed the green and
gold pocket-handkerchief of a lobby and lifting the flap went behind
the burgundy-plastic counter. He bent down, heaved the weight of
the trades directory into view and down on to the counter's surface.
The dust had almost settled as Ramsey reached for it. He stayed his

hand in the mid-action. It might be worth finding out.

'Why the change?' he asked abruptly and looked the porter full in the face. It was to stare at a former all-in wrestler stonily nursing the memories of his defeats.

'What change?'

'Come on. When I first came in here it was like the temptation of Christ. Girls. Boys. Pot. You were trying to fix me up with the riches of the earth. Now – now you won't give me the time of day. What is it? Sore loser?'

The porter didn't shave his skull. A few wisps of hair still ran straight back over its top. His eyebrows were the colour of dirty straw. The eyes blinked. The tautness of his cheek muscles relaxed a truce-conferring fraction. 'I try not to get out of my league,' he muttered quickly. 'I didn't know you had form before.'

'Form? Me?'

The porter nodded towards the window. 'Think cleaning that's my job,' he said.

Ramsey picked up the Yellow Pages. He moved to the window as if seeking light to read by. He flicked pages and then glanced out. A narrowish street. Bourgeois gentility down on its luck and gone in for trade. No garages so cloned cars bumper to bumper on both sides. In one of them, an anonymously dark blue Escort, the shadowy shapes of two men. Ramsey turned another page, looked at the top left entry.

'Who are they?' he said, his back to the porter.

'Old Bill. They've been outside regular as weather every time you've been inside. When you went out yesterday afternoon – whoosh, right behind you.'

'They been up to my room?' He turned as he spoke.

'No.' It seemed the truth. Let them look in any case. There was nothing to find.

'They ain't local bacon,' the porter said. 'I know all of them.'

Ramsey smiled. Going back to the desk, he reached for his wallet. 'Thanks,' he said. The fiver disappeared like a soluble aspirin. 'If I wanted to go beyond pot,' Ramsey said. 'Where would I . . .' The porter's expression cut him off. It was the look of a man blind from birth.

'Like I said,' he said. 'I stay in a league I can handle.'

He sat on the bed and tried to minimise his breathing. Who knew what new forms of life were being cultivated under the bed, behind the moulded bedroom mirror? Not himself. He wasn't about to look. Instead . . . he turned to the pages headed *Physicians and Surgeons*.

Five minutes later the litany of names had so imposed itself on him he was muttering aloud. 'Tanner, Taylor C., Taylor R. . . . Timmerman, Thomas E., Thomas L. . . . Thorne, D. E.' He looked away from the long list with a sudden surge of excitement.

Derrick Edward Thorne! Oily Derrick. Star of the *Rag Revue* about the time they built Stonehenge. 'I'm not the Thorne on your side, madam, but the one in it.' Pause for groans.

Derrick Edward Thorne!

More stairs – this time because a different lift was broken. A different smell of diluted Dettol. But the same dust, apparently. A fag-end there. On the sill of the window, looking out into the scuff-grassed barracks-like square, a crumpled chocolate wrapper. The sickening to the sick.

He gained the second floor, turned, as the sign seemed to indicate he possibly should, and, heels sounding, walked along the depressingly drab corridor. There was a strong sense of a third-rate college for non-conformist ministers. The high Victorian windows seemed to have the Gothic trick of transmitting a minimum of illumination. The corridor debouched into a waiting area. Some speciality must be, or had been, housed up here. Ah yes, ENT. The apathetically huddled mass of about twenty people waiting did not look as if they would be surprised or try to move if told the department had been closed three years ago. Most of them were brown, or black; all of them were poor. It was a long time since he'd been a houseman but surely in his day you occasionally met a patient who looked wealthy – and hopeful. It all compared shoddily with the hospital he worked at in France, with its softened, silence-maintaining rubber flooring, bright strip lighting, stainless steel fittings that were clean. All right, the French hospital was modern, new. But why wasn't this? This was all of a piece with the wilting hotel. And he could almost feel pleased. The mean sadness everywhere apparent on the underside of life here was corroboration that there was nothing wrong with England that staying away couldn't put right.

The desk was deserted. Tea-break, or instantaneous defection to the private sector. But a flash of grey-blue had caught his eye through the glass peephole in the door to the ward. With studied decisiveness he pushed his way into the ward.

At the sound a tall, thin, sallow-featured Staff Nurse turned enquiringly. Tiredness clogged her eyes. She was harassed, peevish, heroic.

'Afternoon, Staff,' he said quickly before she could turn awkward, 'I'm Ramsey. Dr Thorne sent me to fetch Kate Ross.' His tone of voice was as to the manner trained. She let her face relax. 'Oh, yes,' she said. 'She's outside in the waiting room. The tall girl on the corner.'

'Thank you,' he smiled. But he must have given a look of some kind too.

'We needed the bed,' she said. And thereby said it all. He nodded again and went out.

The girl was virtually opposite the door. That was why he had not noticed her on the way in. A white girl, tall and going on skeletal, in a grey sweatshirt, unbuttoned grey cardigan, and tight jeans of a fadedness that matched her appearance. Lank, non-descript shoulder-length hair. Of about half the Staff Nurse's age and quadruple her exhaustion. Ramsey made a point of not getting too intimidatingly close.

'Kate?' he asked.

She looked up from out of nowhere. Mistrust gave her an instant false energy. 'About bloody time,' she said, in a cultured voice that was trying to sound tough. She bent forward, was thrusting a stuffed full supermarket bag at this new-found beau.

'Everything?' he said.

'It was somewhat unexpected.'

'So I heard.'

'Did you?' It was a challenge, stating he was one of them. She was tall, five foot ten, perhaps. The stretched dry skin covered the framework for classic, possibly recoverable, pre-Raphaelite beauty.

'Next time I'll make like a pregnant mum,' she said.

'Sorry. . . ?'

'I'll have the suitcase ready packed.'

This was unfamiliar territory. The lower slopes of Kilburn, perhaps. After they'd gone on past the right turn to Lords he'd surrendered his south of the river soul to the forces of North London darkness.

'You're the navigator,' he said to Kate Ross. She nodded. Not a fool.

'How do you feel?'

'Empty.'

He pulled out past a double-parked van.

'Second on the left.'

He changed down to second and took the corner. Another garage-less pre-World War One street with souvenirs of Dagenham, Cowley and Osaka the length of both its sides.

'Over there. The black gate just past the Mazda.'

He squeezed the tiny Fiat into the hint of a parking space.

'You did that well. Thanks. I can hack it from here.' He kept hold of the shopping bag he was heaving forward from the back seat.

'You haven't done with me yet,' he said.

'What are you? Some kind of social worker?'

'Sociable. I fancy you.' It threw her. There was a hint of amusement in the quick lift of her eyes heavenward. She didn't object as he followed her up the pock-marked asphalt path.

She had the basement flat. They went down a short run of steps. She prised a key from her jeans' pocket. Her fingers were ringless. She turned the key, banging the door open. Neither inviting him in nor slamming the door shut, she went inside. He followed.

There was a small area with doors off and no indication which way she'd gone. Then from the left he heard bathroom noises. He went through a door to the right and in to what must be the flat's main room.

Phew! Did everything this side of the Channel reek or had somebody cranked up his nasal receptivity quotient? He went to a window that looked up on to a slope that some earth-mover had cut out for the subterranean flat's benefit. The catch resisted. It hadn't known use in years, but with force it gave. He creaked the window open. A sort of damp freshness came into the room from the sunless bank of gone-to-seed grass. There was the sound of a toilet flushing. He turned from the window as carelessly zipping up her jeans Kate Ross came back into the room.

'You like fug?' he asked.

'Care to spell that?' But before he could react, she added, 'I love it.'

Kate sat down on the single bed that, draped with some kind of North African blanket, doubled up for a sofa in that bare room. And bare was the word. There was an ancient Welsh dresser for which Isabel would have given her eye teeth if she could thus have bought and prised it from the wall it was built into. But nearly all its shelves were empty. There was a hi-fi system to one end and speakers in two of the room's corners. A Sodastream thingummy stood in isolation on the sanded and sealed floor, whose nakedness two small Mexicanesque rugs seemed to emphasise rather than conceal. Against one wall there was a pine kitchen table, and four spindly chairs, no two of which formed a pair. Several rectangles on the bare walls where pictures had once hung. No television. Not a book in sight.

'But we call it home,' Kate Ross said, derisively reading his thoughts. 'Don't reckon it, do you? And you don't reckon me, you liar. I just took a long hard look. No wonder those harpies wouldn't give me a mirror.'

She grimaced with what once again might have been partly amusement. 'Shit,' she said. 'The best high of my life and I'm not

50

there to take part. Zapped out on the carpet.'

'So it wasn't here?'

'No.'

'Where?'

It was his day for people to give him hard looks.

'Somewhere private,' she said. 'A private shooting gallery.'

'Who called the ambulance?'

'This guy.'

'What guy?'

'Never saw him before. Don't know.' She had literally shrugged, spoken without first erecting that wall of hostility. With almost instantly diminishing disbelief he realised she told the truth.

'And didn't call the ambulance. Drove me round there. Dumped me and ran. So's the others could split. A real soldier.'

'It's so . . . casual,' he finished lamely. 'Unknown people. Some essentially unknown poison . . . a matter of life and death and you shove . . .'

'Are you a Liverpool supporter?' she asked.

He blinked at the non-sequitur. 'No,' he said. 'Nantes.'

She was unambiguously amused this time. 'Snorting. Shooting up. A hot shot blow . . . They're not matters of life and death. They're much more important than that.'

'Like, how?'

'How do you mean how?'

'Describe the feeling.'

Now she smiled broadly. There was green-yellow on the even teeth. 'Can't ever be described,' she said. 'To know it you have to try it.' She paused maliciously, 'Want to?' she said.

He'd lucked out. It wasn't quite the route he'd mapped out but if a short cut presents itself go with it.

'Why not?' he said.

She laughed. Outright and nastily. 'I'll tell you why bleeding not,' she said. 'First it's because I don't have a damned thing to give anyone, starting with myself. No coke, no hash, no bennies, no nothing. Second I don't have any bread to go get something with. I don't have any bread to get bread with if you really want to know! But third, if I did have stuff, if I had a whole bloody wardrobe full of it and it bursting out the doors, I still wouldn't give a single solitary crumb to a piece of narcotics squad filth like you!'

The bed she sat on was opposite the window. The light in that underfurnished room was so dim her face seemed shadowed, or had seemed. But along with the stridency echoing off the bare walls, the enhanced, open enmity in her expression had restored definition to her features. Almost illuminating them.

He sighed and, walking across to her, fished out his wallet. He showed her his driving licence. She studied it a long moment. 'OK,' she said at last, 'so you're a French dick. Well, I've heard they're the best sort.'

She couldn't forbear the laugh that matched her joke. Ramsey gave her a moment to feel pleased with herself before trying old-fashioned truth. 'I'm not French and I'm not a detective,' he said. 'I'm English and I'm a doctor – although that's beside the point.'

It was, almost.

'I live and work in France but I came over here because a friend of mine died a few days ago. He OD'd all the way on coke.'

'You mean he sniffed it then he snuffed it.'

'You put it very well. Very nastily.'

'So.'

'I don't know why it went rotten for him. He wasn't that young a man. Older than me.'

'Ancient!'

'And too modern. It could be, of course, that the last stuff he took had been cut with some kind of . . . of . . .'

'Shit.'

'Yes. In another nutshell.'

'So how does that get you walking into that rat-trap of a hospital to pick me up?'

'I phoned around various old medical contacts. One of them told me about this patient of his – you – who'd OD'd a lot of the way towards all of the way.'

'Dr Thorne,' she said. 'He a friend of yours?'

'Yes.'

'Not a bad soldier,' she said. 'He came into the hospital when the police took a statement.'

'He's a good bloke. I thought, you see, there was a chance the stuff that nearly did for you was from the same source that finished my friend.'

She spread her arms wide like a footballer protesting a booking. The tendons at the front of her neck stuck up scrawnily from the sweatshirt's collar. 'Where have you been?' she said. 'No. Don't tell me, France. Have you any idea of how much stuff is swilling about there on the streets? How many dealers and pushers are in the friendly neighbourhood?'

'Upstream from them, though, it comes in in one-off batches, doesn't it?'

'So does petrol . . . Baked beans . . . You've got no chance.'

He turned and looked out of the window at the dispirited grass. She was no doubt right. He'd tried to take action, any action, to

52

paper over the feeling of being useless. 'And what chance do you think you've got?' he said, his back still to her. She didn't answer.

'Ever been on a Big Dipper?' she asked softly.

He turned back towards her. 'A long time ago.'

'It starts like that. With this bitter taste. Your heart begins to pound. You hear your veins humming – really *hear* them – all the way down to your toes.' Real animation had replaced the flatness in her voice. It was as if she were trying to turn herself on from memories.

'You feel like . . . like your mainspring's being over-wound. You want to rush out, do things, discover continents. Then you know that all the continents are in you.' There was genuine fervour in her expression now.

'You talking coke?' he prompted gently.

'It's the best stone on God's earth. No argument. The warmest, soothingest. The best, bestest, highest there is. They say it's like God kissing you. People save all year. They fly somewhere like Bali – lie in the sun, listen to the surf, watch the kites fly over the palm trees. For how long? Two weeks? Two weeks in the year . . .? Pathetic! A line of nose candy and I can do that any night in the year!'

'So it gives you a lift.'

'Oh, Jesus, does it ever!'

'How long have you been into it?'

'Eighteen months.'

'So you're finding it difficult to come down. You're starting to need help.'

'Ludes. I use them. They do it.'

'Soon you won't be able to sleep.'

'Sleepers.'

'Exactly. More drugs. And after a time they won't work either. You've already flogged or pawned everything loose in your life to pay for what you need but that's the least of your problems. Your nose is going . . . your reflexes . . . your liver . . . you're sick half the time . . . paranoia is building.'

'What are you? Some kind of –'

'Doctor. Yes, I told you. The memory starts shedding brain cells like autumn leaves as well. How old are you, Kate?'

'That I do remember. Twenty-two.'

'Know how long your average doper lives?'

Sullen again she scowled at him. 'You're about to tell me, aren't you, Doc!'

'From first puff to last pop – twelve years.'

'Bull shit!'

'No, true. You're eighteen months in. Before you hit thirty-two all that's left of you will be the dodgy contents of a plastic ash-can.'

'Great! Use it to cut coke with! Someone can snort me and get a cannibal high!' A wild glee had come into her voice but he knew from the ferocity of the obscene image that he had got to her. Again surprising him by her height she got to her feet. She came and stood close to him.

'How about you?' she said. 'Would you like to snort me? Like now?' The soft light had smoothed out the strained edginess in her face.

'You can have me,' she said. 'Bargain rate. I owe you a bit for collecting me.' She reached a hand out and touched his arm. He backed away.

'I'm here in place of your doctor,' he said.

'Men like me. They always have. You weren't lying. You do fancy me, don't you?'

The answer should have been, 'no he didn't'.

'Come on. Forget you're ethical. I'll be honest. It doesn't do much for me now but I'm good at making it last for the man. You'll like that.'

'No sale.'

She gave a great groan. In a sudden flurry of beating arms she was trying to hammer at his face and chest. The arms were thin. Their force, for all her height, quite slight. He held her off and when she wouldn't stop hit her once across the mouth with his hand. She stopped. 'Damn you,' she said simply, without rancour. 'Come to bed . . . Thirty quid.'

He started to go.

'Look,' she yelled, 'you want coke, yes? A sample. The hot-shot stuff.'

'And so do you.'

'No! I need food. Milk, meat, potatoes. I'm skint. I need money for food.'

He stood considering. He was a doctor who had just hit a sick person and now he was a doctor who might do something monstrous.

'Look,' she was pleading. 'I don't have any. I told you. But, thirty quid, and I'll give you his name. My pusher.'

'You'll be to him before I am.'

'No! They're going to charge me. I'll . . . Look, food. I've got to eat . . . Think of the risk I'm taking. You shop him – take him out – I've lost my connection!'

She was desperate now. He stood ignoring her lies and contradictions. Was there really more rejoicing for the one that is lost and then found again, than for the ninety-nine who never strayed? Not for doctors. Those proportions were a deity's luxury. And so many more than one were straying in this instance. If she was a lost soul now he could return to sweep her back to safety later.

'Thirty quid,' she said. 'Twenty!' She was crying because she knew he would refuse.

'Who?' he said. 'Where?'

'There's a wine bar,' she said. '*La Belle Aurore*. Bottom of Primrose Hill. When he's dealing he's there after seven. He's white with dark hair. About twenty-eight. His name is Charlie – or so he says. It's all I know him by.'

For the second time in that mournful, empty room he reached for his wallet. 'Thirty,' he said spading the money at her. In a crumpling grab she had snatched it away. No thanks, only a pathetic fierce defiance. She knew he didn't believe it would be spent on food.

He saw only one consolation. Paper money went more quickly from hand to hand than silver pieces. More words would have seemed a mockery. His footsteps sounded off the bare floor and walls as he left her in the treacherous light.

Later when he called Dany he found her at home. When he was able to make the point that he might be detained in England a few nights longer than he had anticipated he found she was less than amused. He could tell by the impact which, despite the electronic distance between them, the slammed-down receiver was still able to make on his ear-drum.

SEVEN

'Go forth upon thy journey from this world,
Oh Christian soul.
In the name of Jesus Christ who suffered for thee.
In the name of the Holy Spirit who . . .'

Whatever the fate of the departed's soul, the voice of the Vicar rose smoothly upwards towards the ingrowing vaulting in the ceiling. Not that his own contribution to the ceremony had been either pointed or over the heads of the congregation. Like most of them, a politic man, he owed his place not to dark nights of his own soul as he agonised on how the contents of some Jewish quasi-virgin's belly might have been filled or an Ethiopian mother of seven's might be, but because he had never voted with a Synod minority and spoke with that smooth-tongued public-school assurance best acquired at public schools. Certainly cannon fodder, Ramsey thought, from the end of the last pew but one, and this is his big show-case chance.

The entire affair was proving distasteful in the extreme. To begin with the crematorium chapel was another example of Victorian ugliness. It could well have stood in the grounds of the hospital where he'd met Kate Ross. Instead it stood in the centre of a large cemetery that now stood on the outskirts of the country town. By contrast, the village church at Brinkton was a gem. Still with a Norman doorway it stood on Saxon remains. If the rugged elms had not survived the contagion spread from Holland, the yew trees and one thousand year old lime had. Church and graveyard were as pretty as a picture.

It was not a broad church. Neither was it very long. Even for such a hand-picked congregation as this there would have been insufficient elbow room. Nor did it have all mod-cons. The old furnace, used to send glugging tepid water through the pipes, was coke-burning only. Since a modicum of space was essential, and since, from whatever motives, it had been decreed that Exton Waite's personal path of glory should lead not to the grave but to the urn, his coffin had not been born slow through the Church-way path but driven in a Daimler through the suburbs.

'In communion with the blessed saints
and aided by Angels and Archangels
and all the armies of the heavenly host.'

Ramsey grimaced outwardly. Not all the armies had gained entrance

56

but there was a sufficient host here, heavenly or otherwise, to keep Beryl satisfied until the main event of the Memorial Service. She had pride of place here, of course, in the front pew. Tessa, who had insisted on travelling with himself, had proved publicity-minded enough to sit next to her mother. Ted Adams was there and the man he had recognised as the fatter, sleeker Wyn Bennet. Some kind of sense of decorum had relegated the Prime Minister from the front benches for this session. A personal body-guard sat bulkily alongside the nation's leader in the second row. The rest of them, if not patrolling outside, were in the back row breathing down his neck.

They'd been in attendance as, letting Tessa go ahead of him, he'd arrived. Like ushers at a wedding. But what ushers. No smile and 'Bride or groom's side?' but wary eyes, tight mouths, round heads and square faces on wide necks and shoulders. And 'Name?' He had given his and shown some identification and had a metal detecting probe run over his clothes.

'What's in that pocket, sir?'

'Car keys. Here.'

Perhaps they hadn't looked at him or treated him differently to any of the other mourners. Perhaps they wouldn't be remembering him specially. Perhaps they hadn't done a metal scan on the corpse.

'May thy portion this day be in peace
and thy dwelling in the heavenly Jerusalem.'

He felt cheated. The organ struck up 'God Moves In A Mysterious Way' and as the congregation cluttered coughingly to its feet Ramsey thought 'too fucking right.' This had not been a funeral worth hanging about for. As he rose to his own feet he felt obscurely diminished. When, in a distressing totality of silence, the wooden box had disappeared towards what Beryl would no doubt have referred to as 'the facilities' he had thought to himself that this had nothing to do with the Exton he had once known, several centuries ago. He wondered how Tessa was bearing up down there at the front. He could not see properly but her shoulders were straight, her hands not to her face and no doubt she'd be damned if she was going to break down when side by side with Beryl. Isabel, the shop shut, would be crying – refusing to get drunk because that would cheapen her grief but nevertheless feeling excluded in death as she had in life and crying. But hers was the better ceremony; there was the truer adieu to Exton.

Tessa had brought up Izzie's name as they were speeding westwards on the motorway.

'I went to see her, yesterday,' she had said.

57

'Oh?' He'd tried to stay relaxed at the wheel. Having started the day by picking her up he was still in the driving seat.

'Is she still . . . sort of together?' he went on.

'Well . . . yes and no, I'd say.'

'How "yes and no"?'

'Well I think the fact that Daddy is dead – gone out of our future lives – I think she's clocked that deep down. More than I have probably. In her soft way she's a tough cookie.'

'Yes.'

'But the implication. What it means for *her*. I don't think she's begun to face up to that. Ask her now and I'm sure she'll say she's going to do the next thirty years on memories.'

'Things will happen to her. The memories will be there when she wants them.' But not, he knew for certain, complete or good enough. The slabs of the motorway hurtled forward to dive under the Fiat's wheels. Once more he strained not to make his voice sound strained.

'Did she have any thoughts on how it happened?' he said. He sensed Tessa's head turn.

'No. Why should she?'

'Oh . . . professional curiosity. She didn't want to talk about it when I saw her. I thought with another woman . . .'

'No. I mean, it clearly came as a total shock.'

Tessa seemed satisfied. And Isobel had kept her promise.

'The two of you really get on, don't you?' he said.

'Yes, we do. Ever since Daddy took a huge breath and introduced us. It's obvious, isn't it?'

'What is?'

'That she's exactly the mother that I would have picked out if I'd had the choice. You know, never any secrets?'

'Funny – I've always rather seen you as sisters.'

'Really?'

'Yes, really.'

But there was at least one secret now. They whooshed under a bridge and he knew there was another one that he would have to cross soon. After the funeral, yes, but Tessa would have to be told.

They had come off the motorway and quite speedily into the city centre. For a short while the spacious, elegant status symbols on which the wool trade had lavished its wealth had promised that Exton would have a funeral of a certain quality. But their directions took them out to the other side of town. Once the cemetery had been purposely distanced from the living. But the developers had advanced. As they'd driven past industrial estates and electronics plants he'd had a foreboding that Exton would not be making his last public appearance in a setting of either elegance or quality.

'. . . was in the beginning is now and ever shall be, world without end. Amen.'

Amen. That's all folks. That was it. As the organist – no, sorry, cassette – began its subdued voluntary they set about shuffling out. Was it the rules or just respectful mass instinct that let Beryl and Tessa and then the Prime Minister leave first? Being near the back and on the end of a pew he was among the next out. That made him privileged himself. As the Prime Minister's Jaguar, put on radio message cue, drew up outside, a disobedient photographer had clicked off some frames. Must have. Three men, none of them uniformed, were surrounding him and a piece of chemically treated acetate was parting company with its spool. The photographer was invited rather sharpishly into a Rover. Not many other people, Ramsey observed, had had the chance to admire the expertise.

'Safe home!' Although coming from the driveway outside, Beryl's voice carried cuttingly through to the living room. Ted Adams took a pace or two under the low beams, and arcing backwards, stretched his back. From the next room came the chatter of the two girls drafted in from 'The Fox' clearing away the dirtied plates and surviving post-funeral bridge rolls. He was the last human survivor. Tessa, having put in her dutiful daughter stint in well up to snuff – oops! – fashion had just been mini-cabbed away. By all-round tacit consent Ramsey, that rather no-man's landish loner she had in rather obvious tow, had not showed his face at the wake. Pity. It was an interesting face. Worth talking to probably.

Well, the end of an era. End of something. EW had loved this farmhouse. For the past fifteen years when he used the word 'home' this is what he'd meant. God! How many strategies, deals, approaches had been hatched in front of this vast Jacobean hearth from the depths of these equally vast Heals' armchairs . . . There was a footstep. Beryl came in.

'Well . . .' she said letting out her breath.

What to say? He said nothing.

'A very smooth operation in the event,' she said. 'Ted, you've been a tower of strength. How do I thank you?'

He smiled. He knew it to be true.

'How about a Scotch apiece?' he said.

'Just what the – Perfect!' She moved to the decanters. Leaded crystal clinked. 'And the by-election?' she said, her back to him.

'Too early to say. See how this one goes first.'

'Any idea who Central Office have in mind?'

'No. Haven't heard.'

59

She splashed water into one glass, turned and gave him the neat one. 'I'd like to propose a name,' she said.

'Someone I know?'

'Me. Cheers.'

He drank as if on Pavlovian reflex. But it gave him a second to frame his reply. He was by no means taken by surprise and the whole party knew of her behind the scenes work-rate. But the whole party disliked her. Which of course gave him a job for life. For her political life, anyway.

'I'd had the thought,' he acknowledged. 'It's an obvious one. You'd do it splendidly. And there's precedent – almost. Hugh Gaitskell's widow in the Lords.'

'Hardly the same, Ted.'

'Airey Neave's widow was mooted. So was your namesake Beryl Macleod . . . The big question is simply the timing.' Hearing himself say that he knew he'd chosen his own future.

'Isn't sentiment at its highest now?'

'I meant the feeling in the country now. There's a sense that too many seats are effectively in some interested party's gift. Patronage. A whiff of rotten boroughs. I mean there's the Golding scenario.'

'Exactly! The left deal out constituencies to union hacks as if they were golden handshakes!'

He felt her scrutiny press on his eyes. 'Haven't I earned it?' she said. 'Aren't I worth it?'

'Of course. On both counts,' he over-stated.

He sipped more Tallisker. 'I'll float it, Beryl,' he said. 'I think we'll find it's a runner.'

She moved to the mullioned window. 'It will be a continuation,' she said. 'I won't say I have no regrets. I have a million. But at least the past, this way, won't be a write-off. It will be a foundation. Still count.'

So she already assumed success.

'You know one keen regret?' she went on. 'Her.'

There was no point in pretending ignorance.

'Oh, Berl, really – in France, in Italy.'

'Easy enough for her. A dozen red roses and "how was it for you?" But that's not marriage. Marriage is work!'

But the Waites hadn't had a marriage of two bodies in years.

'It's his things,' she said.

'His things?'

'I know there are cupboard fulls of them round at her grubby little establishment. She's no doubt mooning over them this minute. But by rights they're mine now.'

She turned from the window. A vindictiveness had stiffened her squat posture, brightened her eyes.

'I've a good mind to go round there and claim them!' she said.

'She'd dispute your right to. She'll have bought a lot –'

'My lawyer will *eat* her lawyer.'

Hell hath no fury like a woman scorned, he thought. And said. She stiffened even more as, with every reason, she took it personally. But he knew what he was doing.

'How do you mean?' she hissed.

'Beryl – in view of what we were discussing, we can't afford a tabloid scandal. If she were to get emotional, malicious . . . well. If it's a question of precedents, how about the little example of Sarah Keays . . . ?'

He could almost hear her counting to ten.

'As ever, Ted,' she at last lied in her turn, 'you're absolutely right . . . I was over-reacting.'

EIGHT

'Ramsey – you'll have to shout. It's a terrible line.'

'I said I may not be there 'till quite late – ten or eleven. Can you make sure she stays?'

'Not a problem! She's taken time off work! She's staying – oh, that's much better – she's staying the night.'

'Oh, that's super.'

'We'll see you when we see you.'

'You will indeed. Take care, Izzie.'

'And you. 'Bye.'

He emerged from the Post Office in Wigmore Street and following the convenient trail of double-parked Bentleys walked the short distance to Wyn Bennet's surgery. Wimpole, not Harley Street. Subtle touch that. You could even be silly enough to think you were getting your money's worth . . . But on the other hand, not SW3 either. He bounded up the white-washed steps finding it impossible not to feel like Robert Browning. But the security business with a squawk box straightway brought him back to the twentieth century and the certain knowledge that April was not what it used to be.

The door whirred and clicked and he went in. The receptionist had just come in from a photographic session for the cover of *Cosmopolitan* even as her uniform was a Moulton Street original.

'If you'd just like to take a seat.'

He spent twelve past-the-appointed-time minutes comparing the property pages of three up-to-date *Country Lifes*. House prices hadn't just exploded in England during his absence, they'd thermo-nuclear detonated. If Wyn Bennet owned even a few bricks of this place then, like the Cosmopolitan nurse, he was sitting on a fortune.

'So sorry to have kept you. Do come in.' The man himself, standing in the belatedly open inner doorway. He ushered Ramsey through. There was a sink in the corner, a screen and a high couch behind, and a repertory theatre prop of a stethoscope on the big military desk. But otherwise with its mushroom carpet, rosewood chairs, personal computer work base and glass-fronted bookcase the room was an inner sanctum from which to sell shares, market dogfood or launder money. Or push drugs.

Bennet closed the door. As they shook hands the questioning look he had given Ramsey redoubled as if the answer was on the tip of his mind.

'We've met before,' he said. Behind heavy-rimmed black glasses he was a seal of a man. Plump, fleshy and with black hair parted and actually sleeked down with some grease like the swat of the Remove. Had it not been for his suavely up to the minute double-breasted grey suit he would have looked more like a politician than a politician.

'We had a friend in common,' Ramsey said. 'Exton Waite.'

'Of course. The funeral. Rather a grim effort, really, I thought.'

Well it wasn't in the style of this office.

'But then the very fact of his dying was so grim in the first place,' Bennet went on.

'Indeed.'

They exchanged enigmatic glances. Bennet went behind the desk and glanced at a computer read-out.

'Right,' he said. 'A check-up, Mr Ramsey.'

'You could say that. Beryl thought the glyceryl trinitrate tablets were for swallowing.'

Bennet took off his glasses the better to stare at him narrowly. He sat down.

'It's Dr Ramsey, actually,' Ramsey said, 'and, to anticipate you, I never had a colleague yet who didn't discuss his patients with someone.'

Bennet pursed his lips. For a split second he looked like a spiteful fish. Then, ruefully, he smiled. 'It's amazing she didn't think they were for planting in the garden,' he said.

'Shouldn't his work load have been reduced?'

'Of course! It was madness. But these Triple A achievers – so long as fame is their spur and they can only be fulfilled by winning public plaudits for the way they play the real-life power-game . . . I tried to apply brakes. Canute had a better chance with the waves.'

'He was still playing golf . . .'

'Yes. I tried to minimise the danger there by going round with him myself as often as possible. But . . .' He shrugged.

'And, of course, he was doing cocaine.' Eyes flashed. The glasses went back on. Now the fish looked very spiteful.

'You're here under false pretences,' it snapped.

'But not for wrong reasons. To sign a certificate you need to have seen a patient within two weeks.'

Bennet erred tactically. Instead of leaping to his feet, showing him the door, he flipped open a black 'executive' diary.

'I had. Tuesday the ninth. Four-thirty.' The mouth was piscine but the words came out very dry.

'You found that very easily,' Ramsey said. He allowed a beat for the irony and then as Bennet got to his feet bored in again. 'There are entries in *Waite's* diary too,' he said. 'Dexamethazone and Terfenadine – if it's not your speciality, they're anti-inflammatories to reduce

63

the swelling of the nasal passages. To help the voice sound normal. I suggest they are familiar to you. I suggest you prescribed them.'

Bennet was weightly round from behind the desk. Ramsey braced himself to parry a blow. 'Out!' Bennet hissed.

'I take it you'd be happy to argue this out in front of a Disciplinary Committee?' Ramsey pressed. No round-house swing. Wyn Bennet moved to the door and opened it.

'Show Dr Ramsey out, please, nurse,' he said in a pleasantly even voice. But as the sound of a chair moving on expensive carpet came from the outer office he was turning to Ramsey again, his face working in fury. 'This has been a waste of my time!' he said gutterally.

Not of mine, Ramsey thought.

'So send me a bill,' Ramsey said. He pushed past both Bennet and the frowning nurse and on out into the street. Something inside him was buzzing, was excited. He'd enjoyed that. Bennet had slow reflexes. Just as he'd been late in granting an audience so he'd played too late at a couple of Ramsey's in-swingers. Ramsey smiled. As he turned south he checked that the man who'd pretended to be filling in a form in the Post Office was still following him.

Less than twenty minutes later when, having walked down into Soho he emerged with his purchase from Richards, the man was still in long-range attendance. A glance in the mirror of a kerb-straddling van showed him keeping the same distance behind. Late forties. Hair receding. A nondescript greyish suit. Hmmn. Clutching the bag in his left hand Ramsey proceeded in an easterly direction. It was a depressing continuation: 'Stud Centre', 'Nude Encounter', 'Hard Core', 'Pornissimo'. Along the narrow lengths of the sleazy polyglot streets sex was marketed in the same garish yellow and red plastic that MacDonalds and Currys beckoned the masses with. Some signs were crude hand-scrawled efforts. 'Entrance 50p' – after which the charging has to start, it neglected to add. A girl hovered in a Windmill Street doorway. A micro-skirted, loosely crocheted dress conveyed that her profession pre-dated quantity surveying. Her skin was yellowy-white. It gave the impression of being covered with a light patina of grime. She was as slummocky as the jarring signs and the omnipresent smell that made you feel you were walking inside the dome of a slightly off fried egg. God alone knew what drugs and diseases were being dispensed up all these exploitary stair-cases. And who cared? As he side-stepped a motorist hurling four-letter abuse at a traffic warden, and confirmed the tail was still on him, Ramsey felt fatigue settle on him almost as palpably as if he'd put on an over-heavy coat. Who did care? If the four horsemen came scything through West One with blades honed on Aids and heroin and coke, wasn't it a pure, good thing? London needed a new start. First must come the plague.

He broke into Regent Street. As he passed by Wren's St James's in Piccadilly the coat on his shoulders lightened a little. It wasn't all Hogarth. Blake had been baptised in there. By the time he had found an empty bench in St James's Park Ramsey was aware that the sun was out. He felt more like himself. A doctor. A doctor whose friend had died in suspect circumstances. A doctor increasingly hemmed in by the infrastructure of a dubious Establishment. On the next bench along sat the man with receding hair.

Ramsey took out his clasp knife. There was no reaction from the other man. Reaching into the paper bag Ramsey took out a lemon. He sliced it in half, in quarters. He put the quarters on the bench beside him. He took the first of the oysters out of the bag and prised it open. A drop of juice and, ah, shut your eyes, swallow and he was almost in France. *Vive la différence!*

'That how you eat them over there?'

Never shut your eyes when being followed. People can creep up on you and sit down on your bench and eavesdrop on your thoughts.

'Yep,' Ramsey said.

'They don't bother with the "r" in the month thing?'

'No. Want one?'

'No thanks. I'm more of a crisp man myself.'

'*Chacun à son gout.* I was wondering when you'd introduce yourself.'

'Well seeing as it's nice here . . . and as how you'd rumbled me quite a way back.'

Ah, not just a less than pretty face. Ramsey held the knife more firmly as the man reached into his breast pocket. False alarm. The man was proffering a card. A warrant card. Detective Inspector Brook. Ramsey returned the card.

'Drugs squad,' Brook said.

'Ah . . . a DI doing leg-work? I should be flattered.'

'Not really. On a sunny day it beats pounding a desk.'

'Or sitting in a car outside a hotel.'

'Come again?'

'The variable odd couple in the same Escort outside my hotel,' Ramsey said.

Brook's affable eyes became opaque. 'Not my lot,' he said after a moment. 'I picked you up at the hospital.'

Ramsey looked at the solid, self-assured face with the drinker's broken cheek veins. Wyn Bennet's grey suit had looked a million dollars. Brook's was two up from having been slept in.

'Why?' he said.

'There's a junkie inside we're giving a long rein to,' Brook said.

'Suddenly you – a doctor – turn up and collect her. I find that intriguing. It makes me curious.'

'Not suspicious?'

'Suspicious is the next stage. Now you tell me "why".'

From behind Ramsey could hear the muffled roar of traffic along the Mall. A skirmishing kerfuffle of quacking ducks erupted and, as suddenly, subsided on the lake-shore off to the left. Very human, he thought. Quarrelling over a crust or a mate.

'A mate of mine died,' he said looking back at Brook. 'An old friend and ex-patient. Respiratory failure with cardiovascular collapse. Except . . . I wasn't around but from what I've heard I don't think it was natural causes. I think it was down to a go-around with adulterated cocaine. But none of that's my scene. I thought Kate Ross might lead me . . . somewhere.'

'Has she?'

'No.' Ramsey said. It might be an anticipation of the truth. He blotted out the instant mental impressions of her using his thirty pounds.

'Coke, you say?' Brook said.

'Yes.'

'In my neck of the woods there is, I grant you, a non-stop stream of fatal ODs,' Brook said. 'But almost invariably heroin.'

'If there were some maverick cocaine in circulation – wouldn't that do it?'

'If there were, it might.'

'Is there such?'

Brook shook his head. 'Short answer's "No",' he said. 'Not that we're wise to. And a one-off shot could have been contaminated in so many ways. Some users inject – a dirty needle would –'

'That wouldn't apply here.'

'Some people cut it for themselves.'

'I doubt that in this case too. This would have been taken as it came.'

'Well . . . I can't help. Your standard coke cut would be something in the speed spectrum.'

'An amphetamine.'

'Yes. Usually it's mannite or –'

'What's that?'

'Italian laxative. If not that, dextrose or borax, maybe – they're both common.'

Brook looked at Ramsey. 'Thing is,' he continued, 'they'd all reduce the rush. They'd not increase it. Interesting, eh?'

'Are you thinking that –'

'I'm thinking that it may not just be a case of unnatural causes. It may be a case of *which* unnatural causes. Accidental or . . . otherwise.'

He smiled at Ramsey. It came into Ramsey's mind that Brook would never win the Derby but an each-way bet on him for the Cheltenham Gold Cup would be a canny wager.

'You know – know of – a quack named Wakeley?' he asked Brooke.

Brook smiled again. 'Oh, yes,' he said readily. 'Jimmy Wakeley. Pink Jim. He works for five and six.'

'Five and six what?'

'My, my! You are an innocent. MI5 and MI6.'

'He's in intelligence in some –'

'They have a little list. Tame medicos. A fellow falls off the top of the Hilton, breaks every bone in his body, they'll swear blind it was the liver.'

'You're not serious.'

'I'm not unserious . . . Was Wakeley's one of the signatures on the death certificate?'

'Yes. That's why I brought him up.'

Brook sighed with perverse relish. 'Then you've no chance, mate,' he said. 'Stop nosing around. Not when Pink Jim's been giving out autographs.'

From the lake came a mandarinly ironic endorsement of Brook's assertion.

Brook stood up. 'That accounts for the odd couple in the Escort,' he said. 'Abso-no-bloody-lutely chance. Especially when your old friend's body was cremated yesterday.'

He stared hard but not unkindly at Ramsey as Ramsey tried hard not to react.

'You said it yourself,' Brook said. 'None of this is your scene. You don't know where the goal-posts are, who's a referee and who's playing on the other side. You don't even know how many teams are in the game. You can be got on anything.'

He went into parody. 'Are you aware, sir, that littering a public park with oyster shells is an offence punishable by a fine of up to two hundred pounds?'

'There's a waste-bin over there.'

'So there is. There's also no doubt a rear door to your hotel. But I don't like amateurs. Be careful just how you use it.' He nodded and turned away. There had been a stain on the left thigh of his trousers. Once again, in brief, ambiguous derision, a duck quacked.

Ramsey's love of humanity was not running high this evening. Sitting with his back to the wine bar's far basement wall he glanced at his watch yet again and gulped another mouthful of wine. If you swallowed it before you could taste it, it got by as merely foul. Over an hour and a half whether you measured it by the dial of his twenty-five year old Rolex or by the near emptiness of the bottle of twenty-five day old Chateau Ripoff. He'd chosen this cramped corner table because it gave him a full view of the modish, inadequate, space-saving spiral staircase that led '*La Belle Aurore*'s' clientele down to meet their fate. But his stake-out – 'I don't like amateurs', Brook had said – had revealed nothing.

He had acted on Brook's hint. Another fiver to the Michelin man receptionist had got him out of the hotel the back way via a kitchen custom-designed, you'd have said, for cockroach racing. As he himself had descended the spiral staircase he'd felt oddly self-conscious. This is how a mis-cast actor must feel, he had thought. He had all but found himself improvising the role of a television commercial junkie – sniff, twitch and blink. In the event as he'd approached the bar he'd relied on wardrobe – his heavy navy-blue sweater and the still darker blue blouson shell he wore over it. That and a disingenuous sort of honesty.

'If I told you I was the doctor and I was looking for Charlie,' he had said, 'could you point him out to me?'

The bar-man was a tall, dark unhandsome man who had not heard that Burt Reynolds had outlived his hey-day.

'What would you like to drink?' he had answered. He was also Australian. OK – first the membership fees. Ramsey looked at the runners and riders on the blackboard and knew that his wallet was deeply homesick for France.

'I'll try the house claret,' he said.

In fetching the bottle to the counter top the bar-man didn't have to move his feet. Like himself it came up from under although a glance at the label 'St Antoin' suggested it might prove a touch harder to ascribe its provenance.

'That all?' the bar-man said. You could bet your mortgage he was without a work permit and gainfully employed quite illegally, but he exuded a king-of-the-castle cocksureness. Ramsey thought he didn't like him.

'Charlie,' Ramsey said.

'That'll be twenty pounds, sir.'

Ramsey was sure he didn't like him. He took a breath. 'The board says six pounds fifty,' he said.

'So it does.'

'I meet Charlie and I'll get short-sighted.' He had resisted the temptation to use 'Bruce'.

They looked each other over. Stale memories of a million bad films put a pleasingly distancing filter between Ramsey and the barman's macho pantomiming.

'Tell you what,' the bar-man said, 'I don't know you. You could be bad news. Charlie comes in I'll point you out to him. Say you want a meet. He can look at you . . . we'll let him decide.'

'Deal. Here's six-fifty. Balance on delivery.'

He had edged his way to the table with the strategic view feeling foolishly ignorant. Take away the pin-pointing description of a white male under thirty and he had no idea what he was looking for. What did your friendly neighbourhood pusher look like? He was as low on ideas as, without some Eurocheck work at a bank tomorrow, he was going to be on money. He felt conspicuous. 'Not my scene', he had said to Brook and this, all new to him, wasn't either.

Wine bars hadn't been around in England when he'd last been around. Neither pubs, nor restaurants: he wasn't sure how he'd feel about such hybrids even if the wine was drinkable. Women obviously liked them. There were more here already than you'd see in any pub – four over there clearly continuing an office birthday party; two there coming back from the food counter with dubiously multi-coloured salads who seemed not to be uptight about the imminence of light and bitter induced gang-rape. Well, wine bars might be an astute marketing exercise in terms of women's responses but a sense of security was not what had brought him here and might bring Charlie. But 'where's Charlie?' he had to ask himself.

Feet continually clattered on the iron staircase. The place was filling up fast. Lots of blokes now. Two out of three could be squeezed into the loose description and as the staircase's spirals brought new faces corkscrewing down into view, there was a second in each case when he thought his waiting for the man might be over. But wrong. No-one came across. He looked from table to table but no-one looked up from their buzz of chat to return his scrutiny. Bruce the bar-man made occasional glances but his face was no more communicative than Ayer's rock.

A new perception came to Ramsey as time went by. A decade ago he could have fairly safely excluded a good half of the men from his 'possibles' list by the cut of their jib. Sports jackets, club ties, haircuts, perhaps above all shoes would have sent out two dozen subtle signals saying bank clerk, estate agent, plumber, university lecturer. Now, he suddenly realised designer jeans, logo'd sweaters, trainers had resulted in a visually egalitarian society. The haystack for the human needle was consequently – hello, what was that?

Footsteps ringing on the wrought-iron stair treads had missed a beat. Sawn off at the waist jeans staggered drunkenly. Someone had nearly fallen. As a few others glanced up as well, the jeans' owner righted himself. Herself. Damn! Further descent revealed the owner as a girl. Ramsey looked away. And then looked back. The girl had swayed for a moment a second time as she reached the foot of the stairs. Halting, she had blown her nose on a tissue she'd drawn from her sweater sleeve. She looked nothing like Kate Ross and yet she did.

She was short where Kate Ross was tall and plump where Kate Ross was thin. This girl's hips and thighs bulged out her jeans. But she too was poor. As she sidled her broad-beamed way to the bar there was something in her eyes and in the way her mouth worked that put him in mind of how Kate Ross had looked as, with growing desperation, she'd made clear she would do anything, divulge anything, for a few precious pounds. This girl gave off the same aura of desperation.

It had seemed too soft to sit there with his eyes studiously glued to Bruce, the bar-man, all evening. People might have said they were in love. But this was an encounter that, carrying his failure to take up lip-reading in his youth, he watched unblinkingly. The girl asked a question. Bruce shook his surly head. The girl's own head drooped. She asked Bruce the time. He showed her his watch. She said something further and Bruce replied. Somebody else came down the stairs and the girl's head twisted round as if following a tennis shot.

It was a couple. Black. The potential hope in the girl's face was converted to a look even more distraught. She seemed to be giving Bruce an instruction. He shrugged but then nodded. Without another word the girl was pushing back through the crowd-them-in-anyhow tables and climbing the stairs. Ramsey decided to follow suit and follow her.

The drug scene might not be his scene, but if ever he'd seen a person desperate for a fix, the girl was it, or he had no right ever to diagnose again. Besides, it would make a pleasant change to be the pursuer and not the pursued.

He emerged into what had remained a mild night. The short arty street of book and antique shops, a Greek restaurant, and a delicatessen, seemed deserted. But he could hear the girl's staccato footsteps. He looked in the direction of the sound and, as he did, she emerged into the light of a street lamp from behind a parked van. She was walking east. He waited a few seconds longer, then fell in behind her. Almost at once she turned left up a residential street.

She walked as she had descended the staircase: in fits and starts. Her intention was clearly to walk fast but her progress bordered on the slow. She was tacking from side to side across the pavement. Several times she slowed virtually to a halt to right her course. But

70

her forward progress was in any case erratic. Several short sharp steps would be followed by a gradual slowing down, another attempt at acceleration. She advanced like a car with a partially blocked fuel line. Ramsey had to make a positive effort to drag his own footsteps so as to keep his distance. There were absolutely no other pedestrians about. With most people he would have aroused suspicion inside the first hundred yards. But not, he fancied, with somebody in this girl's state of mind.

An overground train rattled through the night very close to hand and now, indeed, they were crossing a bridge hard by a station. Primrose Hill, if memory served . . . yes. Careful, she was turning left. She was heading back westwards. Ah yes, she had had to cross the railway line before she homed in on wherever she was going. If you were a drugs pusher what would you do? Deal from a point around the corner or keep your place of business as far from your own pad as possible? They'd been walking in this slow, slow, quick, quick, slow fashion for about ten minutes and were back in residential streets. What was she? Student? Waitress? Primary school teacher? Unemployed or unemployable? Impossible to guess. This road must be taking them back towards the railway line. Yes, hold it down now, this was a cul de sac. He crossed to the far side of its short length before he followed her down into it.

She went to the very end house. It was a two-storey building. Completely dark. He halted in a patch of shadow diagonally up from it and waited, watching and listening. He couldn't hear her ring the bell but from somewhere a faint splashing sound came and went on the light breeze. The house stayed dark. No light sprang on at any window or from behind the front door. Now he heard something quite distinct. The girl groaned. Huge frustration and need, great despair was in the sound. Her head seemed to fall against the door. Now she walked back down the path to scan the windows. In the upshine from the lamp-post opposite the house stared blankly back at her with its blind window-eyes, not giving a damn about her problems. She groaned again and began to retrace her steps almost at a run. As she passed by on the other side, she was not so much sobbing as gasping. She rounded the corner and he let her go.

He stood considering. If he was right this was Charlie's house. It *could* be Charlie's house if – hello! If one of the upstairs windows a light had sprung on. Sod's law in operation for the girl. Except this was another girl. Another girl who had appeared in the window to draw the curtains close; who did it with one hand, a curtain at a time, because she was eating a sandwich or something. Charlie's girl? Well, looking at the house it was a fifty-fifty chance. Worth going for.

He crossed the street. The splashing sound grew louder and

became continuous. Liquid gleamed in mid-air. At the side of the house an overflow pipe was performing its function. In the empty flat a ball-cock must be on the blink. Shit! Perhaps Charlie doesn't live here any more . . . if he ever had. Right. Go for it.

He took a deep breath and went all the way up to the front door. Three bell pushes on a squawk-box, electronic door release system: labelled one, two and two A. Opposite the 'one' a name tag said Porter. Opposite 'two' an inked name had long since become indecipherable. Opposite 'two A' was a blank. He swallowed and realising he was half-way towards being a candidate for cardiovascular collapse himself, took a deep breath. Then he pushed 'two'. Almost at once, tinny music somehow part of it, a girl's distorted voice blatted in his ear.

'Yes?'

'Sorry, love, it's Charlie,' he said. 'Forgotten my key again. Can you press the magic button for me?'

He prayed the system worked on a two-way distortion principle.

' 'Kay, Charlie. Pressing now.'

The lock buzzed. He pushed, was in. As simple as that. He needn't have worried. Then why, as a thin, cold, cementy smell assailed his nostrils, was his pulse rate up in the Space Shuttle take-off league? He'd better take-off. This was no place to be caught dithering around.

The once broad hall had been encroached upon. To the right an ugly modern inner door had been angled across to create what was clearly the entrance to the ground floor flat. Assume Charlie's name wasn't Porter for the minute. The way onward was upward – up the narrow staircase more or less straight in front. It was carpeted but Charlie wouldn't creep up them. It took an amazingly adrenalin draining effort but he made himself walk up them with the 'nothing to hide' step of any North London drugs dealer. Almost half-way up he realised one piece of luck was working for him. The music he had heard through the squawk box hadn't been imaginary. Less tinny now, and more muffled, it came from the door on a sort of sub-landing. Feeling the door would open at any moment to let loose a request for a cup of sugar, the odd coke, he moved swiftly by and doubled back along some bannisters to the front of the house. Another door had been put in at the time of the conversion to flats. It would be the entrance to flat 'two A'.

It was only about eight paces from the other door. He straightened, took another very anxious breath. He realised he was sweating. He hoped the girl was washing her hair, making a phone call. Charlie wouldn't knock at his own door. Ramsey placed his ear against the door and, reasonably loudly, knocked. Nothing. No sound of a chair scraping back inside. No sudden appearance in her doorway of the girl neighbour, now trying to make up for her over-trusting mistake with the world's loudest scream. Right then, he was . . . at a loss.

He straightened again. The memory of his recent 'movie scene' with the Australian bar-man came helpfully back. 'Dial M for Murder!' Yes. A spare key. He ran his fingers along the top of the door frame. Idiot! This was London's flat land. His fingers came away empty of all but dust. So, the hero smashes the door down with a one-off shoulder-charge and goes on in. In the movies. In life he sustains considerable bruising against a door that doesn't budge and makes enough row to ensure he goes in to prison . . . But it seemed to be a Yale-type lock. Well, perhaps his American Express card would do nicely. It had worked for Michel Piccoli. Maybe the technique had crossed the Channel.

Less worried about being discovered now that he had this local problem to provide diversion therapy, he worked the credit card into the slight but definite gap between the door and its jamb at the point where he judged the tongue of the lock must be. It slid in for about half its length and then met resistance: it would move up and down but not further in. Higher up it would slide in further. Right. He centred it opposite the key-hole again and warping the plastic slightly applied more and increasing pressure. Something was shifting! He pressed harder and with a dry sound of cracking the card split apart in his fingers approximately along the line of his signature. He had been guilty of over-reaching. What would work for Michel Piccoli wouldn't work for everyone.

As he pocketed the two brittle fragments he became aware of a vibration coming up through his feet. Then noise. Another train was coming along the line that he now remembered was an easy stone's throw from the house. Noise and vibration both intensified. The house definitely shook. No doubt when you lived there all the time you got so you could totally ignore it. Still the noise grew. As it seemed to be peaking, partly on instinct, and partly in reaction to his Mickey Mouse efforts with the card, he went for the door flat out. Semi-literally. He backed off against the wall opposite and, bracing himself against it, kicked the entire flat of his foot karate-fashion as close to the lock as he could manage. One – and nothing happened. Two – and the fitting on the inside jamb flying away, the door burst away and open. It made a noise like the fall of the house of Usher. Again on instinct – he was less worried about the reception waiting inside than detection outside – he stepped quickly into the flat and shoved the door as closed as it would now go. He turned to get his bearings in the darkened, slightly street lamp illuminated room and at once, despite his galloping pulse, the hair on the back of his neck stood up.

An even band of light shone from under an inner door across the room on the left. His mind was instantly compartmentalised. The smaller compartment was everyday and logical. He'd seen no light shining when outside in the street, therefore the room behind the door lacked windows. A bathroom, therefore, or a loo. The larger part of his mind was already back in the world of films. He knew what he was going to find behind the door. The tracking shot forward and then the seen-it-all-before shock-horror cliché. Was that the source of his *déjà vu* or did it derive from the sounder basis of his professional experience? How many times had he entered a ward, lifted a phone, only to stop an infinitesimal moment in mid-movement. The death had happened after all and despite everything. But, of course, in those circumstances, you'd known there was always the possibility . . . Here there was only the growingly uncomfortable awareness that however *déjà vu*, this wasn't a film.

He began the tracking shot. Halfway to the door he paused to make sure of avoiding a half-seen coffee table. The pounding in his ears had become a constant. He began to make out two more sounds. The one was the splashing from the overflow pipe – heard this time from the inside as it splatted to the ground. The second was a differently liquid noise. The steady tom-tom rhythm of water dripping drop by drop into more water. So . . . find out! He moved carefully on and reached the door. Using the palms of both hands, and not his fingers, he turned its knob-type handle. With his elbows he pushed the door open.

He had been right. It was the bathroom. It was a rather mean, over-ordinary bathroom for the most part in dated, unrelieved white tile that managed to suggest it had in mind turning yellow. There was a sink, a toilet, a bath. The sink was unexceptional. The toilet would have been, if it had not been that on its down-turned seat was a still-life. A hypodermic, a spoon, a ball of cotton wool and, focal point of the composition, a glassine envelope containing a white powder.

The bath would have been unexceptional if the tap had not been left on, causing it to overflow. Water was glugging steadily away down an overflow outlet not quite up to the job. The old school sum had gone a little wrong. Brimming to the bath's rim the water had found one corner faintly lower than the others. It was from beneath this corner that the dripping sound was coming. Why the tap had been left on and what the precise nature of the white powder was, were questions into which Ramsey felt he had a major insight. As if Ramsey were interrupting him halfway through a practical demonstration in Archimedean basics a man was lying in the bath. A white man. He had no clothes on. His left leg was hooked over the side. The rest of him, aggravating the overflow problem, was submerged. Charlie had died cleanly. But not prettily. Magnified by the water his open upturned eyes looked like diseased lychees.

Ramsey had discovered the hard way that life imitates the movies. It was not the first corpse he had seen but he ventured to believe that had a layman come upon it instead of a doctor he too would not have been hard put to it to diagnose death.

But how long dead? Ramsey moved across the awash floor and touched the leg with the back of his hand. No turkey was ever colder. The foot was already turning blue. What lay amidst the underwater sea-plant floating between the man's thighs was also looking off-colour. But the man's young face still showed lingering patches of what had been a massive rush of blood to the head. The lips were far from being the classic purple they should have been by now. They were still an almost cosmetic pink. Experiencing the eerie feeling of being watched by a second – or was it third? – party, Ramsey picked up a flannel from the sink and used it as he turned the running tap off. The flannel was nastily soggy but not to mind. He used his dry left hand to pick up and pocket the envelope of cocaine. He left the light on as he left the room, and as he did so heard the gurgling water hesitate and then decide against any further expenditure of energy in dashing downstairs. It was not a viewpoint that Ramsey felt like sharing.

'I don't believe it!' Tessa shouted.

But from the vehemence of her cry, and the tears already swimming in her eyes, it was clear that already it was her own protestation she knew she must disbelieve.

'It's dreadful but it's true,' Ramsey repeated. 'You need to accept it. Your –'

'Accept it!'

'Acknowledge it, then. Your father died from over-dosing on the contents of a wrap very similar to this.'

He prodded the square of tinfoil on the table with his finger.

'How long have you known?' Tessa said. The tears were running now.

'I've suspected since we were in France.'

'Then why didn't you tell me?'

'I didn't want to spoil your funeral,' he said. It was a grim answer but he was feeling grim. A doctor expects to have his attention drawn to corpses on stretchers or in beds, and there was a brutal logic to the reply – even therapy. Tessa had gulped, taken some deep, silent breaths. But he was in error. The shock treatment hadn't worked.

'For Christ's sake!' Tessa was suddenly screaming. 'If you knew all that time you should've stopped him! Couldn't you have made him stop?'

It wasn't so much a question as an after the event demand. And directed not at him but Isabel.

Izzie's eyes closed in a face already haggard enough. The old butcher's clock on the wall stated it was past midnight and, waiting for him, neither of them had been to bed. He looked from one to the other. Tessa with her indignant sense of having right on her side was very much her late father's daughter. Izzie, unnaturally still as she absorbed the punishment, just or unjust, into her inner self and used her gentleness and strength to rob it of its power to hurt was being very much herself. The clock ticked self-importantly. When, opening her eyes, Isabel at last spoke, her voice was soft and low.

'Tessa,' she said. 'This will probably pain you a great deal but I don't think anyone could have made Exton stop. Not even you. The letalone lay only in his own will. I asked him, begged him, told him to many times but . . . he never listened.'

Tessa caught her breath. The image of her father's dying expression was as vivid in her mind's eye as if it were all happening again. She now had a certain knowledge of why that terrible guilt had blazed out from his eyes. He was dying aghast he had not confided in her: that she would find out like this. She let out a sob. Izzie misinterpreted the cause. She reached out and touched Tessa's hand with her own. 'It seems now I didn't try hard enough,' she said. 'I shan't forgive myself. I don't expect you to. I was afraid, you see.'

'Afraid?'

'Afraid of seeming to nag him. A . . . a mistress, you see, feels so vulnerable so often. She has no proper hold on the man. He can go away at any time. I . . . I didn't want to seem a scold.'

'But he loved you,' Tessa said raising her head. 'If it hadn't been for his public position . . .' Her voice tailed away.

'What might have been we don't know,' Isabel said wistfully. 'What happened we know only too well. Only – Ramsey, I must say this! – he told me several times it wasn't physiological. Not cocaine, he said. I told him he couldn't keep on burning the candle at both ends – committees, sub-committees, the Ministry, television, writing, everything – but he was proud! He said that was why the candle had two ends in the first place. When he said it wasn't physiological I didn't mind quite so much. Ramsey, it's not is it?'

'Yes,' he said, 'it is.' It was not a night for softening bad news.

'He probably chose to believe it wasn't because it suited his sense of his own intelligence. He couldn't abide stupid behaviour in others.

76

Heroin he would have found intellectually distasteful. I don't think he lied to you. But enlargement of the heart . . . hypertension . . . burnt out sinuses . . . respiratory problems . . . no, Izzie, I won't lie to you either. No-one can classify that lot as anything but physiological.'

Now it was Isabel's turn to weep. Tessa brought her chair closer and put her arm round her.

'Izzie,' she said. 'You're right. I don't know much but I know I couldn't have made him stop either. It would have taken trained people . . . and taking him up by a giant hand and putting him in a world where there were no candles of any kind at all.'

That was the father's daughter too, Ramsey thought. Proved wrong, seeing the chance of an honourable compromise, no politician had been more winningly generous.

'Tessa,' he said gently, 'this wrap. When you first found your father – did you see anything like this?'

'No,' Tessa said. 'One could have been under him on the desk. I didn't have much eye for detail at the time, you understand.'

'No. Of course not.'

'I see now what Strudwick was getting at with his disbelieving questions.'

Ah. She really had come to accept overdosing as a cause of death.

'I understand now why he was on the scene so fast,' she went on. 'And if Dad's detective saw anything like . . . like that, he might have tidied it away.'

'*Dad's detective?*'

'Special Branch. He was having his supper in the kitchen. Bodyguards are useful for emergencies but distinctly come into the "downstairs" category.'

She had managed a wan smile.

'He was soon there,' she said. 'I didn't see him do it but he would have made the crucial call.'

'Who to?'

'The Cabinet Secretary.'

'Why him?'

'It's his job. Sort of cross between an *éminence grise* and a fine leg. If he don't know it, it ain't knowledge. The dirt, the rumours, he sees them, tells them.'

'Tells who? The Cabinet?'

'Them and the wider circle. *Not on, old boy. Have to stop.*'

'If it doesn't?'

'*Afraid I shall have to take it up with the PM.*'

'Is it a political appointment?'

'I *think* he's a civil servant. Technically anyway. I'm a bit confused

77

because there was all that "I won't tell you, so there!" State Secret stuff about leaks and such during the battle of Brittan.'

'Ah, yes. The French enjoyed that.'

'They've always liked farce . . . Not to mention *Armstrong's Last Goodnight.*' She'd been talking with an increasingly determined jauntiness, but it could not last. Her true feelings returned.

'Goddamit, Ramsey,' she said, but more in sorrow than anger. 'I'm seeing Beryl tomorrow.'

'I would guess she knows, but there's no reason to bring any of this up.'

'It's hardly likely to add to the gaiety of a meeting that's starting ten down to begin with.'

'Why meet anyway?'

'She's going on a pilgrimage. She wants to go back to Oxford. Where Daddy and she first met.'

'How amazingly sentimental!' Izzie said, and obviously before she'd thought. She blinked. 'I'm sorry,' she went on in her softer voice. 'What right have I? I'm sure she's very upset. It just seems so, well, unlike Beryl.'

'And drugs seems so unlike Daddy,' Tessa mourned. Her eyes lost focus as they went back in to the past in search of him. Almost as if to create a sisterly diversion, one woman helping another, Isabel made a movement. Her hand moved out to the foil wrap on the table. Her index finger teased at the corner he had already worked loose. The wrap became briefly alive. It skittered a ragged pirouette. A few gleaming crystals lay isolated on the blond wood.

'Like sugar,' Izzie breathed. She stared at the grains with a sort of fascinated revulsion.

'How much is there?' she said.

'A gramme,' Ramsey said. 'About three-quarters of a tea spoon.'

'How much is that worth?'

'I've simply no idea.' Tessa too was staring as if fighting off the urge to succumb to hypnotism.

'Is that what killed . . . does that have any connection at all with the coke that Dad took?' she finally got out.

'There's no direct reason to believe it does,' he said.

'Then why . . . where'd you get it?'

He weighed his thoughts. The immediate can his answer could open held particularly poisonous beans. But left ignorant both women might be more vulnerable to the visitations of the men from the 'keep Britain tidy' squad. He sighed. It certainly was the night of the grim truths. Both women seemed very still as, looking at him, they waited.

'This packet,' he said to at last break the clock's strident domination, 'has one thing in common with the one your father must have used, Tessa.'

'It has . . . ?'

'Yes. The guy who had it is also dead.' He heard two intakes of breath and nothing more.

'I broke into his flat.'

'Broke in?' Isabel said. She seemed the more shocked by this revelation.

'Yes.'

'Literally broke in?'

'If you consider kicking the door in justifies the figure of speech, yes.'

'Ramsey!' He was confronted by two people for whom breaking the law meant getting a parking ticket.

'Isabel,' he said formally, 'how about a drink?' In the event, when slowly, omitting only the more clinical aspects, he told them how he had passed his evening, all three whiskies remained largely untouched. When he had got beyond his anonymous 999 call the tireless clock again held sway.

'You think he . . . this man, whoever he is, *was* – got this from the same source as Exton?' Tessa, less shocked by his own lawlessness, had recovered the quicker.

'Maybe. Just maybe.'

'So what's –

'You remember Klaus Goldschmidt, Tessa?'

She shook her head.

'Well, you were young. Charles Goldsmith now. He owes me a favour or two in that very connection. He'll analyse this for me. If it's impure it may be significant. Take us beyond coincidence.' And me back to Brook, he thought.

Now Isabel spoke. 'But if it is,' she said, 'if it is impure and Exton's was too, well, it won't stop at two will it? I mean, surely there was a big batch of stuff and . . . well, people all over will be using it and . . . horribly at risk.'

She had said what he had been trying not to think about all night.

'We can't assume that. It's what happened downstream from the mother lode, so to speak, that counts. A lot of people dilute it themselves. All in individual ways.'

Tessa shivered. He carefully edged the spilled grains back into the wrap and folded it tight. Particularly he had been trying not to think about what Kate Ross might have been out buying with the thirty pounds he'd given her.

NINE

Ramsey spent a restless night. The *ad hoc* conglomeration of cushions, pillows and blankets on the floor of Isabel's living room left several things to be desired. Draught-proofing and sleep were two. When he did sink into some state of unconsciousness it was not into total oblivion. His sleep was shot through with a sense of foreboding, of things being sinisterly wrong. Eventually two grey eyes, pupil-less but, he could tell, able to see, floated above him. When they started to swim nearer, hinting they might soon develop a pink, all-devouring mouth, some protecting mechanism in his mind woke him up before the nightmare could start in earnest. He sat up and, as he remembered where he was, remembered too that the nightmare had already happened. And in no-one's sleep. He was glad when the dawn's early light giving dim definition to the room's unfamiliar shapes seemed to sanction his getting up.

He padded to the tiny kitchen and, as quietly as he could, made a cup of tea. No sound came from either of the rooms in which Tessa and Isabel were sleeping. It got lighter. The first noises of the world outside going about its business started to make themselves heard. A car door slammed. An engine stuttered, caught, revved. Streets away a siren probed at the city's nerves. It seemed an aptly malign cock-crow. He sat and thought, and above all worried. A glance in the phone directory told him Charles Goldsmith had not moved house but that was not the cause of his anxiety . . . It was still not seven-thirty when, having written a note, he crept downstairs.

From well back within the shop he examined the street outside. They might still think he was in the hotel, but it was most unlikely. They would certainly have linked him to Isabel. A seeing eye might be on dogged duty outside. So far so good. No sign. But from here the field of vision was limited. He went to the door, undid the several locks, and muffled the bell as he went out. No shapes sat in the parked cars. Apart from a BMXing paper boy the street seemed deserted. When he moved off in the Panda no other car followed and five minutes of double-backing through the rat-runs produced no continuity in his rear-view mirror. All right: time to go to Kilburn.

It was barely eight when he drew diagonally across the house where Kate Ross lived. No parked ambulance, no flashing blue light had hammered at his vision when he turned the corner of the street. His grip on the wheel relaxed and he allowed himself to breath again. All quiet on the Kilburn front.

Only not quite, he saw now. Tailgate on high, a Peugeot station wagon was parked immediately outside the house. As he crossed behind it he saw two or three cardboard boxes inside. The landlord kitting up a flat, perhaps. A tenant doing a break-of-day flit . . . He went through the open gate and stopped in mid-stride. It was the door to the basement flat, Kate Ross's flat, that stood ajar. At the top of the short flight of steps leading down to it was another cardboard box. A kettle stuck awkwardly up from it. Well, you wouldn't expect her to do a neat job of anything these days. He bent to improve the kettle's positioning. As he did so there was a movement at the corner of his eye and as he straightened a man was bristling at him from the doorway.

'What the hell do you think you're doing?' he snapped.

He was about fifty. He had spruce, thinning, red fair hair and, particularly about the eyes, a reddish complexion. There was a hint of ex-soldier about him. His accent was what Kate's was when she wasn't acting tough or common.

Ramsey chose his words with some care. 'Do forgive me,' he said, 'I thought this had been forgotten. I was looking for Kate Ross, actually. I'm a doctor. Doctor Ramsey.' He knew that unshaven and be-sweatered, he hardly looked the part, but it usually worked. Not this time, however. There was no conciliation but, rather a redoubling of animosity.

'Doctor! Are you part of that Simon Wood filth?' The red-rimmed eyes were bulging with a barely suppressed violence. The name had rung a faint bell, but first things first. This man was spoiling for a fight. Ramsey was glad to be holding the high ground.

'No,' he said gently, 'I'm a colleague of Dr Thorne.'

The straightforward statement had extraordinary effect. The hostility in the man's face hardened. And then collapsed. There was an unsuccessfully stifled groan and, as the eyes screwed themselves tight, the features might have been sketched on a crumpled bag. The man had staggered sideways against the door jamb. With a brokenly executed move of one arm that in other circumstances would have seemed like a cheap comic doing a gay bit he acknowledged Ramsey again.

'Please . . . forgive me.' The voice regained some control as it continued, 'I mistook you for . . . someone else. I appreciate what Dr Thorne tried to do very much.'

It was Ramsey's turn to struggle for control. From somewhere a skull grinned confidentially at him. His worst fears seemed very close to being realised. He thought he could guess why the man's eyes were so red.

'. . . Tried?' he said.

'Kate died yesterday,' the man said. 'I was her father. Her dad.' His face worked as visibly he fought off the urge to cry once more. 'Father . . . doctor. There's nothing any of us can do for her now,' Ross went on.

'Yesterday?' Ramsey asked.

'The night before last. In the small hours. They found her yesterday. In a pub. In a pub loo! My God, man, in a pub loo!'

'Steady!' Ramsey went quickly down the steps that now had nothing to do with tactical advantage and gripped one of Ross's shoulders with his hand. An icy fist was squeezing at his own tripes but his first duty was to this man on the edge of temporary madness. His bereavement, the degradation of the way it had been visited on him, were clearly close to unhinging his mind.

'Let's go inside,' Ramsey said.

Ross looked at him, understood. The wild glint went out of the bulging eyes. He nodded and turned. The night before last, Ramsey thought. My thirty pounds. But if I'd come running here after I discovered Charlie I wouldn't have been in time.

'Your thirty pounds,' the skull whispered. 'You knew it would happen. For you a ticket to information. For her a passport to extinction.' As Ross led the way not to the empty, echoing room but a bedroom at the back, Ramsey felt soiled. He had betrayed . . . his judgement, his principles, Kate Ross. The ice at his stomach's pit would not be quick in going away, might never go completely. This would not be like the death of a patient you had done your very best to save. It was as much for his own sake as for Ross's that he sought the distraction of small-talk.

'Your car,' he said, 'the back's up. Someone –'

'Let them,' Ross said briefly. 'Junk. I don't know why I'm here . . . Yes, I do. It's to be doing something. I couldn't sleep all last night. Earlier, you see, I was at the mortuary . . . I suppose if you're a doctor you'll know what I mean.'

Ramsey nodded. He visualised the dished stainless steel table with the drainage point at the centre of the St Andrew's cross formed by the gulleys, the filing cabinet drawer that was refrigerated and two metres deep. It was less than the ideal setting for a father to bid his daughter a final farewell.

'Junk,' Ross repeated. 'Look!'

He held up a training shoe. It was next to impossible to determine the original colour. A frayed hole where the little toe had forced its way through brought faint visual echoes of pan-handling down and outs to mind.

'We're a long way from being poor,' Ross said. 'She didn't have to want for anything that really counted . . .'

A part of the problem, Ramsey allowed himself to consider – but what right did he now have to pass such judgements? Ross had sat down on the bare mattress of the bed. Centrally stained, Ramsey could not but help noticing.

'Here.'

Ross was offering him a half-full bottle of Dewar's.

'Thanks,' Ramsey said. He took a hefty belt. The whiskey did nothing for the way his stomach felt, but the gesture had forged a sort of man to man link. Ross took the bottle back. He picked a shoe-box up from the mattress. Inside were photographs.

'What about these?' he said. 'Burn them – or build a shrine?'

'Neither,' Ramsey said. 'Put them somewhere safe and take them out when you want to. You will, you know.'

'You think?'

'Yes. May I?'

He took the box and gently sifted through the six or seven photos. Her bone structure had not lied. Before the drugs had overtaken her she had been a stunning girl: a fair English beauty with promises of fire and fun to offset the cool superficial languor. There was one of her against a railing with some European, Alpine view behind. A casually tall, dark, handsome man had his arm round her. The camera had caught her in mid-laugh. The result was an image that seemed to sum up the hope, the joy, the potential of being alive. The girl in the photo seemed more alive than the shrunken man huddled in onto himself on the bed. But already infinity separated that moment in time from the corpse in a drawer in a mortuary. In its unrecapturable vibrance the photo was heartbreakingly sad.

'Smashing kid,' Ross said as if staring over his shoulder, '. . . privilege to watch her grow up, share in it . . . golden girl, really . . . 'course I'm biased.'

'Funny dad who isn't.'

One photograph had been on the lawn of a big, country-looking house. A family group. A mother.

'You felt there was nothing she couldn't do if she put her mind to it. A friend took her swimming years back. Three months later she was swimming beautifully . . . crawl, back-stroke. Same with the guitar. She did it all as if it was . . . walking.'

Ramsey felt Ross tighten before the change in voice.

'Then it all went sour,' Ross said. His mind had come back from the past of golden lasses to the unbearably present present. His slumped head turned. He looked savagely at Ramsey.

'It'll destroy society,' he gritted out. 'Forget the Bomb!'

'Drugs?'

'Yes! Drugs! . . . Aids, Herpes, some virus or another. We'll do it

83

to ourselves. Mass-suicide! And we'll have deserved it!'

His means of expression was confused but his meaning was very clear. In that damp-seeming room, the taste of Scotch mingling in his mouth with guilt, Ramsey had a fleeting moment of wanting to agree with him. What did it matter anyway? Who cared? And wasn't it more in keeping to end with a plague rather than the Bomb? Not with a bang but a mass-suicide whimper? No! It wasn't. Not for him anyway. Startling Ross, he moved round the corner of the bed and picked up the Scotch. He took another fiery swig. No. He was probably going to be steamrollered anyway but he couldn't just lie down to wait his turn. He'd entered into an agreement when he'd taken on his particular line of work, and standing up against steamrollers was written into the contract.

'Where did she get the money?' he asked Ross.

'Savings, first. Then selling just about everything she owned . . . including herself. Yes! Why not say it? You die in a loo what cover-up can you –'

'Come on. Easy. I'm sorry. I shouldn't have asked.'

'Why not? What difference does it make now. . . ? From me, too, of course, the money . . . There was a pizza house close to her last digs. I paid them thirty pounds a week – to keep her alive.'

'Wouldn't it have been better spent on detoxification?'

'For God's sake! You think we didn't try! . . . We even got her off it once. Three months clean. She'd kicked it, we dared to believe. Thorne had a lot to do with that. He recommended she came back home. She was going to. Then some swine of a dealer slipped her a couple of freebies. End of story. End of . . . everything.'

'When I arrived you mentioned a name. Not Derrick Thorne. You thought I was –'

'Wood. Simon slime Wood.'

'It does ring a bell.'

'His name's always in the papers. The ones that don't count. Dempster's Diary and those barrel scrapings.'

'Oh . . . yes. He's some sort of osteopath?'

'Ostensibly. What he really is is a giver of parties. He must be forty plus but he still makes believe it's the Swinging Sixties. Surrounds himself with young kids. Like a vampire.' Ross stood up. A more controlled anger was now restoring something in the way of self-possession. There was a good measure of dignity about this well-spoken man next to the tacky bed.

'I happen to know – I think I know and I think I can get to prove it – I know Kate got drugs from him on occasion. And I'm going to get him. I'm going to nobble him with a private prosecution. Or die trying. Give me something to live for.'

Interesting.

'Is that possible?' Ramsey asked.

'Given evidence. Given the magistrates agree there's a case. Then it goes on to the DPP. Of course, he's got connections. There'll be a lot of havering about.'

'Sounds expensive.'

'It'll bust me. But my boy is nearly self-directing now and will understand. I just pray he never – Yes, it'll bust me but if I take the bastard down with me it will be worth every penny.'

'If you're right, I'd say that was right . . . How about your wife? Does she know?'

'No. I haven't told her yet. I wanted to pull myself together. She . . . she'll be distraught but, you know, part of her will be almost relieved. It seems a ghastly thing to say, I suppose, but . . .'

'Part of her has long been expecting this.'

'Yes. As with me. And when it happens . . . perhaps it helps.'

'You're not sleeping – would you like me to arrange something?'

'No. No thanks.' Ross's shoulders straightened. 'There's a lot to do. Funeral arrangements. Letters to write. Telling Margaret . . . talking to you has helped, you know. You've been very kind.'

Lost for words, Ramsey shook his head.

'Besides,' Ross went on. 'It wouldn't seem right. We're all into drugs these days, aren't we? Aspirin, valium . . . I'd like to believe you're better off looking disaster or whatever right in the face. Pipe your eye if it helps but face it cleanly. Not under sedation. Don't diminish the scale of your own grief because if you do you're diminishing the scale of whomever you grieve for.'

He looked at Ramsey. 'I suppose that seems ridiculously Kipling-esque,' he said. 'Especially to a doctor.'

'No,' Ramsey said. 'And Kipling wasn't ridiculous.' Nor, he had decided, was Ross. Ross was worth not getting steamrollered for. He held out his hand.

'In happier circumstances next time, I hope,' he said. It was utterly inadequate and yet it seemed to serve.

'Yes,' Ross said. 'Goodbye Dr – er –'

'Ramsey,' Ramsey said.

'Ramsey. Yes.'

The echo of his footsteps as he left the flat this second time had a doubly hollow ring. The skull's taunting was in it. He had comforted a man for the loss of a daughter towards whose death, however infinitesimally, he had himself contributed. He had had his larger reasons. No court would begin to consider him guilty – but he was his own court. The ice in his stomach remained. Doctors weren't in business to do things like that.

85

As he got into the Fiat he glanced at his watch. Only just after half-past eight. It seemed far too early in the day to feel so down. But the foreground of his mind was still ticking over. As he put the car in gear he had the feeling he was staring directly at something absurdly obvious and not seeing it at all. Well, it would come to him. He was in business to diagnose.

The quadrangle seemed small in comparison with the wide open spaces of some she could remember from past visits. The lawn imprisoned in the frame of crushed gravel was not the most finely shaven and shorn she had seen. But the glossy ivy clung fetchingly to the walls. The roar of the traffic seemed distanced in time rather than space. That was it: in its intimacy this college seemed to wall out time more successfully than most. She had a feeling that if she were to turn quickly she would be granted a glimpse through the porch of two Dodgson-like figures, passing along a Turl Street that had reverted to Victorian resemblance of those catchpenny prints you saw every-where.

'He loved it here,' Beryl said as she stood beside her. 'Came of age in every sense. A case of a university really working. Of course Lincoln didn't have the cachet then of the big name holiday camps where the public school high-flyers and the money-bag brats went. But he'd discovered this was *the* tutor he wanted's college and this is what he set his sights on. And, of course, got . . . Let's go through here.'

Tessa followed her mother towards an arched passage through the block of rooms forming the right-hand side of the quad. It was less than six foot high and no wider than one person. As they approached it steps sounded from its far end. They paused and a young man, younger than Tessa, emerged like a figure from a medieval clock. He wore the short undergraduate's gown over a green crew-neck sweater and jeans. He was carrying a Fender guitar case. It was very hard to visualise him as a twenty-first century Cabinet Minister. Her father at that age . . . what had he *really* been like?

Beryl leading, they went through the tunnel of a passage and into a still smaller quadrangle. This had no grass but only rather uneven flagstones. Opposite where they'd emerged rose the bulk of the college chapel. But Beryl was leading the way to a staircase on the left. She stopped and consulted the names painted on the board inside the doorway.

'A4,' she said, 'that was his room.'

The sign informed them it was now occupied by a D. Patel. Tessa could sense Beryl pursing her lips at that. She raised a pre-emptive topic. 'Dad always told me you met at a Commem Ball,' she said.

Beryl ceased contemplating the spectre of an Indian becoming the British Prime Minister. Her expression perceptibly softened. 'We did,' she said.

'By accident or design?'

'By chance. I'd come as somebody else's partner.'

'And you switched horses?'

'Why not?' Beryl smiled at the memory of her initiative. 'Churchill did it.'

'Who was the other man?'

'Ah, the inquisitve child! Who remembers?'

'Mother!'

Tessa could see her mother on the verge of going positively girlish. 'He was someone. He went into the Conference Business and became an alcoholic.'

'On account of a broken heart, no doubt.'

'On account of the alcohol.'

Overtaken by memories her mother had grown flippant. 'I dare say I would have made something of him.' But not that flippant.

'Dad – what was he like then?' Tessa asked.

'Poor,' Beryl replied like a shot. 'Church mouse poor. It rained . . . his shoes leaked . . . wet socks, all of that. Then – the next term – he invited me to hear him speak at the Union.'

'Good?'

'No. Riveting. His DJ was threadbare and spotty but his speech was anything but. Then and there I knew. MP . . . Member of a Cabinet . . . and that I could have a piece of him.'

On these last chilling words – the trickle of affection Tessa had begun to feel for her mother in this reminiscing mood froze. They reduced her dead father to the level of real estate. They had nothing to do with the way that she herself wanted to possess and be possessed by, utterly interpenetrate, just to be with, Ramsey. Beggarman, thief even – it wouldn't matter.

'We'll go in the chapel,' Beryl said.

Putting their ankles at risk they crossed the quad and pushed open the heavy wooden door. Her distaste momentarily forgotten, Tessa let out a gasp of pleasure. From the altar window the Saints in what must have been very close to their heavenly glory shone down into the dark interior. The vivid saturation of the stained-glass reds and blues was almost painful to the eyes. The sun must have been in the ideal quarter.

'It is rather magnificent, isn't it?' Beryl said.

'Glorious,' Tessa replied. She had made her mind up then and there this would henceforth be her favourite Oxford college.

'Flemish, I think,' Beryl went on. 'Fourteenth century. Or one of those. The great thing is they weren't touched by the bombing.'

'That would have been a crime.'

'A war crime, yes. These carvings are incredible too.' Tessa followed the line of her mother's gaze. At the entrances to the lines of pews flanking the length of the walls the disciples rose up again; this time in the form of wooden carvings. They were perhaps a foot to eighteen inches high and, not in the least medieval, extremely realistic. They actually put Tessa in mind not of Michelangelo but the other one, the. . . .

'There's going to be a bye-election, of course.' Beryl had cuttingly interrupted Tessa's search for the name.

'Are you supposed to wave the party flag?'

'You could say that, dear. Central Office want me to fight the seat.'

'Oh.' How she loathed being called 'dear'.

'Your enthusiasm is noted.'

'I'm taken aback. Surprised. But in many ways, of course, it's very logical.'

'Exactly. The immediate question is a tactical one – whether it would seem like a sentimental bid for cheap votes. If that is the general feeling then the thinking is some other Home Counties seat – as and when one falls available.'

'And . . . how, under everything, do you feel about it?'

'Flattered. Tempted. Positive.'

'After the vote-counting, when you had to get down to it on a daily grind basis – could you do it?'

'On my head. I've sat in on more surgeries and constituency meetings than I've had hot dinners. I argued the toss through all of Exton's major speeches paragraph by paragraph. Re-wrote half of them.'

'What about your own maiden speech? Wouldn't you be scared?'

'No more than most. I'd do it better than most.' She would too, Tessa silently acknowledged.

'There's one thing I can't do, though.'

'Oh?'

'However things break, I won't be able to manage with you, Ramsey and that woman sniping away behind my back.'

A numb, seeping sadness stole over Tessa. Until now, she realised, she had been somehow nurturing the small hope that this trip to Oxford might be Beryl's overture to a peace campaign: mother and daughter, alike bereaved, forgetting old scores and discovering new things in common. It wasn't at all. It was Beryl's way of saying, 'can I see you outside for a moment?' Of lowering a boom . . . Tessa stared at a carving trying to remember which of the apostles is the one with the lamb. Mark was the one with the lion, of course, because of

Venice . . . but she had better say something.

'Who do you mean by *that woman*?' she said.

'Whom. You know very well. Your father's whore and, it would seem, your friend.'

'Mother – Daddy died from an overdose of cocaine.'

'So I have been given to understand that Ramsey is putting about.'

'I see Wyn Bennet's been on to you.'

'Well, of course.'

'Mother – I'm quite sure you knew that Daddy was . . . doing cocaine. What I don't think you appreciate is that the last lot he used was almost certainly adulterated to the point of being poisonous.'

'The idea! That I knew!' That, Tessa bleakly realised, was the greater enormity.

'Daddy in effect was poisoned. Do you want the people responsible to go unpunished?'

'Would it bring him back?'

'No. But if –'

'What it would do is tarnish his reputation beyond repair.'

'And yours, of course.'

'It would detract from every one of his achievements. Tessa, listen!'

Tessa's head jerked up. Her mother had positively hissed her name. The glare in her eyes was close to the fanatic's.

'I want your father talked about in the party twenty years from now,' Beryl said vehemently. 'But for the right reasons. The heroic reasons. I want his name mentioned in the same breath as Churchill.'

'And not as Stonehouse and Thorpe. I know, mother. But he wasn't like them and he won't be, and there are others involved now.'

'Others?'

'Other lives. If the cocaine was poisonous. It wouldn't be the only one, would it?'

'I've really no idea.'

'Mother! Don't pretend! There are lives that can be saved. Don't they matter?'

'Exton served on the last Special Committee on Drug Abuse. How do you think the media would handle a gift like that?'

'A scandal. A skeleton out of its cupboard. For what – five days? Until the next big rail crash outside West Bromwich or wherever drives it out of the papers. Is that so dreadful – so dreadful when weighed against saving people's lives?'

'My dear, you have a lot of *Realpolitik* to learn. The plain working truth is that the smallest private issue is bigger than the greatest international one. Earthquakes in Mexico . . . Famines in Ethiopia . . . they're nothing compared with the next gas bill or a speeding ticket or the price of BT shares.'

'Well, that solves one problem.'

'Which?'

The content of your election pamphlet. You've got a real vote-catcher there! In any case, if you're right, who's really going to give a damn about the way Daddy died.'

'I am, God damn you, Tessa! I do!'

Tessa swallowed. She made her words come out evenly and reasonably. 'No you don't,' she said. 'You're concerned about the way people think he died. And you're not concerned at all about the dealers, the pushers, the millionaire barons or even their victims.' Beryl Waite reared back slightly in her Jaeger suit. 'No one forces people,' she said. 'Nobody twists their arms.'

Tessa found herself appalled. 'So don't try twisting mine,' she managed to get out. Then turned. Her heels clacking she walked out of the chapel. She did not look round but as she closed the door after her she had a sharp impression of her mother standing there under the bland, blind scrutiny of the saints and the apostles.

'Was there in fact a real reason?' Isabel asked him.

'Oh yes.'

'Namely?'

'Ramsey hesitated. He knew she'd be embarrassed by his answer. 'It was because of Anne,' he said. 'We'd had it established that her condition was terminal. Anne knew she was dying faster than the rest of us. She didn't fancy doing it inch by inch, day by day, watched by her friends. You know, coming round. Pretending nothing is different when everything is. She wanted to relieve everyone, herself most of all, of all that . . . artificial . . . strain. So we went somewhere where nobody else knew us – the same way a dying cat slips away into a corner . . .'

He hadn't been looking at Isabel but at the blond-wooded table. But now he looked steadily, gently at her.

'That was the reason,' he said.

'And a very good one. The best, perhaps. Certainly the most considerate. I suppose a cynic would say Exton had it lucky.'

'If he were cynic he would.'

'I wish I'd known her – known her well.'

'You'd've got on.'

'I'm sorry if I was opening old wounds. I should –'

'No. Don't worry. It happened. But she was a winner and that's a finite fact too.'

'How long ago was it?'

'Nine years now.'

'And you still miss her?'

'Yes.'

'You could miss her just as completely here as there.'

'Contrary to rumour, people get sick in France too.'

'Isn't it a little bit of a cop out?'

'Oh?'

'Isn't there a dash of playing at up-market hippy about it, Ramsey? Or is that being impertinent?'

'Yes – but you're allowed. Am I what the awful "frogs" would call a *poseur*? No, I don't think so. It's very simple. I like it there.' She had been pushy but it had been in what she saw as a good cause. It was easy to choose not to be angry.

'It's better than here?'

He shifted in his chair. He was glad to see the conversation opening out into the general. Isabel had closed the shop and they were having a salady snack lunch.

'Yes. It's better. I haven't seen anything over here this time around that's made me want to come back. I know this drugs thing – it makes it an artifical situation – but England . . . it's become a selfish place, hasn't it? Self-regarding. There's so much fashion there isn't any style left.'

'London, maybe. You live in a little fishing town. You're not comparing like with like.'

Fair comment, really – For every Soho there's a Belleville.

'Maybe not. But better the devil I've come to know than what I see here.'

Isabel blinked, pursed her lips. She was upset. 'Oh dear, I was feeling quite up because I sold those bisque porcelain figures this morning. Now I feel like one of life's also-rans.'

'I'm sorry. It's me being an up-market hippy. I didn't mean to make your crest fall. Or recall Exton Waite to mind.

'Tell you what. I'll cheer you up. With a riddle. How do you find South West Three in West One?'

'Er . . . I don't know. How do you find South West Three in West One?'

'By telephoning this number.' He pushed the scrap of paper across to her. She looked at it then, puzzled, back at him.

'Whose is it?'

'A Simon Wood's.'

'Simon Wood the playboy?'

'As I believe. Now – dial the number but pretend to be Exton's secretary. Crisp. Efficient. Slightly bored. You know her name?'

'Joyce.'

'Say you're her. Say you're tying up loose ends. Ask whether there's any account still left outstanding.'

'Would Exton have approved of this?'

'. . . Yes. Underneath everything. I promise.'

'All right then.'

'Can you manage it?'

'Ramsey, I haven't been an antique dealer all these years for nothing. Crisp and slightly bored.' She reached the phone to her and dialled. It was answered immediately.

'Oh, hello,' Isabel said, 'is that Simon Wood's secretary? . . . Oh good, this is Joyce – I was Exton Waite's secretary. . . .'

He could hear the tinny reply without being able to make out individual words.

'Yes, of course, I'm sure you were,' Izzie was saying. 'I'll see your message is passed on . . . No, no . . . Send the account to the house.'

Ramsey leaned towards her other ear. 'When was the last appointment?' he hissed. He was right but might as well make it double sure.

'And while I'm on . . . could you just tell me when Mr Waite's last appointment was? . . . Thursday, the eleventh at three. Thank you so much. Sorry to have been a bother . . . 'Bye.' She hung up. He'd killed two birds with one call. Her spirits were definitely raised. She looked at him.

'Ramsey,' she said, 'what have I been doing? You look smug.'

Goldsmith had said make it 'The Grapes' because the beer wasn't bad, the atmosphere nice and you could always ignore the neighbours. It was also far enough off the beaten Guy's drinking track to be safe from his point of view. Close to the afternoon's 'last orders please' the two sat drinking in the little square window overlooking the Thames. No one was sitting cheek-by-jowl with them but there was still enough hustle and hub-bub to give camouflage. Ramsey was sure he'd not been followed.

'So who did you support in the World Cup?' he asked.

Charles Goldsmith, né Goldschmidt, laughed. 'Ramsey,' he said. 'I haven't had a Hungarian thought since 1956. Not since I stole my last egg. Anyway they were rubbish. No one supported England more than I.'

'Also rubbish,' Ramsey said. 'I was for France through and through. Amoros man of the tournament.'

'Tasty, I admit,' Goldsmith said. 'But you've never been an England fan since they sacked you as team manager.'

The two old friends smiled at the old joke. Short, plump – nobody could have looked more Centrally European than Charles and nobody could have been more English in attitude. In dress – Harris tweed jacket, crisp smart shirt – he was the epitome of Bromley man. Ramsey knew he had written letters to *The Times* not only over NHS cuts but about Geoffrey Boycott. Both men knew that without a long sponsoring statement from the native-born UK passport holder the naturalised Englishman could have fetched up in another foreign field almost anywhere. Well, there's two-way traffic in loyalties, Ramsey thought. And finally only one in drugs.

'What is it?' he said quietly.

'Not nice,' Goldsmith casually took the cue at once. 'When you slipped it to me I had a private bet with myself it would be Angel Dust.'

'No. Cocaine.'

'Yes. France or England?'

'Here in London. It's what else besides the cocaine that interests me.'

A haggard bearded man went by *en route* to the Gents. Goldsmith took a pull at his Taylor Walker's.

Ramsey said, 'I know that whatever it is, it's quick acting, clinically cardiotoxic and –'

'Lethal. It's twenty per cent cocaine; twenty per cent mannite, lactose and such . . . and,' Goldsmith's eyes double checked for eavesdroppers.

'And?'

'Sixty per cent Ma-Huang.'

'Come again.'

Goldsmith spelt it out.

'Sounds exotic.'

'It is. It's ephedrine based. Guaranteed to blow your troubles away.'

'And everything else?'

'That's its small drawback.'

The door to the Gents opened on the sound of a hot air drier still blowing hard. The haggard man went back to the front of the pub.

'These cuts – you must know, Ramsey – they mimic the properties of coke. But they're not, repeat not, inert. In the proportions of 20 – 20 – 60 the little lot you gave me isn't a joy-ride. It's a short cut to the cemetery.'

'Crematorium,' Ramsey said.

Goldsmith sat back in his chair. 'Somebody found out the hard way?' he asked softly.

'Somebodies. More than one.'

Goldsmith pulled a face.

'Final question,' Ramsey said. 'An accidental mix or intentional?'

Goldsmith shook his head.

'Oh,' he said, 'there's just no way of knowing. Yes, it could be accidental. This stuff isn't made up in a sterile lab at Boots and tested on thirty thousand white mice. But, yes, it could be deliberate. The profits in trafficking are so huge there's every temptation to make a little go a bit further. So dilute it as much as you can and then more. These are ruthless people. What's a death or a dozen deaths weighed against thousands of millions of pounds or dollars?'

A bell rang.

'Your last orders, please, gents.'

Goldsmith handed Ramsey a sealed envelope. 'There's the break-down in black and white,' he said. 'Don't lose it. It could be *Guinness Book of Records* time for an analysis that complex.'

'Thanks, Charles.' Ramsey pocketed the enveloped directly. Last orders. But no last rites. He stared out at the Thames. Pale sunlight was laying down shimmering rectangles on its muddy brown surface. The sheen hurt his eyes. The river seemed very high. It also seemed that a one-off plot to do away with Exton Waite could definitely be ruled out but in the final path lab analysis the issue was still one of murder . . . Water slapped at the piles right under the window where they sat.

'River's up high,' Goldsmith said. 'The tide must be on the turn. Do you still have your boat?'

When is South West Three in West One? When SW3 is shorthand for a three o'clock appointment with Simon Wood at his Harley Street consulting rooms. Ramsey smiled. History was repeating itself. Once again, his post-card to Dany *en route*, he was leaving the Wigmore Street Post Office to step around the corner for a species of medical consultation. Seeking a second opinion as you might say. Wimpole Street – Harley Street. Whenever Wyn Bennet or Simon Wood felt like paying calls, professional or social, on each other it was hardly worth warming up the Rolls. Or possibly the Porsche. As opposed to SW3, an SW100 944 was squatly on a meter outside Wood's place of work.

London, city of security systems. He pushed yet another squawk box button.

'Yes?'

'Dr Bennet to see Mr Wood.'

The door lock buzzed and then gave. He went in and watched the receptionist's eyes widen. As Harley Street was a little more obvious than Wimpole so she was a slightly coarser sister to the previous *Cosmopolitan* cover girl.

'You're not Dr Bennet!'

'Dr Hawley Harvey Bennet.'

'Is Mr Wood expecting you?'

'He'll want to see me. Here's my card.'

It wasn't a card but a Coca-Cola coaster. On it he had used a marker pen to print 'Kate Ross, RIP.'

The girl stared up at him slack-jawed and thereby lengthened her odds in the Miss World book.

'Take it in and see what happens,' he suggested. The girl got up and wafted herself towards the inner door. There was obviously a casting agency, and almost certainly a recommended mouth to mouth designer. The greys and blues of this haven where butter wouldn't melt suggested that the man had had some off-cuts when he'd finished running up a little collection for Saatchi's.

The door opened. The girl stood there, a blush mantling her scowl because she was defeated.

'Mr Wood says would you step this way.' Resisting the verbal temptation he went past her into the new consulting room.

It was different to Bennet's. It was de luxe but there was a suggestion that work got done there. The high masseur's couch, though by Heals out of Bauhaus, was surrounded by UV and US equipment. Towels were stacked. Rubbing oils and powder stood on an enamel surfaced table. There was a certain hardness to the room. But not to the man who practised there. Whereas Bennet in his bland sleakness had hinted at aspirations to being the Lord Privy Seal, this was Peter Pan. Simon Wood was fighting growing up every inch of the way. And losing. He must once have been very handsome in a blond, public-school way. But now the fair hair had to be blow dried so it would puff up and minimise the growing areas of bald skull. It had to be dyed to eliminate the greyness. There was a stretched quality to the skin over the boyish, chubby cheeks that spoke of face-lifting. The creases about the frank blue eyes were curiously wrong – as if a painter had transposed left and right. The pink healthiness of the cheeks seemed unnaturally arrived at. The mouth, which would always have been the young Adonis's Achilles heel, was fleshy but pinched, ready to turn cross-grained at the drop of an imagined slight. Ramsey had thought to find Wood in a white uniform; in fact the osteopath was wearing bird's-eye patterned Daks slacks, a silk old-gold crew-necked sweater and a double-breasted blazer. The blazer's outer buttons were not done up. As Wood rose from a distant desk Ramsey caught a glimpse of a paunch whose chubbiness outdid the cheeks and made redundant the efforts at perpetual facial youth. Ramsey also saw at a glance that while Wood's day-to-day trade might give him strong hands and firm forearms his essential proclivity was 'limp-wristed'.

At present Wood held the Coca-Cola coaster. Not apprehensive, ready to be angry, he looked at Ramsey appraisingly.

'Was it you who made that bogus 'phone call earlier today?' he asked.

'In effect. Yes.'

'We checked back, you know.'

'I imagine. In your line of business you can't be too careful.'

'Oh? I'm afraid I don't follow.' It was said aggressively. Wood was setting himself to throw an indignant verbal punch. Ramsey decided his eyes were anything but frank. He nodded towards the coaster.

'You knew Catherine Ross,' he said. 'When she was alive,' he added.

'I'd hardly know her afterwards,' Wood said. He said it without thinking, gaily, it could be said. Ramsey decided to let the enormity go. Events would overtake Wood soon enough.

'She came to me with knee trouble after a diving accident,' Wood said. He tried to recover. 'I'm sorry to gather –'

'And we know you knew Exton Waite,' Ramsey cut in.

'Yes. . . . So?'

'Both dead. Both died drug-related deaths. . . . Both bought drugs from you.'

Since his school-boy days and his endless fondling amours Simon Wood had always nursed a feeling somewhere at the core of his being that one day he would be found out. He would get his comeuppance. He stared at Ramsey with unblinking self-possession but inside his head was the growing knowledge that after all these years, on this silly, arbitrary day, he had been caught.

'Waite died from a coronary,' he said in his clinical mode.

'No. He didn't. He died from a cardiovascular collapse brought on by the cocaine you sold him in the course of a three o'clock appointment on the day of his death.'

'Who are you?' Wood said at long last. 'What's your little game?'

'My name is Ramsey. Doctor Ramsey. And it's not a game. I knew Exton when I was a medical student. I was once his GP.'

Simon Wood felt a layer of hope stifle the rising panic inside him. This Ramsey was a club member. 'Then you'll know Exton had a dicky heart,' he said.

'Then there's Charlie . . . Charlie the pusher.'

Wood sensed his reprieve was to be minimal.

'Also dead,' Ramsey progressed relentlessly. 'Also OD'd. Again it was cocaine.'

'Why should I know some individual called . . . Charlie, was it?'

'No, Mr Wood. Not quite the right delivery. Try it again more casually and without that actorish pause.' Still standing, the two men looked at each other.

'And you have evidence for these wild assertions?' Wood continued to bluff.

'No,' Ramsey said. 'I don't.'

Once more Simon Wood felt his gut-feelings seesaw back towards hope. He allowed himself a small-mouthed smile. He does it quite well, Ramsey thought, it's a spin-off from his bedside manner repertoire. But he doesn't do it well enough.

'Are you logging all this?' Wood asked.

Ramsey unwrapped his blouson, held it open. 'No wires,' he said.

'You appreciate the authorities find blackmail peculiarly sordid,' Wood said. 'Especially when attempted on the bases of false accusations. They'll be inclined to give a maximum –'

'Six years,' Ramsey said. 'Minimum.'

'I beg –'

'For manslaughter. Plus what you'll get for dealing. Ten shall we say in all. Of course part of you will enjoy the social life in Parkhurst especially if you like a bit of rough. But it's a long way from the Isle of Wight to Stringfellows and it has to be a really slow day before a con rates a mention in Hickey or Dempster.'

'Manslaughter . . . ?' Wood repeated. Cupid, having become middled-aged, had now turned curiously grey.

'With or without evidence, I'll lay charges,' Ramsey said. His voice thickened slightly as his disgust lent it vehemence. 'My God, that you can have the unmitigated nerve, you piece of fungoid-covered shit, to talk about the "sordid". You – selling on, *peddling*, sub-sordid little packets about whose contents you haven't a clue.'

He moved to the enamel-topped table and picking up a container of talcum powder held it away from him at arms length and upside down. Like sugar from a caster, only finer, building up into a cloud, powder streamed out on to the steel blue carpet. Wood made no effort to stop him.

'Cutting it with this would have been an act of mercy compared with what they did use,' Ramsey said. 'How many?'

Wood made one last stand. 'How many . . . what?'

Ramsey threw the plastic container at him. Leaving a white clown's mark on the Bond Street blazer it bounced hollowly away. 'I mean it,' he said. 'Manslaughter. You've heard of Detective Inspector Brook, I'm sure.'

The way Wood's face flinched was give-away enough.

'Well so have I. He's a mate. I'll go to him. If necessary I'll lie. I'll plant evidence. I'll set up witnesses. With him. The two of us will fit you up. Unless, that is . . .'

'Unless?'

Always leave the other fellow an out. Or seem to. Ramsey had tugged at his line with perfect judgement. Not all of Wood's Harley Street P.R. could keep the sound of hope jack-in-a-boxing back into his voice. 'I don't twist arms,' he said, conceding. 'I shall of course deny this conversation but – man to man, they're free, white – well, usually – and over twenty-one.'

'I explained. You're not a man,' Ramsey said. 'And Kate Ross wasn't over twenty-one.'

'Well –'

'You know what you've been putting into circulation?'

'More or less. Innocuous enough toot. Non-addictive. Nose candy. Coke. Snow. Call it what you will.'

'Why don't we call it poison?'

'But it's not! People can –'

Ramsey thrust a sheet of paper at Wood. The osteopath took it from him on reflex.

'An analysis of what was out on the street at the time you supplied Waite,' he said. 'Sixty per cent Ma-Huang.'

'Ma-Huang!'

'Yes. Put that with twenty per cent cocaine and you're selling pretty much instant death by the wrap. You can keep that as a souvenir. It's a photo-copy.'

Wood had sunk back against his couch. Cupid's face now matched the colour of the white paper sheet along its length. The face worked. 'I didn't know,' he said. It came out in a schoolboy's voice. Simon Wood had indeed been found out.

'Maybe I believe you. But ignorance is no excuse in the dock.'

He let Wood imagine the scene a long moment before he resumed the prosecution. 'You're saying you don't cut it yourself.'

'No! I don't touch them. Parcel them up and get shut of them.'

'Then who does?'

'I don't know!'

'No?'

'No!'

'Then how do you get your supplies?'

'Delivered.'

'How? When?'

'Whenever I need them.'

'If there's no contact how do they know you need more?'

'I leave a coded message on my answering machine. You know, instead of "we'll get back to you", etc., etc., I change it to "I'll get back to you".'

'How does it get here?'

'On motor cycles. Kids. Always different.'

'You mean these messenger service type. . . .'

'No. Unofficial – no paper-work.'

'How did you first get into it?'

'I . . . was approached.'

'Who by?'

'I'm trying to tell you. A man – a company director. He had interests in casinos. Gambling. I . . . I owed quite a lot of money at the time. They said –'

'They?'

'*He*. He was all I ever saw. The deal was they would wipe my slate clean if . . . there was this gap in their organisation. There were customers already in place. Later I could add on more. If I was sure . . . Ramsey, that's how it happened!'

No wonder Brook detested amateurs.

'The spokesman's name?'

'He said it was Michaels. Howard Michaels. But it wasn't, I'm sure.'

'English?'

'I . . . I'm not even totally sure of that.'

'What's his real name?'

'I don't know. I never did. I just suspected . . . the thing is – he's dead.'

Ramsey was inclined to believe Wood. The collapse had been so total. It was beyond a performance. But it was now his own turn to play-act. 'It's all too much,' he said quietly. 'I can't leave you walking around scott free. I have to turn you over to Brook.'

'. . . money? I can . . .'

Ramsey smashed Wood across the face. The negative of the back of his hand stood out as a paler shade of white then started to turn red. Wood looked as if he might cry: not from the pain but because he was not going to be let off. 'You . . . you said *unless* . . .' he managed at last.

'I also asked *how many*?'

'About sixteen.' This time there was no pretence of not understanding. 'Er . . . about sixteen. I can check exactly and –'

'You do that. Now.'

Wood nodded. 'And . . . what will you do?'

'We'll see, shall we? Providing you retire, then . . .'

'Retire!' A whole new corridor of horrors had swung open in front of the bad schoolboy.

'You push one more panadol and I'll see Brook comes looking for you.'

'You don't understand!'

'For you it's incredibly simple. Do as you are told. Stop!'

Wood's tongue flicked out. He licked his lips. For the first time

99

since he'd been struck his hand went to his face. But it seemed an absentminded movement.

'That man – Howard Michaels,' he said. 'The one who's dead. I had a phone call once. At home. A voice I'd never heard – it had an accent, French, I think, Swiss – it said Michaels had tried to cancel his membership in the club. That was the phrase used. Exactly.'

'So?'

'The voice went on. It said they'd decided to dampen Michaels' independence. They'd dropped him in the river. Twice.'

'That would do it.'

'And only pulled him out once.' Wood stared at Ramsey and Ramsey was able to look straight down along the corridor of horrors that began in Wood's aghast eyes. Good, he thought.

'Take swimming lessons,' he said. He turned and went.

Simon Wood stared at the closed door. An enormous, irresistible liquid gush of panic seemed to rise up from the itching soles of his feet and engulf him. It was filling his lungs, drowning him. His dissolving stomach was adding to the flood. The stifling feeling grew so strong that his mind sought disbelief to aid his body. None of it had happened. It was just a projection of what he thought might happen, but it really hadn't happened for real. The panic receded a fraction. He found he had walked to his desk. And he knew it had all happened indeed. He slumped into his chair and put his arms upon the desk and his head on his arms. There was nursery comfort of a sort there. He began to weep. He wept for a long time. At last, scarcely aware he was doing it, he opened a drawer and took out his private address book. There was some relief in action. He tried to focus his swimming eyes. The last feather-light straw was that he would be late home now and Aubrey would snap at him.

Ramsey lay on his bed in the malodorous hotel room and stared at the ceiling as he considered what to do about Wood. The room was growing dim. Outside the great grey ship of the day was gliding on towards twilight and the night. Outside, too, the parked car was still on duty. When he'd returned to his room via the staff entrance a quick look from the lobby had established as much. Had it been there all the long hours he'd been away? It was a matter of complete indifference to him at the moment – as was the question of whether the room, identical in every bare detail to when he'd left it, had been searched. Or bugged. There was nothing to find here. No words of any importance would be uttered out loud. What was Wood to him or he to Wood . . . ? It wasn't a simple balance of crime and punishment. 'What's your little game?' the osteopath had said. It had seemed a cheap line at the time but Wood had spoken more

100

penetratingly than he knew. Quitting seedy hotels by back doors and cross-examining people was a game of sorts. With a growing sense of shame Ramsey acknowledged that he was beginning to enjoy himself.

TEN

'Di . . . Simon. Listen – molto importante! That toot I sold you last week. Used any yet. . . ? Well, don't! Don't whatever . . . It's not kosher. I'm sorry but . . . Of course I'm serious! Deadly serious. I mean that. It's lethal. Really! You must dump it . . . Down the loo . . . Yes, I appreciate that. I'll make it right later. Must fly. Love to Mario. *Ciao*.'

Sweating, Simon Wood hung up. His hand was steady as he crossed another name off his list but his insides continued to vibrate. That left four more. He'd worked out that there were fifteen who might have bought into the dodgy batch. Nine he'd managed to get to the night before. The night or the century. . . ?

It had been the worst night of his life. People just weren't there when there was a crisis. He'd stayed at the office until past ten ringing his way from top to bottom, bottom to top of the list. Only when the wrong numbers had started coming thick and fast had he forced himself to go home. He'd been too sick to eat but Aubrey wasn't to know that. He'd been sulking, and hadn't cooked a morsel. He'd accused him of staying out trolling. As if he needed that, his nerves shredded, his whole body awash with terror and despair. He'd answered back. It had led to separate bedrooms. The two valium had taken hours to work.

Then he'd had trouble waking. He'd surfaced not knowing where he was. He'd had the sense of just having had the most terrible nightmare. One in which he was found out. For something dreadful . . . Then the noise Aubrey was deliberately making in the kitchen had pulled him fully awake and the terrible, total awareness it was not nightmare but fact had scalded through him again . . . He had called the girl, had her cancel his patients, given her the day off. He had come in away from Aubrey's petulance – oh, the bitch! – he didn't *need* that now – to finish off, please, dear God, the list.

He tried to put a brake on his racing, dancing mind. There must still be a way of fixing things, a way of getting off. Perhaps Ramsey's game *was* blackmail and he was out to up the ante . . . perhaps, if no-one else was wasted, Ramsey, if he *was* a doctor, would think he'd done his duty. He could promise – dear God, he'd never do such things again, no, never – he could promise he'd never do the like again. And the others. He was only a '*poste restante*'. He'd never talk. He'd shut up his legit shop too. He'd go away. Abroad. They'd see he could be trusted . . . Sitting at his desk Simon Wood felt a fresh rush of sweat break out upon him as he shivered. He couldn't believe a word of what he was trying to make himself believe. He groaned out loud. His backside squirmed on the chair seat. The next name on the list was Jody Price's once again. That was the number that had yet to produce an answer of any kind.

In his own professional way the Detective Inspector, too, was having a bad morning. It was sunny and clear but Brook's expression as he stood on the kerbside of the turning off Eversholt Street did not suggest he viewed life as made up of sweetness and light. As the patrol car squealed into the side street Brook's manner did not soften. The impression he gave of not finding all right with the world intensified as Ramsey got out and, the patrol car already backing away, walked towards him.

'It would be silly to ask you how you knew where I was staying, wouldn't it?' Ramsey said.

'Just a shot in the dark,' Brook said shortly.

'Is recruiting that much down? Do you have to work all on your own these days?'

'We've done all the book stuff,' Brook said. 'Follow me. You're going to find this interesting.'

Ramsey did follow him. The street was a cul-de-sac. It ended in an ugly, temporary-permanent fence of galvanised metal. A low door was set into this corrugated dead end. Without ceremony Brook went through it first. Ducking his head, Ramsey followed. Narrowness was blown away. The dozen plus lines running into Euston Station extended away in front of him. It was like a solid version of the view of the Thames from 'The Grapes'.

'This way.'

Brook led on. They went along a beaten mud path at the top of a bank. They were walking towards the station. Ahead was a single railway carriage. It had been parked in a siding alongside the bank. Two or three policemen, uniformed and not, were standing about in its shadow. The carriage dwarfed them. Ramsey could see now that it was a sleeper. A shunting engine was coupled to its further end.

'There's no live rail on this track,' Brook said. He sidled down the crude steps cut into the side of the bank with a spade. He was still wearing his crumpled suit. Ramsey followed him down the steps. They entered shadow and Ramsey realised how hot he'd become. Close to, without benefit of a platform, the rolling stock was huge.

'We go in this end.'

Brook accepted the hand a uniformed policeman gave him and grunting, hauled himself up into the doorway. The policeman stooped down again. Ramsey let himself be pulled aboard. 'Thanks.'

The man's insignia put him in the railway police. After the odd approach it was strange to be in the familiar surroundings of a train corridor again.

'What's this about then?' Ramsey said. It was odd to be walking down a corridor and not have it swaying. There was a buzzing sound.

'Forensics finished forty minutes ago,' Brook said. 'Look.' He stood aside. Ramsey squeezed past him. 'Sweet Jesus Christ!' he said.

The buzzing sound came from the flies. The object of their attentions was the blackened, coagulated blood that, from the car's central door to the far end, had sheeted everywhere. The inside of the door was encrusted with it. The corridor floor almost uniformly covered to the far end. It must have looked like a couple of paint cans when fresh, Ramsey thought, just thrown out any old how. His stomach had contracted. You always forgot how much blood people had in them.

'Human, I imagine,' he said. His throat was dry. Brook didn't bother with a reaction.

'A man travelling south last night from Blackpool. He boarded the Inverness train – this – at Preston.'

It couldn't have been Simon Wood then . . .

'He had the compartment next to you. Go on in.' Ramsey hesitated. He all but shut his eyes from fear of what he would see. The fear proved groundless. The door opened on a compartment exceptionable only in that it had not been made up. A man's travelling belongings still filled the ingenious cramming of a quart of living space into a pint of room. Ramsey nodded.

'One thing the British still do better than the French,' he said. He was compensating for his hesitation in front of Brook.

'Dammit, man, we're not on an EEC fact-finding mission,' the policeman said. He pushed past Ramsey. 'Look. Jacket still up on a hanger. An overnight suiter. An executive-style attaché case. Open. Inside a northern edition of yesterday's *Sun*. A paperback even lower on the library scale and . . . two kilos of cocaine.'

'Yes,' Ramsey said. Out of everything he'd seen the two packets first.

'There's also an opened wrap of cocaine on that ledge,' he said. There was. A remnant of powder still clung to it.

'Precisely. Scenario is: sonny boy is coming south to make a delivery. But he's not just a pusher's side-kick. He's a user too. Most pushers and dealers are, of course. It pays for the habit. And it keeps them in line. The big boys like that.'

'So he has his little snort.'

'Yes. His nightcap, let's call it. After that he's flying. Where his head is at is anyone's guess. It still is.'

'He . . . ?'

'Indeed he did. Totters out the door, opens that window, sticks his nut out. Too far out. Bang. Goodnight, Vienna.'

'Christ.'

'He won't help him now. Not in this existence. I bet even as a doctor, Doc, you'd be surprised at how ragged a scrag end that sort of amputation leaves. We've got all sorts of people running around north of Watford to see what's smeared down someone's faithful old 8.22.'

Scofield took the call. He always began with his posh but deeply sincere voice.

'Chandos Motors. How may we be of service?'

'Oh, not to bother, it was a personal call.'

'Mr Jakeman? One moment, I'll just check.' He swivelled and looked across the showroom. Jakeman was with the two Arabs and selling the Mulsanne for all he was worth. For a second Scofield hesitated. But they always split the commission and Carl was straight enough about it. There was no real point in a take-over bid.

'I'm afraid he's with a client at the moment, sir,' he said. 'May I take a message? . . . yes, Simon Wood. He has the number. It's urgent. I'll have him call you as soon as he's free, Mr Wood . . . Not all all.' He hung up, and frowned. The sticker on the Austin Healey re-bore was all askew. The new boy wasn't up to a Mayfair dealership.

The mews was undistinguished, but its back of Queensway location ensured that to live there, owner or tenant, cost a fortune. Most girls in their late twenties couldn't have afforded to have split the mortgage on a three-bedroomed end house three ways. But air hostesses are high flyers by nature. And the perks of their customs-evading trade can tot up at the end of the financial year – all the more so when, in return for the odd personal favour, Jeremy and Hank and Aziz are picking up the tab for so many of life's little necessities. And why not? God knows that the job itself, like its practitioners, is no bowl of cherries. After you've been flying, a little flying makes a nice change. Roz and Jackie were all but through loading the GTI for the sprint down to the airport and points east when Pam appeared at the door.

'Roz!' she called, 'phone!' Roz shook her head. 'I'm gone,' she said. And Jackie was already behind the wheel.

'Better take it,' Roz said. 'It's Simon. We don't want to be caught short, do we? Big girls like us.'

Roz laughed.

'Won't be a second,' she said to Jackie, through the wound-down window. She went back into the house. While their private forms of amusement were not to be sniffed at by the likes of all, rich little rich girls today are increasingly finding a car phone comes into the necessity category.

It was a scruffy pub in the hinterland between the Euston Road and Camden. It had the Indian restaurant wallpaper over every vertical surface. With his rumpled suit, and his rumpled, slept-in face Brook blended with the wallpaper instantly. A third-rate rep well past it, you'd have said. As Ramsey had just found to his cost, Brook's tipple was double malts. Well, the broken veins in the cheeks were part of the camouflage too.

'Cheers,' Ramsey said.

Brook grunted. Largesse had had no impact on his affability index. It remained close to zero.

'In aid of what, then?' Ramsey asked.

'Reciprocal exchange of information in return for your call about Charlie,' Brook said. 'For which thanks.'

'Don't mention it.'

'If I'm asked, who said I did?'

'You have it analysed?' asked Ramsey.

'The Charlie-topper? Of course.'

'And.'

'Usual mix of coke and other cuts.' Brook's face was as deadpan as a forgotten grave.

'But it killed Charlie.'

'There's a *prima facie* case.'

'So it isn't.'

'Isn't what?'

'Usual. The word you were groping for is lethal.'

'In so far as it appears to have blown Charlie to kingdom come, Doc, you may have a point.'

'If you were straight with me, you'd tell me what it was cut with.'

'Would I?

'You'd say something like "Ma-Huang, Incense. Ratio of 60, 20, 20." '

Brook rolled whiskey around his mouth. He swallowed. 'I'm impressed,' he said. He clearly was. But for the first time that morning he had smiled. With pleasure. Ramsey realised he had revealed more than he had learned.

'If you were straighter,' Brook said, his voice back on duty now, 'you'd have told me that you'd been tampering with evidence.'

'I thought I just had.'

'Yes. Better late than never . . . Doesn't seem as if those two kilos are part of the naff bunch, does it now?'

'Not in so far as he opened a door, opened a window. But you can't be sure yet.'

'Does being decapitated have an effect on the heart, Doc?'

'Not if you don't see it coming.'

'Point taken. Know the street value of two kilos?'

Ramsey shook his head.

'Eighty grand according to today's FT.'

'Worth having.'

'If you can keep your head . . . A weekly run on that scale makes the likes of Simon Wood seem quite small beer, doesn't it, Doc?'

Ah. No point in a denial. 'I did get the impression that for all his up-front up-marketry work he was quite small beer. A filling station attendant you might say.'

'You might – and you'd be right. Did he say he supplied Waite?'

'He'd deny it in court but he did.'

'Did you wise him up about the Ma-Huang?'

'Yes.'

'And?'

'He may possibly have shat himself standing up in front of me.'

'He's never wanted for enemies. Did you tell him to sound a general alarm?'

'Yes.'

For the second time in five minutes Brook smiled. 'The thing about amateurs is,' he said, 'they can on occasion, when you're lucky, stir things up. They come out of nowhere and act as catalysts . . . He didn't take you for a copper?'

'I'm sure he didn't.'

'Hmmn . . . thing is, he's a very small fish. The motorcycles come and go. They go back to other fish. But they're small too . . . A good fisherman waits for the big one to get into his net. You should know that – all those trips you make in your old tub.'

'You've been checking on me in France.'

'Would I do a thing like that? Same again?'

'Why not?'

'Miss!' They were silent as the barmaid served the new drinks. Was it force of habit that made Brook eye her hand on the optics like a weights and measures officer?

'Cheers.'

'Good luck.' This time Brook joined in the toast. 'You trust me?' he asked.

'Probably. You're good at your job.'

'Yes, I am. And I happen to respect you for wanting to horn in on it. You get credit for sussing at long range that something was rotten in the Royal Borough. I respect the way you came over to sort it. You have. Now leave it with me. I promise you that in the end, even if it's only a little bit, your friend will be revenged. Go home. Go back to France. Go back to making decent people well again. Leave the scum to those of us who're stuck with it . . . I promise I'll let you know when we've got our result.'

Dany. Calvados. Artie Shaw. A nice quiet noisy game of *boules*. A grave that wasn't forgotten. It all suddenly seemed like a good idea. Ross had said he would be going after the effective killer of his daughter.

'And besides me and my lot,' Brook said, 'there seem to be others who believe the best place for a sleeping dog is lying down.'

'You could have a point,' Ramsey said.

The boardroom table was of a dark, exotic wood grown in one of the many former colonial countries that this EC2 institution had exploited for generations. The cordless phone reflected in the depths of its gloss seemed utterly out of place upon it. It was indeed. Blinded by the red mist that the North Eastern General Manager had engendered that morning, the MD had left it there. The incongruity became all the more marked with the commencement of a hi-tech warble. There was the thud of a falling file and a muttered oath from the adjoining office. Stuart Harrington came fleshily into the room. He was in shirt-sleeves. The broad blue and white stripes of his shirt clashed hideously with the Hispanic fervour of that ultimate aesthetic vulgarity, an MCC tie. Lunch had been demanding. He blundered round the table.

'Yes? Harrington . . . Simon! How are you? . . . Yes, in a meeting all morning . . . Oh, I say, that's too bad! We have a dinner party . . . Tonight! Silver back from Coutts and all the trimmings . . . Of course I can't! No way. It's Lieberson from New York . . . Simon, I'm holding this against you. No Snow White and very likely no deal. The best I'll come out of it now is looking a right schmuck personally! . . . No, I don't! Good-bye!'

Harrington was upset. The chagrin and the heaviness of his lunch so weighed upon him they dulled his powers of lateral thinking. Like the gleaming bone of an African shaman the telephone still lay reflected in the dark wood's glory as, swearing, the MD of the multi-national lumbered from the room.

Only one left. He punched in the sequence of numbers he sensed now he would never forget. As always, he got straight through. Bleep-beep. Bleep-beep. Bleep-beep. Bleep-beep . . . As always, it was Jody Price who remained unobtainable. God! She must be lying in there dead. Simon Wood felt despair congeal the length of his spine. He put his arms on the desk and his head on his arms. There was small comfort now in his regression. The posture made the smell of the constantly renewing sweat in his armpits that much easier to detect. Quite oblivious to the grim irony, he thought he might have a heart attack when, hard by his left earlobe, the phone shrilled.

'Yes!' he shouted. 'Oh . . . Ramsey.'

It was a gentlemanly afternoon, as, on a sunny day in that ghetto between The Mall and Pall Mall, it can often seem to be. As he walked past the Athenaeum, Ramsey became aware that he was pulling back his shoulders and mentally polishing up his accent. He didn't admire the effort. Sod that for a game of soldiers. He made his gait and posture a little less military. Self-appointed private-eyes have more of a lope about them, he told himself sardonically, and not much time for the Establishment. All the same, he was wearing his one suit. The tie on this occasion was not funereal but Touring Theatre C.C. Its very obscurity should put him one up amid the stuffed shirts.

Across the broad, parking-metered street was the house where, he remembered inconsequentially, Kitchener had lived and Northcliffe died. A gruesome pair of ghosts to overlook the sovereign's comings and goings along the Mall. But his destination was here, just beyond the lurking traffic warden. He went up the steps that led to the Silly Billy building which had once housed a king's mistress and now served the Almanac Club.

As he had promised, Ross was waiting in the entrance hall. They shook hands.

'I'll sign you in,' Ross said.

He looked pale and tired but otherwise surprisingly composed for a newly bereaved father. There's no art, Ramsey thought, to read the mind's destruction in the face.

'This way.' Ross led the way into a biggish, rectangular room, not unappealing in its Victorian scruffiness. A vast turkey carpet covered most of a marble floor. Laying it must have been a problem. Fluted pillars standing out into the room suggested that the architect's original sense of weight-bearing capabilities must have been a touch cavalier. The random assortment of handsome bookcases and cabinets about the walls, however, looked capable of a second line of defence against a collapsing ceiling. Library tables in basso profondo mahogany were deployed across the carpet with a pleasing lack of symmetry. So too were the classic chairs of clubland. Clusters were grouped as conversation had earlier dictated. But now, in the late afternoon, few were occupied. The few retired majors scattered about in desultory fashion were an outrageously over-the-top lot from Central Casting.

'Let's try here. It gets a bit warmer by the window when the sun's low.' Ross had detected two otherwise isolated chairs by the wide grey-veined marble fireplace. They could have been pre-set there with intent.

'Drink?'

'Please. Scotch, if I may.' Ramsey wasn't that thirsty but the business of serving would give him a chance to get his bearings. The choice of rendezvous had surprised him slightly – though nothing like as much as getting the actual call. Ross, of course, as his country-member tweeds now accentuated, had gentlemanly inflections and mannerisms, and there had been the photograph of the large 'Sussex borders' house. Poor Kate had worked hard at pretending to be mutton dressed up as lamb. The steward had come and gone and come and gone again.

'Cheers . . .' They'd drunk Scotch on their first meeting.

'Good to see a medical man drinking whiskey.' Ross joked weakly, 'Means it must be OK.'

Ramsey dutifully smiled.

'Purely medicinal. How did you know where to get hold of me?'

Ross couldn't have been that good at waiting until he saw the whites of their eyes. He stared studiously at the gargantuan set of fire-irons. 'When we met. You mentioned the hotel. As you were leaving.'

'Oh yes.'

'It somehow stuck. I . . . it's good of you to come in like this. It's about the private prosecution.'

'Yes?'

'I'm afraid it's looking like a no-go area.'

'But – have you talked to a solicitor?'

'Oh yes. That's the point. My people – known them for donkey's years – they reckon I don't have a prayer.'

'But surely you'll press on. At least until the magistrates have pronounced.'

For the first time since they'd started talking in earnest Ross allowed his eyes to meet Ramsey's. The contact did not last long.

'They advise not,' he said. 'No point.'

'You were so . . . adamant.'

'Then. Cold light of day now. Have to acknowledge a lost cause when you see one. Bloody expensive otherwise.'

'It was "take the bastard down with me . . . die trying . . . worth

110

every last penny" – wasn't it you who said all that?'

As if compelled by hearing his own words brought up in evidence against him Ross again raised his eyes to meet Ramsey's stare. Again they slithered evasively away. 'Er, think it was the alcohol talking.'

The good soldier, the follower of Kipling, shifted in his chair.

'I met Wood,' Ramsey said by way of counter.

'Oh . . . and?'

'Guilty as hell.'

'Beyond any reasonable doubt?'

'Beyond any. When I twisted his arm he –'

'Oh?'

'Metaphorically. He didn't deny supplying Kate. He admitted to pushing coke to a regular dozen to twenty punters . . . But you're happy to let him off the hook.'

'Not happy! I . . . the thing is . . .'

'I may have to shop him myself.' Well, there was a goodish chance this was one place Brook hadn't got bugged. Unless Ross was wired and Brook was behind it. Jabbing at Ross was worth a try, and seemed to be working. The gaze that met Ramsey's now was haunted, even desperate, but it was steady and, you could have said, frank.

'It's not as straightforward as all that,' Ross said. He swallowed.

'When I said "bloody expensive" I didn't really mean money, although, God knows, to get justice these days . . .' His voice trailed away. He was still making up his mind.

'Why don't you just tell me what's happened?' Ramsey said quietly. Ross drank. He nodded. 'Couple of visitors came down to the house. At night. Told me to drop it. As of now.'

Ahh. 'Who were they?'

'I didn't exactly catch the names.'

'Police?'

'That neck of the woods. Told me I was in danger of compromising their enquiries. They said they were about to draw in the net and I could ruin it for them. Months of leg-work, surveillance, what have you, all gone for a burton.'

Brook's argument. He had even used the same image. Of course 'the net closing in' was the absolute cliché. Ramsey looked hard at Ross. 'And you believe you believe this, do you?' he said.

'Yes. Why not.' But the pupils of Ramsey's eyes had somehow flinched.

'How did they threaten you?' Ramsey said.

'Er . . . leave it there, eh, Ramsey. There's a good fellow.'

'Ross. I'm not a good fellow. They probably wouldn't let me in here even if I wanted to join. But I do have a good memory. I never mentioned my hotel to you. I never intended to . . . Ross, don't degrade yourself.'

Ross's cheek muscles tightened. He flushed. 'Ramsey . . . I've lost one child,' he said. 'Nothing will bring her back. My wife's under sedation. Part of her, perhaps the most central part, is dead for ever too. My boy . . .'

His voice broke. Ramsey waited without prompting.

'My son's at Balliol. Got there on his own merits. Worked like a Trojan. He's down for the Civil Service exam next year . . .'

'And?'

Ross's eyes were now a combination of disbelief and fright. His initial spryness had quite leaked away. 'They said . . . they made it clear, Ramsey, that if I didn't back off his papers wouldn't even get marked.'

Ramsey's own eyes must have displayed a matching incredulity.

'That's what they said,' Ross said. 'Almost in so many words. I'm out of things now. I don't have friends in high places to fight back with.'

'No,' Ramsey said. 'I can see how that might be necessary.'

He paused. 'They also, of course,' he said, 'told you to warn me off.'

Ross nodded. He winced. 'You were quite right,' he said, 'it is degrading.'

Ramsey smiled.

'No, not finally,' he said. 'The right message was delivered.'

The remnants of another day were flowing past the window. Ramsey lay on the hard, narrow bed and once more set his mind to thinking. Such a crummy hotel. If he'd obtained an overseas membership of a club he wouldn't be pigging it like this. Hmph! He grunted out loud. But that wasn't his style. He wasn't clubbable. And besides . . . *revenons à nos moutons* . . .

It was odd, that repetition. The police drag-net lovingly prepared, the professional fingers poised to draw it tight on the big fish. Hmmn. Fishy was what it seemed . . . Brook had seemed nothing but convincing, and genuine. He had had him going. Ramsey would shrug himself back into life in Barfleur as if he were once more putting on his age-old and indestructible overcoat. The easy comfortable rut. Total comfort – Dany once assuaged. *Mon Dieu* – that would take some doing. Underneath all her mischievous surface huffing and puffing there was a layer sensitive to slight – real, imaginary or unavoidable. But it could be done. Life would go back to the comfortable lagging around the bruise on his heart that would never fade.

112

Only – he didn't like being taken for an idiot. He didn't like being conned – in the English sense. Who was to say there *was* a police undercover operation set to swoop? Brook, yes. But Brook by his own account didn't like amateurs. He would want him out of the way. And if *he* were bent . . . Low profiling was one thing: low profiling while lethal wraps were being passed about like chewing gum was of a different order. And Ross's night visitors. Who were they? Friendly but worried police? Hardly. With their less than civil threats they sounded far more like friends of Beryl the bye-election peril. In view of what Tessa had told him, Beryl would want the lid kept on tighter than ever . . . But was it egotistical? Was he the one now spoiling for a fight for no better reason than, as he'd admitted, part of him was beginning to find this cloak and dagger conundrum more edgily interesting than that comfortable overcoat of the life he'd wrapped himself in these past years? He lay and thought. It lacked style to be visibly pushed around – style and class. And he did have that address . . . It was like *vingt-et-un*. You always wanted to stay for one more round before you walked away. Perhaps if Wood had no better news in the morning he'd stay at the table for one final don't-tell-me-when-to-quit go-around of the cards.

ELEVEN

Aubrey's Samba was having its top replaced so he asked for – in fact, positively demanded – the Porsche.

'It may be a beautiful blue but it's no use at all if it hasn't a hood,' he had said. 'In any case your waistline will appreciate a walk through the park on a nice sunny morning.'

Bitch! Well, if he was contemplating a divorce . . . but, no, when he thought about it, he couldn't bear the thought of being solo again, and when he wasn't trying to be witty Aubrey was really a wonderful person. A friend.

And perhaps a walk would make him feel better, calm his nerves. He would walk slowly and then perhaps the constant fluttering in his stomach, and the itching of the soles of his feet would go away. The great thing was to live from day to day, to carry on as normal. On the legit side. Little by little as the crisis subsided so would his crisis of nerves.

He entered the park to the east of the zoo and walked due south. Secretaries and other types were walking to their dreary jobs. People with one foot in the grave were walking dogs. He began to revive. Aubrey had been cruel to be kind. It was a bright morning and at least he had banished the unspeakably hum-drum from his life; sailing close to the wind did give you the sort of adrenalin rush that people like this could never know. He frowned. He had always prided himself as passing for straight unless he chose otherwise. The sight of this suave, smiling troller bearing down to accost him indicated his worries were making him careless.

'Simon! How are you?'

Simon Wood stood rooted to the spot, literally slack-jawed.

'Such a beautiful morning. We could be in Oklahoma, eh? Why don't we sit on this bench a little while and have some breakfast? Yes?'

The brown paper bag the man held out was in strange contrast to his immaculate, faintly-striped, double-breasted suit. But Wood was oblivious. Without resistance or protest he followed the man to a sun-dappled vacant bench. He had never before set eyes on this casual user of his name. But he had heard his voice before. The grammar and syntax were almost perfect; but the accent rivalled Aznavour's in its cadences. Its charm could eviscerate well-being from the brightest day.

114

The man had produced paper napkins. With a grave smile he offered Wood one.

'You will join me, I hope.'

Wood shook his head.

'You are quite sure? Avocado and bacon. Fresh. Knock your taste buds over.'

'I said "no thank you"!'

The man sighed. Fastidiously he spread a napkin over his knees. Using both hands he carried a bulging sandwich to his mouth. Holding it like a harmonica he took a bite from its corner. It all took a long time. Wood's stomach began churning again. It began to turn. He was suddenly bathed in that flood of perspiration that anticipates vomiting.

'You phoned and said you were worried,' the man said.

'Wouldn't you be! People dying!'

'But people die all the time.'

'Not from snort they got from me that I got from you!'

'Hoo! Easy!' The man patted his stomach. 'Such accusations are not good for the digestion.'

'I've been finding that out!'

'It is true there was a minor cock-up in the kitchen, but –'

'Minor cock-up!'

'It has been put right.'

'Three or four bodies later. I could go down for manslaughter!'

The man looked at him quizzically. 'Don't be such a hysteric,' he said.

'A man walks in off the street and knows all about it and you . . .'

'*All*? He knows *all* about it?'

'More than enough. He –'

'Well he is why I am here. Tell me about him.'

'He said he was a doctor. I think that was true. He talked the language. He said he was a friend of Exton Waite the MP. He –'

'He said that?'

'Yes. Also Catherine Ross.'

'Another of yours?'

'Yes. Another dead one.'

'Police?'

'No. I don't think so . . . I don't know, do I!'

'And what did he look like?'

'About forty. Tall . . . dark . . .'

The man leaned across and squeezed Wood's thigh.

'And no doubt handsome,' he said. His grin was boyish but the gleam in his eye malevolent. He was handsome too. His parted hair was neatly trim above a relaxed, even face with a positive, straight nose and an amused-looking mouth. The bright eyes and clear complexion suggested a conscience to match. Wood pretended he could afford to ignore the gesture.

'He was, actually,' he said. 'In a – highwayman sort of way.'

The man smiled broadly and cocked his head. 'Highwayman, eh?' he said genially. A Claude Duval. 'Sounds *most* attractive.' When he straightened his head he was no longer smiling.

'What did you tell him?' he said.

'Nothing!'

'Nothing? Oh, Simon. . . ?'

'I told him about Howard Michaels. How he, er, recruited me. Because, you see, I knew that was a dead end.'

'Did you now? Well, that was very clever of you, Simon . . . What else did you tell him?'

'I told him about the delivery system.'

'Oh?'

'That way I could pretend to be so far downstream he couldn't expect me to know anything else. And that's the truth, really; you know as well as I do.'

'You didn't tell him about our little telephone number?'

'Of course not.'

'Good.' The man took another bite from his sandwich. He ruminated. Simon Wood found he was clenching his hands into such tight fists his palms were hurting. He forced himself to relax. But he had to say it now. 'I want out,' he said.

The man stopped chewing and turned to look at him. It was a baleful look.

'That's not your decision,' he said at last. 'You are out when they say you are out. Not one second before.'

He had regained his smile. 'Why exactly do you think Howard Michaels *is* a dead end?' he said.

'I . . .' Here came his fit again.

'Yes. He wanted to retire too. Well, in a way he got his wish.'

Wood hadn't believed his blood could run yet colder. 'It isn't me I'm thinking about,' he lied. 'Not only. It's the whole operation. If I've been rumbled, if I get pulled in . . . it's better I stop having contact of any sort . . . For a while anyway.'

The man's face was neutral for almost the first time in their encounter. At last he nodded. 'That does make sense,' he said at last. 'We close you down now, open you up some time later. Yes. I can sell them on that.'

Now the grin.

'It will be safer,' he said. 'Now. This doctor – does he have a name?'

116

'He used the name "Ramsey". It could be his own.'

'Ramsey. Right. Do you have any reason to think he will visit you again?'

'No – but he's due to telephone!'

'Yes?'

'He knows there is a list of buyers who might be using the . . . cocked-up batch. I've been warning them off. There's one I haven't got to yet. He called yesterday and he said he'd call again this morning to confirm she had been warned too.'

'He is telephoning you this morning?'

'I just told you. Yes.'

'Well, now, that is useful.'

The man's smile had never been warmer.

The girl still unaccounted for, and so still at risk, was called Jody Price. Tuning out the stony-faced look from the driver of the Cavalier he had beaten to the one visible parking gap, Ramsey cut the Panda's engine and looked across at the block of flats. He had misgivings. He shouldn't be here. He was still indulging himself. This was police work, or down to Wood. But the eagerness with which the socialite osteopath had coughed up the address over the phone had been silently eloquent. It suggested that obtaining no reply from a constantly rung and ringing phone, Wood would never summon the nerve to visit the scene of his crime. He practised on living bodies. Breaking down a door to walk in on the body lying stiff and misty-eyed in the unnaturally noiseless room wasn't his style in house calls. Whereas he, Ramsey, of course, did it all the time. As he crossed the street towards the Victorian block of flats Ramsey promised himself that if he did find a second corpse within the next few minutes he would seriously consider rounding out his collection with Wood's.

Another sign of the times and place. Another squawk box. 'Price' lived on the ground floor. He held his breath and pressed the button. The response was almost instant.

'Be right with you,' the distorted voice crackled and the street door lock clicked open. He pushed the door wide. He was sweating. He realised that he needed to breath deeply. To the left was a staircase leading up. He hardly saw it. Back beyond and almost under it was an open door. A girl was struggling to get herself and two large expensive-looking suitcases out into the corridor. Jody Price was alive and well. Wood had got to her and she was now doing some kind of a runner. You couldn't expect a Wood to say that she was gorgeous but he might have mentioned she was black.

He moved quickly forward and reached for the leading suitcase.

She surrendered it readily enough.

'Thanks. Overdone it again.'

'Jody Price?'

She shook her head. Dumbfounded he looked at her.

'Hall's Cars?'

Now he shook his head. He let the case down on to the ground just as she reached forward to take it back.

'Jody does live here, doesn't she?'

'Who wants to know?'

She had a London accent, the Cockney by no means eradicated by upwardly mobile ambitions. Built like an Olympic high-jumper she seemed well capable of holding him off for a few rounds.

'My name's Ramsey,' he said. 'Dr Ramsey.'

'Oh yeah?'

Neither impressed nor convinced. She'd been brought up very street-wise.

'She's a model, right?' he said.

'Yeah. So am I. And this model is off to Frankfurt right now.'

'Do you know the name "Simon Wood"?'

'Maybe.'

So she did. Voice and face were utterly deadpan, but she'd used the wrong word.

'Simon –' He stopped. Light was blocked off from behind. He turned his arm half-raised to ward off a blow. Needlessly. The man silhouetted in the doorway was the stony-faced Cavalier driver.

'Hall's Cars,' the man said. 'Miss Price?'

'Right.' She turned back to Ramsey. 'I'll be back tomorrow night.' She reached down for her case.

Ramsey clamped his hand over hers. 'This can't wait!' he said as urgently as he knew how. He was very conscious of the driver.

'Hey, man, you're hustling me,' she said. It was a return to Railton Road. The driver was on top of them.

'You want a hand with those bags, Miss?' the driver said. He said it looking at Ramsey. A decent chap. With rather wide shoulders.

'The last . . . treatment Jody obtained from Mr Wood,' Ramsey said. 'It's poisonous. The pharmacist made a mistake. If she takes it she'll wake up dead.'

The girl's eyes opened wide in her all cheek-boned face. She thought.

'We'll be right there,' she said to the driver. 'We can manage the cases outside.'

He shuffled, backed away.

'Prove you're a doctor,' the girl said.

He reached out his wallet and showed her his *carte de séjour* and driver's licence.

'They're in French,' she said doubtfully.

'I live in France. Work there. My photo's on the licence.'

'You're part of the chain, aren't you . . .'

'No! I'm a doctor! I've found –'

'So who was Papanicolou?'

Daylight. A chink of it, at least. 'Papanicolou,' he said, 'was the Greek gynaecologist who developed the pap smear test – for detecting early carcinoma of the cervix . . . And how do *you* know?'

'I was a nurse for three years. Until they turned down a pay-claim. Best thing that ever happened to me.'

Her eyes were as shrewd as they were beautiful. 'You look like a doctor I was crazy about,' she said with a sudden grin.

'So I'll believe you. Jody shares with me but she's not here. She and her fella have gone off on holiday.'

'No!'

'Yes. Listen, how bad is –'

'Totally bad. Where've they gone? Abroad?'

'No. "Up-country." They're off shooting somewhere. Not movie shooting but shooting shooting.'

'But where?'

'Hold it down. She left the address on the TV. You take the bags out to the car and I'll go get it for you. Deal?'

'Deal.'

She smiled, turned to go inside, turned again. 'Her boy friend's name is Morgan,' she said.

'Morgan what?'

'Kifflyn Morgan. Morgan's his second name.'

'Kifflyn?'

'Kifflyn. But he's rich, so it's all right.' She grinned again. 'Are you married?' she asked.

'Yes,' Ramsey said. 'Ever so.' He bent to pick up the cases.

'Shit,' she said. She went away inside. Stifling what promised to be too pleasant a fantasy at birth, Ramsey hefted the cases outside. She must be modelling armour plating, he decided. The driver had double-parked in the end.

'Sorted it out with her, then, mate?' he asked as he opened the boot.

'Oh, let her go,' Ramsey said. 'Better off without her.'

Neither appreciated they were being watched.

It is hard to put a Panda into a four-wheel drift but, finally finding the entrance to Kingsmead, he damn nearly did. Tyres screeched. Gravel flew. He had to fight the steering, will himself not to brake for a moment, before he had it back on line. That sobered him. If he'd

119

rolled it, or a milk-float had been paddling down the other way, all his endeavours would have been for nothing. Jesus! Road-works, contra-flow systems, three lanes arbitrarily funnelling into two – he'd never grit his teeth at a *péage* again. The English motorways had to be the best argument for going for a turn-pike system. In France he'd have done in an hour what had taken two. And when off the bloody thing at last just try finding the house!

'Ar . . . Kingsmead . . . now that does ring a bell . . . now let me see . . .' He'd had to stop seven times before, at last, a postman had told him like a shot. Thank God. He'd had no chance of ringing a bell himself at Kingsmead. The address Jody Price had left gave neither telephone number nor host's name.

It wasn't over yet. The driveway looked as if it extended into Wiltshire; what had to be a big house still looked quite small. Wait a minute. By the horse chestnuts a gardener, of sorts. Ramsey halted in line with him.

'Excuse me.' He called out.

The gardener stopped forking soil. There was little of the natural rural grace of Merrie England about him. He was about nineteen. He wore jeans, a studded leather jacket and acne. He seemed unable to speak. He clearly spent his Saturday afternoons seeking to do to away supporters at Reading what he was now doing to his fork. Ramsey got out of the car.

'Excuse me,' he repeated, 'I'm looking for the shooting party.'

The boy glowered, pointed with his fork.

'Found it, ain't you,' he said. 'I have to rake that gravel.'

Ramsey turned his head. A gaggle of some eight or ten guns – back for lunch, presumably – were turning into the driveway at a slower speed than his. As they came nearer Ramsey saw pristine Barbours, jackets that cost more than most suits, flat caps that were nothing like workers'. He also saw that there was no woman among this well-heeled skein. He saw them begin to eye him. They managed to give the impression that drivers of Pandas were legitimate targets whether sitting or not. As they drew almost level one of the leading trio called across to Ramsey.

'Yes? May I help you?'

Ramsey could guess why there had been no name along with the address. Jody Price couldn't spell in Arabic. But the question had been posed with reasonable enough politeness and he tried to reply in kind.

'I hope so. I have a rather urgent message for Miss Jody Price – or else for Mr Morgan.'

Satisfied, the man in the party who looked favourite for owning such an estate smiled and gestured. 'Mr Morgan is the gentleman bringing up our rear.'

'Thank you very much.'

'You're welcome.'

The group as a whole picked up speed and clumped scrunching on. Morgan, who had clearly heard question and answer, came across towards him. The man was still three yards away when Ramsey first smelt the liquor on him. He regretted the next two paces proportionally.

'Who the hell are you?' Morgan said. It was distinctly loud but, for all that, a touch indistinct.

'My name won't mean much,' Ramsey began. 'But –'

'I imagine not!' Morgan compounded his rudeness by fetching a hip flask out of one of his seventeen or so pockets. As he threw his head back Ramsey resisted the temptation to direct the container in pursuit of its former contents. He needed the shit as yet.

Morgan wore a gilet he'd most likely bought at Harrods over a taupe designer hunting shirt in brushed moleskin. His trousers were by Armani *via* Viet Nam. He was stocky, broad. He had a large, crudely handsome head framed by thick black hair which he wore not quite to shoulder length. Looking at him you were supposed to think this was an international soccer star who occasionally won Formula One Grand Prix events. What you actually thought was that the sexual revolution had not entirely dealt a death blow to the ancient art of wanking. It was fitting, Ramsey thought, that while a broken shot-gun over Morgan's left shoulder must have cost several thousand, the absence of any game in the right hand minimised problems in the use of the hip-flask. Morgan wiped his mouth.

'How'd you know my name?' he deigned to say.

'I'm looking for Jody. Where is she?'

'What the hell is that to you?'

Ramsey put on his sweet smile. 'Listen arse-face,' he said, 'it's about the coke. And if you don't stop pretending you're the lord of this manor I'll take that gun, shove it up your anus and discharge both barrels one at a time.'

He took a step forward and Morgan took a step back. His mouth worked for a moment. 'Are you a narc?' he said eventually.

'No. Where's Jody?'

'Back in London.'

'In London!'

'I think. Probably. She left this morning, since you seem to care so much. In a high dudgeon. Or was it a pit of fique?'

'How long ago?'

'Right after breakfast. Right after the night before. A lover's quarrel. Something to do with how many times. That's why I'm stinking at this moment.'

'Where'd she go exactly?'

Morgan swayed and shrugged. 'I don't know. Home, I guess.'

'She wasn't there mid-morning.'

'So she wasn't there.'

'Did she take the coke with her?'

'Who said anything about coke now – other than you?'

'Come on.'

Morgan smiled. Ramsey had the sense he was trying to sober up fast.

'You come on, amigo,' Morgan said.

'OK. Listen. Listen good. I'm a friend of Simon Wood. The last coke he sold her. It's duff. It's poison. It's lethal. It's already killed other users.'

Morgan's eyes narrowed. If he swayed again it was mainly from shock. 'Jesus,' he said.

'Does she have it with her?' Morgan shook his head.

'No,' he said, 'She bought it for me. It's at my place. I got it for an office party. My round. Christ, I nearly broke into it to give myself a little treat.'

Revenge was not an attitude close to the surface in Ramsey. He was pleased to discover he had depths. 'Do you usually serve cocaine?'

'Clients expect it.' Morgan was almost indignant.

'Just what line of work are you in?'

'Advertising.' Now Morgan was full of himself. 'You don't read about it in *Campaign* but a little Happy Dust and some of the biggest accounts in London have changed agencies.'

'That speaks volumes for your executive abilities.'

'Now look –'

'Destroy it!'

Morgan looked askance.

'There's . . . a lot of it,' he said.

'Therefore a lot of potential victims. Flush it and fast!'

'Yes . . . but who pays? Who's that down to?'

'Put in a claim with the Legal and General.'

'It's a lot of bread. How do I know I should believe you?'

'Simon says get rid of it. Call him and get it from the horse's arse. How old are you?'

'Thirty-three if you have to know.'

'That's a lot of your life I've just saved.'

Morgan blinked. Ramsey turned to go. Then the phase two scenario hit him. He whirled around. 'Where it is – is it safe?'

'Absolutely. It's stashed.'

'Does Jody know where?'

'Yes . . .'

'She have a key to your place?'

'Yes. We have an adult relationship so there's no reason . . .'

'Right now there's every reason.'

Morgan's bloodshot eyes opened very wide. 'She was going home,' he said. 'She wouldn't.'

'You *think* she was going home. She left here cursing your guts. She could well be in a "don't get sore get even" mood. Or get high. Do I need to draw you a storyboard?'

'What do I do?'

'Get on the blower fast. If there's no answer, her place or yours, get into your car and go down the motorway praying it's only because she's out getting laid.' Ramsey looked at Morgan and grimaced with distaste. 'I don't like soiling the car,' he said, 'but I'll run you up to the house.'

It was on the drive due east back to London that something clicked in Ramsey's mind and the balance shifted. It came to him that the pussy-footing, the politicking, the killing, had to stop. No one would like it much – not Beryl Waite for her obvious reasons, not Brook for his arcane, or Tessa and Isabel for their personal ones. But enough was enough. It was time for him to blow the whistle.

He grinned sourly to himself acknowledging the irony. He had been more guilty of pussy-footing than anyone. Whatever men there might be running around wrapped in unofficial D-notices he had no vested interest in hushing things up. Terrible things had happened. Exton had been spread-eagled in agony across a desk. Catherine Ross's mother would spend the rest of her earthly days catching her breath from the pain at the hollowed-out centre of her being. Wood was walking around free. But it was none of these enormities that had really tipped the scales. Rather it was Kifflyn Morgan's supercilious assumption that sniffing yourself to conquest business and an early grave was strictly routine, and his moral outrage anyone should object. Goddammit, it was almost this miserable apology for an auto-route and the way the English used it that had somehow made up his mind. Who said the French were the *assassins* of the road? Look at that prick in an XR4i . . . It was damn nearly England their England that had tipped the balance but the die was cast now. *Vive la balance*! He would inform on the whole pack of them. Sort of. If he informed to Lord Tom, Sir Dick or Chief Constable Harry there was no guarantee the whole issue wouldn't be sat on and himself in the dock on a trumped-up back-street abortion charge. He needed a witness. And the best witness was Simon Wood, backed up by Isabel. Simon Wood he'd have to take in under – what was it in England? oh

123

yes – the Common Law Power of Arrest. With luck the streak of slime might try to resist and he could have the pleasure of kicking his sodomite balls out through his ears.

Christ! Look at that! In front with signal lack of attention an artic had side-stepped into the centre lane so as to overtake a removal van. The Panda had almost as much acceleration in top revs as a wheelchair but with nothing in the fast lane for a freak moment he moved on over. Then there was something in the fast lane. In a blaze of lights, a blare of horn something was spreading itself sideways across his rear-view mirror. It had been a dot that came from nowhere at well over a hundred miles an hour. It was now sitting six feet from his tail as, fighting the strange wind-buffets, he tried to get the Fiat to crawl out in front of the artic. It would take several hours. To pass the time while passing he gave the driver behind the finger. That achieved eye-contact and he found himself glaring at a Kifflyn Morgan with one hand on the wheel and another on the phone.

At last he was a length clear of the lorry, two lengths. The lorry began to drift back into the slow lane. He took its place in the central. Morgan's Audi Quattro hammered by to become another dot receding to invisibility at illegal speed. He watched it go with mixed feelings. The man was at least trying, if he didn't total the Audi. But he was still asking to be pulled over with every flying mile. That would be it. The level of alcohol in his blood stream could mean that a lot more would be lost than just his licence . . .

Ramsey kept the Fiat at a respectablish eighty, about all it would do on the flat. Maniac after maniac continued to pile past him far too close to the lunatic in front. As he started to think about Tessa it was a source of some slight pleasure to realise that one of the few other sane drivers about was in a classic old Citroën Pallas 21. It had hoved into silhouetted view on top of a rise a way back and had since made no effort to melt its Michelins away. It was nice to think that there were still a few people left in the world proving that good taste and commonsense went together.

Slewing the Audi in a right-hander that had oncoming traffic braking, Kifflyn Morgan gunned on along Elgin Avenue. Left and – Great! A hole. Oh, shit! He'd graunched his near-side alloy. But what the hell. It was a company car. An hour and ten minutes door to door. Pretty damn good going even if he said it himself. He strong-armed the Battenkill duffle out of the back and decided that he felt OK. Screw shooting. He was a city rat. It was all a wild goose chase this taking care of Jody, but not to worry. It was good to be back. He'd put in some time on the BAT pitch.

He let himself into the hall of his 1840s tea-caddy house.

'Jody?' he called. No reply. No sign of her. She'd not been within a hundred miles. Putting the bag down he walked into the living room and there, sitting in his wing armchair was a complete stranger. A round-faced lout in a tradesman's suit. Morgan glared at him and doubled his fists.

'Who the hell are you!' he said.

The man, unmoved, had the cheek to eye him slowly toe to head.

'Guv,' he said, as their eyes met. For a second Morgan thought he was being addressed but the sound of a foot-fall from the kitchen made him turn his head. An older man with a face whose broken veins explained the stains on his suit walked into the room. He too looked at Morgan.

'Kifflyn Morgan?' he said.

'What's it to you?'

'This is what it's to me.'

From behind his back the crumple-suited man brought into view the opened packet of "Special K". He extracted the polythene wrapped contents from the box. The joke had gone sour. Not cornflakes. Two ounces of coke.

'Answer the question,' the second man said without a trace of emphasis in his voice.

'Yes. I'm Kifflyn Morgan.'

'This your gaff?'

Gaff! For heaven's sake!

'Yes.'

'Your name on the lease?'

'Deeds if you don't mind!' Let's turn this into a two-way confrontation, eh?

'No, I don't mind. Detective Inspector Brook. Drugs Squad.'

'Here.' The other policeman produced an ID card. Morgan made a point of reading it slowly. No flashing it in and out and in for him. He felt his mouth going dry and realised his head was a lot less clear than he'd have liked. But the great thing was not to panic. That bastard in the driveway had set him up and it was going to cost him a packet-plus to come out on the other side. The agency circuit crowd would bust an expense account gut over it all but actually, in the end, it would work for him. Like Frank's little contretemps and Peter's he'd actually gain status from the affair, respect. The thing was to keep these peasants of policemen in their place. They were plainclothes but they had the uniform of their authority. They thought they'd give him the heavy talk. But Jules hadn't forked out on the odd hot dinner at the Boulestin for nothing – not when Sir David was troughing it at the next table.

'Satisfied?' The policeman in the chair pocketed the ID.

'Now show me your warrant,' Morgan said firmly.

'Don't have one.' Brook replied with a faint shrug.

'How interesting. And who asked you in?'

'The person you were calling out to when you walked in. Miss Price.' It started to dawn on Morgan he might not have been set up. That . . . 'Where is she?' he asked.

They both looked at him as if he wasn't there. But where was she? 'I said "where is she"?' he said.

'He must've missed the ambulance, guv,' the younger one said.

A scalpel lanced through him. 'Ambulance!'

'Taking her away,' Brook said.

'He must've missed it.'

'She managed a call out first,' Brook said.

Oh God. Oh God, God, God. Please, a dream. All a dream, please. Let me wake up and I'll never touch the stuff again. Ever. I swear.

'Looked an attractive girl.'

His knees turned to water. It wasn't a dream. He moved to the matching chair and slumped down. 'She's a model,' he heard himself say. Why did he say that?

'Was she?' Brook said just as flatly as before.

Oh God!

'Where do you score?' Brook said.

Morgan looked up. He had heard the question clearly even though it came from miles away. At such a remote distance he could think of no reason for not answering it. 'She bought it,' he said. Then realised what he'd said. Brook jiggled the polythene bag.

'There must be . . . fifteen hundred quid's worth here.'

'My money. It was for a party.'

The seated one laughed. 'He must be a rock star. Looks like one.'

'That right?' Brook said. 'Are you rich and famous and we haven't recognised you?'

'I'm in advertising, sod you!'

'Ah. No wonder my Telecom shares are looking so sorry for themselves. People like you doing the PR.'

'I don't have anything –'

'Cocaine – need I remind you – is a Class "A" drug as defined in Schedule Two of the Misuse of Drugs Act.'

Kifflyn Morgan raised his head a second time. 'Am I under arrest?' he said.

'Well under, sonny.'

Morgan swallowed. He tried to fight his way back to some kind of surface where oxygen wasn't in such short supply. Come on, he told himself, you pulled in Consolidated on the strength of one sustained spit-balling bull-shit. Think how you felt going into that.

'I want to call a solicitor,' he said.

'Be our guest.' Brook handed him the cordless room-to-room. Morgan punched in the digits.

'Oh – calls him a lot, guv. Must have form.'

'He's a personal friend, damn you!' Morgan said. '. . . Ah, is Jules there, please? . . . Kifflyn Morgan here.'

'Paddington nick,' Brook said.

'Sorry?'

'That's where you'll be charged.'

Oh God. No, not a dream. Why was Jules so – 'Oh, Jules? Kifflyn . . . Er, no. Listen, bad news. I've been busted . . . Yeh . . . Drugs. Can you meet me at Paddington Police Station? . . . OK. Soon as you can, sport. Thanks.'

He killed the hand-set. A faint surge of hope warmed his guts. 'He'll be about half an hour,' he said.

Brook had been looking at his best-books bookcase. 'Heller,' he said. 'Nobody better. Go to university?'

'Yes.'

'Copy-writer?'

'Account exec.' In spite of everything Morgan's voice had swelled in tone.

'Ah. Important job.'

'Pretty important, yes.'

'Earn more than the Prime Minister?'

'Funny sort of question if I . . .'

'Do you?' Brook insisted.

'Yes, as it happens. I don't say I'm worth it but it's the going rate.'

'And the name of the game. Do you know that Indian restaurant across from the Polytechnic?'

'Yes.'

'If I told you they do a great Chicken Biriani but the kitchen's like a Bombay sewer and the owner and his wife are being treated for pox – would you eat there?'

'No . . . no, I wouldn't but –'

'So why,' Brook suddenly shouted, 'do you shove any old shit up your nose or into your arm?' A passion had at last gripped him even if it was only bred of disgust. 'People have been pissing in it,' he went on, 'shovelling in laxative, builder's rubble, borax, quinine . . . rat poison. Why should *they* care? You're the sucker and they wouldn't piss on you if you were on fire. People croak, starve to death, have their brains beaten in . . . they don't give a monkey's. All they worry about is the money. Their money.'

The point seemed so unanswerable that, lest he seem a fool,

Morgan felt he should answer. 'My solicitor has rather a lot of form too,' he said tartly.

'Perry Mason time, guv.'

'First offence, sonny?'

'Don't call me sonny! Yes.'

'Well your brief will well know that first offenders in possession usually only pull a fine and a warning. Criminal record, yes, but a warning . . . But, oh dear, this is a "Class A" drug and there's too much for one person.'

'But I explained! I –'

'Big mouth, guv.'

'And maybe the court'll believe you . . . The top whack for trafficking is fourteen years.'

'Fourteen years!' Terror descended on Morgan ten-times multiplied.

'Of course, if as I say, you've got a good brief . . . mind you, given the state of your ex-model friend . . .'

'He's so sick on his own account, guv, he's forgotten all about her and her chances.'

'But . . . you told me . . . the ambulance had taken her off because . . . Jesus Christ, you sons of bitches, is she still alive?'

Brook looked at him steadily. 'You're the son of a bitch, sonny,' he said, 'and you know it. She left here in a deep coma. They were headed for intensive care, life support and all those fun and games. Ladbrokes have it six to four against they'll be able to save her but Joe Coral are quoting ten to one on that if she does open her baby blues again she'll have deep, permanent, irreversible brain damage. She'll be a vegetable. Get the picture, son of a bitch? It'll be exhibit A at your trial. I wouldn't bet on walking away with a warning if I were you. I wouldn't even count on bail.'

Inconsequentially, Morgan remembered he had a lunch date next Thursday with Conrad at Langan's. Not on now . . . not at all on. And possibly being head-hunted on to the board of what would then have become ICHP and M was now the least of his worries. Oh God. He felt sick. Physically sick. Sitting between the two detectives Kifflyn Morgan began to cry.

The thing was to phone. He owed that to Isabel. But from where? Chances were her phone might be bugged. Chances were his room was. A phone box and a call back was the answer. Somewhere around Talgarth Road where the motorway system degenerated into bumper-to-bumper crawl he found an old style booth. Opening the heavy door was to be engulfed in the heavy stink of urine. A scrawl across the actual box informed the world that CFC RULE. A dangling cord suggested they probably did so by hitting people over the head with stolen telephone receivers. Rule Britannia. In his day there had been heavy penalties for receiving. He stepped back out into the lead-fumed air. Cracking wise wasn't solving his problem. Wait. He was only two minutes from his hotel and they wouldn't have bugged the lobby . . .

He'd only be ten minutes. He parked out front. The Escort had apparently given up its stationary watch. There was no sign of it. When he pushed in through the front door the Michelin man porter-receptionist almost allowed a look of surprise to waddle across his greasy chops.

'They've gone,' Ramsey explained.

'They're like Allegros,' the receptionist grunted. 'They never go.'

Ramsey went to the pay-phone in the corner of the lobby. He primed it and dialled Isabel's number. Better to be eavesdropped by a villain than by a Whitehall errand boy.

'Granville Antiques.'

'Izzie? Ramsey.'

'Ramsey! Where are you, we –'

'Izzie – anyone in the shop?'

'No.'

'Close up for the minute. Go to the phone box on the corner. If it's working call me back here.' He gave the number. 'Got it?'

'Yes. Ramsey – are you in trouble? Danger?'

'No. Just staying out of it.'

'Right. I see. Call you back soon as I can.'

He hung up. The receptionist was staring at him with bland, unabashed curiosity. 'Warm for the time of year,' Ramsey said.

'For some, it seems.'

Ramsey went to the window. Ten minutes is a long time to wait when you're waiting. Outside cars went by, people walked along. None of them so much as glanced at the hotel. No silenced Walther .32 suddenly spat fire. No bullet creased his think tank. Unexpectedly, after the long anticipation, the phone rang.

'Ramsey?'

'Yes.'

'Sorry to have been so long. No tens. What's it all about?'

'Just in case there were gremlins on the other line, Izzie.'

'I gathered that much. What don't you want them to hear?'

'Izzie, that SW3 character.'

'Yes. With you.'

'He's guilty as all get out. In it up to his plucked eyebrows. He supplied Mr X.' There was a long, thought-filled silence.

'Did he . . . what have you done to him?'

'Nothing. I'm going to. He's not the king-pin, nothing like, but he can't be left . . . practising. Izzie, I'm going to turn him in. Maybe he'll lead *les flics* higher up the trail.'

'What about . . . our late friend. Won't his name come out if there's an investigation? A trial?'

'I think so. That's why I rang, Izzie. I want your permission.' Again the silence.

'Ramsey – you know that cartoon in the shop?'

'The Wilkes one. Yes.'

'A man came in yesterday and started looking at it. He started comparing politicians then and now. He brought up Ex . . . our friend's name. Said he bet there was a story there. But never speak ill of the dead. These things are always best left to lie . . . Then he offered me three times the asking price of the cartoon. Said I'd undervalued it.'

'Well, well, well. You take his money!'

'Yes, sod him!'

'Izzie, that's the other reason I called. South West 3 admitted his game to me. But he can deny it. Beryl and Company may see it's all hushed up. They may play tricks on me. I need you to stand up and say you knew our friend had a nose for this sort of thing.'

'Yes. I realise. In that case how I came to know will probably come out too. Page One in *The Sun*. I'll stop being me and become "his mistress".'

'Yes. Will you do it Izzie?'

'. . . Yes.'

At last he could relax his grip on the phone.

'You're really rather –'

Beep! Beep! Beep! Beep!

Oh shit. He heard amplified clunking at the far end of the line and the hotel's entrance door swing on its hinges. He swung round quickly. Someone, a man, had just gone out.

'Hello? Ramsey?'

'Still here. You're very nice Izzie.'

'Yes. Well get on with it.'

'*Subito*. Is Tessa still with you?'

'No. She went back this morning. Look, I know it seems silly, prosaic, but she was making dire noises about life without a car.'

'I'm going to visit SW3 right away. This evening at latest. Assuming they don't, er, incarcerate me as well, she should have it back tomorrow.'

'She'll be pleased. I'll phone and let her know.'

'No. Don't do that.'

'Of course not. Stupid of me.'

'I'll get it back to her. Right now I'd better go and tidy up the garbage.'

'Yes. Ramsey – I hate you. It's a real bummer. But you're right. People shouldn't be helped to die.' Before he could say another word she had hung up. He stood imagining her standing in the filthy box forcing herself not to cry; putting a brave face on things before she began the walk back to the shop. Knowing he had no reason to, he felt mean.

The receptionist was still staring with two-faced unconcern. Hear and see all evil. Speak it only when paid to. Ramsey fished out the car keys. As he crossed the lobby again he suddenly had the sense of being in France. '*Disque Bleu*' fumes hung in the air. More than ever, he felt homesick. Well, good! It would put an edge on his appetite for what he was about to do.

Yet another one. This was how the end of civilisation would be formalised. People inter-facing with the people they were too afraid to meet through electronic hardware. He pushed the button.

'Yes?' came the squawk.

'Dr Bennet,' he said. The 'open sesame' of Harley Street. The mechanism clicked and before anything could click back he was barging through the door. The receptionist looked up from her chair. Her eyes dilated with mindless alarm.

'John Bodkin Bennet,' he said. 'Where's Wood?'

'He . . . he's not here,' she said. 'You can't go in there.' She was right in the first part. The inner sanctum was empty. He turned back to the outer office and confronted her across the desk.

'There's no one here at all.'

'Good!' she said. 'He cancelled his patients for this afternoon,' she added, hoping for a small victory. 'I must ask . . .'

'He never hear of locums? What's his home address?'

She bridled, got fierce herself. 'I can't possibly tell you that!'

Ramsey came round the desk. 'Yes you can,' he said, 'because if you don't I'm going to have you out there stripped on the pavements of Harley Street giving all and sundry visible proof of the fact that you wear tanga briefs!'

His hand shot out and grabbed the low-slung vee of her prick-teasing white uniform. His first two fingers curled inside the link strap of her bra. He pulled with not enough suddenness to tear the fabric but enough force to bring her forward to the edge of the chair and up. She strained back. Something ripped. She stopped straining. Ramsey lowered his face close to hers.

'The address,' he said.

She shook her head.

131

'If I do it to you,' Ramsey said, 'I promise you, you won't enjoy it. I'm a doctor, you know. Like Jack the Ripper.'

She started to cry. 'Seven Seagram Street,' she said.

He jerked hard again and something else tore. 'How do I know you're telling the truth?'

Her head twisted. She whimpered. 'I – I don't . . . there's a gas-bill in the drawer. I was supposed to pay it.'

He let her go. 'Fetch it out.'

She did. She had been telling the truth. He moved to the modish phone with its battery of inter-com buttons. It did not take too much strength to separate it from its cable. CFC would have granted him instant membership.

'Now,' he said, 'go home. Don't phone him from outside. If you do I'll know about it. And then I'll be back tomorrow with a warrant. Catch my drift.'

He backed to the door. He didn't like what he'd done but he wasn't sure that he hadn't enjoyed it. The girl was shaking.

'Bastard copper!' she managed. It came out pure Hackney. Not all bad, then, he thought as he went out. More in her than met the eye.

TWELVE

His mother's jock-strap, Dorothy had had the rag on these last days! What with muttering in his sleep, starting at every phone call, flipping from one television channel to the next and back again hour upon hour . . . They'd not gone out for days. No concerts, no theatre, no nice restaurants. He seemed to have spent absolute aeons slaving away over a hot microwave and the thanks he'd got from his lord and master you could tattoo on a detumescent prick and still have room for some hot telephone numbers. It was picky, picky, all day and all night. Now she had come home early from her glorified massage parlour. Again, if you please! God knew it wasn't down to her being on heat!

As he splashed soda into the two glasses of Sancerre, Aubrey Howe threw a quick glance at the nominal head of their ménage. Not a pretty sight, he had to conclude. Simon Wood was standing in the centre of their living room staring at a pictureless television screen and seeing God only knew. His face was screwed tight with anxiety and it did nothing for his crow's feet. Or rather it did too much. He'd flung his jacket over the Eames chair and, because he wasn't thinking about holding it in, his stomach was pushing the blue shirt out over the top of his Gucci belt. She'd really thickened round the waist these last six months Aubrey thought. He poured wine into a second glass and took stock. With the hiss of more soda it came to him. He hadn't lived twenty-six bright summers to exist as a doormat dogsbody. It was time to be moving on. But not just yet. Not before Turkey.

He left the wine bottle on the breakfast counter top and brought the glasses round from the see-through kitchen. He extended one to Wood, who didn't move. Gratitude! Now she didn't even know he was there!

'Here,' Aubrey said softly.

Wood came out of his trance. His head jerked and then, his face clearing, he got a smile on to it. Aubrey would never perhaps know what a brave feat that was. 'You spoil me,' Wood said.

'Don't I just! Cheers.' Aubrey was all boyish eyes a-smiling.

'Cheers.'

'Careful of the Casa Pupo now.'

As if heeding his own warning Aubrey moved to the cream linen Heal's sofa against the wall. He sank into its vast plumpness and patted the cushion beside him. 'Come and sit down,' he said.

Indeed careful with his drink, Simon Wood did as he was told.

Aubrey was now all sincere concern. 'What is it?' he said.

'What . . . what do you mean "what is it"?'

'You know, Simon. You just haven't been yourself lately. Not the merest bit. Is it the shop? You don't have that medical lot breathing down your neck do you?'

'No. Nothing like that. No trouble up at mill.' Wood had actually managed a joke.

'Simon – you're not brooding over our little spat about the Hockney are you?'

Wood reached out and squeezed Aubrey's hand. 'Of course not,' he said. 'Long forgotten.'

'I was wrong. Go ahead and buy it.'

'It doesn't seem so important now,' Wood said. He winced inwardly at the truth of his remark.

'Do what you want. Go ahead and get it.'

'Well . . . it's very us. We can afford it.'

'We?' Aubrey said. 'Now don't start patronising me.' It was roguish on top but bitch underneath. Wood knew the tone exactly. But cornered as he was in the outside world, he was so tired. He so badly needed a friend. He tried to depersonalise the conversation.

'The gallery say it's a good investment.'

'Well, as Mandy said, they would wouldn't they. Personally I think his bubble's about to burst any review now. After all, he traces.'

'Oh come on now!' Not seeing he had been provoked Wood regretted his tone at once.

'Well, we're right back where we were then! Buy the bloody thing!'

They sat in silence. Wood felt very empty and very young inside. Please God, let one thing go right.

'If you *didn't* buy it . . .' Aubrey resumed.

'Yes? Say it.'

'We could still go to Turkey.'

'I've been to Turkey.'

'Not to Ephesus, you said.'

Wood was silent. He saw now what was being stage-managed. He despised himself for letting himself be manoeuvred but it was not so bad a feeling as feeling all alone. And, the way things were, a trip abroad, a sustained trip abroad, could never come more opportunely. Yes, that was it.

'All right,' he said brightening, 'You've convinced me. We'll think big this time and –' The door bell rang. Wood jumped out of his skin so sharply Sancerre and soda sloshed across his Daks trousers.

'Tsk! Tsk! Tsk!' Aubrey said. But, the winner, he could afford to be considerate again.

'I'll go,' he said and got up.

134

'No, don't! Oh my God!'

'What *is* it?'

The bell rang again. 'The Porsche is in the driveway,' Aubrey said. 'You can't really pretend not to be in. I'll go and see who it is and get rid of them.' He was enjoying seeing Dorothy wet her knickers.

'All right. If it's that man Julia rang up about I'm not here. Absolutely not here. Keep the chain on whatever you do!'

'You know me, love,' Aubrey said, 'whatever I do I always keep a chain on.' He went out of the room. His slippers squeaked on the hall flooring.

Wood forced himself up and went into the kitchen for a tea-towel. He heard voices but could not make anything out. He dabbed at his thigh. White wine will come out, he thought confusedly, especially with soda in it. Aubrey came back.

'It's not him,' he said.

Thank God!

'There's two of them. One's French.'

Wood felt the floor start to give way.

'They seem very nice.'

'You didn't let them in!'

'I said I'd see if you were in. Just like a proper butler. And, yes, I've left the chain on.'

Wood gathered himself. He had to keep them sweet. That French swine had agreed a low profile was best for all concerned. Come on, it was no worse than hoping the lad in front of you wasn't going to turn out to be under-cover Vice Squad. He put down the towel and, mouth dry, walked to the front door. He looked through the gap the safety chain permitted.

'Simon! How are you?'

It was indeed the suave, confident Frenchman. With him was a nondescript, slighter man in his forties. Foxy-ish. Common.

'Hello . . .' Wood said and felt foolish.

'I have some good news for you,' the Frenchman said. 'May we come in?'

Wood didn't move. 'What is it?' he said. The Frenchman smiled.

'Well, first let me apologise for my behaviour this morning,' he said. 'In the park. I was worried, frankly. Too many movies in me, eh? My name is Martin Lambert, by the way. Such a good name, don't you think, when one works both sides of the Channel.' And he had pronounced it, almost, in the English way.

'This is my associate, Mr Beach,' Lambert said. 'He is part of the firm.'

'Sandy Beach,' Beach said. He shrugged a little pathetically. 'Sorry, but it got stuck on me at school. What can you do?' He had a north country accent.

135

'What's the good news?' Wood persisted.

'I have talked to our friend. Well, my superiors. They say your point is well made. A little caution is called for.'

'Oh?'

'Yes. They have asked me to reach some sort of accommodation with you. Naturally they do not want to lose a valuable team-member permanently, but . . . Lambert paused and looked over his shoulder at the street. He looked at the safety chain.

'It would be more . . . discreet,' he smiled.

Wood reached for the knob of the chain and then as he released it felt his fingernail tear as it was wrenched from his grasp and the crashed open door smashed into his forearm. He staggered backwards into the hall and on and on as the palm of Beach's foul-smelling hand against his nose drove him towards the living room. His heels could get no traction on the floor to help him resist. Miles away the front door slammed shut.

'Keep going lover boy,' Beach said, unnecessarily.

Arms whirling as he fought to keep some kind of tilted-back balance, pain stabbing at the centre of his face, he was sent sprawling onto the sofa. Aubrey, brought to the centre of the room by the brawling rush, stood open-mouthed.

'Not a word!' Beach hissed at him . . . For the moment the command was also unnecessary. Aubrey Howe's terror was dumbfounding.

Looking back down behind him Lambert strolled into the room. 'Amitco tiles,' he said. 'Very nice. The telephone, Sandy.'

Beach walked to the wall-hung telephone above the kitchen counter. From the breast pocket of his faded sports jacket he produced a cut-throat razor. Wood felt his veins itch the length of his body. There was blood on his trousers now. His nose was bleeding. Beach effortlessly sliced through the phone lead. He turned to the stricken Aubrey. 'You. Lover-boy. Upstairs!' he said.

Like a transfixed rabbit Aubrey could only shake his head. Beach reached into his side pocket. His arm lifted. The sap made a soft, sighing sound as it swung through the air and a sharp, flat sound as it hit the side of Aubrey's jaw. He reeled back against the counter sending the wine bottle crashing to the floor behind. It didn't break but Aubrey's jaw was probably fractured. Already a bulge and a bruise were deforming the stock-in-trade symmetry of his features. He was doubling up. Pain seemed to be splintering his need to scream against his teeth.

'Upstairs!' Beach said again. 'Be honest – a pretty thing like you enjoys a bit of rough once in a while.'

Feeling like fainting, Wood saw that all the time Lambert was

136

watching him. More like a sheep to slaughter than a rabbit Aubrey shambled across to the door.

'Hold it,' Beach said. He turned to Lambert. 'The television,' he said.

Lambert took a pace, bent, and show-jumping leapt into view. Beach shook his head. Lambert played with the gun. A talking head and then a pop video.

'Good,' Beach said. 'Nice and loud.' He motioned Aubrey on. The boy's sick eyes locked with Wood's.

'Simon,' he began thickly. 'Ugh!' Beach had hit him in the kidneys and on out the door. The volume from the television was ear-splitting. Lambert's face came near.

'So pleasant – a detached house,' he amiably shouted. 'When you can afford it. Stay put and you'll suffer no further violence.'

He backed into the kitchen. Wood watched in hynotised horror. He was back at school. At the end of this glass corridor that stretched for many years a man was opening a door, pouring something into a measuring jug, running a tap. The man walked back up the corridor holding the jug. The corridor changed into a glass room. The man sat down on the edge of a chair with a jacket on the back. Perhaps it was his jacket and he was a prefect. Except he already had a jacket on and he was taking out a cigarette and lighting it, which was against the rules. The man sat there for ever. Then for ever came to an end.

The glass room suddenly shivered into ten thousand knife-edged slivers that fell silently away. A sound had done it. It was a sound like no sound Simon Wood had ever heard before. Keener, more piercing than a whistle, *animal*, it had shrilled out above the television's boom. It was a golden arrow, a hideous golden arrow, in a blue sky. Then the sky went dark. The scream was cut off.

'*Merde!*' said the man Wood remembered was Lambert. For the first time he lost his impression of being amused. Wood gasped. The dreamlike quality of his terror was being momentarily replaced by the returning immediacy of his real nightmare. He watched, waited. Without warning Lambert switched off the television. Silence rang through the house. There was a footfall. Wood looked towards the doorway and fainted. His senses had fled at the sight he saw. Beach had on Aubrey's white towelling bathrobe. He'd put the hood up. He might have been a monk, a boxer. But he was not. He was a negative, a Satanic Father Christmas. The front of the robe, its long wide cuffs, were shriekingly dyed crimson.

Beach and Lambert looked at each other.

'It wasn't like boning a haddock,' Beach said in a thin voice.

'The scream! It could have been heard!'

Beach shrugged. 'I put him out first. But doing it brought him round.'

137

'All right. So let's get on with it.'

Beach took off the robe. It fell on the rug. Lambert lifted Wood into a sitting position. Not unkindly, Beach began to slap his face. After a few blows Wood began to stir his head.

Yes, he was at school. It was when he'd been forced to do games. The discus had hit him. He'd thought in the darkness he was dead. He was floating above himself all curled up on the ground with the others standing round. Then he'd floated down into himself and started to wake up. Here he was waking up again . . .

Simon Wood opened his eyes and found himself staring straight at horror – the big close-up faces of Lambert and Beach.

'You fainted,' Lambert said. 'Here, drink this.'

Mechanically Wood reached to steady the jug Lambert was holding. Then he remembered why he had fainted. He remembered he had seen Lambert mixing something in the kitchen. 'No,' he choked out, 'it's poison.' He tried to dash the jug away, to spill it, but Lambert's grip was too strong. He withdrew the jug from Wood's reach. He smiled.

'Nonsense,' he said. 'A sedative. Help you sleep on the plane. We know you're upset about your friend but he might have talked.'

'He didn't know anything!'

Lambert smiled. 'Ah,' he said. 'Here. Drink.'

The rawest instinct to survive, to stay alive, surged possessingly through Wood. He flung his forearms up and out with a strength he had never known was in him. Lambert and Beach were both set back on their heels. Wood thrust upwards from the sofa. He nearly made it. But the depth of its cushioning was too much for him. His knees were too far back. As he scrabbled at the air, neither up nor down, Beach hit him on the skull with his sap. Wood's stomach swam up into his head as he started to collapse.

They wouldn't let him. Beach caught him by the nose. Brutal pain forced him upright and then back. His neck was forced back against the sofa's head-rest, his head canted back beyond. His throat was locked back. He was suffocating. He couldn't use his nose to breathe. He opened his mouth.

They started to pour the liquid down his throat. He shut his teeth, gritted them. They hit him in the belly very hard. He started to gag, and choked. Iron bars were tightening across his chest. He had to breathe. It was like being under water.

Simon Wood opened his mouth and they poured more liquid down. It had no odour and no taste. It didn't burn. His mind went blank and all resistance went out of his body. He was nine again and drinking water from the iron cup on the school fountain.

Almost at once his head began to loll and his mouth to dribble. His eyes were quite devoid of fear now or any other reaction a brain possessing the ability to reason might produce. He no longer had a worry in the world.

'Let's get on with it,' Lambert said. While Beach retrieved the blood-soaked robe from the floor, he began to rip Wood's shirt open. Crooning, the newly created idiot was oblivious as Beach thrust the bunched robe against the torn shirt and bare torso. He smeared it about Wood's grinning face. Straightening, he unbunched it somewhat. From the pocket he took the razor and opened it. The brightness of the arterial blood on the blade was already darkening to rust-black. Using a section of the robe still relatively white Beach wiped the razor clean, not of blood but of finger prints. Holding the blade through the robe's fabric he pushed the handle towards Wood. Wood ignored it. Lambert took his right hand and guided it to the handle. He formed the hand into a loose fist. He worked the handle into the fist. He pressed the fingers tight.

'Good,' he said.

Beach pulled the razor free and tossed it across the room. As it was in mid-air the doorbell rang. The two men looked at each other.

'The scream,' Lambert said. Beach shook his head.

'Too long.'

He looked down at his hangman's hands and anxiously back at Lambert. Lambert might have been considering whether to order the salmon grilled or poached. Wood began to giggle.

'Gun?' Lambert said.

'In the car. No guns, you said.'

'Yes. Always best. Except now.'

'They'll go away.'

'Yes. Probably.'

'Suppose they've a key!' Lambert still seemed to be considering trifles. He threw his half-smoked cigarette across the room.

'Go out the back door,' he said. 'Wait in the garden for two minutes. If I have not –'

The bell rang again.

'– called you back into the house by then go to the car and start the engine running. I will see you there. Two minutes. No more.'

Beach looked apprehensively at Lambert. Then he nodded. He went out into the kitchen area and holding aside the kitchen-to-floor roller-blind, opened the rear door. He went out and the blind flapped back into place.

The bell rang again. It continued to ring. It stopped ringing and was replaced by a new sound. The letter box flap opening.

'Wood, I know you're in there,' a man's grim voice called. 'You have ten seconds before I start breaking the door down.'

Lambert seemed not to think. He slipped off his jacket as he started walking.

He'd half expected this. Ramsey clutched the car jack tighter. This door at least had no entry control but it looked old-fashionedly solid. He took a pace back from the porch. The curtained front room windows were well within reach. The question was would – He broke off his train of thought. He could hear footsteps inside.

The door opened slightly. Ramsey moved back on to the porch. Through the narrow gap which was all the still-secured safety chain permitted Ramsey saw the bulk of a man in shirt-sleeves. He was, in fact, in the process of buttoning one.

'I'm sorry you've been kept waiting,' he said, 'but there is really no need to carry on like that. What do you want?'

For a split second Ramsey was thrown. The man, displacingly, was French.

'I need to see Simon Wood,' Ramsey said. 'It's urgent.'

'Oh?' The man coolly surveyed him as he buttoned the other sleeve.

'And is Mr Wood expecting you?'

'No. But he doesn't –'

'Whom shall I say is calling?'

'Bennet. Dr Bennet. Tell him it's a matter of professional urgency.'

'Very well, Dr Bennet, I'll see if Mr Wood is in.' The man-servant smiled frigidly and swished away.

'Simon,' Ramsey heard him calling, 'there's a Dr Bennet outside saying he must . . .' The voice trailed away. Ramsey set the jack down . . . Well, well, well. Wood liked to swing not only the gay way but with French dressing too. Who said you couldn't get the servants these days? Or wasn't it that this had become the era of the gentleman's gentleman? What could they have been up to that had so delayed this *Cage Aux Folles* fugitive from opening the door . . .

'. . . round about eleven at the latest.'

The man-servant was coming back. Ramsey reminded himself that he had a short sharp shock to deliver to Wood. An arrest. Taking on two might be tricky. He glanced down but the chain was rattling.

'My apologies if I seemed abrupt, Dr Bennet,' Wood's man said, 'but these days . . .'

His shrug was very French. He was wearing a jacket now. He had the chain off at last and opening the door wide, stepped aside.

'I was just on my way out,' the man said, 'so I'll say "good night". Mr Wood is in the back room. Second door on the right.'

'Thanks.' Ramsey nodded. The man smiled and, shutting the door after him, went out into the evening. Ramsey turned and walked down the hall. Perfect command of English idiom but an accent very –

The first thing Ramsey saw was what at first glance he took for a vast raspberry sorbet and then saw was a blood-soaked heap of towels. The next thing he saw was the man he'd come to arrest. He was sitting on a sofa nearly as bloodstained as himself. His left hand was trying to clutch his genitals through his trousers while his right aimlessly brushed non-existent flies away from his head. King Lear in all his madness wasn't in it.

There wasn't time for horror. Ramsey took in the room in one rotating glance. He ran to the kitchen area. No one behind the counter. Running he retraced his steps and skidded to the front door. He opened it a cautious fraction. Nothing. He opened it wide. Cars parked to left and right along the short, ritzy side road but nothing moving, no one. The Frenchman was away and gone.

Fool! Ramsey slammed the door. Whoever talked like that thirties Hollywood butler these days! What an idiot to let himself be taken in! Although, credit where credit was due, grace under pressure wasn't in it. Cool such as –

A new sight interrupted his thoughts. Ramsey had just seen the smears of blood on the stairwall. They literally set him back a step. Seeing the stains it came to him Wood's condition might be the lesser of evils. It came to him there might be others in the house upstairs. Dead victims, or living killers. He stood looking at the stains as the silence shrilled in his ears. After what seemed a long time he found himself climbing the stairs.

His way was well sign-posted. There was blood on the beige carpeted treads as well as the walls. There was blood leading across the broad landing to one of the four doors that opened on to it. That door was open and lights were on in the room beyond. The other three doors were shut pregnantly. At any second, they all clamoured, we will burst open and a gunman will jump out to finish you. Ramsey held himself together. Sweat was pouring off him and yet a millimetre under the skin he felt icy. He decided to open the three doors first.

He did it very quickly. It was the only way. An impossibly marble-camp bathroom. An office-study. A neat spare bedroom with a single bed. All empty. No guys with guns behind the opening doors. All right. The moment of truth. He stood in the middle of the landing again and let his eyes, his feet, resume following the trail of blood.

At the threshold of the master bedroom it stopped. Appeared to. The bedroom carpet was black. It was a room for kinkiness. As he pushed the door wider Ramsey saw reflected in the wall of mirrors a still life torn from some torturer's manual like a limb pulled off by a threshing machine. Now there was time for horror.

141

The sheets on the bed were pale blue. Had been. They were now a saturated sheen of crimson, brown, and a darker, blackening red. A male corpse lay on the bed on its back. Arms and legs were splayed wide. It had taken a moment, even for a doctor, to determine it was a male corpse. Where the genitals should have been there was nothing but a black-red hole. Someone had cut off the penis and scrotal sac to leave the impression of a monstrous, monstrously distended black vulva. Ramsey retched. His own contracted balls were trying to seek refuge in the belly above them. The repositioning of the amputated organs in the corpse's mouth eloquently suggested that the operation had probably not been with benefit of anaesthetic.

Ramsey sought visual refuge. He lifted his eyes up – and the scene screamed at him again. The ceiling was mirrored. He jerked his head to the right and a pier glass bounced an infinity of horror at him. For an instant Ramsey thought he too might go mad. The inside of his skull seemed mirrored and the endless, static image was going to ricochet across his brain for ever more. He clutched at the door. He shut his eyes.

After a moment it was all right. Perhaps anyone but a doctor would have gone mad, he told himself. But it's all right. You can see it clinically and it's all right. He opened his eyes and made himself walk forward to the head of the bed. He looked at the face of the blood-let boy who had really been Wood's lover. It was as so often with violent death. Looking up beyond the butcher's jagged parody of felatio Ramsey could see a face that in its chalk-whiteness seemed curiously innocent and surprised. He felt the temple with the back of his hand. Still warm . . . Well, a police job.

He went quickly downstairs. Wood hadn't moved. He still babbled. But now Ramsey saw the razor. As he picked up the phone another hot flush of shock swept through him. While he went upstairs Wood might have turned berserk again and come psyching up the stairs after him. If he had ever gone beserk at all. Ramsey had just detected that the phone was dead. Christ. What should he do now?

He moved to the sofa and saw on the cushion next to Wood the discarded measuring jug. It was on its side. A residue of colourless liquid stretched along its length. There were stains other than blood on the sofa and Wood's tattered shirt. Hallucinogens . . .? Ramsey perceived that rather than having freaked out homicidally Wood had been force-fed a cocktail making pernicious nonsense of the expansive theories of Dr Timothy. He looked at Wood, or what had been Wood. The man had been slime. A murderer at one remove; a passer-by on the other side *en route* to his illegal bank account. But was this living death sentence a punishment that fitted the crime? Well, who was he to judge? In any case, just possibly the punishment could be mitigated. It was ironic. He had come to take Wood in to the police. Now if he drove him fast to the Royal Free there might be an outside chance of reclaiming some brain cells.

A machine gun went off. Ramsey threw himself to the floor, but nothing splintered. No bullets buried themselves in wall or upholstery, no windows shattered, no acrid stench of cordite was burning out the smell of *Disque Bleu* the Frenchman had bequeathed the room. Ramsey raised his head. The roller-blind's toggle-cord was still swinging from side to side. As he got to his feet Ramsey could see his whole body reflected in the glass of the now-visible back door.

The change in feeling was total. Curtained the room was safe. Now it had become a well-lit goldfish bowl in a sea of dark. Charged with violence the night did have a thousand eyes and the real machine gun McCoy might be out there in the dark. Quitting time.

Ramsey approached Wood very carefully. If he had any motor co-ordination at all it might be wrestling time. He might be possessed with the power of ten thousand djinns. Or – he might fall flat on his face. Ramsey stooped down and grasped Wood's forearm. He gently pulled. Wood got to his feet like a good little boy. Ramsey frowned. He was a pitiable sight. He had soiled himself. The shirt was a torn, bloodied flag. Ramsey picked up the dark jacket from the chair and draped it over Wood's shoulders. He propelled him gently into the hall. He left the lights on. He stretched past Wood to open the front door. He would call the police from the Royal Free. The car wasn't far. Ah, the jack.

As Ramsey bent to retrieve it, Wood acted exactly like a footballer shielding the ball with his body. He backed into Ramsey, nearly knocking him over. He did it again. Hard. He started to pivot and slump. The hallucinogens were too much for him. As Ramsey forgot the jack and stood to support this twisting zombie, time suddenly exploded and divided. Part of it went incredibly fast and part of it slowed to an eternal slowness.

Tyres squealed, lights blazed and a car roared away. Wood spun round in an ineffably slow, heavy sag of a pirouette. The jacket fell off his shoulders. His virtually bare chest made it easy to make out in the light from the hall that to match the atrocity perpetrated on his lost lover he now sported two flowering, gushing holes on his own bosom. He was a dead weight in Ramsey's arms. As Ramsey lowered him to the ground he realised in slow time that if there was a God after all, he had perhaps decided to temper justice with mercy. But in fast time from the intersection with the major road there came an outrageous squealing of tyres and brakes and a kerrumph that sounded beneath the screams and shouts and tinkling glass like an exploding land-mine. Ramsey laid Wood's head gently on the ground and started to run.

It was about seventy yards. He was not the first on the scene. Several cars had stopped, street doors had opened. Cries of alarm were beginning to ring the collision round. Panting, he paused a few yards off to weigh the situation up. Somewhere in there was a man with a gun.

It had happened right on a corner. The ballistics were easy to read. Forced into the middle of the narrow road by the cars parked either side a Fiesta had gone nearly head-first into a long-wheel based, roo-barred Shogun turning into Seagram Street. A mini-bus, parked on the corner itself, would have obscured the views of both drivers. The result was as, given their respective weights and masses, smart money would have bet. The Shogun was set back a thousand or so around the front off-side wing. The Fiesta was probably a write-off. Its bonnet was about half the length it had been at the outset of its brief last journey. It must have been motoring – going as fast as you would expect a getaway car to be going.

The Shogun must have been full. At least four people in it. Its height allowed Ramsey to see heads moving, turning inside it. The Fiesta's passengers were harder to make out. The crowd blocked the view.

A woman turned away from the half-stunned, half-delighted crowd. 'My God, I think he's dead,' she began. Her hysterics gave Ramsey his cue.

'Out of the way, please, I'm a doctor.' He pushed forward. As always, people stood aside, relieved to be relieved of any decisions or judgements.

'It's him, mate,' a man said and pointed to the Fiesta's passenger. Ramsey saw that the Fiesta's lights were on and the passenger side window all the way down before, as he pulled the buckled door open by main force, he realised there was no driver behind the wheel. He straightened up.

'Where's the driver?' he shouted. 'Who's the driver?'

'The swine ran off,' a young girl's Sloane Street voice cried out. 'The swine saw what he'd done and ran away.'

Ramsey hunched down into the car. He'd felt free to ask his question because a single glance at the angle of the passenger's neck had told him the man was dead. Not wearing a seat belt, he had catapulted into the windscreen with such force his head had starred the unbreakable laminate its entire length. As the windscreen had buckled and popped twistedly out of its frame the middle-aged man's head had snapped back and sideways across the corner of the seat back. Pierpoint couldn't have done it better.

Pretending to doctor, Ramsey thought fast. Why the window was

144

down and the man had not had his belt on was obvious. Both choices had been to aid marksmanship. His hand scrabbled on the floor for a gun. Nothing. They wouldn't have banked on Wood coming through the door first. It was easy to see why when the crunch came the driver had slewed the Fiesta round to favour his side. A cool Frenchman. He'd taken enough time to take the gun. Yes. There was blood all over this little runt's hands. And not his own.

'It looks bad,' Ramsey shouted over his shoulder. 'Has someone phoned for an ambulance?'

A tangled chorus told him it was being done. Meanwhile he had his own motives for continuing to search for a corpse's pulse. He bent forward and put his ear against the dead man's chest. And his hand into his jacket's breast pocket. Bingo! Leather. A wallet. Now. Take it easy and take it fast. Good. Safely gathered in.

Now. One last question. How cool was M. Cool? Had he had the *sang-froid* to return, hover on the edge of the crowd? As he got up out of the car would there be a discreet surgery-like cough and a fourth corpse in Seagram Street that night? The chances were against. The odds would be too stacked. He could be recognised as the runaway driver. He could be seen shooting. He would be in at least mild shock. He could well have a severely bruised chest, broken ribs even, judging by the shape of the steering wheel. Right. Steady the Buffs. Ramsey stood back up out of the car. No harsh, dry cough sounded. Nobody killed him.

'I've got some Sodium Triumvirate in my car,' he said. 'I'll go and get it.'

The wallet bobbling lightly against the waist-band of his blouson he backed, then turned, away. He felt the on-rush of shock trying to make him light-headed. He fought the attack off. He couldn't afford a car crash of his own. In the distance a siren started to sound. It was a good thing the street wasn't a cul-de-sac.

The Chinese chef who, without benefit of work permit, grubbed away in the hotel kitchen had seen Ramsey in transit so many times he had come to think he was some upstairs member of the staff. He could not know what shuddering, nausea-inducing images his lightning fast cleaving of the chicken carcass was conjuring in the passer-by this time. Ramsey found himself gagging as he came into the lobby through the 'Staff Only' door. The vivid, crimson deathbed lacerated his mind's eye again. Fresh perspiration began to trickle down his back to replenish the staler sweat already congealed there. He shook his head and the image away. Clear thinking now. Clear, clear, thinking. Only possible in the light of recent events in the most secluded, solitary, unadvertised hide-away in the world. Page one was to check out.

Almost from conditioned habit he went to the window and, as the never-sleeping porter looked at him, looked out. The light from the street lamp showed the Escort was not back on duty. A Carlton had taken over its usual spot. Empty. He started to turn away. The Carlton was one along from the high-shouldered bulk of a big old Citroën. Funny that was the second he'd seen that day. Even in France you . . . Wait. The second – or the same?

It had brushed his mind with the lightness of a snowflake falling. He'd been turning away and almost not noticed it but in a day when he'd twice smelt *Disque Bleu* in the air, once in this very lobby, he'd twice seen a big old Citroën. He looked at the porter and the porter looked at him.

'Any messages?' Ramsey said as he moved to the desk.

The porter didn't bother to turn and look in the pigeon-hole. 'No,' he said.

'Fine. I'll have my key,' Ramsey said.

The porter swivelled to reach the key and swivelled back again. He didn't continue the movement by handing the key across. 'I was wondering, Doc,' he said, 'if you could bring your account up to date.'

'What? Now?'

'Yes. If you wouldn't mind.'

Red had been the colour of the evening. A red alert had begun to sound in Ramsey's brain. He knew his nerves were stretched to the limit but the mind could work faster on a fine-drawn tension. So he was on the point of checking out. But nobody alive knew that.

'Strange time, isn't it?' he probed. 'I mean, I'm planning to stay here several days yet.'

'Yes, right. No problem,' the porter said. 'Only it helps the book-keeper, you see. We do our weekly books mid-week. Helps with the VAT.' He looked at Ramsey in a way that reduced Mona Lisa to a gossip. But there was sweat on his upper lip.

'I missed you earlier,' he said. A lie. He had waited in this lobby for a phone call for ten minutes. Earlier. A smell of *Disque Bleu*.

'Ah, got you,' Ramsey smiled. He feared he had. Wood had been turned to a gibbering vegetable to stop him talking. Who else might talk? That Doctor who had been going around asking questions, stirring things up. Who turned up on doorsteps. Who reappeared on doorsteps with a human shield when we tried to top him. Get it right this time, *mon vieux*. Silence him too. It was the night for checking out. Right now sitting expectantly in his room with all the patience of a professional would be a man. A self-possessed Frenchman. He wouldn't be smoking now. He would be breathing silently through his open mouth. And to ensure a perpetual silence from the room's returning occupant he would have brought along the precise tool for the job. A silencer.

Ramsey smiled again. 'Can I borrow your pen?' he said. He reached into the blouson's inner pocket. The surface of the stolen wallet was tacky. Ramsey had small doubt as to what with. Nor it seemed had the porter. A definite expression had at last showed on his face. Fear. He flinched as Ramsey brought his hand out. It was empty of all but blood stains.

'Damn,' he said. 'The traveller's cheques are in the glove compartment. Be right back.' Dragging his car keys out he went through the 'Staff Only' door. Fast. His shoulders felt very broad and the centre of his back soft and magnetic. Yes, he'd be right back – right back with his forefathers if he came back.

Familiarity breeds familiarity. The Chinese cook grinned and waved the cleaver at his new colleague. Well meant as it was, it did not slow Ramsey down.

THIRTEEN

Her picture – there it was with all its green and blues, its lines running up and across. As a draughtsman's representation of the *manoir* – adequate. As an attempt to trap the passing play of morning light upon the *manoir* within a fixed, eternal rectangle of canvas – a joke. Futile. It was a waste of time even as a pastime. Dany sighed and laid down her brush. The sword stabs of sunlight against the conservatory that turned its windows into opaque, reflectionless mirrors, the way the sunshine became soft against the brick and seemed to be seeping into the very fabric it was crumbling – she hadn't begun to convey the impression. She felt the ghost of Monet chuckling over her shoulder. It was still only mid-morning but she felt tired. It was far more than tiresome, it was hugely tiring to wait out the man you loved being away in a foreign country. She could have borne not seeing Ramsey for several days with no more than her surface joke-complaints if knowing he was only a few kilometres away. But England! Yes, not so many kilometres away but in terms of the emotional remoteness it could have as well been Java or Sumatra. She picked up the brush again and a tube of cadmium yellow. Everything was unfair. Ramsey was unfair. The light was unfair. In England the insipid light allowed all the anaemic water colourists to wash over –

'*Le Docteur Ramsey, madame.*'

Louise, her maid, had come to interrupt her and with the best of all reasons. Dany's heart leapt up knowing its forlornness throughout the past days had earned the rich reward of his unannounced return.

'*Où?*' she said and since no woman is a Carmelite to her maid did not try to hide her eagerness.

'*Le téléphone, madame,*' Louise said, saving her the need to pull her own wry face of regret.

'Ah . . .' Dany let her breath out in a long, slow sigh, which didn't lighten her disappointment. It was, part of her mind noted, far deeper than her chagrin at not being anything more than a dabbler with paints. Monet would have told him to call back after sunset, she thought as, wiping her hands on her smock, she half-ran into the house. She snatched the phone up from the hall table.

'Ramsey! Where the hell are you?'

'In England still. A village in the South.'

'When are you coming home?'

'Soon. How's Gabin?'

'You pig!' She was quite unable to help herself.

148

'What's wrong?'

'*You*, Ramsey. You say 'soon' instead of 'today' and you ask after your flea-ridden mongrel before you ask about me.'

'It's obvious you're your old self, Dany.'

'Ramsey – I am not old!'

'*Figure de rhétorique*. How are you?'

'He's out in the garden pining for you. Like me.'

'Dany – I've just a couple of more things to do.'

'Are we talking days or weeks?'

'Days. Maybe no more than two. But I need a favour.'

'Of course.'

She had suddenly sensed he wanted to be serious.

'I want you to look after someone for me.'

This was heavy duty. 'Who?'

'The daughter of my MP friend. You remember?'

'Yes – I remember. But you remember: I'm not the maternal type. I'm not good with kids.'

'She's not a kid.'

Ah . . . Sunlight was streaming through the open doorway to layer a golden parallelogram across the black and white tiles. As she wasn't going to like what she was about to hear she would look at that and pretend she wasn't listening any more. 'How old is she then?' she heard herself go on.

'Twenty-four.'

More black tiles were covered than white tiles. How appropriate.

'. . . Dany? You still there?'

'Is she pretty? Well?'

'. . . It's not easy. Use your imagination.'

'I just have been!'

'She's standing less than two metres away.'

'So – your eyesight is failing?'

'Well, then, yes.'

'Yes, what?'

'What you said.'

'I forgot what I said.'

'Oh, Dany! *D'accord elle est jolie. D'accord elle est sympathique. Mais, c'est une gosse, tu m'entends?*'

Yes, she had got the message all right. And men of a certain age could get very sentimental over daughter figures. Sentimental plus. She strained to catch the off-phone exchanges half-reaching her.

'What was all that about?' she said.

'*Elle veut savoir ce qu'on se dit.*'

'So talk English, Ramsey. Why should I look after her?'

There was a pause. 'It's not safe here anymore, Dany.'

The sunlight on the floor went very cold. She had never known anyone less given to melodrama than Ramsey. She forced herself to sound casual. 'Not safe?'

'No.'

'Then what do I do?'

'Could you meet her off tomorrow's boat?'

'Cherbourg?'

'Mid-afternoon.'

'I'll be there. Ramsey – you didn't tell me it would be dangerous'.

'I didn't know.'

'Don't do anything stupid – like trying to do something brave.'

'Would I behave like that?'

'Yes. *Tu ne vauts rien, Ramsey, mais je t'aime.*'

'*C'est ça. Cause en français. Ça exprime mieux les petites tendresses.*'

'I can't make love to a corpse, Ramsey.' She had spoken better than she knew. Standing in the presumably bugless reception area of the Ladbrooke Hotel on the edge of Basingstoke, Ramsey lost all vision of the impersonal surroundings. Once again the Jacobean tableau of the blood-drenched bed, the creature who had died as he'd lived, returned to cauterise all other thought. His own flesh crept. The Frenchman had seen his face. It did not take too much imagination to see himself the subject of such butchery.

'. . . Ramsey? *Tu m'écoutes?*'

Dany seemed suddenly immensely far away and immensely desirable. The realist in him had to acknowledge it was not only the romantic that made him want to be with her. Where she was right now seemed a long way from men with razors.

'Yes, still here,' he said, as he thought this. 'Tomorrow's boat, OK?'

'Yes. Don't worry. But take care!'

'I will take care, I promise.'

'Yes, and I will worry, I know. *Je t'aime*, Ramsey.'

'I know. And it's returned. *Au 'voir*, Dany.'

'Soon, please, Ramsey. Soon!' She had hung up. He did too. He turned to Tessa. It was interesting that in Tessa's presence he had felt inhibited about telling Dany outright that he loved her too. Was it a straw in the wind? He frowned inwardly. He was far too old to resume playing 'how happy could I be with either were t'other dear charmer away'. He nodded at Tessa.

'Done,' he said.

'Fine . . . I suppose,' she said. She looked searchingly at him. 'I'm blowing the entire rest of my entitlement on this,' she went on, 'are you really sure –'

'Tessa! You read about Simon Wood.'

'Sounded right out of Joe Orton.'

He hadn't told Tessa of his personal presence at the Seagram Street slaughter-house. 'I promise you it wasn't suicide,' he said. 'People are making unholy fortunes dealing in drugs. When they get crossed they don't go running to the BMA for protection. They take care of it themselves. With guns if necessary.' And other things, he added to himself. Tessa was still looking dubious rather than fearful.

'Then go to the police!'

'I intend to.'

'When?'

'Soon.' Suddenly everything was 'soon'.

'Why not right now?'

'I need to check one or two things to make sure I can make them take me seriously. Including checking on them. If Brook is a tame cop I want to know who the tamer is. In the meantime it'll do you no harm to lie low.'

'Then what about Izzie?' she said.

He felt his face tighten. It was a good question and he wasn't sure he was getting the answer right. 'There's a direct line from Simon Wood to your father to you, to me,' he said. 'An out-in-the-open line. I went to Wood and so on. For obvious reasons Izzie's association with your father is known to very few. Beryl and the Whitehall whipper-ins may see to it that her VAT returns get a good going over but – otherwise – she's out of harm's way.'

He hoped he could believe what he was saying. They had moved to the reception desk. Through a window a girl in an inner office signalled she'd have the charge for the phone call worked out shortly.

'Love to have been a fly on her wall,' Tessa said.

For an instant Ramsey imagined Tessa as nurturing prurient visions of her father and Izzie. It must almost have showed. 'Dany,' Tessa said.

'Oh. Not many flies on Dany's walls.'

'Where'd you meet her?'

'In the South China Sea.'

'Oh, of course. You had the next cabin on from Jean Harlowe and Clark Gable.'

'Something like that.'

'What's she like?'

'Not you as well.'

'Natural enough question, I should have thought.'

'Well . . .' he made a point of choosing his words over-zealously, 'she's gracious . . . graceful . . . sophisticated . . . fastidious . . .'

'Haven't you missed out "attractive"?'

Ramsey shook his head.

'She's not?'

'Oh, no, she's . . . exquisite.'

The clerk who brought out the receipt for the overseas call could see at a glance that the Frog and his bit of local crumpet were having a row.

Fleetwood! Ses églises! Ses paquebots! Son phare! Son Mac! Yes, well, Ramsey thought, it was going to have to be a damned well-written guide book to get the touring holiday maker to deviate from his original Avignon to Carcasonne itinerary enough to take the Morecambe Bay route. And it wouldn't be worth the extra petrol. Fleetwood didn't even compare well with Barfleur. Packed between the wall-painted Dubonnet and Riccard ads of the French golfing village was, for better and worse, a tight-knit community. The fishing boats buffeted out to sea with a sense of pent-up energy. But here everything seemed desultory. There was the feeling of being on the floor of a vast factory where three-quarters of the work force had been laid off. The solitary trawler making off towards the Irish Sea seemed to dawdle, reluctant to forsake the land. God knew why. Standing on the sea wall Ramsey surveyed the view. It was not a pretty sight. The tide was out. In front of him a short strip of shingle gave way almost at once to an ongoing expanse of mud flats, less brown in the grey morning light than oily black. Littering this salt-ridden waste land was a virtually endless gamut of detritus. Rusted oil cans, muddied, broken bottles, a drive shaft, half a lawn-mower were hardly encouragement to a scuba diver to put on his gear. And the larger stuff, stove-in rowing boats or intact pleasure boats lying anchored dourly, waiting for the tide to refloat them, hardly conveyed the Romance of the Sea in their stranded state. To get to them now, in any case, you'd have to wade crotch-deep through mud going on quicksand.

Only the gulls, perhaps, matched their Barfleur counterparts. A screaming, scavenging squadron of them was off to the right wheeling above the harbour's commercial installations. Regularly in ones, in groups, they would divebomb the two trawlers unloading their catch or, driven by greed, skim down into the long open-ended hangar-like building where the dealers had their stalls and into which the newly boxed fish were being trollied. Over there at least the factory was up to full production capacity. Not so to the left. There along the curve of the bay was the frontage of minor hotels and 'B and B' houses. One glance at those the previous evening had sent revived memories of dank, childhood, cabbage-smell ridden holidays goose-fleshing down his back. He had driven on until, just off the front, he'd found a pub that did accommodation. The Morphet Arms didn't have a 'Routiers' sticker in the window but with a signed photo of George Farm behind the bar it couldn't be all bad.

Ramsey shivered. The wind off the distant sea was coming in wet and cold. Some croissants and decent coffee would go down well now but he could settle, he supposed, for a bacon sandwich and a cup of tea. Later he would pick up a sweater and by that time the public library would be open.

There was a severe depression over most of the Western Atlantic that day. The sky over Cherbourg was no less grey than at Fleetwood. Standing on deck towards the prow of the ferry, Tessa watched the cranes and spires of the French port take on rising definition without enthusiasm. It wasn't going to be a bonus holiday because he wouldn't be there. When he did return it would be the signal all was clear of danger back in England and she was free to pick up the threads of her career. The boring loveless threads . . . She suddenly felt terribly alone. Her father was gone. In future he would always be an absentee from her life. And Ramsey saw her as a kid. It wasn't sex, but she needed an arm to come cuddlingly around her and hold her tight and tell her that she wasn't awake. It wasn't sex, but it would be no good if the arm was a woman's. She wanted her Dad back. She wanted Ramsey. She had neither and the future was going to be as grey and implacable as the day. What future? Fuelling the rest of your life on contempt for your mother didn't add up to living. She felt the wind whipping at her short hair with satisfaction. What was the point of trying to groom yourself when you were futureless and about to be met by the man you loved's mistress and she had a voice that breathed sex down the phone and was gracious and graceful and, dammit, exquisite?

Dany stood in the immigration-arrival hall straining every nerve in her body to appear insouciant. Unknown to her, she was succeeding magnificently. Customs officers, hire-car drivers awaiting arriving passengers, porters, all looked at the woman in the Gianfranco Ferre suit and envied the man she had clearly come to meet. Such was her apparent assurance not one considered moving across to try trying it on for more than a few wistful seconds. This was a lady who knew exactly what she wanted, little man, and if she hadn't, by some incredible stroke of golden fortune, indicated it was you, then save your breath, time and energy.

The customs men were better at detecting contraband than feelings. Dany could not remember feeling so insecure in years. There was no fool like an old fool. Ramsey was not a fool, you'd ever say, and certainly not old. But thrown together in some cloak and dagger romance with a little *gamine*, who knew what mood might not have taken him? A thin, tomboyish girl half his age – might he not see in her arms, her bed, the possibility of drawing fresh energy from her youth? Sex with such a girl might be the revitalising fountain of youth. New textures, new resistances of the flesh . . . Painful imaginings started to come and she was glad when the sight of two cyclists wheeling their bicycles signalled the exodus of the ferry's passengers. Business men . . . families . . . French . . . American, surely . . . and now a girl walking towards her. Dark. Lithe. Definitely a touch of tomboy but for all that totally adult woman.

My God, Tessa thought, Ramsey understated – she's absolutely ravishing. She's stylish beyond all style!

Mon Dieu, Dany was thinking, she's so natural and alive. She's so young.

She took a step forward and managed a beautifully judged smile of low-key sincerity.

'Tessa? Yes? Hello. I'm Dany.'

'Hello, and thanks very much for being here.'

'Oh, it's nothing. My pleasure.'

'He described you very well.'

Dany smiled again. This time ruefully. 'We mustn't devote our conversations to discussing Ramsey,' she said.

'No?' He was, after all, Tessa thought, the one thing they had in common.

'No!' Dany was saying. 'I promised myself. Now – let me take one of your bags. There.'

Ah, Tessa thought, she does feel threatened.

'How was the journey?'

'Slow. I seem to have been travelling since yesterday.'

'I know,' Dany said, 'if I could I'd fly everywhere and leave the sea to the fish.'

A little later, under that same universal grey cloud cover, the crew of the Fleetwood trawler 'Jack London' were temporarily happy to leave the fish to the sea. Some twelve miles out off the Welsh coast they were engaged in a manoeuvre to which the British Trawlerman's Association would scarcely have given their safe-practice seal of approval. Despite the quite choppy seas the Force Four had blown up, the 'Jack London' was ploughing steadily towards a sister trawler out of Brixham. There was no activity, no net emptying, no boxing, on the deck of either vessel. The hands all stood watching as starboard bow to starboard bow the two vessels began to pass at a distance of no more than twelve feet. As a wave lifted it momentarily higher a sailor aboard the Devon ship seemed to pay the smudge of Welsh coastline off in the distance an oblique compliment. With a quick scrum-half's motion he sent something hurtling across into the 'Jack London'. Not a rugby ball but a khaki canvas and webbing pack – but deftly caught, for all that, by a burly deck-hand standing amidships. As water began to widen between the two separating trawlers he was already taking the pack up to the 'Jack London's' wheel house. On the deck the other hands, relaxing it seemed, once more turned their attention to the nets.

The deck hand entered the wheel house toting the pack in front of his chest as if trying to judge its weight.

'What would you say, Terry?' the man at the wheel said looking at him.

'About ten pounds, skip,' the hand said with a grin. 'Felt like fucking fifty when I caught it.'

'Just so you didn't drop it. O.K. Leave it there.'

The hand left the wheel house. The captain secured the wheel. He was a grizzled, stocky man whose heavy forearms and bulging gut would have suggested a front row forward to people not seeing him here in his native habitat. He moved now, balance no problem, to the pack. Carefully he opened it. As carefully he removed four one kilo packs of white powder. He grunted with satisfaction. Looking at his seamed face people would have said he was a hard man but not necessarily an evil one. He turned the empty bag towards the window so as to look right into it. Again he grunted. As the tilting horizon rapidly changed its diagonal in the panoramic view the window gave, Captain Gibson of the 'Jack London' moistened his finger and collected up some loose cocaine grains from the bag's bottom. Almost unconsciously he lifted the finger to his mouth and began rubbing it across his gums.

It had taken him just a few seconds to locate the street on the map in the library's reference room. Finding it in real life was scarcely any harder. Fleetwood's old lighthouse tower provided a bearing almost as dominating as the Eiffel Tower. He walked down the longish street circumspectly and on the opposite, the even numbered, side to where he expected the house to be. It wasn't as he'd imagined it. These houses were small, tightly crowded terrace houses huddled under their slate roofs against the blows they knew Fate would rain down on them. Inside, where their stairs angled round up to the landing, there would be the space built in to allow a coffin to be manoeuvred round the awkward corner. But you could guess that over the years a high proportion of the dwellers in these houses had not died peacefully in their beds – certainly not the recently deceased owner of number 7.

Ah, that made more sense. At the far end of the street, a developer must have acquired some more land or knocked down older properties. About a dozen more modern, sixties-style semi's extended on from the older houses. Interesting, it was the original houses that gained in character from the side-by-side comparison. And interesting, too, the extra work put in on number 7. Another room had been extended out over the garage. The front porch had been sealed flush by the addition of an outer door. A cheap-looking but doubtless expensive double-glazing job had replaced the style of windows still evident in the neighbouring house. In the driveway stood a D registered Sierra. On the street outside was a C registered 2.8 injection Capri. In the evening air it looked high-powered. Well, if Beach had been in its front seat three days ago he might not now be in a zippered nylon bag in a refrigerated drawer.

He rang the bell. The chimes were totally as you would anticipate. A shadowy male figure appeared behind the frosted glass of the outer porch door and then on the doorstep. Ramsey had to work hard not to take a step back in surprise. He'd seen this face before. Last time it had displayed a huge incipient contusion on its forehead and an open-mouthed surprise at the strange angle the neck beneath it had chosen to adopt. Now instead of the rictus there was a tight-lipped, enquiring look, but the foxy features were very much the same. This was clearly the dead man's son. About twenty-eight, twenty-nine. Not tall but powerful across the shoulders.

'Yes?'

'Mr Beach?'

'Mr Beach Junior, yes.'

'Good evening. I . . . I'm sorry to disturb you but my name is Ramsey. Dr Ramsey. I was the doctor who happened to be passing at the time of your father's accident.'

'Ah . . . So?' The foxiness had sharpened into outright suspicion.

Ramsey looked up and down the street. 'Look – I wonder if I could come in for a moment.'

'. . . I suppose. Mum! We've got a visitor!'

Having called out over his shoulder the son of the man who'd tried to murder Ramsey held the outer door aside.

'Thank you.' Awkwardly Ramsey side-stepped into the porch and then through into an essentially orange and cream hallway. A plump, dishevelled woman in her mid-fifties was already advancing towards him from a rear kitchen.

'Who is it, Rocky?'

For all she looked at him, Ramsey might as well not have been there. Amplified chatter, applause, was coming from the front room.

'It's the doctor who saw Dad's accident, Mum.'

'Ooh!' Now she looked at him. Not shrewdly, he would have said. His first impression was of stupidity. And not a vast amount of grief.

'Well you'd better go in the front room, Mr . . .'

'Ramsey.'

'Dr Ramsey, Mum.'

'Doctor. Yes. Well, go on in. Switch the telly off Rocky, it's only Wogan.'

No, not much grief. He followed the son into a room where purple had gained supremacy over orange. The three-piece suite in predominantly that colour was too large for the lilac and black carpeted floor area, as was, indeed, the twenty-six inch television set on a stand above a winking video recorder.

'Would you like a cup of tea, then, Doctor?'

'No. No thank you, Mrs Beach.'

'It's no bother.'

'He doesn't want one, Mum. He's got a message for us. Is that right, Doctor?'

Hmmn. So Mr Beach Junior was a take-charge merchant. The Capri would be his.

'Sort of,' Ramsey said. 'There are two reasons I dropped in on you.'

'Oh yes?'

'Doctor – why don't you sit down?' He did as Mrs Beach had suggested. The large mirror over the coal-effect gas fire had shown them standing ridiculously on top of each other. Mrs Beach sat too. The son stayed on his feet next to the white and gold quilt-fronted cocktail cabinet.

'You with the ambulance team, then?' he said.

'No. It was a complete coincidence I was there. I was just out taking a walk.'

'You saw the crash?' Rocky was quite excited, was watching him keenly.

'Not really. I was about fifty yards away. I heard the bang and started running.'

'You see this driver they never found?'

'No. Not at all. It was dark, remember. I heard later he'd run off but when I got there I was trying to help those in the cars still.'

'We don't know what Dad was doing in that car do we son?' Mrs Beach said.

'It's a mystery.'

'Police say it was hired but probably by someone giving a false name.' Mrs Beach sounded positively awed by her own proximity to such matters. Ramsey began to suspect her sudden accession to some kind of importance was delaying the shock of being widowed.

'Right mystery and no mistake,' the son repeated. He looked at Ramsey and blinked very little. 'What was it you had to say?' he said.

'Well I just wanted to reassure you – I thought it might help to know – he didn't suffer. It was instantaneous.'

'Oh, ta very much, very kind of you indeed,' Mrs Beach said. But, as he'd foreseen, the son was looking at him incredulously.

'You came all the way up here to tell us that?' he said. 'We're on the phone up here these days, you know.'

'Rocky!'

'No, it's all right, Mrs Beach, really. Your son's right. If it was just that of course I'd've phoned. The other thing that . . . look, this is a bit embarrassing.'

'Oh?'

'You see – I got into the car to see if there was anything I could do for . . . Mr Beach. As I said he –'

'Yeah. You said.'

'On the floor – on the mat – was a wallet. His as I found out later. When I saw it, you see, I put it in my pocket.'

'You what?'

'Yes, I know what you're thinking, Mr Beach, but it wasn't that. This may sound funny to you, but I could see some notes sticking out of it and I thought to myself if the police get hold of that they'll have it away at once and no-one the wiser.'

Rocky Beach looked at him appraisingly. 'You reckon,' he said.

'Yes. As a doctor I've had quite a bit to do with the police. You know – assault cases, battered wives, kids into glue-sniffing, and so on. I know it's not a nice thing to say but I've come not to have too much time for them.'

'Who has?' Mrs Beach said sententiously.

'So where's this wallet now?' Her son kept to the point.

'Here.' Ramsey produced it. 'It's my theory your father was putting it in his pocket and that's why he didn't have a seat belt on. Take it. It's absolutely as I found it, I promise. I only opened it to find your address.'

Rocky Beach took it from him sharply. Opening it he brazenly counted the money it held. A hundred and forty pounds, Ramsey knew.

'I wonder if, after all, I could have a cup of tea,' he said.

'Of course. Least we can do. Rocky, go and put the kettle on, will you, love.'

Rocky Beach scowled as if well understanding Ramsey's gambit. 'Why didn't you send it?' he said.

'I was going to. But it was going to be so hard to say what I've just said in a letter. And I was coming up North anyway so –'

158

'Oh?'

'I'm on a short golfing holiday.'

'Like playing where?'

'I was down at Lytham day before yesterday. Tomorrow I'm hoping –'

'Rocky – put that kettle on.'

Not happy, the son left the room. Ramsey pointed at what he'd purposely not looked at again since he'd first sighted it on entering the room.

'That's your husband there, isn't it?' he said.

'Yes. That's Sandy,' Mrs Beach said. On the mantlepiece was a blown-up snapshot of Beach and two other men in fishermen's gear standing on the hatch of a trawler.

'I had no idea he was a fisherman,' Ramsey said. 'You don't think of that in the middle of London.'

'He was for years,' Mrs Beach sniffed. He realised she was about to be possessed at last by a sense of loss.

'Was?' he said quickly.

'Gave it up three years ago. After our pools win. Nearly ninety thousand, you know.'

'Really?'

'Yes. But it goes through whole families. Sandy's brother Alan – he was on the boats and then there's his cousin, Ray, and before that . . .'

'Is Sandy's boat still working?'

'Oh yes. The "Jack London".'

Great. 'Is she out now?' he asked.

'No idea, have we Mum?' Rocky Beach had come back into the room and with him a tension utterly lost, Ramsey was sure, on the mother.

'No, couldn't say,' she said.

'You're the exception to the rule, then, are you, Mr Beach?' Ramsey said.

'How'd you mean?'

'You're not on the boats.'

'No, not in that sense.'

'Marine engineer, my Rocky,' Mrs Beach said. 'Does ever so well by it.'

'Real old boaster, aren't you, Mum?'

'Bought himself a catamaran. You should see it.'

'Second hand. I got it cheap.'

Oh yes, Ramsey thought, and could feel Rocky Beach feeling him think it.

'I'll go and make the tea,' Mrs Beach said. She levered herself up and left the room.

'It hasn't hit her yet,' Rocky Beach said. 'That's why I'm here.'

'Good for you. The shock takes people that way sometimes.'

'That's your professional experience, is it, Doctor?'

'Yes. People try to shut out bad news.'

'And you don't have much time for the police, you say.'

'Not a lot, frankly. I mean, I had this friend. Another doctor. He got into all kinds of trouble over some prescriptions he wrote. He had very good reasons for writing them but it ended up with him getting disbarred.'

He tried to look at Beach as equivocally as he knew how. His efforts produced a sniff. 'Yes, still, they've got a job to do haven't they?' Beach said. 'We wouldn't like it more than like.'

Ramsey shrugged. From the kitchen came the rattle of cups. He pushed his brain into overdrive as he tried to devise some neutral topic to get them through the next ten minutes.

So she had come full circle. She was back to listening to time slowing down in Ramsey's cottage. Alone. Not totally sure why she should be here and playing any of this waiting game except, if she was honest with herself, the feeling in her heart of hearts that it kept her, how to put it, *connected* with Ramsey. Face it, that was why she was here. Dany had made her welcome at the *manoîr* with a chic casualness that implied they'd known each other for years. But confronted with a home as impeccably civilised as its owner she had started to feel overwhelmed. Dany's signals seemed to be that they would see each other every day; become friends. Certainly. Well perhaps, Tessa had thought. And why not? But she refused to do everything *à deux*. A few hours pottering at the cottage – well, it needed airing – was made-to-measure isolation. She had not been able to say that Dany's *manoîr* evoked no memories of Artie Shaw's clarinet climaxing in *Crescendo in Blue*. She didn't like to think what tunes had been played and danced to *chez Dany* . . . She was quite sure. As instructed, they had driven down to the town square and discovered Marcel playing *boules*. As easy as that. Tessa had given the mute Ramsey's note. He had read it, smiled toothily and touched his forehead. By that she might understand she had a 'minder'. Whatever the melodramatic excess, she had slept the better for it.

Gosh, the cottage was stuffy. It airlessly smelt of leather and wood and dust. She opened the side casement of the huge window looking out over the marine painting of the harbour. The clouds had mostly gone. Those few left were white and sunshine was streaming in through the windows on the other side of the house. Oh, the petunias! They had looked as if they might yet revive put on a life support system. Still in her house-coat she went into the kitchen and –

it was as good as anything – filled the kettle. She opened the front door. Marcel was leaning against Ramsey's Light Fifteen across from it, working a pattern of beautiful intricacy with his yo-yo. Seeing what she was about to do he somehow had curtailed the arabesque and pocketed the plaything in one curt move and was coming over to her. Gently he indicated he should water the flowers in the hanging bowl. She let him have the kettle.

'Café?' she exaggerated with her mouth.

He nodded happily. Standing waiting for the kettle in the sunshine she dared to realise she might be happy too.

The room had not been made up yet. Ignoring the lop-sided chest of drawers he went straight for the scuffed, once expensive, grip. Already unzipped it was stuffed with clothes: sweaters, shirts. New stuff mainly. There was an inside pocket; papers inside it by the feel of it. He unzipped it and worked them out. Passport! Yes, his photo. Funny – the name was Ramsey and it did say Doctor. Maybe a piece of hake but a bloody good one if it was. Traveller's cheques, Swiss francs. Funny again. Or was it he just knew where the smart money went these days . . . What the hell was this. All in French. *Carte de bloody séjours*. Not another fucking French connection. He took a Pools envelope out of his Levi jacket and as quickly as he was able copied what seemed the address on the card. Good. He put the papers back the way they'd been and the grip back alongside the washstand. He checked the wardrobe just in case. No, not a sign of a golf-club anywhere and no golf gear in with the clothes. No bag or anything in the car, either. He'd checked that as he'd come across the car park. Very funny. Not a complete liar, it seemed, but a long way from being straight. Standing stock-still for a moment in the centre of the shabby room, Rocky Beach sniffed.

Once again seagulls skirled and screamed in the sky. A scrap thrown their way and they were diving down for it, side-swiping each other to snatch it clean away. There were plenty of targets to keep them wheeling overhead. Three trawlers had come in on the dawn tide. Viewed close to, the quayside and adjacent wholesalers' market gave the lie to his impression of the day before that Fleetwood was a town operating at quarter pace. Fork-lift trucks zigged and zagged under the great open, hangar-like sheds. Boxes rattled along roller tracks. Vans backed up, hooted and accelerated away. Porters in shiny, greasy caps and with sacking about their shoulders crissed and crossed in organised chaos. Chains clattered like giants' rattles as davits swung and more box and basket laden nets were swung up from the boats to the men waiting on the high quay wall. The smell of fish was everywhere and nowhere. Amid the gull screams, the 'mind yer backs' shouts, and the sudden snorts of capstans, he had already ceased to notice it.

From the shadow of a vast vertical steel support pillar, Ramsey watched with satisfaction. A visit to the Harbour Master's office was now going to be superfluous. One of the trawlers newly tied up alongside was the 'Jack London'. It was unloading now, and seemed to have had a good trip. Basket after crammed basket of gleaming fish was being manhandled away from the quayside where she lay. Well, that proved nothing – not even if he was following a completely false scent amid all the fish.

Sandy Beach, after all, killer in error of Simon Wood had left the 'Jack London' some three years ago. What was cause and effect was hard to say. He could have left because the alleged pools win that had bought him his tatty, vulgar nouveau-richness was in fact money coming in from an entirely different source. A man for whom gutting fish was commonplace might find it easier, for instance, to set himself up in business as a hired killer. The 'Jack London' might be as honest a craft as ever put out to sea. But Rocky Beach didn't encourage such a theory. He had been tight, hostile, and probing throughout their meeting. Defensive first and last he had seemed no more upset over his father's death than his mother, as complacent in grief as over her possessions. Moreover, he had not seemed particularly surprised, which in a way was more indicative . . .

Ramsey stiffened. He drew closer to the pillar and into its full shadow. As if conjured by his thoughts on the son, Rocky Beach, leather blousoned and foxy-red haired, was threading his way along the quayside. Sure enough it was at the 'Jack London' that he stopped. As if he'd done it many times he swung on to the top of the iron ladder protruding up above the wall. His hair caught the sun, then dropped from view as he clambered down. Well maybe the 'Jack London' was as honest as the day was long, when the day in question was Christmas at the North Pole . . .

With a light thud Rocky Beach jumped across on to the deck of the 'Jack London'. The three hands working the hatch all looked up at the impact but it was McCrae's eyes that Beach chose to catch. He flicked his own in the direction of the wheel house. McCrae, ruddy-faced and curly-haired, and big with it, stopped coiling a rope and shambled after him. He seemed clumsy but he was only a pace behind Beach as they reached the wheel house door.

Inside, the radio playing softly on long-wave, Gibson, the skipper, was still writing up his log-sheets. He looked up as their bodies bulked out his light.

'We've hit trouble,' Rocky Beach said. 'Could have.'

Gibson's enquiring look didn't change. His big hand reached out and turned off the radio. He needed a shave. The grey stubble accentuated his age and his very evident tiredness. The old fart's getting past it, Rocky Beach thought.

'The police turn up your old man's record?' Gibson said finally. He didn't sound alarmed but you didn't know if he'd worked out he ought to be.

'No,' Rocky Beach said. 'This bloke. Nosing around. Came to the house last night asking questions.'

'Police?' McCrae said. His accent was neither Scots nor Northern Irish but it turned the one word into two.

'Don't know. Says he's a doctor. He's got paper work that backs him up.'

'Oh?' Gibson said. 'He so generous he let you check it?'

'He's staying at the "Morphet". Big Jack let me have a little look round.'

'Ah. Canny.'

'But why'd he come to yer house?' McCrae said.

'That's it. He said he was there when the crash happened. Wanted to tell us the old man never knew what hit him . . .'

'And?'

'And he had Dad's wallet. Said he didn't want to let the Bill snaffle it.' Gibson and McCrae looked at each other.

'He's got to be the police,' McCrae said. A hint of fun seemed to glint in his eye. 'Why don't you let me take him out?'

Gibson held up his huge, squat hand. Liver spots did not add to its delicacy. 'Easy,' he said. 'No over-loading the winch. What did you make of him, Rocky?'

'I don't know. Thing is him being a doctor. He could've been there when you-know-who bought it. He kept hinting he *was* dodgy – as a doctor, you know. You know, er –'

'Struck off,' McCrae supplied.

'That's it.'

'Could he be from another firm?' Gibson asked. Rocky Beach shrugged.

'It's possible,' Gibson said. 'Or if he's in the business he might have heard a whisper from some other medic there's ways up here of getting rich.'

'But we don't want him, do we?' Rocky Beach said.

'No. No. I never said that. Bring it up this afternoon. Meanwhile we all behave as normal and leave any next move to him.'

'What if he makes us an offer?' Beach said.

'We're reasonable men, Rocky, I'm sure,' Gibson said with no trace of a smile.

163

'And if he *is* trouble?' McCrae insisted.

'Then we'll take up your offer, Alex,' Gibson said. 'You can strike him off once and for all.' This time the tired Captain allowed himself a short smile at his joke.

Having Ramsey in common and nothing else they nevertheless seemed to have everything. Tessa found she experienced no feeling of constraint in Dany's company. For a brief while this surprised her but the reason was too obvious for her not to see it very quickly. Both of them might harbour plans, hopes, and fantasies but if, reduced to sexist fairy-tale terms, they were two princesses waiting for their knight to rein in his charger and made the decision which one to carry off, they were so unalike that no local jockeying for position could give either of them a material advantage. Chalk and cheese, they could only abide his choice. And if he chose chalk there was no way cheese could either influence his decision or transmute herself. Nor did they have magic spells to turn each other into toads or, if they did, it would have been tacky to resort to them. Before their first car journey together was over Tessa had begun to detect a very genuine ring to Dany's responses. She might wrap up her actions in a feminine-masculine blend of fashion and tough-guy talk but the core of what she said and did seemed invariably to contain consideration for those around her.

'Are you sure I didn't twist your arm too much and you'd really like something stronger?' Dany said. There. A good way of making her point. There was no way that that was affected.

'I don't mind in the least being a British cliché,' Tessa smiled. 'It's tea-time and tea is what I feel like.'

'The cup that cheers,' Dany said, 'and to hell with the liver.'

Away from the front of Port En Bessin it was still warm enough to sit outside. The low sun came under the Stella Artois advertising awning and shed a glowing warmth on their arms and legs. Dany had that blonde's golden tan which promises it goes all the way through to the bone. She was wearing a pocketed shirt-blouse, slacks that were not quite a matching olive and a man's gold Omega. She looked good looking like Lee Remick looking good.

'You'd like to see the hospital where Ramsey works,' she now said. It came out like a statement freely volunteered.

'Yes. yes I would.' But only now had she realised it was something she did want.

'We'll drive back that way. I'll smuggle you in. But not, I promise, via the maternity wing.'

'That would be a touch premature.'

'For me too, alas.' A distant look softened the focus in Dany's eyes. For a moment they weren't worldly. Tessa was afraid an old regret might spoil the sunlit moment. By way of diversion she said the first thing to come into her head.

'May I ask you something?' she said.

'Well, you can always *ask*.' It was said with a cool, smiling roguishness and the old regret had gone. The eyes were wary again.

'You won't laugh?'

'I don't promise not to. But probably not.'

'Ramsey told me you met in the South China Sea – is that the truth?'

'He told you that?'

'Yes.'

'Then why do you need to ask me?'

'I . . . well, I asked him where he met you and –'

'I'm flattered.'

'Yes, well I was jealous, wasn't I?'

'I hope so.'

'And he said "in the South China Sea". And I didn't believe him.'

'Why not?'

'I thought it was his polite way of saying mind your own business.'

'Ah, I see . . . well, you should have.'

'Believed him?'

'Yes. It's true. It was nearly four years ago. We were working for *Médicins du Monde* – patrolling the sea searching for boat people.' Tessa mentally blinked. She could see Ramsey in the job instantly but Dany, surely, didn't inhabit the same galaxy as the saline drip.

'I didn't know it still went on.'

'Oh yes. It's just not news any more.'

'Isn't it dangerous?'

Dany considered. It was if she had inhaled the thought and was waiting to breathe it out. 'It didn't turn out to be dangerous for us,' was all she said.

'He's never talked about it.' Tessa realised she must sound quite disgruntled. Dany smiled and reached for the holder to her glass.

'Ramsey doesn't talk about a lot of things until you know him,' she said. She glanced at Tessa.

'And not much then,' she gently added. She sipped her tea.

There are worse places to be on a late afternoon-early evening than Wilmslow Railway Station but, equally, a fair number that are usually more attractive. The somewhat handsome, well-built business man sitting on the bench seat was clearly using his copy of *The Financial Times* to occupy his thoughts usefully until circumstances made for a more congenial environment. He read steadily, oblivious to the few other travellers pacing the down platform in the happy knowledge they were still some half-hour ahead of the evening Manchester commuter rush. When a somewhat ageing tearaway type had enough social gall to plonk his briefcase on the bench and sit down beside it, the business man did permit himself use of the brief stranger to stranger eye-contact convention allows at such moments. Clearly not liking what he saw, the man returned to the columns with which he plainly felt he had more in common. The tearaway shifted on his seat, scratched the side of his head, looked at two girls on the opposite platform. Martin Lambert and Rocky Beach sat side by side without talking for some minute and a half.

'Name's Ramsey,' Beach then said. He said it very softly even though he was looking away from Lambert at the time.

'He says he's a doctor. Lives in France.'

'Ah, yes. Does he look a little French? About six foot? Slim, dark hair?' Lambert's breath did not so much as stir the paper that he continued, it seemed, to read.

'Yeah. That's him.'

'Where in France?'

'Wrote what was in his papers down, didn't I.'

'Good.'

'He said he was there. Said he saw the old man get it.'

'He was telling the truth. We were trying to get him.'

'Fucking arseholes.' From up the track came a sustained metallic braying. The London-bound Inter-City was swaying in.

'Where is he now?' Lambert said.

'Pub in Fleetwood.'

Lambert closed and meticulously folded his paper. He did it just in advance of the whoosh of air that swept down the platform alongside the rattling train. With so much noise tearing the air it was quite safe, indeed necessary, for Lambert to raise his voice.

'When he moves from the pub, hit him,' he said. 'Hard. Permanently.' He began to walk towards the nearest carriage door. The briefcase, it had to be said, looked far less incongruous alongside his subdued pinstripes than it had against Rocky Beach's jeans. They in any case looked far more at home among the assorted clothes of the handful of newly arrived ticket holders shuffling towards the barrier.

FOURTEEN

Ramsey used the full tilt back of the glass as a chance to glance at the clock. Pub time would put it about ten minutes fast. Give it five more minutes then. Good, trip to Blackpool or not, the day had crawled.

'So what's a deckie earn today?' he continued.

The big landlord of the big, sadly near-empty pub grunted in what might have been his approximation to humour. 'Thinking of taking it up?' he said.

Ramsey grinned and held up his hands. 'Too much Fairy Liquid,' he said. And you could say the same for the bloody beer, he thought. 'Hardly in a deckie's class, eh?' He nodded at the photograph. 'Or in Mr Farm's.'

'Ah, now you're talking. Ever see him play?'

'At Stamford Bridge once. Stopped a header from Roy Bentley, I've no idea to this day how he managed it.'

The landlord stopped swabbing the bar's sticky wood with a cloth. 'He stopped a lot they wouldn't stop now,' he said. 'Mind you, I can't think of a header of the ball today comes anywhere near Bentley.'

'Right. And just think of what he earned compared with your Lineker's and the like today.'

'Lineker,' the landlord said in half-derision. 'Doesn't have Barrass marking him, does he? But he gets a touch more than twelve per cent of the catch for all that and I suppose I don't begrudge him.'

'That the going rate?'

'Yep. About three hundred a trip, these days. A lot more than in mine . . . but so's inflation.'

'Still not a fortune, is it?'

'Nope. And then you got to remember all the times it's too rough to put out. Too rough to stop out. Force Six in the North Sea's uncomfortable. In the Irish Sea it's unworkable. Lose a net – that's eight grand down the swanee.'

The landlord raised his eyebrows. Ramsey pulled a face. 'Enough to turn you to crime,' he said. He drained his glass.

The landlord's eyes grew canny. 'Ah, well, we leave that to the police,' he said.

Ramsey grinned. He sent the empty straight glass shimmering back across the bar. 'Think I'll take a stroll and see if I can get myself a little tired,' he said. 'See you in the morning.'

He went out. In the corner the old man and woman sitting over one half of Guinness never so much as blinked as he went by. The

167

landlord stifled a yawn. Another eight minutes before he could finish off another evening that was only going to work out at a loss. The slight, wiry middle-aged drinker at the far table got up and brought his shorts glass up to the counter.

'Same again, Kenny?' the landlord asked.

'No. Call it a day. And give us five tens for the phone, will you, pal?'

Hugging the shadows he approached the dock down the Coronation Street of a side road. Just before the corner he halted. The entrance gate to the dock area had not been closed. It was probably seldom if ever moved. He'd established earlier that a lot of crews slept aboard their berthed vessels. There were lamps high-lighting random areas about and just beyond the gate but that wasn't too bad. Where there were lights there were shadows. The casual eye couldn't adjust for both at once and under his blue-black blouson he was wearing a black roll-neck sweater. He could see one, two, men moving about inside the well-lit reception office next to the gate. It took an act of faith to really realise it but the reverse did not apply: the lighting was not two-way. For them the windows would be mirror-black and there was no way they could see him. He felt his stomach contract. He had remembered the roller blind shooting up in the house in Seagram Street and the feeling of being trapped in a goldfish bowl and about to be impaled. If they had gone for him from the garden . . . Come on. This was now, not then, and no time for faint resolve. He moved forward in a quick diagonal across the road. At once he felt a positive quickening of excitement lift him. The soles of his feet felt nicely on edge in the light-fitting trainers. The weight of the monkey-wrench rammed in the waistband of his trousers made him feel high-powered.

He was inside the gates. No problem. But still with a long way to go. The quayside, the fish market hangar were quite a way ahead up the rutted, beaten earthtrack. Immediately to the right was the romantically down-beat sprawl of a rust-ridden scrap heap. Across to the left was a trailer park. Artics parked higgledy-piggledy made it look like a graveyard from pre-history. One silhouetted combination had been left with its tractor tilted forward in four-square obeisance. Someone had half-axed the beast's head off. A coiling tendon stood clearly out against a light. Ramsey smiled. The tractor's posture reminded him of the Pope kissing the earth at Lyons.

He stopped smiling. In the mid-distance headlights had suddenly turned a right-angle to come jolting towards him. He moved swiftly, awkwardly to his right across treacherously uneven, metal-strewn ground. But safely enough. His ankles remained intact and as the battered Sherpa bucked past he was well beyond the sweep of its beams. Gathering his breath he started to move on. Only to freeze. Very close he heard a human grunt. There was a scuffling sound. Panting. He relaxed again. Somewhere in the shadows of the scrap-heap a couple were making love in age-old mean town circumstances. One of them, the girl, was finding the experience satisfactory. Well good luck to them. He moved quietly on.

Three stealthy minutes later he had reached the great hangar-shed of the fish market. Curious. You'd think that at night, empty of its haggling, morning pandemonium, it would seem bigger. But it didn't; it seemed smaller, shrunken. Well, perhaps it was the temperature. In spite of his warm clothing, in spite of the sweat on his temples, he shivered. There was a damp tang coming in off the sea on the steady breeze. Ah. A band of light it was impossible not to cross. He did so purposefully, a deckie returning from the pub. Now he had regained the pillar he had used as cover several centuries ago that morning. Good. The 'Jack London' was still there. Beyond riding up higher against the quay wall on the tide, she hadn't moved one inch. Her dark length was as quiet and devoid of motion as Lester Piggott's face in a tight finish. But bad. The crew in the trawler one mooring along were making a night of it aboard. Lights blazed and the noise of a television commentary came distantly to him. Well maybe good after all. The noise might cover a multitude of break-ins. Look out!

More headlights were carving up the distant night. Coming his way. He flattened against the pillar. A small car . . . a mini-van. *Merde*, a police car. Stopping. Hell, it was the sort they carried dogs in. As the two young coppers got out Ramsey reached for the monkey wrench. With infinite caution he worked it free. Ditch this and it would be eighteen months off his sentence! He reached for a handerchief. The absence of finger-prints . . . Hang on. Relax. The two coppers had only come up here for a fast smoke. Well, it was to be hoped it would be fast. Silently Ramsey sighed. The night was still young and there was plenty of time for it to put years on him.

The Penta, The Crest, The Holiday Inn. They continually rang the changes but always around the Heathrow perimeter. This time the briefcase that, along with certain information, had changed hands at Wilmslow's station had temporarily fetched up on a sofa in a suite at the Sheraton Skyline. It was now empty. Its contents were undergoing a transformation in the centre of the room. A 'C change' as Lambert had heard it called. Sitting at the other end of the sofa, he yawned. The trouble with this system was that once the production line started rolling you were in *à perpétuité*. No room service. No going down to bring yourself up an attention-drawing tray of drinks. Still, not too long now.

The centre of the room resembled at first glance an emergency operation. Two masked, gloved and overalled women were gathered about two tables brought together there under the main lighting fixture. The addition of a patient might have made them fugitives from *M.A.S.H.* But there was no patient and the small scales had never belonged to Justice.

A polythene sheet covered the tables. At one end rolling pins and a marble slab ensured the cocaine crystals Lambert had delivered were being pulverised to a smooth even powder, similar in texture to that of the Boots' glucose also in plentiful supply. Close enough consistency was guaranteed by means of tea-strainers through which the still pure coke was sieved into a Pyrex mixing bowl. The odd obdurate crystal went back to square one. The fine enough coke was then being weighed on the laboratory scales by one of the two women. Weighed and reweighed, as she made certain its proportion to the glucose was not over-generous. One-ounce cuts were the object of the exercise. Some two hundred and fifty would result from the original two kilos of pure cocaine and the pile of rubber-banded polythene sandwich bags was growing. A fine white dust hung in the air but the nearby presence of a stack of black plastic bin-liners and a small hand vacuum suggested that, come the morning, the chamber maid would be in no danger of forming an untoward addiction. For the moment the bagging up operation had outstripped the up-stream processes. One of the women straightened up and sighed. She placed both hands on the small of her back and arched her spine backwards. She moved over towards Lambert, the perfect picture of a disposably gowned angel of mercy.

'We do have the right stuff this time?' he said drily.

The woman nodded. 'I ran an alkaloid on it,' she said through the mask in a surprisingly young voice. 'It's American Standards Association ninety per cent pure Columbian gem of the ocean.'

Lambert grunted. He didn't like her cocksureness. 'That bad batch,' he said. 'We're still having problems on account of it.'

The woman stretched her arms out like a scare-crow or a Christ.

'That wasn't me,' she said. Behind the mask she might have grinned. 'I didn't drop out of Warwick for nothing.'

Lambert nodded. He watched her as she went back to the production line. She was cocky but it was true they had never had trouble from her. And, valuably, she was not a user herself.

He yawned again as he looked at his watch. The two movements caused the paper in his breast pocket to crackle. He smiled as he completed the yawn. A French address on an English pools coupon

170

was a curious coming together. But useful . . . very useful. Cocaine made strange bedfellows.

The police had moved on. Two dog-ends somewhere over there marked their malfeasance. In fact they'd done him a favour. In the long eternity their two tips had glowed away, no movement had come from the 'Jack London'. Ramsey felt very cold but even more highly charged. Making sure the wrench was firmly wedged again he loped quickly to the quay-side.

The iron ladder was burning cold against his hand. He swung around its top and was down below the top of the quay wall inside a second. He paused, then jumped down on to the deck, landing on his toes. It made a noise like the fall of Nineveh or no noise at all. The commentator's voice, word for word audible now, didn't miss a beat as it whipped itself up into a synthetic frenzy. Oh yes, the Bruno-Norman fight. He'd better move fast, that wouldn't be lasting long. But still it seemed there was no one aboard. No one had come at him with a marline spike or a Polaris. Time to press home his advantage. He made for the companion-way.

It was tight down here: a bottle-neck. This is where they would jump him. His throat seemed very vulnerable. Small though it was, it was with a sense of expanding relief that he opened the door of what must be the crew's cabin. A lighter shade of dark came through a port hole. On the sea-facing side. He could risk a light. From his blouson pocket he took his ENT torch. This was not what its pencil-wide beam had been designed to look into but the object of his search was still, in broad terms, a matter of medical malfunction. Maybe he should have brought a scalpel too.

Silicone-breasted centrefolds on the wall, greasy playing cards, oil skins, two non-matching trainers, a torn pair of jeans whose pockets were . . . quite empty. He made what he speedily realised was a less than scientific, random sampling kind of search. The seat locker was empty of all except a pile of magazines and a smell that, strong enough to overcome the general stench of fish, took him straight back to school and the gym changing room. He lowered the top back down. Well, you couldn't expect anything here. He moved into the adjoining cabin – the Captain's.

There was hardly anything more for the Skipper's comfort than for the crew's. A vestigial increase in privacy was about all: a battery razor, a balaclava, a book of cross-words – surprisingly neatly completed. A leather-framed photo of a woman with two teenage daughters who from their neatly groomed, not unstylish appearance looked as though they had every reason to be proud of their Dad. In the pockets of the jacket hung on the door, nothing. He examined the

171

fluff in close-up under the bright thin beam but it looked only like fluff. Under the bunk's mattress, nothing. Nothing under the pillow. He tried the mini-cupboards set in under the seat and alongside the mirror. A discarded toothbrush, a tube of Savlon, a broken watch-strap, a ball of twine.

Nothing.

There remained the wheel house. That meant retracing his steps. The known is usually more terrifying than the unknown. The narrowness of the companion way, the extent to which, in the dark, he could be taken at a physical disadvantage swept over him as he doused his light. For an instant he thought as a child again. Monks in high pointed cowls were waiting outside to tighten the cords of their gowns about his throat . . . Come on! It was absurd to be frightened over fantasies of his own imagining when very real only too human threats to his safety were infinitely more likely and potentially much closer. And it was absurd to have come so far and not explore the most likely place to house evidence of the 'Jack London's' involvement in drug-running. Breathing through his open mouth so as to make no human or demon-arousing noise, holding the wrench before him at arm's length like a holy relic to ward off spirits, he groped towards the foot of the companion way. The noise of the television began to restore him to the world of the everyday. The sky, visible as he mounted, showed a rent in clouds whose edges were silvered by moonlight. As he regained the deck, unheard and unnoticed, it seemed, his crisis of claustrophobic nerves left him. He was himself again as he made for the wheel house.

Damn! Locked! And his credit card technique was no 'open sesame'. Hmmn. The outer end of the Yale-type bolt was quite proud. If he could get the wrench around it maybe he could twist the entire . . . No. There was a collar around the lock. The fight was between rounds. Somebody was needing to pull out all the stops in the grand stand finish to what had now come down to a test of character. He pushed with his shoulder and foot against the door. At the bottom there was considerable give. He knelt down. Yes, near the bottom he could get the handle of the wrench between the sea-warped door and the jamb. Right. Deep breath. Keeping the wrench as horizontal as possible he started to work it upwards. It was heavy going. He could feel the door taking the strain, more easily than he could. About a third of the way up was all he could manage. He caught his breath again. He was hot now, sweating again. And from some points on the quay surely visible. One more time. Gritting his teeth, straining, then straining some more he levered the wrench back toward him. With the report of a pistol firing the door shot away from him. He all but fell back, then, re-recoiling, dived across the

172

threshold. The floor hit him hard but he was in. He got to his feet and pushed the door to. Ah yes, the interior lock fitting, the female bit, had come right out of the jamb.

More exposed here but . . . all the same. He risked the torch again. Yes. This was more like. Radar, sonar, Decca stuff, a domestic TV, a sea-going radio-transceiver. A chart storage desk full of . . . charts. This entire ship was too predictable. The log. Crouching on the floor he examined it. The entry for the last trip spoke of twelve baskets of top quality plaice. Well it would wouldn't it . . . Pencils, a set-square, dividers . . . A paper-wrapped cube of sugar. He stiffened and warily tried the cube against his teeth and tongue. Sugar. Not even laced with L.S.D. Beaten. He hadn't proved a thing. That in itself didn't disprove anything but . . . well, maybe he was in danger of over-staying his welcome. Just possibly he could force the bit of lock catch back on hard enough to disguise he'd ever been aboard.

His pencil beam swept the floor. What would the lock's trajectory have most likely been? Ah there it was, hard to make out on that bag. He stooped to retrieve the lock and only then realised the webbing and canvas army surplus sort of bag was something he'd missed. He rummaged inside – empty. But something small and sharply hard in the bottom seam.

Bingo! He crouched on the floor. With some effort he punched and pulled the bag inside out. Grains of white powder had worked themselves into the coarse texture. Yes! He could feel his pulse accelerating from sheer excitement now. He picked up a few grains on the tip of his moistened finger. He transferred them to his tongue. No question. From his hip pocket he took an envelope. He salvaged as many crystals as he could quickly manage into it before repocketing it. He turned the bag the right way out and stood up. What to do with what he'd found was still to be decided but, directly or indirectly, this stinking kettle of fish had a lot to do with Exton Waite's death, with Kate Ross's and with God alone knew how many other sordid, agony-racked endings. One way or another he'd see they got what they had coming.

No. As well as being lucky he'd been silly. There was no way to fake that door hadn't been forced. Just get out while the getting was good. He slipped out of the wheel house and back along the deck. He clasped the iron-cold ladder in the quay-wall and started on up. All of two steps. A sudden flood of light and surge of music stopped him in his upwardly mobile tracks. The boxing had finished. Somebody had come out on the deck of the trawler moored next along.

'Big jessie,' he heard a Scots voice say. Huddled to the ladder like a monkey on a stick he could not look to see what was happening. If the night had a thousand eyes again they were all boring into the back of his neck. Holding his breath he heard muffled sounds, indecipherable against the music and then, abruptly, the unmistakable noise of a man peeing forcefully into water. It went on and on. At last there was a dwindling away, a sighing, a sound he could now make out as a zip being zipped and a grunt of satisfaction. Steps padded across a deck. The light and music levels were alike reduced as a door closed. Ramsey sighed. Whatever the man's relief it was as nothing to his own.

He climbed a few cautious rungs and raised his head above the parapet of the quay wall. Nobody blew it off. All clear. The no-man's land strip of road-cum-work area between him and the high black safety of the fishing market shed glittered malignantly under the down-shine of a scattering of lamps. But there was no shirking it. So go! He pulled himself on to the quay and, not quite running, crossed in a straight line. There! He had gained the shadows of the vast hangar and was still in one piece. OK: the shortest distance for him and his new-found evidence was now a straight line.

He moved off. With his fifth step an engine roared and head-lamps cut a horizontal trench through the darkness. It blindingly flowed around him. He was impaled like a Junkers in a search-light. Even as he began, twisting away, to hope it was the police high-beaming him like this, he half-heard beneath the engine's idling a whining, whirring, rattling. His head snapped round. Outside the light's field a ghostly bulk was rising up. Bearing down rather. Exploding out of the darkness a fork-lift truck, its fangs at belly height, was charging at him from no more than four yards away. Adrenalin rushed instinct to him in an attempt at self-preservation. Centre for Guy's once again he dodged to the left and took a half-step toward the truck. It swerved a late fraction and on that instant he came hard off his left foot with a giant side step to the right. It would have cut no ears in Madrid but the horns of the truck were gone by. He had a corner of eye impression of a man wrenching a wheel and then a horrendous violent shrieking of metal told him the truck had hit something as solid as itself.

Not his worry. He dodged again out of the light and straightway saw two men, one very wide and heavy, one tall and heavy advancing on him. Both of them carried box-hooks at the ready. He turned as he fumbled the wrench out. Not good. The truck had hit a pillar. But the driver was unhurt. On his feet, his own box-hook cocked, he too was closing in. Behind the headlights found them, lost them again as, revving, the car manoeuvred.

'Stow that,' the broad man shouted. 'We haven't sold tickets.'

The car lights were cut along with its engine. If he could make it to the other trawler. But they'd side with their own kind. And for the moment the thin, third man – shit! he'd been drinking in the 'Morphet' – was cutting off that line of retreat. A Western. It was a Western. It wasn't a corral but they were closing in on him. He sidestepped along. If he could get his back against the next pillar.

'Find what you want, snooper?' the broad man sneered. There was a matter of fact Northern menace about the way he said it.

'I'm after a job,' Ramsey said. 'You know. Not fishing. Ask Rocky.'

The tall, curly-haired man laughed. 'You're about to be made redundant,' he said.

'I'm a doctor. I can be –'

Something punched him hard in the left shoulder, waited and then tore agonisingly at his flesh. Jesus! While he'd been bluffing the third man had pounced. As he tried to retrieve his hook Ramsey chopped the wrench down on his wrist in flat-out animal reaction. The pistol-crack of the bone breaking was less than a half-second ahead of the man's falsetto scream. He spun away and as the hook clattered to the concrete Ramsey spun too, back and downwards. Just in time. The broad man's hook hissed as it swung past his head and then his torn shoulder was butting agonisingly into the man's gut. They locked motionless for a moment and then, as hard as he could, Ramsey smashed the wrench home hard against the side of the man's left knee. The man gave a loud shout-groan and then as he fell ponderously away his weight was gone from Ramsey. A chance took its place. The tall man had lost heart, was recoiling. There was a gap.

Ramsey went for it. Taking off from his semi-crouch he gave it everything he had. His wrench made it a relay race. He was past the tall man on sheer speed aware of pain in his left shoulder and blood spurting into his shirt and not aware of it at all. Jesus, the hangar was vast. As he heard shouts, the car revving up, he realised it was endless. The nightmarishness of it all hit him. The pain in his shoulder was spreading across his chest down to his belly, his knees. His heart had no gaps between its pulses as it swelled. It was so simple! He couldn't run fast enough. He was in his forties not twenties and underneath the agony tearing at his gasping lungs the leg speed just wasn't there.

The town was so close. And so impossibly far. God! Light flooded everywhere as the car got him in its lights again. Desperately hoping nothing would catch his feet, break his shins, Ramsey swerved to the left of the line of pillars to prevent his being run over. If he could make it to the scrap-heap! A game of hide and seek would lower the odds!

It wasn't going to be on. The car, a Capri, with Rocky Beach, went hurtling straight by. It skidded around broadside opposite the heap.

From there it also commanded any run to the dock gates. He was stymied in two directions.

And collapsing. He couldn't keep this up. The trainers were a mockery. He had stepped into young men's shoes. There was a cone of darkness off to his left. He skidded to a doubled-over halt in its black sanctuary. He straightened, doubled over again, straightened. Blood burnt his throat as he rasped air down into his sand-papered lungs. Silence was out of the question. He was spent, his chest was heaving like an anaesthetist's bladder. This was the peaks of Everest without oxygen. The car was ahead of him. And behind him he could hear voices. And, yes, hell, torch beams were beginning to rake the huge shed in an eliminating cross-fire. Maybe thirty seconds before they pin-pointed him. There was maybe one chance. The trailer park. It might be open to the sea. He could swim for it. Or at least there, perhaps, he could try for the game of hide and seek. He still had the wrench.

A few more seconds. He put the wrench down, awkwardly pulled a handkerchief out of his left pocket with his right hand. He wadded the handkerchief and got it up inside his sweater to his left shoulder. Nasty. Superficial but ragged. A lot of blood gone. He pressed the handkerchief against the wound. Unbelievable. In the far distance a bus was turning a corner. And here he was. In danger of losing his life. All right – the voices were getting close. He bent to retrieve the wrench and once more took off from a standing start.

A minute ago he wouldn't have believed it possible but he was instantly back up to some kind of speed. As concrete gave way to beaten mud, shouts and the sound of the car pursued him. He was in among the trailers. Gritty, rutted dirt tried to throw him off balance. The great bulks were parked unsystematically. He slowed to go round one dead ahead and, oh God, the exhaustion was worse than before, found he simply couldn't start sprinting again.

His heart was begging to explode. He felt as if, suffocatingly cutting off his air intake, he might throw up. He ducked down alongside the artic's huge rear axle. His brain raced in time with his pulse. Plenty of shadow, plenty of places to squirm away into. But not that far behind he could see the torches criss-crossing relentlessly on beneath the undercarriages of trailers he'd already passed.

The sea must be close here. Its waters lapped audibly. He turned his head. Light glinted on waves not forty yards away. And he was a better swimmer than most. For a few more seconds while sweat and blood began to congeal across his chest he rested collecting himself. Then he found he had to make a run for it yet again.

Twenty yards from the edge of the trailer park he realised he had made a fundamental error. The way to the sea was not open. A wire fence about the perimeter was taking on meshed definition. It was about three metres high. It bent inwards at the top as if to ward off soccer thugs. The mesh was fine. There were no heavy cross-strands. As shouts came again from behind and less diffusely he looked left and right for the support poles. No help. They were slender and the far side of the wire.

Beyond rational calculation now, he gathered himself and found energy and air from some last pocket deep inside him. He ran at the fence and jumped. His fingers gripped for the mesh like a monkey's. His trainers scrabbled for a toe-hold. Perhaps if his shoulder could have taken its share of the strain, if his lungs had not been extended beyond endurance, if it had been daylight, if he had had time, he might have made it. But now there was no way. Defeated, he dropped back to the ground. Once again he was confronted by a gang of men closing in on him. Four now. Rocky Beach had joined the party.

'Let me have him,' said the man whose wrist he'd broken. He was carrying a length of pipe now. They were all carrying things to hit him with.

Panting, Ramsey, the doctor, stood crouched over like a species of ape. He swung his arms from side to side. He raised the wrench to shoulder height as, head swivelling, he tried to judge who would strike at him first.

In the background a trailer broadside on had P. Devlin and Sons, Wexford, as its straight up and down livery.

'You once went to the opera there with Anne,' a voice far off down a long road in Ramsey's head said to him. He was amazed to hear it but knew neither it nor the memory had anything to do with him now.

It was a small, English gesture and arguably foolish too, but she had insisted on making herself mistress of Ramsey's cottage for an entire day and entertaining Dany to dinner. In Barfleur even her choice of menu – potato and leek soup, sole bonne femme – must have seemed ridiculously commonplace. Dany had seemed to divine that the invitation, however trite, meant something. She had accepted at once and with a smile that did not seem a cosmetic adjunct. And she had stayed late. Although conversation had dwindled to an easy, unforced silence, she was showing no inclination to go yet. Perhaps, Tessa thought, it was a rare pleasure for her to be here at the heart of Ramsey's domain when the owner was not filling the foreground for her with his brooding, kind, enigmatic, wonderful presence. Oh shit! Don't think of him. Think of someone you don't like.

As Tessa lifted the glass to sip more armagnac the image of her mother in the chapel of Lincoln College came, unbidden it seemed, to her mind. So she didn't like her mother then. Well, cheers, what was so new about that bit of information? Well, perhaps this was a small formal acknowledgement to herself of a status quo that would persist for ever now. Whatever primrose path to Parliament Beryl now trod she would have none of her mother. The day in Oxford had ended in, if not a clean, a complete amputation. She had lost two parents this year. Sad. There had been times when she had been little and her father –

'Brrrr.' Very dramatically Dany had shivered.

'Gosh,' Tessa said, glad of a topic come to hand. 'Someone just stepped on your grave?'

Dany looked at her earnestly. 'I'm sorry?' she said.

'It's an English expression. When people suddenly shiver. You're doing it because someone's just walked over the bit of ground that one day will be your grave.'

'Oh. I've never heard that,' Dany said.

'Well – it's a bit old-fashioned these days.'

'Very much so in my case. I intend to be cremated.' Dany smiled a remote smile as if to take the edge of seriousness from her declaration.

'Perhaps we should be getting along back now,' she said.

Both women got to their feet. Ghosts, of course, do not exist, and extrasensory perception is a concept maintained by the craftily lunatic fringe to ensure academic funding. It had been a pleasant evening. There was no need for Dany's expression to become, indeed, grave. It was a matter of total coincidence that at the moment she experienced her frisson the man both she and her companion loved had received a blow from a piece of lead piping along the slant of his jaw and, several hundred kilometres away to the north, had plunged forward unconscious to the ground. It would have taken a clairvoyant of a very high order to know that a miracle of biblical proportions would be called for if anyone were to walk over to the grave that the men dragging his body away had in mind for him.

FIFTEEN

Dawn did not break that morning; it oozed into the world. Grey sky, grey sea, grey mist, and grey mud flats merged dankly together in a smudged charcoal drawing of the estuary. When the small, tight helicopter came in low and fast from the south it might have been a kindness if it had completed its imitation of a gun-ship by spitting cannon fire at the lone trawler inching carefully out to sea along the one navigable channel left by the retreating tide. Then at least, a jagged yellow-orange, a blood red, might have brought colour into the monochrome print.

The helicopter chopped up the air with increasingly vicious butchery as it neared the town. Aft on the trawler a deck-hand watched it approaching with a sullen, lumpen resentment. It was low enough for him to make out the faces of the two men in the bubble and for them to see his. With the disdain of all have-nots for those above them in life, McCrae spat heavily into the sea.

In the Westland the man beside the pilot grunted his sour appreciation. He glanced to his left in the direction of the far-off sea. Covered with what might have been an oily scum it looked as smooth and solid as a sheet of lead. Rain, it seemed, would rebound from it and then form puddles. Unimpressed, the man looked at his watch. The pilot caught the gesture. By way of answer he pointed straight ahead. Beyond a straggle of edge-of-town houses a playing field was tilting up to meet them. Detective Inspector Brook was out of the chopper and running towards a car before the blades had finished rotating.

Ramsey had heard, and almost felt, the helicopter passing overhead. Its blunt sound had vibrated down into the captain's cabin where, wrists and ankles bound and linked, they had thrown him. It was a noise quite distinctive from the growling throb of the trawler's engine. Forgetting the pain in his jaw he pulled a face. Life's final irony. The dark wings of the Angel of Death had beat close about indeed.

He was under no illusion as to what was programmed for him. For the moment, underneath the numbness and the cold, his body was a collage of pain centres. They took turns in assuming predominance as he tried to brace himself on the floor against the ship's slow, not quite predictable wallowing. His stiffened, throbbing shoulder was not the worst. After he'd plunged forward into that sea of black obliviousness they must have kicked him about. Soon he would be plunging, dead-weighted, into a real sea. It would be cold and shocking but he'd scarcely notice that. A basic animal panic would engulf him as totally as the water. The steel bands he had felt about his chest the night before would be as nothing now. The weight of all the world would seem to rest upon his chest as his lungs, desperate for air, refused on reflex to admit water. Unconsciousness might be long, eternal seconds coming. That was how it had always been with the victims of drowning he had encountered. There was virtually no water in their lungs. The body had preferred asphyxiation as the lesser of two terrors. And he was cursed with being a strong swimmer, used to staying under water. Well, he must be resolutely clever. As he hit the surface, before his body knew it, he must gulp in water.

For the moment he was not frightened. Later, he knew, he could be. But for the moment he did not mind the third stage of his non-being. After the last unconsciousness had rescued him from the final few seconds of insanity he would become what else but food for fishes. As good for fishes as for worms. He did not mind the image of his collapsed skeleton picked clean and scoured as bright as cuttle-bone. And, who knew, he might still experience the phenomenon of seeing the course of his entire life flash before him as he went down.

Well, no, he wouldn't. That was a tale told by old wives who'd never drowned. Best to review it now. It didn't add up to too much. Perhaps on account of a bone he'd set here, a fever diagnosed there, it just ended up on the profit side of the ledger. But small loss to anyone, truth be told, himself included. To go now before the body's wholesale decay, the onset of clinical senility was not without advantage. But he felt a small bolus of angry frustration souring the centre of his feelings. He would die feeling diminished because bested by this sorry crew. They would see themselves as winners and, small though it was of him, the feeling of having lost would be there to qualify his fear or taint his resignation. Unless he could think of Anne.

Anne was the last, the only, thing that he should meditate upon. He would remember her that day, which day, it didn't matter, in Greenwich Park. A perfect day of clear-breezed summer. Shouts of cricket far away and in the foreground, lithe and dark and laughing in a light blue work-shirt a carefree, healthy, as it seemed, Anne. Death would make for no mystical reunion in a children's never-never land. But death would not be all loss. Failing to re-join him with Anne, it would at last take away the dull, ever-present bruise of separation from her. The light blue shirt. That was the snapshot he must die holding in his head . . .

In the wheel house, Gibson the skipper was steering through the shallow waters with laboured care. It was as though knowledge of a precious cargo made him self-conscious about decisions he would normally have done as a matter of unthinking course. As if seeking diversion he nodded at the slight man with his right arm in a sling.

'Kenny,' he said, 'get McCrae along in here.' Kenny went out. Presently McCrae was standing in the doorway looking enquiringly at Gibson.

'Now?' he said.

'Yes,' Gibson nodded. 'Chain him up. We'll drop him as soon as we're past the banks. Give him plenty of weight.'

A crude grin of anticipated pleasure broke up McCrae's churl's potato face. 'Don't worry,' he said. 'He'll go down with more chains on him than Ron Atkinson.'

He went out. Lengths of chain were coiled aft the wheelhouse. McCrae began to sort those with the heavier gauge links. Kenny, the man with the broken wrist, watched him from the rail.

'Want a hand?' he said. It wasn't meant as a joke but it ended up as one.

McCrae smiled his idiot-toothed grin. He shook his head. 'You'd better be careful with what you've got left,' he said and laughed again. Kenny didn't think it that funny.

'Got to get this fucker set before it sets stiff all wrong,' he said.

'Soon be back in. Short trip today, eh,' McCrae said. 'Engine trials.'

Below, in the captain's cabin, Ramsey knew the time was come before the door was unlocked. The clanking bump of the chains announced it eloquently enough. Like Captain Hook, he thought, but his throat was very dry. I would like to be able to spit at them at the last, he thought. The door opened. The one built like a thin gorilla came in. His breath as he knelt beside Ramsey was like a gorilla's too. He produced a knife. A long thin knife. Ramsey hadn't considered they would kill him first but perhaps a fractional kindness still had a place in their make-up. The man put the knife on the floor. He began to undo the rope trussing Ramsey together.

'Can you swim?' he asked in a low, fast voice. His accent was suddenly not from some Celtic borderland. Ramsey didn't care to trust the spurt of amazed hope that was shooting through him like brandy.

'Can you?!'

Ramsey nodded. So did the man.

'It's your only chance. Fifty yards from here it'll bottom out.'

'Why? Why are you –?'

'Let's just say I can't brook seeing an amateur killed in cold water.'

181

Even if he has deserved it.' Ramsey felt his whole face ache from the effort his eyes made to open wide.

'Can you stand?'

He only just could. He was numb and his joints had forgotten their purpose in life.

'Right. Can you swing your right arm?'

'Yes. I'll tread water if I –'

'To hell with that. You've got to hit me. In the face. Hard, sod you. You understand why?'

'Yes. I'm sorry if I've –'

'Get on with it.' Still unsteady on his feet Ramsey hit the man who called himself McCrae.

'Again!' Ramsey hit him three more times.

'You're a bleeding doctor. Will that mark me up enough? It sure as hell feels like it.'

Ramsey nodded.

'All right, now's as good as any time. Go for it and go for it fast!' It was easier said than done. The trawler was picking up speed as it met the swell of the sea proper. As well as wallowing it was plunging forward to aft. In negotiating the tiny corridor to the foot of the companion way he was bounced painfully several times off either wall. He gripped a tread of the companion way with his right hand, gingerly raised his left arm. It creaked and hurt like buggery but it moved. Crouched, listening for footsteps overhead, he climbed in daylight the swaying rungs that he'd last climbed in darkness when they were still. He sneaked a look outside. The ship rolled down to port and at the bottom of the grey sky's upward roll he saw grey land come into view. That way, then. Not quite yet believing in his reprieve, wondering if on hitting the water he might get cramp in earnest, he found he was hurtling across the deck at surprising speed and, as a shout rang in his ears, diving into space.

It was an ill-judged dive. He hit the water too flat and in a trough. The air was knocked out of him as if he'd been punched and it was the pain of this, the gasping need to replenish his lungs, that his brain registered before the iciness of the sea lanced him to the marrow.

It was Kenny's shout that he had heard. Careering against the side of the wheel house in his one-armed awkwardness, he recovered to half-stagger through its door.

'Go about, go about!' he screamed. 'The bastard's got away!'

'I can't here, man! I can't!' Gibson yelled back. He had seen what had happened. He was scrabbling to unlock a drawer. He succeeded. He pulled out a World War 2 issue Webley .45, the vast break-in-half cannon of a revolver. He was raking away now inside the drawer. The gun still needed loading.

'They'll hear that on the shore!' Kenny exclaimed.

'Maybe. I doubt it. No other way now. He knows too much.' In spite of everything he had loaded the gun with a calm, impressive speed.

'Then hurry for Christ's sake! There's a mist blowing across!'

'Out the fucking way!' Gibson was out on to the deck. McCrae was staggering towards the starboard rail moaning as he held a hand to his bleeding face. Gibson moved to the port side of the wheel house and braced his back against it. His target, the man in the saturated clothing, was afloat and swimming but seemed to be making no progress. He hung on the upswell of a wave like a piece of driftwood. There was a chance. It would take a hell of a shot but there was a chance. To wing him with one of these fat squat bullets would be to guarantee his drowning after all.

'Holy Mother of God!' It was McCrae's voice that had called out.

'Jesus! Jesus Christ!' Now Kenny. Gibson became aware of a throaty, growing thrumming different to the chug of his own idling engines.

'Don't, man! Don't!' Kenny had rounded the wheelhouse, his face white and hysterical. He pointed to the starboard, ocean, side.

'For Christ's sake!' Gibson stormed. But he moved to the corner to look. His mouth tightened. Slowing down as it came gliding out of the mist was a coastguard launch.

'Oh, Susan!' Gibson said. He threw the Webley overboard. It sank like a stone with chains on. 'Susan,' Gibson said again.

'. . . six fifty . . . seven . . . seven fifty . . . eight. Any more on eight? Eight, eight, eight –'

Looking like a houseman in his white coat, the auctioneer was trying to do his usual best as he worked his way down the line of baskets of dead fish. But the bidding was nowhere near as brisk as usual. This rare morning he had competition, and a distraction to which the eight or nine well wrapped up fish merchants were willing to accord priority.

Centre-piece of this distraction was not the black police transit nor even the several uniformed policemen standing about the quayside. The focus of attention was the trawler the 'Jack London'. Or, possibly, the manner of its berthing on this occasion. It was not being brought in by its usual crew. That would hardly be possible because they were standing, all four, handcuffed together on deck. One had a broken arm, it became clear, another a nastily beaten face. As the trawler tied up it also became clear that she had been piloted in by a customs officer. He'd made nearly as good a job of it as Gibson would have done.

'All right, moving on to ling,' the auctioneer said. 'Oh, sod it! We'll finish off, gents, when the cabaret is over and we can all get down to proper business. That way I can watch too.'

Edging forward with the growing crowd of porters, fishermen and buyers the auctioneer watched as one by one, heads appearing first, the four men mounted up the iron ladder and on to the quayside like candidates for the guillotine. They were not however separated from their heads by the police who received them, but merely rehandcuffed in pairs before being bundled into the black van. It didn't happen without a growing, growling swell of discontent.

'You'll be all right, Kenny. Don't let 'em grind you down,' a voice called out from the crowd. Several of the uniformed police turned their heads and pursed their lips self-importantly. But the cry seemed to fall on deaf ears when it came to the copper who seemed in charge of it all. Perhaps he hadn't understood. The couple of times he'd spoken it was clear he was some high-up from London where they gave the southerners all the best jobs. The van drove off.

'Now, gents, let's be having you,' the auctioneer said. 'Fun's over.'

Ignorance is often bliss, but complacency is invariably dangerous. Rocky Beach was in a state of both as, later than usual, he drove to his overt place of work that morning. He slammed the Capri into the R. G. BEACH parking slot in front of the snazzy new waterside industrial unit with a considerable sense of satisfaction. Lambert had said hit the bastard hard and they had. So hard he was going to turn very soft very fast. They'd shown them down there they could handle a little local difficulty up here in nothing flat and wrap it up all neat and tidy. No loose ends. In its own way it was just as neat a bit of engineering as the mod. his shop could do on a standard Mercury. He locked the Capri – you never knew, even here – and went into the works. Reg and Dave were well into it hoisting the big inboard out of that weird Thanet conversion so he gave them no more of a wave. Besides two customers were waiting for him in the partitioned-off little office in the corner. That was good. But it was not so good Reg leaving them to stew like that. They could've been there hours. He tried to sum them up as he approached the glass partition. Middle-aged. Not loaded. Maybe not customers. Maybe Reg had let them be because they were reps. Ah well. Soon say no.

'Morning, gents,' he said instead as he opened the door, 'you being looked after?'

'We said we'd wait for you,' the greyer one said.

'That's nice.' He slipped his jacket off. 'How can I help?'

'Is your name Beach? Robert Gavin Beach?'

184

His stomach turned over as he started to see it coming. 'What is it?' he tried. '*This Is Your Life*?'

'It could be yours, just about, son,' the same one said. 'But I'm not Eamonn Andrews.'

'Then who the hell are you?'

'Detective Inspector Brook. This is Detective-Sergeant Allinson.'

'Oh . . . right. What's this about?'

'What this is about son is that you're being nicked.'

'On what charge?'

'Intent to cause grievous bodily harm. Assault with a deadly weapon.'

Rocky Beach tried to keep his brain ticking over. Think, think, think! It was bad but he wasn't in that deep.

'Is that right, Sergeant?' Brook was lazily saying.

'All right for openers, yes sir.'

'Openers . . . how'd you mean – openers?'

'Well later on – yes, thank you, Sergeant – we'll no doubt be putting you in the frame for offences under the Misuse of Drugs Act, 1971.'

'You've got to be joking!'

'From where we stand you're the joker.'

'What am I supposed to have done?'

'Well, if you've got an hour or two, let's see – Possession . . . trading . . . possession with intent to supply . . . importing.'

'Bollocks!'

'Now, now. Your turn later. Right now it's our duty to caution you. Sergeant.'

'Mr Beach. You do not have to say anything unless you wish to do so but what you say may be given in evidence.'

Rocky Beach swallowed hard. This was a lot more than a little local difficulty. He was feeling ill. It was hard to keep your head when its inside was swirling around like a cement mixer. 'Why me?' was all he could manage.

'Not just you, son, is it?' Brook said. 'It's full house time.'

Beach's foxy features visibly blenched. He moistened his lips. It was not a pretty sight. 'Full . . . house?'

'Oh I wouldn't be funny about a thing like that. Gibson, McCrae. Russell. Jenks.'

'The best back four Fleetwood ever had, sir.'

'Not any more. And now we've got the ball-carrier too.'

Without really noticing he'd reached for it, Rocky Beach discovered he was putting his jacket back on again. Worth five times the chain-store whistles they had on, cheapskate back-hander bastards. Wait a minute. He wasn't dead yet! As he turned back to face Brook his attempt at discretion only brought the full craftiness out in his sharp, know-all face.

'Can we have a word?' he said to Brook. 'The two of us?'

Beach saw the copper latch on to his wavelength at once. It was only for form's sake he pretended to think it over.

'I might have some information that would be of service to you,' Beach said. 'At this present moment of time, however, I'd like it to be off the record.'

'Sergeant,' Brook said. Well, he'd given him an out, hadn't he? The junior cop left the office. It was Brook who made sure the door was closed.

'Well?' he said coming back and standing close.

'We're both men of the world, Inspector,' Rocky Beach said.

'I imagine so.'

'All right, tell me. What am I looking at? Ten pennorth?'

'As things stand, son, anything less than fourteen and I for one will be heart-broken.'

'Ah . . . but supposing it got so things stood differently . . . could we do something about it?'

Brook looked at him steadily. A crafty little look came into his own eyes and then transferred itself to his mouth. Beach forced himself to hold Brook's gaze. 'Are you suggesting what I think?' Brook finally ventured.

'Depends what you're thinking, don't it?'

Brook's face hardened. 'Don't piss me about, son,' he said, 'him out there can't lip read.'

Beach gulped. All right. Now or never. 'I've got money in the Isle of Man,' he said. 'Enough for two. Half's yours.'

'Half?'

'It's more'n you can get through if you're not a lunatic.'

Brook stood there trying the idea on for size. 'And just how do I qualify for these, er, retirement benefits?' he asked.

'Well . . . you look the other way for two hours.'

'Just two?'

'Two'll do it. The pubs'll be open soon. Call it four pints.'

'Well . . . I am thirsty at that.' Brook considered the prospect a moment longer. Then, almost viciously, he was yanking open the door. 'Sergeant!' he called.

Allinson came back into the office looking from one to the other. Brook had taken up a position further away from Beach than during their *tête à tête*. Now, in almost a parody of a flashing exhibitionist he was holding open the jacket of that cheap suit. Beach's wayward stomach contracted into an icily clenched fist. He was easily able to see the miniature recorder poking out of his inside pocket. He was dished, he knew it. Fourteen years away! Abuse was his only consolation now.

'You bastard!' he shouted. 'You poxy, cock-sucking bastard. You wound me up! You –' He got no further. The machine switched off, Brook had stepped across and hit him once, surprisingly hard, in the stomach. Beach lurched and gagged. He leaned on the desk for support. Brook turned and glanced outside. The two mechanics were putting a lot into their present task of pretending to be working.

Brook turned back away from them.

'We'll run a check, won't we, Sergeant?' he said. 'Unlikely. But just in case.'

'Yes, sir.'

'And of course we've got the Isle of Man to go on now.' Brook smiled and then as he approached the still gasping Beach stopped smiling. 'I'm not without ambition, Rocky,' he said, 'and not so very moral. Being a cop has cost me a marriage, most of my friends and years of sleep. I don't even think I enjoy it any more. But it's all I know. And, there's one thing does please me. And that's the fact that thick, know-it-all haemorrhoids like you can't buy me. There's nothing I'd take from slime like you. Not women . . . money . . . big fast cars . . . not even your matchbox collection. Nothing!'

On the glass wall of the office was a heavy engineering company's calendar. The month's patron pin-up was all coarse country tits and pubic hair. As they put the handcuffs on him Rocky Beach realised with a start of horror that he could be over forty before he had the real thing again.

He seemed to have been swimming for hours although a calculation somewhere inside him was nightmarishly saying it had only been for seconds. All to no point. He was making no headway at all. It was as if he were crucified face down on the shuddering cold swell of the sea. A sitting duck. The space between his shoulder blades was as wide as a goalmouth for anyone striking with bullet or harpoon. The nerve ends there had already closed in tingling anticipation of the blow he could do nothing to avert. Besides he was going to drown after all. He should have paused to take off his blouson, the heavy sweater beneath. Saturated instantly and icily they had quadrupled in weight to pull relentlessly at his upper arms. The light-fitting, water-logged shoes gave his feet no purchase in the water. As it rocked and tossed him, submerged and buffeted him he found he could neither swim nor float.

His shoulder wound had opened at once. He could feel blood running out of it turning from warm to freezing in the space of each pulse-spurt. The pain and stiffness made it almost as hard to breast-stroke. He went under again. Choking he somehow jerked splutteringly to the surface. But it was only a question of time. The build-up of acid, of raw pain in his arms was like when you did press-ups and you simply, in the short end, ran out of strength. He didn't have it in him to keep on.

Somehow, though, he did. The nightmare insisted he should. It dawned on him in the midst of his pain that a shot had not come. A lurch in the waves had slid him under a bank of mist. On his side he could manage a sort of dog-paddle. It took different muscles past the point of no return then further and further until groaning in protest he swallowed another throatful of salt water and all resistance taken from him, sank downwards in a final paroxysm of choking.

To touch bottom! On tip-toe he could just make contact with the sea-bed while keeping his head intermittently above the surface. For a long time he seemed to make progress. He could press off from the bottom with a sort of ballet dancer's upward lunge and scramble forward on what he began to sense might be an in-running tide. Then the floor began to shelve more sharply and his problems began anew.

He could stand now, had to. But the floor was mud. The estuary silt made it first cousin to quicksand. To put pressure on it was to start to sink in at once. He pulled a leg already ankle-deep out of the mud and found the other up to mid-calf from the added pressure of his effort. He pulled in quick panic at that and for all its tight lacing his shoe was wrenched from his foot. The water was only around his thighs now but as he slewed shivering out of the mist pocket his heart sank. Ahead was a vast desert of mud-flat stretching on to near eternity. Already his hamstrings felt as though they were percolating the blood they could not renew.

Like a man on artificial limbs he lurched stabbingly on, only able to gain about nine inches with each pull from his hips. Bright blood was emerging from the wrist of his blouson to drip and be washed away in the brown tide. His left foot refused to budge and, committed to the forward motion, he fell headlong to be submerged yet again. A wrenched ankle, he realised as he floundered gasping to his knees for air, was now another in his catalogue of hurts. At least the fall had pulled him free. He staggered on.

Thirty yards later he was on his knees. Literally crawling, he spread the pressure of his weight more evenly over the mud. But it seemed to emphasise the coldness so much more. His teeth were chattering so rapidly so much beyond his control he knew he had passed the demarcation line between cold and hypothermia. The blood drying on his left hand was mingled with the filthy mud he pawed at. Each oozing, loose print in the mud was releasing a fetid stench of bad eggs buried for suppurating centuries. He stared at his left hand and it wavered out of focus. He lay full length, his cheek against the stinking sludge. This was it. He couldn't go on further. He should because he would die of cold or – oh, God! – the tide *was* coming in. The sea was already licking about his feet.

The elemental terror of drowning repossessed him. He was transfixed again, this time on land, his every muscle turned to jelly. On land for the moment, but the water was rising about him. It was the ultimate nightmare come true. He was still a half-mile from shore. Perhaps if he could get his poor tortured lungs to scream the breeze might carry his cry the distance. With an effort that might have raised empires he lifted his head. He opened his mouth but – horror – the cry was stuck in his throat. He –

'Easy. Easy, man. You're OK now.'

Bathed in sweat, his left arm in a sling, Ramsey was rescued by a dark voice and a soft, firm hand on his forehead. He shuddered oxygen into lungs that still seemed awash with salt water. As the nurse took on definition she remained dark, a warm, glowing, West Indian brown.

'Thanks for waking me,' Ramsey gulped.

'That's OK. Heart attacks are hard on us. What were you doing – reliving it?'

'Exactly. Edited highlights.'

The nurse grinned. She was small and young and slim. She had amazing features. Not just the nose but the entire face beneath the wide forehead seemed *retroussé*. The effect might have been bizarre or comic, but augmented by the large, faintly oriental eyes – eyes you could drown in, Ramsey regretted himself saying – and looked up at from a bed the face emerged as strikingly, blazingly, beautiful. It was the face of a black queen who could have usurped Sheba's throne and her place in Solomon's affections. It was the face of a nurse in Fleetwood. As his nightmare fled back into his subconscious Ramsey, restored to life, wondered if he had ever seen so wonderful a face.

'Want to talk it out?'

'Oh – I think it'll stay away now. Somebody went for me with a boat-hook.'

The girl's face lit up with delighted mischief.

He tried to lever himself into more of a sitting position. Pain from his shoulder swirled into his neck and chest with sufficient bite to make his eyes water.

'Easy.' Gently she used his good arm to help lever him up. She fluffed a bolstering pillow behind him. She smelt far nicer than the sickening mud. And she wasn't going to miss out on her real life scoop.

189

'I guess you hadn't just spilled his beer, though,' she said. Her accent was half Port of Spain and half Oswaldtwistle.

'Not exactly, no.' He was trying to make out the name on her tag but she was too sideways on. 'What's your name?' he asked.

'Anne,' she said.

Ah, well. It happened all the time.

'Was it over a girl?' she asked.

He didn't want to lie to her but he didn't want to spoil her gleeful anticipation. And he lacked the energy to let her down gently. He nodded. Her smile made the lie radiantly worthwhile.

'What's she look like?' she asked.

That was far easier to deal with. 'In no way in your class,' he said.

The face lit up again at what its goddess owner took only as a compliment. She wagged a long, slender finger at him. 'It's saying things like that to every girl you meet that gets you into having stitches in your shoulder.'

She considered him. 'It's a pity you've already had your tetanus jabs,' she said.

'You haven't missed much,' he said. He grinned. Then he stopped grinning. Walking into his line of vision from beyond the bottom of the bed had come Brook. The nurse – Anne – saw his eyes shift their focus and turned to look at Brook too.

'Who are you?' she said in a voice prepared to be stubborn.

Brook showed her his warrant card. 'Police,' he said pleasantly. 'Your Casualty Officer said it was all right to talk to this patient for a while.'

'Mr Sharma?'

'Mr Sharma. Yes.'

'OK.' Satisfied, she moved to the door. Ramsey began to guess why he was in a private room. Anne turned in its doorway to fire a parting shot at Brook.

'Just go easy,' she said. 'There may be some residual shock.'

'Don't worry,' Brook said with amiable grimness, 'there will be. Depend on it.'

She wasn't to be bested. 'He's too nice a one-armed bandit to lock up,' she said before she went.

'About which there are two schools of thought,' Brook said. 'I should have done it days ago.'

'Yes. Thanks for scraping me up,' Ramsey said.

'Don't mention it. Then maybe I'll forget I did.'

Ramsey decided to let that ride. There was an angry silence which, finally, Brook could not abide. 'For the umpteenth time,' he exploded, 'just what do you think you were doing!'

'People die of lethal drug doses. A man dies of shock and loss of blood after being sexually mutilated. A man dies in my arms of a shot almost certainly intended for me. I'm attacked with everything but the kitchen sink and within minutes of –'

'You leave it to the police.'

'Do I? Do I? Is it the police, though, or the Friends of the Government's Reputation Society? We don't want *this* on BBC1.'

Brook went red and then pale. 'I don't have to take that from you,' he said throatily.

'Why not? It's what it seems like from where I stand.' Except he wasn't standing. He didn't like being literally talked down to. He pushed to raise himself higher in the bed. The pain scalded its way back and creased his face.

'Hurt?' Brook said vindictively.

'Not a bit.'

'Serve you bloody right,' Brook reached in his pocket. He spaded a five card trick of Polaroids at Ramsey. Ramsey dealt them patiently out on the blanket in front of him. Rocky Beach and the trawler crew. It sounded like a group but the flat flashlighting had made their faces look both scared and villainous. Ramsey looked his question up at Brook.

'We picked them all up this morning,' Brook said, his anger slightly mollified.

'McCrae too?'

'He'll go inside and listen, won't he? He's good at that. If he wasn't you'd be food for bloody crabs right now.'

'I'll buy him a drink. Lots of drink,' Ramsey said soberly. 'He saved my life. As far as I'm concerned that makes him unique.'

He sank back into the pillows. He could feel something hard and spiteful ebbing out of him. It was a raggle-taggle, messy end to things but it was near enough an end for all that. Exton Waite's death if not avenged had been trigger for a sort of justice.

'So apart from the Frenchman I told you about on the phone, it's over,' he said.

In another burst of fury Brook snatched the photographs back from him so ferociously they buckled. 'Too damned right, it's over,' Brook said. 'It probably damned well is!'

He leaned down over Ramsey, his veined face livid. 'We didn't just want Fleetwood, you berk,' he hissed. 'We wanted Fleetwood, London, Amsterdam, France. *And* the rest. We wanted to unravel the Coke Run all the way back to Columbia. Well now the thread's snapped off. We moved in to save your amateurish little life and had to let it all go off half-cock. *You* – single-handed – have sent a year's work, thousands of pounds' worth of painstaking investigation, straight down the pan. And even now you've no conception. We're never going to get that Frog!'

Ramsey lay very still and looked at the wall. 'I'm sorry,' he said at last.

'Pardon?' Brook said.

'I'm sorry.'

'Put like that it doesn't sound very much,' Brook said, 'does it? It doesn't sound enough.'

'So why did you do it then?'

'Do what?'

'Move in to save my amateurish little life. I'm no great loss, let's face it.'

Brook did not come back with the obvious, agreeing gibe. He shuffled on his feet, looked embarrassed even as his eyes failed to hold Ramsey's.

'McCrae didn't want to see you killed in cold blood,' he muttered.

'And the others?'

'What others?'

'For God's sake! The ten, thirty, eighty poor bastards who got hooked, maybe irreversibly, during this year you've been spending on "painstaking investigation". The three, six, dozen who've been killed outright by that flat-out poison. They don't matter, eh? They don't count, I suppose.'

'That's the price you pay,' Brook said a little less than confidently.

'The price *they* pay.'

'All right!' Brook said steaming up. 'But at least they went into it with their eyes sort of open. You can say they knew the odds.'

'So they got what they deserved.'

'No . . . but they got what they knew might be coming to them . . . You, you blundered in feet first, both eyes closed.'

'Closed! I twigged –'

'Near enough closed as I just explained. Also . . .'

'Yes?'

'I reckoned somebody owed you one. Those men outside your hotel. Nearer the Home Office than the Yard. All that trying to close you down. At the end of the day you can say I had some time for a man who wouldn't take "No" for an answer when a friend of his died in a dodgy way and "No" was the run-around everyone was giving him.'

This time the silence had a played out feel.

'OK.' Ramsey broke it at last with, 'so I owe you quite a few beers too. But know who you're drinking with, Brook. If they brought Adolph Hitler in here to me right now and he was ill I'd give him a pint of my blood if no one needed it more urgently. Maybe you can play God with people's lives while you play a waiting game but I'm a doctor. I just clean up whatever's straight in front of me.'

'It's called penny-wise and pound foolish,' Brook said.

'No, it's not –'

'But I haven't come here to compare professional ethics. Just possibly you can help us in a damage limitation attempt.'

'How?'

'This famous five can be held on a charge of attempted murder.'

'God knows they can.'

'GBH. All of that. If you complain to the police here, turn up in the magistrates court tomorrow, we can officially keep drugs out of it. I won't be there. Just possibly – *just* possibly – the rest of the chain, the other runners, will see this as a freak hiccough. They won't know quite what to make of you. Especially with your flying back to France the next day.'

'Oh. I see.'

'That's the second reason I'm here. There's an RAF trainer that at the British tax payer's expense and with me waving you off in person is going to land you in Caen.'

'Really.'

'Yes. You're a doctor. You know all about recovering. So – are you prepared to make a statement that will enable the local force to bring charges?'

'Of course. If you get me a pen and . . .'

Brook smiled. He reached into his inner pocket and brought out a vertically folded sheaf of A4 paper.

'You'll find it's already witnessed,' he said. 'Here. You can press on this tray.'

A thought struck Ramsey as he took hold of the pen. 'What about bail?' he said. 'Supposing they –'

Brook grinned wolfishly. 'Just think of their occupation,' he said, 'and how close they are to a port. Then ask what magistrate from these parts is going to grant them bail the police opposing.'

SIXTEEN

To step out of Ramsey's front door was to have the breeze tug at your hair from every direction. The breeze or a Force Nine gale. The *manoir* by contrast was a sun-trap. The wind had to get up a tidy bit before it blew bold-faced enough to climb over the high mellow wall and run its rings around the orchard. That was one plus to staying there. Tessa could see fleecy-lamb clouds scurrying along quite rapidly in the mostly blue sky, but behind the windbreak walls a leaf, let fall would twirl to the ground in a straight line. Beside the conservatory, safe from sudden masculine intrusion she was sunbathing topless and, by a judicious feat of string-pulling, all but bottomless too. Gazing at the sky was making her feel insignificant, she decided. And her eyes ached. Sighing with contentment as the sun baked its way down to her bones she lolled back in the recliner and shielded her face with a copy of *Elle*.

When a few moments later she heard a footfall she was not concerned. She had learned to recognise Dany's tread. She made no move to take away the magazine.

'Is that wise?' Dany said.

'Is what wise?' Tessa said, removing the magazine after all and sitting up. She had no wish to appear rude if Dany wanted to talk.

'Frying yourself in the sun,' Dany said.

'Probably not. But I love the feel of it. And you're deliciously golden.'

Tessa swung her legs off the recliner and sat edgeways on it. 'Truth is,' she said, 'I'm probably over-compensating.'

'Oh? What for?'

'For always feeling second best to you when I've got clothes on.'

'There's absolutely no need to feel that I assure you.'

'Ho, isn't there?'

Dany sat down on a white wrought iron chair. She wore a cream blouse and a tan casual skirt and they each could have cost anything from fifty francs to five hundred. It was relevant. Whatever the original cost she looked a million dollars, Tessa thought. She voiced the thought.

'You always look so good,' she said. 'You can be pretty depressing to be with.'

Dany shrugged as she tried not to show her pleasure at the remark. 'You have to dress,' she said vaguely, 'You might as well do it properly.'

She smiled at Tessa. With a connoisseur's authority that made her seem almost masculine she said, 'At the moment you seem to be dressed to very good advantage yourself.'

Tessa half-blushed at the returned compliment and to cover her confusion at least swung herself horizontally back on to the recliner. Dany looked at her lying there. She sighed inwardly. She knew the remark had not been ill-directed. It was true that if she had been lying naked alongside Tessa most men would have placed her first in a comparison. Her calves were softer, her hips a vital fraction plumper, her breasts considerably fuller and with prouder, larger nipples. Paris would have given her the apple. And yet her body had these days, she knew, a manufactured aura. She worked religiously at her exercises and maintained a strict, if gourmet, diet. Twice a year she spent ten days at a health farm. Tessa's body, by contrast, had a naturalness about it. A bit tomboyish, yes, a bit sinewy in the fashion of English girls good at games, but somehow lithely spontaneous, charmingly . . . unpremeditated. The exercises got harder every day. She had thought this year that the flesh on her upper arms was refusing to be banished away. The time might come, she thought, when Paris might not be worth a mass of self-inflicted tortures. Never, she counter-decided, I shall fight every centimetre of the way.

The immediate vexation came back to plague her thoughts. That man! Days away and now, rather literally, arriving out of the blue with only a few hours advanced warning – arriving at the one time when she was otherwise engaged. Well, in a way. Busy as he was Jean-Paul would always fit her in at another time somehow. But perhaps if she left things as they were it would be better . . .

'Did you hear the phone ring a while back?' she asked casually.

'I think so. Vaguely.'

'It was some friend of yours, I think.'

'Oh? Who?'

'Somebody called – Ramsey, I think it was . . .'

'Dany!' Tessa sat up sideways so exuberantly her breasts jiggled and bounced like apples in a bucket. She was quite oblivious this time.

'Dany! He called and you've been keeping it all to yourself! You didn't call me to the phone.'

'I suppose I should have,' Dany said lazily, 'but to tell you the truth I didn't see much point.'

'Oh!'

'After all – he is going to be back here mid-afternoon.'

'Dany!' Tessa's whoop of joy must have carried well beyond the high walls. Very English and . . . young, Dany decided. It confirmed her in her little strategy.

'He's arriving at Caen. At three. He'd like us to meet him.'

'We'll be there with bells on!'

'Hmmn?'

'Never mind. Just an expression. Of course we'll meet.'

'Well there's just one little problem – I have a hair appointment. I could cancel it, of course. But heaven knows when he'd find time for me next.'

'But Dany surely –'

'Do you think you could go? You could take his old blunderbuss of a car.'

'But of course I could go! I've driven the car enough now and it's not *that* far.'

'No. You're sure you don't mind?'

' "Mind" is the last thing I feel about going.' Dany smiled her thanks and hid her thoughts. If absence makes the heart grow fonder she would take out an extra hour or two's insurance to underwrite her exclusive, because prior, erotic claim on Ramsey. He would look for them both at the airfield, find only Tessa and missing her own instant presence be all the more impatient to see her, repossess her. In the sunshine she felt the old, familiar, ineffable, thick warmth starting to build at the base of her spine. She scolded herself. It was still a little early in the day for that. She counter-balanced the first tweak of desire by telling herself she was being mean. But all was fair in love and sex. And besides, the appointment would be entirely functional. Jean-Paul would make her hair look ravishing.

What was that expression the British, the Americans, rather, had? Oh yes. Playing hard to get. Well, she wasn't playing quite *that* hard. But after *une aussi longe absence* a little good old-fashioned finesse would cost nothing while sharpening desire. Not that her own needed more whetting . . .

The wicket gate ajar, Dany strolled in the garden, secateurs in her hand. She wore a pale green summer dress and very little else. Jean-Paul had excelled himself. Only a very discerning woman with reason to look would know, she knew, that an hour ago she had still been at the hairdresser's. For the fourteenth time, perhaps, she looked at her watch. It was reasonable to suppose Tessa would be back by now.

This time her impatience was rewarded. A car drew up outside. Only not Ramsey's Citroën. The asthmatic wheezing of the idling engine wasn't his. She went to the door set in the larger gates and her heart somersaulted with joy. The vehicle was a Peugeot 504 diesel. It was a taxi. And Ramsey, his back to her, was paying off the driver. There is usually something in our pleasure we would rather not

196

reveal. Dany's was enhanced by her instantly seeing that Ramsey was alone.

'Ramsey!' she called out. He turned and the pleasure was qualified at once. There was a yellow-brown bruise at the side of his face. He was gaunter. He wore unfamiliar new clothes. He was wearing a blue-grey jacket over his shoulders like some *poseur* of a television director. But with a good excuse. His left arm was in a sling.

He must have seen her face change. 'It's nothing,' he said. 'A little accident.'

He walked towards her as the taxi drove away. She found she was still holding the secateurs. Very deliberately he took them from her and let them fall on the gravel. He put his one good arm around her back and pulled her to him. He kissed her. He kissed her for a long, searching, rediscovering time. It became more than her flesh and blood could stand and not do more. At last he lifted his head.

'Where's Gabin,' he said.

She could have kicked him, when seconds before her instinct had been to stroke. 'Marcel has taken your flea-bag to the beach,' she said. 'To run off some of the fat all his high living here has put on him.'

Ramsey grinned. 'It doesn't put any on you,' he said.

He moved to kiss her agin. But she wanted a small revenge as well as information. 'Where's Tessa?' she countered.

'You tell me,' he shrugged.

'She was there to meet you, yes?'

'No. No one was. I was *désolé*. Home is the hunter and – zilch.'

'She was taking your antique.'

'If she's bent it I'll spank her. Still, it wasn't exactly a scheduled flight. It did get in ahead of time.'

Dany looked at him. 'She'll be back soon,' she said. 'But perhaps not too soon. Come and spank mine. Now. Please.'

So much, she thought, for playing hard to get. He took her in his arm once again. 'You bring out the Josephine in me like this,' she said.

They kissed again more fiercely but, since they now had other plans, more briefly too. 'You'll have to do all the work,' Ramsey said.

She rubbed her palm against his ribs. '*Vive l'empéreur*,' she said.

Tessa was considerate. In the soft light of the lace-curtained bedroom Dany straddled Ramsey. She kissed the savage bruises she was aghast to find on his body. She kissed his body where it was not bruised. She rode him to another storming finish. She snuggled her warmth to his. It was bliss. Absence had made everything grow fonder. The relish and savour was keener than ever. Only one microscopic blemish qualified it all. He had kept his watch on. It was the wrong way round on his right wrist but he had not taken it off; sometimes he didn't. That always angered her. When she saw him being mean with time she felt he was being mean with her too. Consciously intending it or not, he was reminding her of her place. Leaning across her to trace the end of his arm projecting out from under her neck he looked at his damned watch now.

'Do you think Tessa's being incredibly diplomatic or has just got herself incredibly lost?' he said.

Dany kissed him before he could manoeuvre himself back off her. 'Knowing your car, she's probably incredibly greasy right now,' she said.

'Would she be at the cottage?'

'It's possible. She's spent hours there since she got here.'

'Really . . .' He didn't do it well. Dany clocked his quick blink. It was 'he knew that she knew that he knew' time. In the last quarter century a lot of women must have fallen for him: you would have thought he could have been more dead-pan than that.

She pulled his arm out from under her.

'Why don't we check the cottage out?' he said. 'We may bump into Marcel.'

The moment her CX turned the corner it looked as if something was wrong. Ramsey's own Citroën was parked in its usual spot looking as if it had not been driven in five years. And Gabin looked like a temporary stand-in for a stone dog as he sat in an upright, semi-*qui vive* position beside a front door that was open. He saw Ramsey at thirty yards and came at him first like a greyhound and then like a bear. Ramsey angled his disabled shoulder away from the dog's leaping, joyously panting bulk as patting, stroking with his right hand he gradually calmed him down.

'*On t'a gâté, Gabin,*' he said. '*Tu as engraissé. Dès maintenant, c'est le régime.*'

Gabin's clumping tail indicated henceforward he could live on companionship. Ramsey tickled behind his ears.

'You wait here a moment, Dany,' he said and said it far too casually.

She decided to comply. Gabin looked absurdly too big for his antics as, in leaping fits and starts, he frolicked about Ramsey's heels. She held her breath as Ramsey paused on his own threshold.

'Please not,' Ramsey was saying to himself. 'Please not.' The lacerating vision was sheeting blood down the screen inside his head. He shook his head. The vision did not go. There was nothing left to do but go inside and find the new obscenity.

There was nothing in the study-living room. It was so unchanged, the fresh flowers at the centre of the table leapt to his eye as the exception proving all else was normal. Tessa's handiwork. It meant that in the bedroom nothing might ever be normal again. He was trembling. The scuffling of Gabin's paws on the ground only heightened the screaming silence. He found he could not walk into the bedroom with one simple stride. He had to push the door open first. He did it with his eyes shut. When he opened them there was a body on the bed.

It was Marcel. Alive. Seeing the door move, light change, he was squirming in a silent, self-induced spasm. He had been bound hand and foot, hands to feet, exactly as Ramsey had been tied up on the trawler. And gagged. His eyes bulged wide as he saw Ramsey. Ramsey went to him and, heaving Marcel to his side, began to deal with the ropes. They had been tied by someone who knew his knots. It was impossible to loosen them one-handed, and impossible to signal to Marcel to lie still and be patient. Ramsey freed his left arm from the sling. It hurt like hell but he was able now to tell Marcel to relax. There was a large mark the colour of a rotting pear completely covering Marcel's left temple. Ramsey touched it with his good hand. He saw Marcel's eyes contract with pain. But nothing seemed to be broken.

'One second,' he signalled.

He went to the front door and called for Dany. He went to the kitchen. When, heart in mouth, Dany entered the cottage, she was confronted by Ramsey, the sling about his neck, standing grimly before her with a huge Sabatier knife in his hand. For a split second he looked like a fancy-dress pirate.

'It's Marcel. He's been attacked. Tied up. You cut him loose.'

'*Mon Dieu*. Where's Tessa?'

Ramsey flashed her an utterly harrowed look. 'God knows,' he said. 'Quick.'

She loosened Marcel's gag. The sickening, gutteral garglings which were the nearest he could come to speech rasped from his throat. Ramsey signalled to him to stay quiet. When Dany had finished cutting the ropes away he stretched Marcel full length on the bed upon his back.

'Massage his ankles where they were tied,' he said.

Dany did so. The ropes had bitten in deep. Once more a nurse, she worked hard at the swollen flesh. Ramsey was talking deaf and dumb to Marcel more intently than she'd ever seen. More grimly. She tried to concentrate on the mechanics of the massage. She watched her fingers instead of Ramsey. The fingers were no longer hers. They moved independently of the woman who sat waiting the outcome of

199

this dumb, life-and-death exchange with a widening abyss of horror growing within her like an alien.

After many long years Ramsey straightened up.

'A car pulled up outside,' he said flatly. 'A man got out. Alone. Holding a map. Lost. Tessa and Marcel were just leaving to meet me. They went over to the man with the map. Then he saw Tessa turn and scream. Of course he didn't hear a thing. As he turned he felt a terrible pain and then nothing. He came to here.'

Dany shut her eyes. 'When?' she asked.

Ramsey stared sombrely at her. 'I know what you're thinking,' he said. 'But our making love didn't make any difference. It happened before I landed.'

'We would have got here sooner.'

'Yes. We would have got here sooner.'

A laser beam knifed through both their skulls. It was the telephone. Ramsey shut his eyes a moment. He motioned to Marcel why he was leaving the room. Dany resumed the massage. It was of some minuscule benefit, to her.

'Allo.'

'Dr Ramsey, I presume.'

As soon as he heard the male voice Ramsey did not have to ask himself why he was gripping the phone so tightly his hand hurt. He had heard it before. He had stood hearing it suavely deployed across the threshold of a doorway to a house just to the north of Regent's Park. The voice's owner did not seem in the least put out that, truly lost for words as he tried to beat back the rising waves of fear, Ramsey had remained silent.

'One moment, Dr Ramsey,' the voice went on, 'I have a Miss Waite on the line for you.'

A moment. A plasticky grating noise. An eternity.

'Ramsey?'

'Tessa!'

Her voice was evisceratingly thin, tearful, frightened. 'Yes, Ramsey, it's me . . . I –'

'Tessa. Are you all right? Have they hurt you?'

'Yes . . . No. Not really. I'm . . . all right.'

'Where are you?'

'I don't know. I –' There was a gasp. The sound of a very distant tide withdrawing down a shingled beach washed down the line to him. He heard a grunt, a sound like a wet towel striking a bath. He heard what seemed to be a stifled scream. Then the sinisterly comic French accent was uncomfortably close to his ear.

'You see. She is quite all right. Well, as well as can be expected. So far.'

'. . . so far.'

'Yes. So far. I imagine you went upstairs the last time we met. You have some conception of how she might not be all right later. After all, England was the home of Jack the Ripper.'

Ramsey's mouth had gone so dry he did not trust himself to speak.

'You are still there?'

'What do you want?'

'Excellent. You are ahead of me. It is all about, you see, some colleagues of mine. In the north of your country. There is a wicked slander going about they tried to hurt you . . . You are listening?'

'Yes.'

'You know it is untrue – that it is not right my friends should be in prison. The charges against them are nonsense. They should be dropped.'

'I – I can't influence that. It's the police who brought the charges. They're the only –'

'So I understand. But it follows that you are their key witness. Their only witness. Yes?' The image of McCrae untying him shot into close-up from the banks of the high-speed images overlapping in Ramsey's mind. But what could McCrae do here?

'If you inform the police you realise you were mistaken – mistaken identities, eh? – they will not have a case. Besides, Miss Waite's father was quite an important man, yes? I am sure he was a friend of your Home Secretary. I am sure Mrs Beryl Waite is a woman of great influence.'

'What will you do to her?'

'In the circumstances that is an absurd question.'

His chagrin at having asked it was a partial help. Resentment began to put some steel into his fear-steeped swirl of thoughts. 'I don't think I begin to have any influence,' he said. 'But if I can do something – it could take weeks.'

'Yes. I understand that. But we are patient people. We can wait. But in any case I think we may all find ourselves pleasantly surprised at how fast the wheels of justice can turn under certain circumstances . . . The answer to your foolish question is, of course, that we will kill her. Eventually.'

How could his throat be so dry when his belly was awash? 'How . . . how do I let –'

'Do not call us. We will call you. First we will give you time to think about it. To search for a way out. When you have realised there is not a way out you will be more sensible and . . . enthusiastic on our behalf. *A tout à l'heure.*'

Click! A kilometre away, three hundred kilometres away a pebble had bounced off a wall. The phone at his ear began to purr. As he replaced the receiver he became aware that Dany was standing in the doorway. Her eyes were dilated with fear and wondering. He supposed his own must look the same.

'Tessa's been kidnapped,' he said tersely. 'She's alive but in great danger.'

Dany's face made a stand against collapse and then, as her jaw quivered, failed completely. As if to hide the disgrace of breaking down she flung herself at him and, sending a stinging pain into his shoulder, buried her face in his chest. It wasn't what he needed.

'It's my fault,' she finally sobbed out. He pushed her gently away so he could look at her.

'That's nonsense,' he said. 'It's mine.' She shook her head.

'You don't understand . . . She's nice. I like her. She's too nice. I was jealous of her. Of her and you. I thought if she went to the airfield without me you would miss me – start taking her for granted. I could easily have gone with her. Easily.'

He gripped her shoulder hard. 'Then you would have been badly hurt – maybe killed,' he said. 'And that would have destroyed me. Because I love you. There is no earthly need for you ever to feel jealous of another woman.'

She looked at his blurred image and for an instant was able to persuade herself he meant what he said unreservedly. But she could only choose not to believe. She would go to her grave jealous of Anne.

'Nothing you did or didn't do earlier today has made any difference to what has happened to Tessa,' he went on. 'Now think about things for a moment and you know that's so. Come on Dany, you're a nurse. You've been trained to keep your head and your heart apart.'

She had stopped crying. Her hair, he noticed, was tousled and forlorn. But the vital element of cool detachment that he so admired in her had been restored.

'Ramsey,' she said softly, 'what's going on? Who's kidnapped Tessa?'

'It's complicated. Right now there isn't time to explain. I have to call a policeman in England. And right now you have to go back to being a nurse. I want you to take Marcel to hospital. His head needs an X-ray. Can you do that for him please?'

She swallowed, and nodded.

'I'll tell you everything – *everything* – tonight,' he said. 'At your place. OK?'

'OK.'

'I'll help you get Marcel into the car.'

'He may throw up once he's on his feet,' she said and he knew she was herself again.

When they had gone off he poured himself a small medicinal brandy. He was not really worried about the crack Marcel had taken. The X-ray was insurance – and diversion therapy for Dany. The real blow Marcel had sustained was to his own esteem. The faithful squire had failed master and fair damsel alike. Ramsey had spent some moments signalling 'you were not to blame' to the sad-faced man he counted among his best friends. Dany had fastened Marcel's seat belt for him and Ramsey had felt his exoneration had not convinced. He rapped the empty glass down on the desk. The blame was all his. Less than composed himself, he dialled New Scotland Yard.

Technology for once worked for him. A switchboard and he was put straight through.

'Brook.'

Sod's law was on holiday. 'Brook, it's Ramsey.'

'God's strewth, I've only just said goodbye to you.'

'I'm in France now. Back home. It's gone very nasty.'

'Oh yes?'

'The daughter of that cabinet minister . . .'

'The dead one. Yes, I'm with you.'

'She's been kidnapped.'

'Where from?'

'Here.'

'Who by?'

'Them.'

'What was she doing there?'

'You won't like this. I sent her over here so she'd be safe.'

No. Brook didn't like it. The silence was protracted. Ramsey could sense the slow burn travelling down the line to brand him culpable. When Brook finally spoke it was an anti-climax. Almost.

'I don't know what to say to you,' he said wearily. 'I tell you time and time again until I'm bored with saying it to leave things to professionals. You – first on the phone, then face to face – keep going on about some French smoothie who you reckon is the worst of the lot. Then, without mentioning once to me you've done it, you send this kid off to where of all bleeding places.'

'I didn't mention it because I thought you people would know.'

'Some people might have but my people didn't. I didn't.'

'France has a population of about fifty-five million.'

'The majority of whom can read a phone book.'

'Look I had no idea –'

'No you hadn't. But we're wasting time. How do you know she's been kidnapped?'

'They phoned. Let her say a few words.'

'And what do they want?'

'They want me to get you to release the "Jack London" crew.'

'Because you made a mistake?'

'Yes.'

'Wait a minute. Let me think.' Ramsey waited. The brandy was warm in his stomach. It seemed impossible not to breathe noisily.

'All right,' Brook resumed. 'it's bad. It's bad but it's not all bad. In a good many kidnap cases when it's about money you might just as well put the ransom on the victim being dead before the first contact's been made.'

'Jesus, if –'

'Not this time. They don't want money. There's no percentage there. They're professionals too. But they're worried professionals.'

'Worried?'

'Worried the people we've got will talk.'

'Have they?'

'Not yet. They've been well trained. But we've got an inside straight there, as you know. But this is interesting. A giveaway. One of them must know more than we thought. Enough to get us a fair way up the chain. When he sees how much bird he's looking at we may be able to do a deal.'

'But they want me to back off. That's the whole point.'

'Ramsey, the attempted murder charge is neither here nor there. I'm not saying this, mind, but very shortly there's going to be a combined cross-channel two-way family favourites operation. You with me?'

'I think so. This time you're going trawling.'

'Right. That's three hundred per cent confidential.'

'But if you do that . . . when it happens . . . they'll kill Tessa.'

'Possible. Even probable. You've queered my pitch all over again.'

Ramsey's throat tightened. For some precious moments Brook's matter of fact manner had hinted at some kind of miraculous deliverance. It seemed there was to be none. He had put Tessa in a death cell.

'Ramsey?'

'Yes.'

'How are they getting back to you?'

'Phone.'

'Right. It won't be for twenty-four hours at least. They'll want to make you sweat. Here's how you play it. You won't like what you hear much but it's what I'm telling you as someone who's been around the track before. Now it's life and death will you do what I say?'

'Yes.'

'The thing is to turn it around.'

They ate something that evening. Since Dany had prepared the meal herself it was probably delectable. It didn't stick in his throat. He cleared his plate. But after the sombre ritual of dining for dining's sake was over he would have been hard pressed to say what he had consumed.

Marcel was OK. The hospital had wanted to err on the side of caution, but Marcel had been adamant about not staying in overnight. He wanted, Ramsey knew, to go off and drink himself into a memory-erasing stupor. Ramsey had not issued a preventive warning. If it was bad for his arteries, it would be good for his crushed spirit. Instead, obeying Brook's instructions, Ramsey had had the ironic experience of telling a deaf-mute to keep his mouth shut about what had happened.

But over the anonymous dinner, he and Dany had talked. He had neglected to notice the flavour and texture of his food as for the first time, from Tessa's initial arrival to his own wounded return from England, he told her everything.

'Animals,' Dany had commented bitterly. 'And you – what are you now?'

He had felt himself bridling at the apparent linking.

'What does that mean exactly?' he had asked.

'You went to England a doctor. You come back . . . what? What would you call yourself now?'

'An interfering meddler, I suppose.'

'It's so cruel. So unfair. If you couldn't have protected her, and looked after her, you shouldn't have involved her.'

'I did it for the best. I'd no idea it would follow us back here.'

'You were lacking in modesty.' Not understanding he scanned her face. She had put her hair to beautiful rights.

'You shouldn't have chosen to play God. What do you think is happening to her right now?' This time he knew precisely what she meant but he did not want it stated between them. But a mean, even sadistic streak had got into Dany. She persisted relentlessly.

'Tessa is young. Very attractive,' she said. 'And whoever's got her won't be paralysed from the waist down. Whatever their sex.'

He felt blood pound in his throat. 'Do you not think I've thought those thoughts, imagined those images every minute since that call first came?' he said thickly.

'Have you slept with her yourself?'

'Yes. Very briefly. Two years ago.'

'Ah. Thank you. You lied to me this afternoon, didn't you?' It was scarcely a question.

'When?'

'When you said you loved me.'

'That was not a lie,' he said sincerely.

'When we made love this afternoon you kept your watch on.'

'Did I?'

'Here. You would never have done that with Anne.'

'Dany – I loved Anne. I love you. The love is different because you are different people. The main difference – and it is one that no-one can do anything about – is that she was first.'

'Quite an advantage. The even bigger advantage she has, of course, is that she's dead.'

'Dany!' He knew there was justice, accuracy in her observation but that didn't stop it piercing him like a lance.

'Oh, God!' Dany reached across the table and grasped his forearm so hard it hurt.

'I've never said that out loud before,' she said, 'and now I've said it just when you least needed to hear it. I'm so sorry.'

'It's all right. I know what you mean.'

'You were away so long. You come back and it's wonderful for two hours and then everything is horrible, dreadful and when you need help I am only insecure and selfish.'

She was right once again. Looking at her across the table's dim light he was put in mind of Isabel. He knew why. They were type and anti-type. Under Dany's chic and competence there was a deep layer of vulnerability. And he was about to add to it.

'I'm not being brutal,' he said. 'I'm not retaliating but I think it would be a good thing if you went away now – back to the apartment.'

'Paris . . .?'

'Yes. They've obviously been watching the cottage. They must know the local scene. You could be in danger too. Away, you'll be one less thing to worry about.'

'What about you?'

'It doesn't matter about me.'

'It does to me!'

'For God's sake, Dany,' he heard himself shouting, 'if I'm going to be tortured let me be tortured on my own!'

Two days later Dany left for Paris.

'It will be harder for me but easier for you so I will go,' she said. Beneath the vulnerability was still another layer.

'Phone me,' she said as she kissed him, 'whatever the news.'

He watched her car disappear and it was a death in miniature. He was hollowed out by the sight of it diminishing. The vulnerability was all his now. Brook had been right. Making him sweat it out they had not got back to him.

That evening, as if possessed of an intelligence of its own that had monitored his state of mind, the telephone elected to ring.

'Well?' One word. But redolent with the same suave smugness.

'I think we can do business.'

'Excellent.'

'On condition.'

'Really? *You* have conditions?'

'Damn right. These conditions: one, I still don't know how much influence I have with the British authorities. Some, maybe. But, two, it will be possible for me to have a lapse of memory . . .'

'Go on.'

'But only, three, if you release the girl immediately.'

'I see you have a typical English sense of humour.'

'No one's joking. You've got nowhere to go, nowhere to man-oeuvre. The legal paperwork can last for ever. I'm –'

'It is your job to speed it up.'

'Stop interrupting and listen. I'm only going to say it once. Get the girl back and I'll do what I can. I don't know where you are so I'll give you forty-eight hours. You can get someone twice round the world in that time. I'll be in the *Bar de la Marée* this time the day after tomorrow. If she walks in I'll keep my word to you. I'll try. But one last thing. If she's hurt – harmed in any way – then the deal is off. If she's hurt or if she doesn't turn up then I go to the police both sides of the Channel with everything I know.'

There was the silence on the line that is never a true silence. Then the verdict. 'Dr Ramsey – I don't believe we can conduct business together on that basis.'

Click! Somebody else had flicked a pebble against the wall.

Tough-guy talk. Put it back on them. Make them realise how far out on a limb they were. Well, he'd ridden to Brook's orders and now all he had to show for it was a shirt soaked in perspiration and a tightness in his chest that felt like being in a switched-off iron lung. Sod Brown! Sod him! Sod him! And, as instructed, call him! He dialled the number Brook had given him for evenings. If memory served, it put the DI in the Peckham area.

'Brook.'

The pick-up had been so fast, he could almost see the cramped, old-fashioned, divorced copper's flat. 'Ramsey. He just called.'

'And?'

'I told him his move first – like you said. He said no dice.'

'He would off the top of his head. I told you to expect that.'

'He sounded like he meant it.'

'It's his job to sound like he means things. How long did you give them?'

'Forty-eight hours.'

'Good. Shows you're not *too* concerned.'

'Brook – I'm going out of my mind!'

'No, you're not! You're under extreme stress but you are not going out of your mind.'

'And if she doesn't show up?'

'She probably won't.'

'Won't?'

'If she doesn't it means one of two things. It could mean they've killed her.'

'Brook!'

'I'd say there's about one chance in four on that. So far as I can establish with the French police they've kept their noses pretty clean over there. They'd prefer to keep it that way. Remember they've still got a guillotine oiled in Paris.'

'What are the other chances?' Ramsey managed to ask.

'Probably she won't show up because they – and there will be several involved – are squabbling over what to do with her. When they realise well and truly she's a commodity that's not negotiable, the chances are they'll let her go.'

'Chances!'

'You want me to write you a personal guarantee? Now, this is important.'

'Yes?'

'They will probably phone again. To pressure you. Don't talk to them. Don't haggle. You'll hate yourself but hang up. Pressure them.'

'Jesus, Brook –'

'If or when she doesn't show up call me again. I'll get the French police to stop sitting on it and then –'

'They know?'

'Of course. Off the record. They'll put it on the record and make a lot of high profile noise going around asking questions.'

'So she'll be killed.'

'That is the risk. But the realisation we mean business, *you* mean business, that there's going to be no hiding place should make them let her go. We'll get it in the papers so that they can read between the lines that if she turns up safe the heat will be off.'

'Will it be?'

'I told you. We've got other heat.'

'I'm not convinced by any of this.'

'There's no other scenario. If there is you tell me.'

From within the disconnected iron-lung it was not possible to offer an alternative. Ramsey held the phone tighter to stop the room spinning. 'Brook,' he said, 'the other day somebody accused me of playing God. They were talking to the wrong person.'

'If God existed I'm sure She'd be a realist,' Brook said. 'How's the shoulder?'

'Fuck you too,' Ramsey said and hung up.

Two nights later the patron of the *Bar de la Marée* had to send for Marcel. Ramsey was too drunk to make his way home alone. It was unheard of. But then his woman had gone off to Paris. He had been in the bar for six hours discouraging all company. In fact nobody had joined him all night.

A French cop came to see him. Chief Superintendent Durand from Bayeux. He was dapper in a manner Brook could not have arrived at in a million years. A fashion-plate Jacques-the-lad, Ramsey distantly noted. In a sympathetic voice Durand asked all the right questions in a way that clearly showed he already knew the answers.

'We will conduct enquiries throughout the area,' he said.

And now existence for Ramsey resolved itself into travel around the loops of two elemental spirals. One was Time and the other Space. The curiosity was, though, that simultaneously he was travelling in two opposite directions. With Time the loops were getting larger and larger as the minutes expanded into hours and the world and all in it turned slower and slower. But Space went round in ever decreasing circles. The town, the cemetery, the boat, the cottage, his bedroom, his bed. Everything was moving in on him. And yet in this strange claustrophobia it took longer and longer to move between places that had become closer and closer. At times he could almost see the spirals corkscrewing up, crystalline, into the sky from out of the sea. The one an opening cone, the other a tightening round pyramid, they were inscribed three-dimensionally on the air. Yet also they intersected in his head. One day when he had spent hours staring at the sea trying to run to the horizon and, vaporising itself, to become one with the sky, Marcel tapped him on the shoulder. Ramsey had looked at his watch and found he had been at the end of the breakwater only a matter of minutes. Vaguely – it didn't matter, you see – he supposed he was going out of his mind. Marcel seemed to share the same opinion. His hands moving much more slowly than usual he delivered his solemn opinion to Ramsey.

'You must go back to work.'

Occupation, diversion: it was the therapy he always prescribed. For others. Now the physician was due to heal himself he knew such shallow tricks were quite beside the point.

'A glass,' Marcel signalled. 'Tomorrow the hospital.' They walked back into the town. And there, quite casually, not even suddenly, was Tessa looking into the window. She was standing outside the boucherie in the side street that led to the square.

'Tessa! Tessa!' calling her name he ran towards her.

At first she did not look round. Then, when he was right on top of her, she did. Indignant, terrified, it was a considerably older woman who did not resemble Tessa at all. Her lips moved, but someone had switched off the sound.

'*Je m'excuse . . . je m'excuse*' he mumbled or shouted after her as she hurried away. Then someone smashed a fierce blow across his face. He recoiled and looked to see his adversary. It was Marcel. He was crying. He pointed to the window.

Ramsey divined he was to look not at the laid-out cuts of meat but at his own reflection. It was a shocking sight. A stranger with a four-day growth of beard, unkempt, hair on end, with food stains down his sweater, stared at him askance. Ramsey shook his head. So did the stranger. It came to Ramsey that he was concerned about going out of his mind. It was a dishonourable thing to do. If he was going to be riven by guilt for the rest of his life he owed it to Tessa to undergo the experience undiluted. He shook his head again. This time it was not to reflect upon himself but to smash the two crystal spirals. He succeeded. He sensed himself seeing them crack and shiver, and as the needles they had become dissolved away, Time and Space were put properly in their place.

'Work!' Marcel shouted.

Ramsey nodded. 'Better now,' he indicated. 'Let's start with a shave.' His stitches needed taking out in any case. The next morning the hospital gave him the fast-lane treatment due a '*cher collègue*' and, his shoulder being as good as new, the *raison d'être*, he went in to see Dubreilh. It was instantly arranged. He would resume work in the morning.

The rest of the day he spent at his desk writing. The last piece of paper he covered was the hardest to complete. It was a letter. The hardest part was penning the opening. Finally he decided that if Beryl Waite's name was on the envelope he could omit the hypocrisy of any salutation. He started with the first line of his text.

You will have heard by now from unofficial sources what has happened to your daughter. I strongly believe that you will be aware that this is directly connected to the circumstances by which your husband met his death – circumstances which, I also believe, you are totally conversant with. This is to inform you I have today lodged papers with solicitors in both England and France setting out everything I know. In the event of your daughter not being found alive in thirty days of the above date or in the event of my own disappearance or demise, my solicitors are under instruction to release my papers to the press of their own respective countries and of Germany. I suggest if you or Mr Adams have any useful connection with those performing similar functions to the late Simon Wood, you employ all influence at your command in bringing pressure to bear. If the worst – as I fear – has come or will come to pass the shit hitting your fan will make the Parkinson and Archer scandals look like the trivial pursuits they are.

I imagine this will be the last communication between us. R.

That night the phone rang. It was a short conversation.

'Allo?'

'Well?'

He replaced the receiver before a third word could come from either end. The sensation of pain he felt and the strange noise he had heard had been allied, he perceived: their common source was the grinding of his teeth. But it had meant, he dared to hope, that Brook was so far right: that Tessa was still alive.

Work. He returned to his healing practices at eight the next morning. Being clean shaven and two armed hardly made a new man of him but he rediscovered that the human mechanism is amazing beyond prediction. What if he were heartsick. On automatic pilot he functioned as soundly as if he had indeed come back from the holiday which one purblind gas-man said had 'done him the world of good by the look of it'. The first day back he routinely prolonged the life of a taxi driver who came in complaining of pulled muscles in the chest but who was, in fact, emerging from his first heart attack. The second day, along with an ambulance crew, he safely delivered a premature but living, perfectly formed, baby. A farmer's eleven year old son came in minus most of the left arm he had left behind in the drive mechanism of a mechanical reaper. They kept him alive. A television repair man, father of two tiny children, was brought in inexplicably unconscious. The brain haemorrhage never allowed him to come out of his brief coma. When he told the brickyard foreman that they had caught his mother's incipient pneumonia well in time, he had felt he was back in Maupassant's time. The man's peasant eyes had narrowed in disappointment. No matter. Marcel had been right to turn his own prescription upon himself. Work was a famous specific. Because its mechanics crowded in on him, because his brain needed a respite from the near intolerable awareness, there were brief, random moments when he actually forgot Tessa. On the Sunday morning the phone rang.

211

'Well?'

All but destroyed again, it was he who threw the pebble against the wall. The effort it took should have moved a mountain.

They had chosen their time well. Sunday. He was not on duty that day. He wouldn't be summoned by the clanging bells. Maybe he would go in and help out in Casualty. It was always busy on a Sunday morning on account of the farmers who economically saved up their minor injuries for the day of rest. But instead he went to the boat. He could mess about patching it up instead, and perhaps he'd get through the day. He set out along the sea wall to the mooring. His hold on reality was less than total, he realised. The call had unnerved him once again. The wall and the sea looked as if he were viewing them through someone else's glasses. At the far end of the wall was another woman – the fourth now, or was it the fifth? – he had momentarily taken to be Tessa. The girl's total immobility proved it was someone else. He blinked. He saw that it was neither someone else nor a mirage. It was, dear God, no one else but Tessa.

'Hello, Ramsey.'

Her eyes were like a lemur's. Huge chocolate-mauve circles ringed them. She was lifeless. But as he hugged her to him, and she started to weep, he knew she was alive, restored. This time a long time passed and it seemed like no time. He had forgotten you could risk believing such happiness was true. At last they moved apart.

'You all right?' was all he contrived to say.

Childlike she nodded. But then rolling up the sleeve of her blouse she showed him the inside of her right arm. The length of its central vein were the bruises and punctures of a hypodermic. The left arm was the same. He held her tight again. No, never believe in happiness.

'What?' he said.

'Heroin.'

'How many times?'

She pulled her face away from his chest and looked gravely at him from her dead eyes. 'I gave up counting. Every few hours.'

As though the effort had drained her, she closed her eyes. Very gently he kissed her eye-lids. 'It will be all right,' he said. 'You'll see.'

They stayed in their embrace. He began to acknowledge that part of him was glad at what they'd done to her. She would need a doctor. Performing that function for her was going to be his own final cure.

SEVENTEEN

No longer crouching to ring with bad news, the phone became a friend again. He called Durand who was ecstatic because, he implied, his strategy had worked. Then, his eyes seldom leaving Tessa as she toyed with rather than ate the onion soup, he called the man who did deserve credit.

'Brook.'

'Ramsey. She's back.'

'Alive and well?'

'Alive. They've shot her up with heroin.'

'Oh. How serious is that?'

'It's nasty but not serious.'

'Can you handle it for her?'

'Yes. I think I owe you a pint, Brook.'

'Yes, you do. But just do me a favour in return.'

'Name it.'

'Don't do anything. Just stay at home. Do your job and let me do mine.'

'You're preaching to the converted – converted the hard way.'

'Good. Keep a weather eye open, though.'

'Oh?'

'They just might get on to a revenge kick when the going between Fleetwood and points south gets rough.'

'Right. With you. I'll watch it.'

'Good. 'Bye now.'

'Thanks again.'

With what he knew was an effort of considerable will, Tessa focused her still unnaturally pin-pointed eyes on him. 'Nasty but not serious, eh?' she said.

'That's about it.'

'Are you referring to my condition or our relationship?' It was a joke of heroic endeavour.

'Our relationship, I trust, is nice and easy.'

'Ramsey – am I going to be all right?'

'Yes.'

'I'm not hooked?'

'No.'

'Because if I am going to be a junkie from here on in I'd rather be told –'

'Tessa! Don't talk like that!' He drew a chair up close to her and,

213

taking her hand, squeezed it hard. 'Look at me,' he said with real urgency, 'and take the words in. It will be nasty, like I said. Rough. Rough but not as bad as you fear. Don't help it by panicking. There are things I can give you to help. You're someone who's got the equivalent of a king-size dose of 'flu coming up. King-size plus, maybe. But hang on to this. Nothing I give you will probably help as much as this fact. During the Viet Nam war thousands of Americans got addicted to heroin. The high was better than being shit scared. Today over ninety per cent of them are clean. And that's after they'd been on it for months.'

'You say that's a fact?'

'A cast iron, super-solid, American apple-pie fact.' With the dark rings about her eyes, her white skin, she looked about eight years old as she grinned her attempt to make him think she was encouraged. He leaned forward and felt her forehead with his palm.

'Hot?'

'Burning,' she said.

'Otherwise?'

'A bit achey, doctor.'

'Where?'

She rubbed the small of her back with her hands. 'Here. And I have pains in my legs.'

'OK. Get undressed and into bed. I'll put out some pyjamas for you. It's Sunday so I'm going off to the hospital for twenty minutes or so to get some stuff.'

'I didn't realise it was Sunday.'

'Why should you have? I'll lock the door. Don't let anyone in. No one at all.'

In spite of her fever she shivered. He saw fear beginning to ebb back into her. 'Just twenty minutes,' he said. 'Then I'll be telling you a bedtime story.'

'That's a nice feeling,' the eight-year-old said.

In fact he took twenty-five minutes. He owed it to Marcel to swing by the *Bar de la Marée* with the good news. When he told him, he thought Marcel would cry again. But when he left him the deaf-mute was edging forward to claim a place in the next *boules* game. It would be his first attempt to play since the day of the kidnap.

When he got back Tessa was sitting up in bed, her knees drawn up to her chin. 'I'm scared,' she said. 'My guts feel like water.'

'Two inevitable reactions,' he said. 'But when you know they're the norm you can start to handle both of them.'

He held up the bottle. 'Methadone,' he said. 'Less noxious. Less addictive. It's like weaning. We start with twenty milligrams every twelve hours. Then, about day three we reduce to ten. Then five.

214

One day you won't need it.'

He measured the syrupy liquid into the plastic spoon. 'Here.'

She gulped it down.

'How did you feel after the injections?' he casually asked.

'First time – sick as a horse. All itchy. Even my clothes made me feel uncomfortable.'

'Yes. Here.'

She shuddered. But not from the taste. 'After a while I was looking forward to them.'

'Here.'

'Tessa,' he said, pouring again, 'did they touch you?'

'Rape me, you mean.'

'Yes.'

'No. One time when I was flying one of them came in. I think he was going to. He started to paw me.'

She blushed. 'The truth is,' she said, 'I didn't much mind. It didn't seem important one way or the other.'

'No. Here.'

'Another one came in. There was a row. They went out. The first one never came back.'

'Were they French or English?'

'French. But they knew some English.'

'And they held you where?'

'A room. A bare room.' Again she shuddered.

'Any idea whereabouts?'

'No. They put a scarf round my eyes. Held me down. We were in that car for ever. I thought they meant to kill me.'

'I know it's hard. Could you guess how long for ever was?'

'. . . two hours perhaps. It felt like going round in circles.'

'Here. Last one.'

She swallowed it then yawned. 'Tired,' she said.

'Yes. Sleep now.'

'Where will you be?'

'A shout away.'

She smiled and stretched down into the bed.

In sweater and slacks, under a rug on the camp bed he slept fitfully. On and off. Towards two in the morning he was awake listening to the wind getting up, the waves hitting the rocks. He glanced at his watch and, doing so, thought of Dany. Had he lied to her to ease her insecurity? Cowardice on his part because – gagging coughs from the bedroom switched his own thoughts to low priority. He went into the bedroom.

Tessa was sitting up again. She was clasping her knees to her chest.

215

Her hair was spikey. Drenched in sweat she had thrown off the bedclothes. Fear suffused her too.

'Rough?' he said.

'Rough. Stomach cramps.'

He picked up the towel and gently wiped her face dry. He pushed the damp hair back from her forehead.

'I'm sorry,' she said.

'What for?'

'For being such a nuisance.'

'Rubbish.'

'Perhaps a little more Methadone . . .'

'Not yet.'

'Christ, Ramsey,' she was suddenly crying fiercely, 'it's no time to go tough on me!'

He realised her sweetness had been the low-level cunning of an addict's apprentice con job.

'Please!'

'I'll give you something to make you sleep,' he said.

'I feel like something sweet.'

'I'll see what I can do.' He went to the bathroom and got a temazepan for her. He got honey from the kitchen. In her haste to get to the honey she swallowed the tablet almost violently. He motioned at the jar.

'I'll leave it here.'

Her head shook from side to side. Because she was shivering.

'Cold now?' Doctors always ask stupid belated questions.

'Freezing.'

He made her lie down and pulling the bedclothes up tucked her in. Her head jerked round.

'Ramsey,' she said, her voice shot through with panic. 'I'm dying!'

'You're not,' he said shortly. It came out over-abrupt.

'Do you want me to try and warm you up?' he said by way of compensating.

'No,' she said. 'Don't touch me.'

Coughing, she turned away. He stood watching, feeling yet again the duality every physician must live with. The god-like impersonal professional in him knew that thanks to his expertise she should, in time, be all right. The human knew that for the only time that meant anything to her now, the present, he was powerless to help.

The sound of the lavatory flushing woke him. Gone nine. Late. As he swivelled upright Tessa came into the room. She had a blanket wrapped around her but it didn't stop the smell of dried sweat on the crumpled pyjamas reaching him. She looked like death warmed up.

216

'All right if I have a bath?' and sounded it.

'Of course. Want me to run it?'

'I think I can manage.'

'We'll give you an edge. You're due your next four spoonfuls.'

The very news put some life in her. She gulped the dosage avidly.

'Have your bath,' he said. 'I'm about to prescribe orange juice, coffee and day-old croissants.'

Her face wrinkled. 'I don't think I can stomach that,' she said. 'Literally.'

'Yes you can. Doctor's orders.'

The orange juice took the longest because it was fresh squeezed. Twelve minutes later he was balancing a tray precariously on his left hand as he knocked on the bathroom door.

'Are you decent?'

'I certainly am,' she called.

He went in. It was as well he had got two hands back on the tray before he saw her. Her idea of decent was quaint. She was still in the bath and stretched out full length. A modicum of foam floated on the water's surface but it was rather less than Botticelli would have employed in leaving Venus a shred or two of token modesty. Botticelli would have ordered the hands more discreetly too. She grinned up at him. 'Decency is a moral state,' she said. 'I *am* your patient, after all.' The hot water had revivified the marks on her inner arms. He concentrated on those.

'I warn you,' he said grimly. 'There's a randy phase coming up.'

'Promises, promises.'

'Spontaneous orgasms. The works.'

'Can't wait.'

'And you're going to feel terrible again.'

'. . . spoil sport.'

'I have to go out for a while this morning,' he said. 'Anything you want?'

She thought for a moment. 'Chocolate,' she said. 'Lots of it.'

'You've only just come back.' Stocky, grey, bespectacled, Dubreilh turned from the window and looked harshly at Ramsey.

'I know. I'm sorry. If it's possible to forfeit, er, exchange my next year's holiday for the time now I'd be quite happy to agree.'

Dubreilh had positioned his desk so that the glare from the office window shone distractingly straight into your eyes. Ramsey's ached. Dubreilh moved back behind the desk and sat down.

'You said it was a personal matter,' he said. 'Can I prevail on you – strictly within these four walls – to be a little more explicit?'

'A friend of mine died recently. His daughter, grown-up, has got hooked on heroin. She needs me to get her off it and I'd like to do it in his memory.'

Dubreilh looked at him from the far side of the glare. 'Is this the English girl the police were swarming around asking questions about?'

'Yes. She turned up.'

'As the whole district knows.'

Dubreilh smiled. 'Dr Ramsey,' he said, 'you are a dishonest man. No – don't protest! You know very well that I know very well that if you wanted it you could secure a position in a far more prestigious and better equipped hospital than this. Even one by the sea. I really have no choice, do I . . . ?' Dubreilh raised his bushy eyebrows in ironic bafflement.

'That's very kind of you, Vincent.'

'Nor do I approve of personnel here working non-stop through the year. All work and no vacation makes the doctor what he should never allow himself to be – sub-standard.'

'Vincent I –'

'The matter is closed. Is she badly hooked?'

'I think the odds are on our side.'

'Good.'

Brook had made his 'tough it out' strategy stick. Ramsey had no sense of foreboding as laden down with brioche, salami, soup packets and, above all, chocolate, he returned to the cottage.

'I'm back,' he said as he kneed the front door open. No answer was the stern reply.

'Tessa?'

It was suddenly not funny. The bathroom and the bedroom doors were both ajar. He put the groceries down on the floor and went into the bathroom. Nothing. She was in the bedroom. She sat on the floor, her back against the wall and her legs splayed. She hadn't dressed since getting out of the bath. Her mouth was open as she crooned a tuneless sound she was hearing from far away and her eyes, pinpointed into darts, stared right through him to the centre of the earth, moon and stars.

218

EIGHTEEN

Once they were out from the shelter of the breakwater, the trailing dinghy began to smack up and down against the collision of their own wake with the swell. The boat began to pitch but steadily, predictably. In the prow, tail wagging, Gabin was revelling in the breeze hurling strange scents at him. Tessa, her back wedged against the groundsheet covering the camping gear out on the open deck, was in a diametrically opposed frame of mind. Leaving the wheel to Marcel, Ramsey went forward and crouched down beside her.

'What is this place, anyway?' she sulked.

'An island. With a fort. Fortified, rather. It was to the French in the days of Nelson what the Martello towers were to us. Then the Germans used it. But apart from the rabbits it's been uninhabited since World War 2. I've not been here for years.'

'It sounds terrific . . . How long are you planning to spend on this sceptred-fucking isle?'

'As long as it takes, Tessa. Marcel will do milk runs for us.'

'Ducky! It'll be just like the Eddystone lighthouse. No one will be able to get at us and with you as my round-the-clock gaoler I won't be able to get at anyone.'

'Or anything.'

'You don't trust me, do you?'

'You've proved I can't.'

'Ramsey moves in a mysterious way his wonder-cures to peform!'

'We can't go in all the way. We'll have to ferry the gear and supplies the last bit in the dinghy.'

'So?'

'So stop play-acting and think about being useful.'

Later, with the driftwood fire burning steadily a sensible distance from the small ridge tent she had become more reconciled. Reconciled but physically little improved. After the afternoon remission of the regulation Methadone dose she was once more in the throes of the withdrawal symptoms. He lay on his back looking at the glitter of stars restored to a pre-urban brightness. How unfriendly they became if you weren't using them for navigation. After a while he was staring at the cold, indifferent infinities between them. Ongoing nothingness not giving a damn. The last time he had visited the island with anyone else it had been with Anne. By that time he had had to carry her ashore.

'I'd like to see the stars one final time – properly,' she said. 'It's so boring being sick.'

'I feel sick,' she said now. The stars blinked and he realised it was Tessa who had produced the echo.

'I'm exhausted. But beyond sleep. I'm all over twitchy. Inside and out. Talk to me.'

'I think I've worked out why they've done this to you.'

'. . . Why?'

'The man I saw in London. The one I think kept the others off you. He fancies himself. He would think this . . . witty. A good joke.'

'The bastard.'

'You can have the last laugh, Tessa. Two when they get him.'

'Will they?'

'Brook has something coming to the boil.'

'I hope it's that swine!'

Good. He'd managed to crank up her determination a notch or two. 'Let's go over it again,' he said. 'What about sounds?'

'. . . Normal, everyday sounds.'

'City sounds? Country sounds?'

'House sounds. Doors going. Loos flushing. Water in pipes. Loud foot steps.'

'Think. Think hard. Give me one unusual sound.'

'Relentless, aren't you?'

'Come on! You said you wanted to talk.'

'I've changed my mind.' They lay in prickly silence a long time. He levered himself up to put another branch on the fire.

'Hens,' she said. 'Clucking. And a cockerel.'

'You're sure?'

'Oh for God's sake, Ramsey. Of course I'm not sure. On account of the fact I'm scared shitless I'm going off my chump, I'm quite positive it was one of those monstrous nightmares I couldn't wake up from . . . that I was – how would you put it – aurally hallucinating!'

'Tessa, if you thought –'

'Thought! How do I know what I thought? Or think? I've got the cramps, the sweats, the trots and God –'

'I'll give you some Lomotil.'

'Great! Lomotil for this. Valium for that! And I'm trapped on this ever-decreasing circle. Ramsey – I want to go back!'

'I told you. We go back when it's over.'

'God damn you!' Staggering a good deal she got to her feet. Convinced by such suddenness it must be time to scatter more rabbits Gabin started up from his stertorous slumber. Tail wagging, he followed her beyond the fire's circle of light.

'Oh sod off! Stop following me, you stupid thing.'

220

A snuffle. Not a best friend any more, Gabin slunk back, black out of black, from the night. He padded over to Ramsey and began disconsolately, to lick his hand. Then his ears pricked. Ramsey could hear it too. The sound of retching as someone seemed to be trying to fetch their very stomach up.

But his instinct had been right. The island made a crucial difference. It was incredible how irrelevantly remote its few kilometres of off-shoreness made the rest of the world. As they circled the beaches and coves collecting wood, running out lines, all else dropped away. D.H.S.S. selfishness, Paris bomb outrages, what Botham or Platini or Reagan did – none of it mattered. The radio burbled on about such stuff from time to time but they paid no heed. There was no point. The clean, salt wind came off of the sea to tell them it had been doing this throughout creation and all else was vanity. The silver-blue sea laughed at the White House and the Kremlin's presumption. All was false except for the four elements and people one by one.

Still it was not a straight progression. The fourth morning, returning bare-foot from the spring-fed well that made their sojourn possible, he found Tessa scrabbling through his doctor's bag with a furious, shabby, furtiveness.

'Lost something?' he said.

She lurched to her feet. 'You've hidden it!' she accused.

'Obviously.'

'You bastard! You still don't trust me!'

'And with every reason. He walked past her, picked up the bag, collected the scattered tubes and bottles and put them back inside. He put the bag back in the tent. As he straightened up he saw Tessa was crying. She was feeling sorry for herself.

'You don't understand! You can't!'

'So tell me.'

'I ache. From the end of my hair to my toenails. When I'm not sweating, I'm freezing. When I'm not freezing, I'm sweating. I feel permanently sick. I have stomach cramps. The clothes on my back hurt me. *Hurt* me. I feel like a . . . peeled egg.'

He looked at her.

'Lomotil . . . valium . . . breakfast?' he said.

She rushed at him beating at his chest with a powerless desperation. He easily caught the two flailing arms. 'You're a sadist, you swine!' she sobbed. 'You pretend it's kill or cure but you know there's no cure and you're enjoying it!'

He knew it wasn't her saying this. 'You're getting cured,' he said.

'I'm not! I'm not! I don't feel any better.'

'You don't feel any worse and you're down to ten milligrams a dose. Ten more in three hours.'

'I can't wait that long! I can't.'

'Yes you can.'

'How? How can I?'

'Because you have to.'

Three steps forward, two and a half back. Slowly, painfully. It still came out as progress. On the fourth night she only got up to be sick three times. Soon, he knew, the rate of progress would start accelerating. 'Let's try fishing from the dinghy,' he said next day. They anchored a couple of hundred metres out and dropped four lines. The sun shone. The sea sparkled. Tessa in blue cotton shirt and cut-off jeans was well on the way to an in-depth tan. A picture of health, you would have said, as she devoured a bar of Lindt. She rinsed her hands over the bobbing side and wiped them on her jeans. She looked sideways at him so archly that for a second he thought she was going to take off her shirt.

'When I came calling two years ago,' she said instead '– you haven't forgotten, have you?'

'It's etched on my memory.'

'You already knew Dany?'

'Yes.'

'Where was she?'

'In Paris. At her flat.'

'And you were already screwing her?'

'I don't know which of us that cheapens the more.'

'Oh, don't worry. I'm not being holier than thou. I just about raped you.'

'That's true,' he said. Suddenly they were both smiling. Like the rate of the franc against the yen, that was all in another time, another place. Beyond her he saw the plastic bottle duck sharply down.

'You've caught one!' he said.

She pulled in the line. The hunter's elemental satisfaction had momentarily made her completely well. As he worked the hook free from the surprisingly large plaice a gull swooped low with coarse cries of outrage. It circled and hovered in the hope of some spoon-feeding. Tessa clutched Ramsey's arm.

'That's something else,' she said. 'Seagulls. Crying. Lots of them.'

'So it was by the sea.'

'Hens put it in the country.'

'A small house or farm on the coast. But in a small place strange comings and going, stand out. I would have bet on a town myself.'

Early next morning she woke him as she left the tent. It was the first time that night and as she'd pushed past the flap he'd seen streaks of grey in the sky. No point in trying to doze off again before she returned. He clasped his hands behind his head.

It was funny. If she'd been healthy, or if he'd been younger, the air would have been saturated with sex. If, for instance, they'd been two students tenting their way across Europe. And, of course, his body still wanted her. It reminded him of the fact every time he awoke like this and found himself as ramrod hard as any student. A part of him had enjoyed seeing her in that bath, had wanted her to remove her shirt that afternoon, had wanted to have its prick teased and then put to proper use.

But she was his patient, unofficial though it might be. There were rules about those things. But it was more basic even than that. He wasn't such a nice guy. The paradox was that complete proximity was a turn-off. The bodily intimacies, shoved under your nose, were a guaranteed anaphrodisiac. It is difficult to lust after someone you see stalking into the interior with a trench-spade and a toilet roll: who has failed, this time, to prevent some of her vomit staining her sweater: whom you've seen spitting phlegmy toothpaste into a tin mug. He smiled to himself. The island idyll had been too like a marriage to give lust a fair crack of any kind of whip.

The tent flap slithered. Gabin growled. Tessa was inching back in to her sleeping bag.

'First time,' he checked.

'Yes. Damn near made it through the night.'

'I think we could say you did. Too late to go back to sleep. Half an hour for it to warm up and I'll make some coffee.'

'My hero . . . Ramsey?'

'Yes?'

'You've stayed here before, haven't you?'

'Yes.'

'With Dany?'

'No.'

'With Anne.'

'Yes. And then by myself after she . . . afterwards. It's a good place to be alone.'

'I'm not coming back – not if I live to be a million.'

'It's going to be the scene of a genuine triumph for you.'

'Hmph! One thing though . . .'

'Yes?'

'I'm glad I wasn't alone when I was here.'

The next night and the following three she slept the clock round well into the broad daylight. That was on five milligrams. Taken off

223

altogether she spent forty-eight hours more without feeling more than a degree under.

'I've felt worse from the dreaded P.M.T.,' she said that afternoon. They were walking on the beach. Her tan was now confirmed and her smile as she spoke beat the sea's into second place.

'Will you marry Dany?' she asked from out of the sky's blue. She was relaxed enough, it seemed, to rearrange her order of preoccupations.

'Why don't you stop beating about the bush and stop being so obscure?' He tried to fend her off.

'Will you?'

'Is it any of your business?'

'Yes.'

'Yes, I suppose it is . . . We've never discussed it.'

She stopped strolling, obliging him to stop too and to look round. 'I can't believe you,' she said. It didn't sound insulting.

'There is a husband,' he said.

'Oh.'

'I've a question for you,' he said.

'Namely?'

'Marcel is due tomorrow. How would you like to go home?'

When she believed she could believe he was being serious her smile outshone the sun.

It was as well Marcel was due the next day. They had run their supplies down very low. Centrepiece of their meal that evening was potatoes ashily baked in their jackets. They were too hot to handle right out of the fire. They sat waiting for them to cool off, under stars closer than ever. Tessa realised that, gradually, what at first was only to be endured had become romantic.

'Perhaps you're right,' she said breaking the silence. 'I might remember this place with some affection after all.'

'You have reason to now.'

'Even though we forgot the eight gramophone records,' she joked. But then she shivered.

'Cold?'

'No. The truth is I'm sort of scared about going back to that other universe over there – being plunged into the mainstream.'

'If you're frightened they might come after you again, Brook –'

'It's not that. Out of sight, out of reach – it's easier to avoid temptations here.'

He put an arm round her. 'You're going to do fine,' he said. 'And the day after tomorrow we'll whirl you about so fast your feet won't

224

touch the ground. The boat needs a service. We'll take her to Dieppe.'

He paused. 'Better face it, though,' he said. 'You're cured.'

NINETEEN

'Help!' Tessa said, 'I'm getting dizzy. It's all too fast!'

It was traffic speeding by in a dangerous kaleidoscope that dragged your eyeballs along after it. Store fronts clamoured silently for attention. Pedestrians rose up out of the pavement in front of you, sidestepping away only after collision seemed inevitable. She felt gawky, deafened. The street was full of noises.

They stood in a doorway in Dieppe's main shopping area. When the boat was safely delivered to the engineers, and Marcel, who had brought the car overland, was safely off on the Abbéville train to see his sister, she had wanted to do some shopping. A fortnight or so of roughing it entitled her to some new undies and maybe a decent blouse or two. Only she didn't feel safe at all. This was a strident, threatening world.

'What's happening to me?' she bewilderedly asked Ramsey. All he could do was smile.

'My fault,' he said. 'It's the contrast after being all alone on the island. This is too sudden. I'm feeling it too. We need a decompression chamber.'

But she had a deeper, underlying fear. 'Ramsey,' she said, 'I've got this terrible urge for chocolate. Does that mean –'

This time he laughed outright. 'It neither means you're hooked or pregnant. It means you're the same as I am – starving. That's the answer. A restaurant is the decompression chamber we need. There's a good one just a couple of streets away. We'll sit in the window and get used to the world going by again.'

It was called *Gachons*. It was small and crowded but the *patron*, a tall, balding young man smiled broadly when his eyes lit on Ramsey. There was a voluble exchange she didn't catch and, *voilà*, they were indeed accorded a seat at the window.

As they sat she detected a certain something about Ramsey she had never seen in him before . . . smugness, that was it. He had the air of a tennis player who had just hit a spectacularly extravagant winner. She switch-backed down into instant depression. It was unfair, no doubt. She was still a fair bit strung out, perhaps, and the knowledge that she must soon go back to England and what passed for life there was circling ever closer but –

'You've been here before,' she heard herself saying.

'Yes. Many times.'

'You should've let me choose.' He stopped smiling. She had heard the pettiness in her voice. But her point was valid all the same.

'You don't like it,' he said.

'It's not that.'

'So . . . what is it?'

She shook her head. 'You wouldn't understand.'

'Why? Am I that insensitive?'

'We always go to places *you* know.'

'Wooh!' he said, relaxing a little. 'Hold on. One – this is my neck of the woods. Two – if there are three restaurants in a street –'

'*Voilà, m'selle, m'sieur.*'

Great placards of menus had appeared before them.

'It's nothing to do with this,' she said shaking her menu, 'whether their coquilles are better than someone else's. It's–'

'What is it then?'

'Where you take me. They're places you've been with others. Dany. Or Suzanne. Or Françoise. Or –'

'Hey stop it! You're confused. It's not Alain Delon you're sitting opposite.' He was trying to keep it light but she could tell he was hurt and angry. 'I'd like, just once, for there to be a place, however grotty, that was ours,' she went on. 'Yours and mine, and no ghosts from your past.'

'Done,' he said too heartily. 'The next meal – a real greasy spoon. Belgian chips. Incinerated "bifteck". Some corner of a foreign gaff that is forever Tessa's.'

To both their consternations she began to cry. 'Hankie,' she sniffed. 'Quick.'

He handed her his. 'What is it really?' he said.

She fought her way back to coherence if not composure. 'I love you, Ramsey,' she at last allowed herself to say. 'And in a few days I'll have to go back home. No! Let me finish! . . . When I've gone, Dany will come back. I'll be there. You'll be here. You won't want me over here in France again, I know. I know you won't.'

'Who's told you that?'

'No one needs to! And I won't want to come back, anyway. To watch you and her together. Can't you see?'

'You don't like her?'

'I hate her. She's smashing and I hate her . . . I've loved you for ten years.'

'Tessa – a little distance on things, please. Ten years ago you were a kid – braces on your teeth, pigtails . . .'

'I never had pigtails!' she almost shouted. He seemed to fight off a smile. It had sounded so infantile she felt outraged herself. The waitress with a *panier* of bread and the cutlery temporarily rescued her. But she didn't want that; she wanted to show she could rescue herself. What the hell if the waitress spoke English!

'You're a doctor,' she said. 'You're immune to things.'

'Am I?'

'We were alone together on the island all that time.'

'You hated it, you said.'

'I hated it because of the way I was. Don't you see? I sweated and stank and vomited and worse – all in front of you. In earshot. You were wishing the wind was blowing the other way just when I wanted you to look at me and see something beautiful beyond compare.'

She'd got it about right, he thought. And taking the long view it was no doubt a good thing that the unlovely mechanics of living cheek by unsanitary jowl had been there as a safety valve.

'Tessa,' he said. 'Leave Anne out of it. You know wherever I go there's a ghost at my side. She's here now. She was there on the island. She was on the island the week she died . . . Of all people in the world, or out of it, she knew things like a person heaving their heart up into a bowl is neither here nor there. She would have approved of me approving of you fighting a plucky, gutsy fight.'

'That's beside *my* point. I wasn't trying to win my girl guide "Fortitude" badge.'

'*Alors, m'selle, m'sieur – vous avez choisi?*'

Arbitrarily, appetite all gone, they ordered. Tessa reached mechanically for a piece of bread. In mid-motion she froze. From the harbour there sounded the fat, deep, organic blast of the cross-channel ferry. 'Ramsey!' she breathed.

'What?'

'The ferry. The siren.'

'It's probably about to leave.'

'No. That's another sound. Like the hens, the seagull. I remember now. I heard it when I was climbing up that dreadful yellow papered wall. The vibrations seemed to get right inside me. I'm sure that's the same one. I must have been hearing it from somewhere very close to here.'

He began to sense a spark of something in the air.

'Let's eat,' he said. 'fortify ourselves. Let's get our balance. Then we'll walk around.'

It was hopeless. Every car, parked or passing, was now the ideal for a bunch of hoods. Because it was big and fast. Because it was small and anonymous. It was the same with the houses and the *pensions*. They all flatly returned any scrutiny, their façade demanding to be taken as innocent until proved guilty. And where was the evidence?

'Tessa,' Ramsey said. They were in the rue de Lorraine. He was pointing to rail tracks crossing the street.

'They would have made the car rattle,' he said. 'Do you remember any rattling or jolting?'

She could only shake her head. Aimlessly they wandered on up the street. A futile exercise. It had, though, re-acclimatised her to the pace of city streets. They turned left into a small square.

'I'm sorry,' Tessa said. 'It's hopeless. My hair ought to stand up on end. I should feel drawn by this evil magnetic force.'

'Especially here.'

Why so?'

'We're in the *place de l'Enfer*. The "Square of Hell".'

'Yes, well, I'm as psychic as a brick – wherever I am. Face it, Ramsey, they probably had me holed up in Newhaven!'

'It's out of the breeze here. We'll do a promenade all the way round then head over to the car park while we can still afford the bail money.'

'These are tallish houses,' Tessa said, 'and because of the stairs we went up it must've been quite tall. And I don't remember a steady sound of traffic like there would be over most of Dieppe. It's quiet here too.'

She stopped walking, trying to gauge the sound level against her memory. Then she was standing rigid staring at Ramsey's staring eyes. He had heard it too. On the relatively quiet air there carried the sounds of squabbling hens.

'Ramsey!'

'Over here, I think. Yes?'

'Yes. Oh, Ramsey – I wasn't hallucinating!' They quickly cut a corner of the square to reach its southern side. The noise had stopped. Then it resumed. Louder.

'Ramsey. Just along there. An empty house!'

He was already looking at it. Paint flaking from its woodwork, it was the shabbiest in its row. Its blank windows blindly mourned that no one lived behind them.

'It's high enough, I think,' Tessa said in a small voice. She clutched Ramsey's arm.

'The room you were in – did it have a window?'

'It was boarded up. Crudely. Just with planks. Except for the very top. There was a light.'

'Neither of those top two ones are boarded up.'

'No. Oh my God!'

Her hand had tightened on his arm to the point of hurting him. 'Ramsey – the window on the left. Our left. Look in the top corner. What do you see?'

He squinted.

'There's a crack in it, isn't there?'

229

'Look harder!'

Sunlight was glancing awkwardly off the glass. It was like trying to look at a badly placed picture in a gallery. He moved his position to the other end of a parked car. A man came to the door of the house opposite and glared at him suspiciously. Up his! Ramsey squinted up diagonally at the window again and, obligingly on cue, the sun went behind a cloud. In the top left corner of the window something tiny moved. A spider.

'It's a spider's web,' Ramsey said.

Tessa looked at him white-faced. 'That's the house!' she said. 'There was this enormous spider in the window. Terrifying. He got into my nightmares. I saw him build his web up hour by hour, day by day. Ramsey – what do we do?'

What indeed. He could feel fresh energy pulsing to be released from his fingertips and the balls of his feet. Adrenalin sparkled through him renewing his high voltage. They could talk to the neighbours; maybe talk to local estate agents, postmen; perhaps he could force the door . . . No. Enough was enough. Brook's voice was laconically loud at the back of his head. 'Meddler.' That had been the word that had most got to him. Rightly. He wouldn't meddle now.

'We'll report this to Durand,' he said.

'Durand?'

'The Chief Superintendent at Bayeux. It's on our way back. He wants to talk to you anyway.'

She smiled. They started to walk from the square. He could now admit to himself that as he'd spoken a great surge of relief had washed the pent-up excitement away. It all became easier when you left living to the servants! It was perhaps this state of euphoria that prevented either of them remarking on the car which, as they turned right into the rue de Lorraine, started up in the square behind them.

They were a kilometre or two on from having turned inland at St Valéry-en-Caux. Tessa had fallen to talking about her father.

'You greatly disappointed him, you know,' she said. He did know but, as he glanced again in the rear-view mirror, he was curious to hear it at only one remove from Exton.

'He thought you had great things in you. Going off. Burying yourself. He knew there were reasons but it disappointed him all the same – on your behalf.'

'Headlines aren't the yardstick of having done or not done great things,' Ramsey said. 'Besides, he was a far more disappointed man than I'll ever be.'

'. . . really?'

'Really. I remember him at the age of nineteen doing prime

minister impressions for the Experimental Theatre Club Review. He loved the applause. Twenty-five years later he's a Cabinet Minister being slagged off in *Spitting Image*.'

'He could take that.'

'Oh, sure. Water off a duck's back. What he couldn't take was the increasing, certain knowledge he was a British minister at the time of the country's lowest ebb in nearly four centuries.'

'Did he feel that – he never –'

'The last time we met. In Paris. He was vital, 'up', alive. Then it all went. All that talk then of *sovereignty*, of *Britannia* – so much whistling in the dark, he said. "What are we?" he said. "Selfish beyond belief. The pits." '

'That was the coke talking, wasn't it?'

'I don't think so. I think that it was the other way round. That's how he felt and the coke made him stop feeling that. There's also something else I feel . . .'

'What?'

'Don't swing round to look but I'm ninety per cent certain the car behind is following us.'

'No!'

'It's been there since we left Dieppe.'

'What is it?'

'A big Renault. Three men in it.'

'Three men . . . it could be coincidence. Cars leave Dieppe all the time.'

'I don't think so. This isn't an obvious route to travel. That's why I chose it. And they've got more speed than us. They could easily have come past.'

'So we can't out-run them.'

'No. I can maybe out-handle them in this. Only . . .'

'Only what?'

'French roads are so damned straight. It means getting on to country roads, lanes. That means getting ourselves isolated. Getting us in a lonely place may be what they most want.'

'Ramsey – it's getting lonely enough right here.'

It was true. They were on a local rather than regional road. It went up and down dale but in a line so straight you could still hear the heavy stamp of the legions if you tried. It was late afternoon. The fair sprinkling of cars, overtaking, whooshing towards and past, had dwindled to a very few. He'd held off tensing Tessa up all over again but now he was almost certain they were in danger it was better she knew now than – shit! They had breasted yet another hill to see before them a long slope down, the balancing climb up, and between the two-kilometre stretch of honour-guard poplars not a solitary oncoming vehicle.

'How did they get on to us?'

'There was that model Renault in the square. I think it's the same one. Tessa, it's coming on.'

He put his foot down all the way. The cylinders had been re-lined within the year, the heads polished. The compression was probably as good as the day the Light Fifteen was sold. But that was nearly fifty years ago. The Renault was coming on fast now. Gaining.

'Tessa. Nothing to lose now. Look round and see if you recognise anyone.'

He kept his eye on the road and the rear-mirror as the revs went near to maximum. He sensed rather than saw Tessa clambering round. He sensed rather than saw the terror pinching her face when she turned back.

'The driver. He's one of them. The one who started to paw me. The one next to him. We saw him in the square. He came out of a house.' It was no wonder she could be so sure. The Renault was only the length of a cricket pitch away as, savaging springs, they tore out of the down slope and at once began to climb. The Light Fifteen was howling. It felt tight as an overstrung guitar. But the Renault's modern power would tell even more in a climb. Yes. It was pulling out. The passenger window was being wound down. He remembered why Rocky Beach's father had had his window open.

'Ramsey! They're going to overtake! What'll we do?'

'Put our faith in M. André's *traction avant*.' To the left a country lane snaked off in a diagonal twist across the hills rising up from the valley. It bisected a line of trees.

'Hold on!' Praying to the god of connecting rods and transmissions he stood on the brakes. Michelin patterns shrieked their way on to the road surface as the Renault careered by. The Light Fifteen hadn't deviated an inch from its original line. It was still sliding, the Renault still wallowing, as he double declutched, went from top into second, got it right and, the wheel hard over, screamed across the road into the lane.

'They're backing up!' Tessa confirmed as he changed up again.

'Yes. OK. We've got chances now.'

Excitement, triumph were swirling around with all the other feelings on his stomach and his head. Eat your heart our Prost! He was getting his one-man band kicks anyhow. On this just about made-up surface, if the bends kept coming as tight as this he might be able to stay ahead long enough for them to come to people, other cars, houses . . . He concentrated on going through two right handers and a left as fast as possible. They were in the trees now. The trunks sped past like vertical tracers. The revs grit their screaming teeth.

'All right?' he yelled at Tessa.

'No! For Christ's sake, no!'

He took a corner wide, accelerating without an inch of deviation and saw his hopes had been premature. A long straight run took the lane up out of the wood and on to the brow of the hill. And in the mirror, yes, was a glint of fast movement a bend back. Change down. Good. If they could make it to the top they must run into a broader, perhaps populous, road. The Renault couldn't overtake along here for a broadside shot. But it was closing fast again now.

Jesus!

'Ramsey!'

He'd seen it. A split second before they'd burst from the woods a tractor had started to edge forward from a field on the right and across their path. Then the howl of their engines must have got to it. A face whipped round. A boy. With a shuddering lurch the tractor had stalled. Impossibly close. Over half-way into the lane.

He probably couldn't have braked anyway. Praying the wayside foliage didn't conceal a ditch he steered to the left and half up the verge. Kerump. Kerpow. The steering wheel juddered shock through his forearms as the sky tilted. His bad shoulder yelled its pain as like a ducks and draking stone the Citroën stopped travelling courtesy of its wheels and bottomed out three teeth-snapping times. For an instant he was sitting higher than Tessa. As glass shrapnel showered in a vicious confetti about his neck and air tore into the car from outside he thought they would over-turn. But wrenching his arm again the sky slammed noisily back into place. The front wheels bounced and gained a spinning grip and as he eased off the accelerator, they were back in the middle of a clear road. He listened for the sound of a flat-out crash from behind. Above the tempest roar of engine and wind he couldn't hear it.

'Are they through?' he shouted.

'No.'

'Crashed?'

'No.'

'You OK?'

'No. I'm terrified. They just shot at us.'

He risked a glance at her. She was staring straight ahead breathing in and out on every pulse. A trickle of blood glistened beneath her left ear. 'Ramsey – there's a terrible smell of petrol!'

He had already picked it up. The gauge might almost be going visibly down. '*Courage!*' he shouted. 'Here's a road.'

He shot on to it, very nearly turning left regardless because that was the easy way to go. But up ahead just beneath the ridge of the hill was a cluster of houses. And right on the horizon a country station.

He put his foot all the way down. Safe. If they didn't blow up there were phones and officials at a station.

A sign he didn't read. An old man with a startled face on a bicycle. Then skidding slightly on gravel he was braking in a small forecourt. A waiting taxi driver started to yell at him. Taxi? Here? *Merveilleux*!

'Quick, Tessa, quick!'

As the train drew to what seemed a sedately quiet standstill they were bundling on to the platform of what was only a tiny halt. Someone shouted. The train began to move. He all but threw Tessa up on the high step and then an arm that must have belonged to a stevedore from Le Havre was pulling him aboard. He flopped on to a seat gasping like a just-landed salmon. He wouldn't have minded if someone had hit him on the head.

'*Vous êtes un peu pressé, monsieur,*' a voice said.

He looked at the seat opposite. It wasn't a stevedore but a farmer's wife. She looked at him with distaste as he fought for breath. There were few faces in the open carriage but he realised that such as were there were all staring at him with unabashed curiosity.

'Look!' Tessa panted out.

He looked back over his shoulder and out the window. The Renault was alive and well and just running into the hamlet. They'd see the leaking Light Fifteen. They weren't out of the woods yet. He looked back at the woman opposite. Perhaps she was a stevedore.

'*Pardon, madame, le train est en direction d'où?*' he said.

'*Oui, très pressé,*' she grunted, '*Rouen.*'

234

TWENTY

To switch trains and double back to the coast. To press straight on to Paris. To go to the police in Rouen. When they had begun to breathe normally again they started a low-voiced weighing of options.

'Rouen's the most dangerous for us,' Ramsey said. 'They can do it in that car as fast as this train'll take. But it's the most dangerous for them too. They won't be taking evasive action if they're haring in after us.'

Tessa stared out at the level, boring countryside that was spread out in the late afternoon sun. Very flat, like Lincolnshire, she thought inconsequentially.

'I owe them something on the "don't get sore get even" principle,' she said. 'Come on, for God's sake let's try and finish it off.'

Ramsey nodded.

'You don't want a sense of left-overs walking around looking for you back in England,' he said.

The train rattled on and she didn't think he'd seen her bite her lip. The tracks alongside them started to multiply. Squat ugly buildings grew taller and continuous. They were pulling into the vast barn of Rouen station. Ahead-of-the-game commuters were beginning to stream towards their trains across the distinctive art deco concourse. Ramsey returned from squaring up their fares.

'We'll gamble five minutes on a phone call to Durand,' he said. 'Go into the bar over there and blend with the wallpaper. I'll be as quick as I can.'

She walked quickly to the bar just inside the station's left-hand entrance. It was neither packed nor empty. A stool at the bar seemed the best bet. She would have her back to the window and could be hunched up.

'*Deux cafés au lait,*' she ordered.

Ramsey was back in dead on five minutes. But pulling a face. 'Couldn't reach Durand,' he said. 'He's away from his desk on quote important affairs unquote.'

'I bet. Like getting away early I expect. Did you talk to anyone else?'

'Too tortuous,' Ramsey shook his head.

'Brook?'

'Too tortuous to phone England from a pay phone. Thanks.'

Ramsey gulped his coffee. 'What we'll do, we'll hole up in a nice

235

anonymous hotel, two simple tourists, and get a phone all to ourselves. Question is, how . . .'

'I've got some money if –'

'How to get to the hotel. Taxi-drivers have memories and not too many scruples. But our friends must surely do business in the biggest town in the region. If I'd been in their shoes – car, that is, – I'd've stopped for whatever it took and phoned ahead to a mate.'

'To have us met, so to speak.'

'Yes . . . I think the taxi is the lesser of two evils. Tell you what we do. I'll go and get one. Give me three minutes. The rank should be almost directly outside. See if you can seem to attach yourself to a group or someone who doesn't look like me as you walk out.'

She finished her coffee with a growing sense of being nakedly on show. The fat, pursey, business type along the counter, the boy in the fake leather jacket – they were obviously there keeping tabs on her. But they both stayed put as she left and it seemed to work quite well. She drew alongside a smart young girl high-heeling rapidly, to judge from her scent, to a date. And had judged it perfectly. Ramsey was just ducking into a taxi. A dozen strides and she was sliding into the rear seat next to him.

'I've asked him to take us to a modest, clean hotel,' Ramsey said. 'A bit away from the centre. You didn't seem to be followed.' The taxi crossed the square and headed toward the Rue Jeanne d'Arc.

'I was here on a school trip about the time they invented printing,' Tessa said. 'I thought then it was all a bit more Madame Tussaud's than Joan of Arc.'

'In the centre, maybe. But it's a good, tough, working town. Look at the walls.'

They were passing the Museum and Library in the Square Vesdrei. The World War 2 small arms fire continued to leave its mark. 'Us or them?' Tessa asked.

'Argies, I should think. They're supposed to be the true enemy these days.'

'Or drug smugglers.'

'Sssh.' But the driver's greased head had not moved as he accelerated through a red light.

'Being typical tourists we seem to be getting the Piccadilly to Leicester Square via Neasden route,' Ramsey said after a while. 'But it's useful. I'm sure we're not being tailed.' He swivelled back forward in his seat.

'I didn't realise the river was so wide here,' Tessa said. They were crossing the Pont Corneille.

'Oh yes. Rouen is to the Seine what Tilbury, say, used to be to the Thames. You get ocean-going ships coming up-river to unload. And then upstream canals and what-not take you on to the Schildt and the Rhine and so on.'

'So you can get in to the Danube and all the way down to the Black Sea.'

'In the right sort of boat, yes.'

'Bloody useful, I should think, if you're in our friends' business.'

'Good point.'

'You couldn't get too far upstream in those barges, though. They're enormous.'

He leaned across to see where she was pointing. Across on the Quai Corneille close to the goods yards four barges were moored side by side. You could have played football on the acreage they covered.

'Coal barges,' he said. 'MacGregor – you should be living at this hour.'

The taxi stopped almost at once. '*Hotel Nord*,' the driver said. '*Voilà*.'

'We get the round trip reduction, do we?' Ramsey asked in English as he paid him. The driver grimaced in contemptuous thanks as he gunned away.

'I over-tipped him,' Ramsey said, 'but he'll have us tagged now as green tourists – roles we'll now have to switch.'

He was weighing up the small, narrow hotel. It had had a modern glass frontage inserted into its fin du siècle brickwork to produce something approaching the effect of a stainless steel false tooth. A collage of credit card logos on the plate glass door added to the impression of a chequered history. *Plus ça change*. He was back on the Earls Court-Shepherd's Bush borders.

'I'm typecast as a tourist.' Tessa was saying. 'Why change?'

'You have your passport?'

'No.'

'They'll want it for registering. We've no luggage either. It's not the weekend but pay in advance and dirty weekend time.'

She looked quickly away. 'I'm sorry,' he said. 'But that's how it's got to be.'

'Yes, well, we know we're playing parts,' she said. 'Come on, let's get off the streets.'

Ten minutes later they were ensconced in a room whose musty aerosoled smell could have been bottled as essence of Earls Court. These days, Ramsey thought, you can travel round the world and always find the hotel's got there first. He took in the room visually as well. It contrived to be both beigely anonymous and out of date. The not-so-large double bed still squeezed the rest of the scant furniture to the walls. Someone had been greedy. A larger room had been partitioned. But far-sightedly greedy. A flimsy connecting door made pretensions to a 'family suite' still technically tenable.

'That's where the maid sleeps – with the children,' Ramsey said as he tried the door. It shivered top to bottom at his tug but was locked. Tessa drew the curtains.

'Not much to write home about but it's dry, safe and there's a phone,' Ramsey said. 'Right, let's get on with it.'

Durand in Bayeux was still out on important business. Lines to England were all tied up. Twenty-eight minutes later when they did get through to Scotland Yard Brook was not in either.

'No. No message,' Ramsey said and hung up.

'No?'

'We'll try his home number first.'

'And if he's not there?'

'Give it another hour and try Durand again and if not start talking from square one to the police here while still trying Brook in England.'

Money is money. Rémonecq was pleased enough by the over-the-odds killing he'd made at the expense of the two English people who seemed to assume he couldn't understand their language. But when he got back to the station rank and learned from Cibot that some operator was asking questions about late afternoon fares and using a well-filled wallet to jog memories, Rémonecq was not backward in coming forward. A sou was a sou. A franc is a franc.

The cynically dead-pan receptionist had regretted the hotel had no restaurant.

'There is breakfast,' she had said. 'In your room or the lounge.'

She had taken the notes and the coins. 'If you stay that long,' she'd added.

'Hungry?' Ramsey asked.

'Starving,' Tessa said from where she sat on the bed. 'I shouldn't be after that lunch but I am.'

'It's being cooped up, waiting,' Ramsey said. 'Your stomach gets self-conscious.' He looked at his watch.

'Here's what we do,' he said. 'We'll play it safe and not mess around with restaurants. We've blown out three times on Durand now. I'll go out and speak to the police. It'll take a while, I'm sure, but either I'll come back with some wine and sausage and stuff or I'll come back with a copper or knowing the coast is clear.'

'All right,' she said, not liking the sound of it too much.

'*Meanwhile* – meanwhile you get back to Scotland Yard. I don't suppose you'll raise Brook but get on to his department, someone near him, and give them the story so far. Any help he can deliver'll be most appreciated, etcetera. And if you've got it flaunt it. Remind them who your dad was.'

Tessa nodded. He picked up the inevitable bookmatch from the beside table and got to his feet.

'I'll leave the key here. Beethoven's Fifth on the door means it's me. If things change, I'll phone.' She smiled and he went out into the narrow corridor. Once again he had given her a pastime. One floor up. He'd walk down. If he were true to type now, he'd go out the back way through the kitchen. Except with no restaurant, there'd be no kitchen to speak of. But there must be a back way. Oh to hell with it! He was in the deserted lobby now and there was the door ahead.

'Inspector Brook's office.'

A woman's voice. The business world had shut up shop for the day and she had got through at once.

'Is Inspector Brook there?'

'Who's calling, please?'

'My name is Waite. Tessa Waite. Exton Waite's daughter.'

'I'm afraid Inspector Brook is out of the country, Miss Waite. Can I help at all?'

'Well, yes. Yes. It's urgent. But I'm afraid it's quite complicated.'

'I'll do my best.'

There was a knock at the door. 'Just a minute. There's someone at the door.'

But it had not been the opening of the Fifth Symphony. '. . . Who's there?'

'M'selle Waite? Miss Waite? Commissaire Durand.'

'. . . Is . . . is Doctor Ramsey with you?'

'Er, 'e is at the, er, *commissariat.*'

'One moment!' She lifted the phone to her mouth and tried to talk as rapidly as the tide of fear rising through her would allow.

'Listen. I'm –'

'Yes. Still here.'

'I'm at the Hotel Nord in Rouen, France. Normandy. I think –'

'Could you spell that, miss?'

She could hear a key probing at the lock.

'For God's sake! Rouen. R-O-U-'

The door flew inwards and the man whose face had leered in her drug-induced fantasies dived across the room at her. The scream she began became buried in the bruising weight of his hand across her mouth. Then a knee was trying to crack her spine in two as her face was rammed brutally into the stiff, harsh material of the bed's coverlet. She kicked, tried to roll free. A stunning blow to the side of her skull sent her senses swimming and she heard the telephone

239

receiver klonk on something. She felt her arms being forced up behind her back and, as she lost consciousness, knew that the nightmare was not a dream and that this time there was no other captor to make her attacker stop.

His luck had held. When he'd left the hotel they'd once again failed to gun him down, bury him under an avalanche. He'd turned right, down the hill in the direction of the river. The phone book had suggested that there was a sub-police station close by in this quarter. But contrary to his present descent down the centre of this narrow, cobbled street, spelling it all out to the local *flics* was going to be an uphill struggle. Once they'd penetrated his accent there would be xenophobia to cut through as well as the usual scepticism and sheer let-him-cool-his-heels-awhile red tape. Tessa was going to have a longer wait than he'd let on but the chances were it would be that much shorter if he took the time now to go in to the main station and tried to corner somebody senior and civilised. He loped on downwards. At the bottom he might pick up a taxi or ask about buses.

Perhaps if the car had just come on down the hill normally it would have got him in one. But the driver had chosen to cruise down, lights and engine both off. Because there was nothing else about, no doubt. But because there was nothing else about the squelchy, squeezing crunch of the tyres as the wheel crushed something on the cobbles sounded out in its unusualness like a klaxon. Already alarmed, he turned. About forty metres behind and above the big Renault was stalking him. As he registered as much, its engine fired and he was caught dead centre of its beams.

His eyes still the spheres of a thousand dazzling further detonations he started to run. They had guns. He tried to zig-zag. The slope leant him speed but it threatened to trip him face forward on its cobbles. And the race was hopelessly unequal. His own shadow in front of him was growing shorter with every stride.

Crouched almost double, lengthening his stride, he knew they had him. He remounted the strip of pavement but a thudding clonk behind told him they had too. Again the garrotte about his lungs and – my God! – straight ahead, parked more on the pavement than road – a car. He'd be snapped off at the knees.

His body took over. He was well balanced as he hurdled up on to the Peugeot's bonnet and with the next stride gained its roof. He teetered clownishly for a long, long split second and had then jumped two-footed to the boot. It was the impact of the Renault, mating nose to nose with the Peugeot in an incredibly loud shrieking tear of twisting metal and crazing glass that drove him staggering forward off the boot. He landed on his feet. His forward-flailing, foot-scrabbling not quite sprawl took him a dozen metres further on before his legs at last gave best to the overall momentum and he pitched forward to embrace the juddering shafts of pain the cobbles offered up to him. But lucky at that. As he rolled around he saw the Renault had driven the Peugeot back a good two lengths. He also saw the Renault's passenger door being forced open. A gun appeared above the car's roof-line held aloft Excalibur-like. Then the owner of the arm was rising upwards too.

Ramsey roll-scrambled to his feet. He resumed his downhill sprint. If he had pains they were a long way off in his childhood where real bullets never blew tunnels through backs the sudden size of barn-doors. He risked a backwards glance. The gunman was coming after him and coming fast. But they were all but upon the Quai now at the bottom. Traffic from right and left was brisk. But unarmed. Go for it! Pat Nevin lived! Amid a blare of horns, a blaze of lights, a screech of burning rubber he had dodged across the wide-laned carriage-way. His pursuer was stuck on its other side. No, dammit, he had spotted a gap. He was coming on.

Darkness be my friend. The street was well lit. The river was dark. He could outswim the bastard maybe. Ramsey dropped down on to the side of the Seine and at once he knew where he was. This was the railed section where the goods trains loaded up. Over there were the barges. He made for them. Rails and cross-ties cropped up regularly to trip him but it was his own stamina that was now his greatest enemy: his lack of it. He was slowing fast. And he'd miscalculated. When you weren't under the streetlights looking down, it was a good deal less pitch black here than it seemed. The spatter of running leather behind him seemed to be getting louder. The blood was pounding in his throat so heavily it was hard to hear. Had the sound stopped? A bullet singing a war-song past him as he swerved to miss a junction box told him that for an aim-taking moment it must have. And now he saw why. Sooner than he'd realised here was the upsheen of black water and the barge nearest the bank. He long-stepped aboard it, his lungs two torture chambers of screaming shreds and patches. He could do nothing, decide nothing, until the burning inside had abated.

He went straight from the first barge onto the second. There was some superstructure aft; a cabin, a wheelhouse. Shadows. If he could stay his gasping for air, breathe silently again, he might have chances yet. Crouching he hurried aft. Off to his right he heard a thud, a scrape of leather, panting. Good. He wasn't the only one in need of a second wind. As lightly as possible he stepped across to the third barge. One trouble was it would be hard to get into the water quietly and he wouldn't reckon on being able to stay under that long. It would be Fleetwood all over again. He'd be a sitting duck and this time there would be no waves to make life hard for a marksman. Besides – for the first time he had pause in which to examine the grim truth he'd known from the second the Renault's lights had blazed – if they had him, they had the hotel. If they had the hotel, they had Tessa. He crouched low by the wheelhouse trying to spot his pursuer. There! Moving on to the second barge's prow, halting. Eyes still on him, Ramsey started to feel around for something loose, heavy. Anything. If they had Tessa then he had no choice. And, in any case, attack was the best form of defence.

Nothing came to hand. The wheelhouse door was padlocked. Hang on. The man was backtracking to the first barge. Why? Giving up? No. He was having to eliminate each wheelhouse area first in case he left a route back to the Quai open behind him.

Ramsey backed to the far side of the third wheelhouse. At the very end of the barge a rowing boat was mounted on davits. Not high. An oar would be ideal. But none was in sight. Probably stowed inside under the tarp. But there was a rowlock standing just discernibly silhouetted against the faintly lighter sodiumised sky. Maybe. As the man with the gun disappeared the far side of the first wheelhouse, Ramsey chanced his arm. Two strides and he was pulling hard at the rowlock. It wasn't bolted in place. It made a noise like thunder leaving its hole, it seemed, but maybe not. He was crouching back in the shadows with a hefty lump of metal in his hand.

Yes. Got away with it. The man with the gun was still working on the first wheelhouse. It wasn't easy for him either. Hide and seek around a cube calls for a lot of lateral thinking. The gunman was erring on the side of caution. Let him. Ramsey had his shoes off now. Leaving them on the river side of the third wheelhouse he squirmed on his belly out along the rim of the same barge. He could taste coal dust sweetly-sour and gritty on his lips but he had a position some ten metres from his shoes well before the gunman had circled the second wheelhouse. If he just kept up the same pattern when he came across . . . Ramsey felt his throat tighten and then relax. As the man stepped over to the same barge he was on Ramsey felt curiously cool. It was going to be all right. It would happen just as he'd planned it.

It took forever but it almost did. The gunman edged clockwise round the wheelhouse like a street-corner gangster in a movie. He kept throwing quick glances over his shoulder. But never down. When he resumed inching forward he didn't see the shoes, his feet kicked them. He exclaimed and bent down. As he half-straightened peering at the water, Ramsey rushed him. The man started to turn but he didn't get a shot off. Ramsey brought the rowlock down harder than hell on the centre of his forehead. The distinct crunch coincided exactly with his grabbing the man's right wrist. There was no resistance. The gun came into his own hand as if in a well-rehearsed baton exchange as, once more, he crunched the rowlock down.

The man stared at Ramsey with eyes that didn't see him. He was young. Less than thirty. If it hadn't been for the dent in his forehead, the blood running from both nostrils, he would have been good-looking in a flashy sort of way. It looked that way at night with the light behind him. His lips moved. A bubble of blood grew between them and burst. It seemed to propel the man backwards. In a line, straight at first, then increasingly erratic, he walked backwards to the aft end of the barge. His knees buckled. He half spun towards the fourth barge as if seeking to cross to it. But it rode higher in the water by about nine inches. It was too much to negotiate. The man's foot caught and, quite gracefully, he pitched diagonally forward into the Seine.

'Rowlocks,' Ramsey said.

He looked at the gun. It was an automatic. A big one. Heavy. God knew what sort but this ought to be the safety. Pointing the gun away from him he moved the catch. Wincing, he aimed at the river and pulled the trigger. It hardly budged and no recoil broke his wrist. Good. Cracked it. He put the gun inside his blouson. Taking out the same handkerchief he'd lent to Tessa he wiped his blunt instrument clean of prints before replacing it. He put his shoes on fast. God knew there was need to.

TWENTY-ONE

Not caring about being seen, he loped across the barges, onto the bank and up to the road level again. The gun bounced and jostled across his ribs. He started to cross the Quai at a more circumspect jog this time but when he was half-way across his attention became split and he halted. Horns blared again. Oncoming lights on his right dazzled yellow. But towards the bottom of the hill leading to the hotel a different coloured light was pulsing stridently. The police were at the scene of a car crash. A gap occurred in the traffic stream. He took the chance. But the gun was weighing heavier as he gained the foot of the climbing street. In motion before he'd completed the thought, he turned right and walked parallel to the river. His face was stinging and certainly grazed from his fall; he picked up God knew what in the way of dirt, filth, coal dust on the barges. No policeman was going to let him walk by unchallenged. And here he was packing a rod true gangster fashion – and with no intention of not packing it. Going the long way round the block would be safer and quicker.

The next street up. He took it at a rapid walk and resisted the temptation to run. It took a great effort. A cold murderous voice, cooling the hot excitement, the *enjoyment* in his blood, was whispering the things that would by now have been done to Tessa, was conjuring images. But he was labouring hard enough as it was. Sprinting up the hill would do for him completely. He had to be in some kind of shape if further action was still required of him. Further action. The iciness spread through him. But it was not just the iciness of fear. As on the barge a cold resolve was growing in him.

He was above the level of the hotel now, and had reached a cross street. A run of local shops extended to the left. There was a bar. He hesitated. It would take more precious time. But it would confirm beyond doubt.

'*Un cognac, s'il vous plaît. Et un jeton, aussi.*' He sank the brandy in one shot. Fumbling the bookmatch from his pocket he went to the phone.

Perhaps no one was on reception. The number rang and rang. Give it three more – 'Hotel Nord.'

'Could I speak to Dr Ramsey in room 205, please.'

'One moment.' With a slightly different tone a second phone took up the ringing.

The sudden shrilling of the squat, old-fashioned phone right by her ear caused Tessa to gasp chokingly through her gag. It had sent shock through her like a sword from head to toe. It had roused her bruised, bleeding, sore, from the blessed coma in which she'd fled her pain and fright. There was nothing she could do by way of answering the phone. The man had tied her to the bed with her own tights. He had no intention of answering it either. As he had been doing since an ambulance went blatting by and, grinning, he'd gone to the window and looked out, he was sitting in the cane chair smoking. His gun was on his knee. The phone kept ringing and ringing until she knew that although none of it mattered now it would never stop.

Ramsey hung up. As he went outside the gun banged against the door. Yes, he had that. But what to do? What to do? Walking quicker on the cross street he moved even faster as he turned the corner approaching the hotel from above. It wasn't far from the intersection. Yes. That might work. He felt the strain on his hamstrings as he abruptly halted. Necessarily. Taking out his handkerchief he licked at it and proceeded, as best he could, to clean his face. He smoothed his hair back. Then he pushed through the hotel door.

He saw two things simultaneously. The key was there in its pigeon hole, and there was someone on duty. A heavy-shouldered, elderly man watching the flicker of a tiny black and white television.

'Room 206, please,' Ramsey said with just an edge of command.

'M'sieur.' The receptionist had taken his eye off the screen for less than two seconds in handing the key across.

'Merci, bien.' Ramsey went up the stairs.

He hadn't wanted the lift to make a noise but with each step he took his breathing seemed as bad a sound source. And his tell-tale heart. As he gained the narrow corridor he paused to let the thudding die away. Useless. The bland doors down the run of faded carpet made the short length pregnant with death. This was no place to steady your pulse. Telling himself the noise was all inside his own head he crept down the corridor on tip-toe. Outside room 205 he halted. He had never listened so hard in his life. God, for a stethoscope now! But, no. Nothing. He crept on to 206. As if performing brain surgery he inserted the key in the lock. Easy, easy . . . now! He opened the door an inch. A foot. The bed was not folded down in the darkened room. The curtains were open. The room was empty and he was inside and, amazingly, the door hadn't creaked. Not putting on the light he left it ajar now. He removed the gun from his blouson and placed it on the bed.

The connecting door in the flimsy partition. Good. No wardrobe blocked it. In front of it stood one of the wooden and webbing strap trestles that hotels provide for standing suitcases on and no guest ever

uses. Ramsey approached it. Taking care not to collapse it, lifting it
ultra-high above all non-existent obstacles he placed it on the bed. It
took no more than ten minutes. It took little longer to slide open the
one small bolt locking the door. All right. He moved to the bed and
picked up the gun. He drew in great draughts of the bedroom's musty
air . . .

In 205 Tessa was back in the gentle, perfect past again. Sunday
lunchtime. Her father had motored down to take her away from
stodge and train smash for a proper lunch at the White Hart. She
could smell his after-shave. Its scent would linger long –

'Tessa . . .'

The knock at the door had come first but it was hearing her name
that catapulted her back to the unspeakable present. The man was
out of his seat in a stride and the cut-throat razor back in his hand. It
sliced through her gag, then rested at her throat as he nodded at her.

'Tessa?'

'Yes . . .' she croaked out. She had meant to say 'Run! Go! Save
yourself!' But all she could do for the man she loved with the razor at
her throat was say 'Yes.'

The razor left her throat. It sliced through the tights. She was
lurched to her feet.

'It's me. Ramsey.'

'Coming.'

She was. The gun was in her ribs as an arm cruelly bent up behind
her shoulder-blade and force-marched her to the door. The gun
moved from her ribs, pointed at the door knob. No! She wouldn't!
After he'd killed Ramsey, he'd kill her. He put the gun to her temple.
Something metallic clicked. She moved her free hand forward in
spite of herself and everything and turned the door knob. She opened
the door. On nothing. To her left someone crashed a giant match
box.

Ramsey crashed through the connecting door with an animal's
momentum. His crouching on-rush knocked Tessa aside and the man
with the gun backwards. It was easy. It was like on the barge. Again
he had the man's left wrist. But this time the wrist was straining up
and back, arching round. Ramsey remembered to hit the man. He'd
forgotten that. He hit him again. With the flat of the gun. Again. The
man still held tightly to his own gun. Ramsey hit him again and the
rhythm grew on him. He kept hitting the face in front of him. He kept
hitting it long after the man had let fall his gun, long after bright
crimson blobs were freshly decorating the wallpaper and skirting
board. He had a better way of hitting now even though his arm was
tiring.

Tiring . . . he began to make out a high, almost continuous

keening scream. No, it wasn't his . . . it came from Tessa. She was slumped against the wall. Her leg was trapped between him and the man. She was splashed too. Splattered with blood.

He looked down at the man. The throat and jaw were still all right. But above the mouth the skull had been much flattened. The top of the head had got a bit loose. Bubbly grey sponge material drinking up blood like blotting paper was giving the head a fan-shaped halo. Bright shades of white bone enhanced the impression. The sponge seemed to be pulsing as it spread out on the carpet. Ramsey found he was panting very heavily. But he still giggled. Was this a forceps delivery that had got cocked up? No. He knew it wasn't really. He knew what it was. He wondered if he'd get into trouble because he was giggling when he ought to be screaming too.

The room was bare. It was small too and somehow the emptiness made it smaller. There was a plain, drawerless table jarringly set in the dead centre. A thousand Gauloises and Gitanes had burned down to sear its top. A table had no feelings. There was one window, shadeless, blindless, bars on the outside. A grey, firing-squad dawn light filtered through the window. There was an oiliness to it. It was like being under dirty, greenish water at the bottom of the deepest well. He could feel it weighing on him, viscous, almost tangible.

Ramsey sat on one chair against the wall, opposite the window and away from the table. Another chair was empty. A uniformed gendarme was stoically standing to guard the door. His early-morning shift had glazed a nasty patina upon his heavy, youthful, features. Ramsey wondered what his own face looked like. Rotting veal if it accurately projected the way he felt. He'd been up all night; questioned repeatedly. He looked at his watch. Seven-thirty.

He could feel the two images preparing to flash vividly on to his inner eye again. One of them. Either the close-up of the black red primitive vulva where a manhood had been totally rooted out or else the pulsing spread of sponge fanning out from the top of the broken, flattened, skull. Two now. He couldn't tell which it would be. They had come and gone at lacerating random throughout the night. He braced himself. Then he was rescued. He heard footsteps in the corridor outside. The door opened.

The room became crowded with people: Durand, Brook, Tessa. With astonishment he realised he was not surprised to see them. They had found Tessa some clothes to wear. A skirt, a blouse. Or were they her own? He didn't know. They didn't seem to suit her.

Brook had been the last to come in but he was the first to speak. 'Are you all right?' he asked. His voice seemed very beside the point.

247

'Yes. I'm all right,' Ramsey replied. Why not? What else to say that would stop them talking?

'Miss Waite has made a full statement,' he heard Brook saying, 'and the French authorities have no further reason to detain her here. Arrangements have been made for her to return to England this morning via Le Havre. The express leaves Rouen at ten. Someone will travel with Miss Waite.'

Ramsey realised that since they'd all come in he had only really looked at Tessa. She looked terrible. As bad as when she'd been drugged. He saw now she had started to cry. He supposed he should get to his feet. He started to get up.

'Don't!' she cried out. Her tear-filled eyes opened wide and shone through the thick air with an expression he couldn't decipher. Then she had turned and rushed from the room. Durand looked anxiously at Brook then followed her. Ramsey again started to get up. Brook pushed him gently back. He didn't resist.

'Later, son,' Brook said, 'when you've got yourself back in one piece. Besides – I'm afraid we still need your help.'

They stood on the downstream side of the Pont Corneille. Passing motorists would have glimpsed two men and thought them to be pleasantly idling a few moments away as the brown river's seawards current mesmerised them.

'You're not at all all right, are you?' Brook said.

'The air's helped,' Ramsey said. 'I'm a few shock layers nearer the surface. I do have this small persistent problem, though.'

'That you've spent a lifetime trying to keep others alive and now you've done someone in.'

'I think that's it. Two, actually.'

The motorists were all wrong. No one was idling. Down from the bridge the river was swarming with activity. On the four barges uniformed police were arguing with a bunch of stevedores. Downstream from them a police launch had anchored itself fore and aft broadside against the current. It was signalling to a tug towing a long, endless string of barges upstream to stay well over towards the Seine's other bank. On this side closer to the bridge a larger launch was anchored more conventionally in line with the current. It bobbed in the wash from the barges and the frogman delayed his backwards flip into the water a moment.

'They showed me their photographs,' Brook said.

'What photographs?'

'Of the hotel room. What was in it.'

'Oh' was all he said. But his own inner photograph bled inside him once again.

'It looked like a kosher butcher's. What got into you?'

Ramsey was silent. He'd not been able to answer the same question the thousand of times he'd asked it himself.

'Was it what he'd done to the girl?' Brook prompted.

'Not really,' Ramsey was aware of saying. He supposed he didn't want to seem ill-mannered. 'I came through the door so fast I only really got a one-up from subliminal look at . . . Tessa. I was concentrating on his gun. I think I hit him first because I didn't want to shoot him. Then I was hitting him for all the people whose lives he'd helped warp. But in with that was just that I'd had enough. Of being chased and leant on, told to lay off. Of being pushed around. By then I'd just blacked out and I'd turned the gun round so I could use it like a hammer and I must have been hitting a clinically dead man harder than ever.'

Brook didn't say a word. Ramsey stared at the river. He got the odd impression the current was flowing the wrong way. 'I've got some other photographs,' Brook said.

'I don't want to see them! I've got my own up here!'

'Other photos, I said. Not that. Here.' Brook handed Ramsey a 35 mm contact sheet. There had been about eighteen or twenty stark images of men's faces on the roll. Footballers? No, too old, some. Pop stars? No. Not prettied up enough by the lighting.

'Fleetwood, Fishguard, Fowey, Brest, Cherbourg,' Brook recited. 'Not a bad little trawl.'

Another piece of reality slotted back into place in Ramsey's head. Mug shots. This kind of photo made everyone look like a criminal.

'For once in your life, if you were going to do what you did do, your timing was immaculate.'

Not the right word, Ramsey thought, seeing his crimson action painting on the wallpaper again.

'And your target. He was on the list. Like him down there, we think. It'll take a high-level exchange but I think you can rule out Devil's Island. They'll let you walk.'

Ramsey shrugged.

'They might make it a condition you return to your native sod. Leave theirs anyway.'

Funny. That seemed to matter. 'I'm not sure about that,' Ramsey said. 'Let me see that sheet again.' His brain was connected to the moment again. He looked at the faces properly this time.

'You've missed one,' he said. 'A biggy.'

'Who?'

'The Frenchman I saw in London. The one who tried putting the black on.'

'Sod it!' From below there came a shout that was almost the echo of

249

Brook's cry. A steel line had been attached to something under the water. A winch was at work on the larger launch. A body heavy in its saturated clothes broke the water. It rolled on to its back. The fish-belly colour of the face, the purple-black lips did not disguise that, living, the man had been flashily good-looking.

'Yes,' Ramsey said.

'I'd better get down there.' Brook started to go.

'Wait.' Ramsey called him back. 'How much damage has this done to them?'

Brook looked away, shuffled. 'The honest answer. Think of it as an octopus. We've hacked off a bit of one tentacle. Plenty left.'

'And tentacles grow again.'

'Look over there.' Ramsey did. Vast and low in the water another caravan of barges was being towed upstream. The tug's whistle rent the damp air.

'Look how big they are. They've got cargo on that could have come from anywhere in the world. What's a few extra kilos of whatever hidden here or there to their bill of lading?'

Brook had gone. To the left an ongoing clank in series told of a goods train moving off. But Ramsey kept his gaze unblinkingly on the river. He had realised why the barges were coming upstream at this hour. He had a sudden picture in his head of the Seine linking up with the Rhine, the Danube, the Black Sea; of a vast grey-brown artery sheening its way across Europe to a Black Sea delta. The current was running the wrong way. The barges were coming in now to take advantage of the sea running up from the Seine's estuary. They were bringing in whatever they were bringing in on the flood tide.